W9-DJI-810

Tiger by the Tail

Casey Claybourne

BERKLEY BOOKS, NEW YORK

TIGER BY THE TAIL

A Berkley Book / published by arrangement with
the author

PRINTING HISTORY
Berkley edition / May 1999

The Penguin Putnam Inc. World Wide Web site address is
http://www.penguinputnam.com

ISBN: 0-425-16321-0

BERKLEY®
Berkley Books are published by The Berkley Publishing Group,
a division of Penguin Putnam Inc.,
375 Hudson Street, New York, New York 10014.
BERKLEY and the "B" logo
are trademarks belonging to Penguin Putnam Inc.

PRINTED IN THE UNITED STATES OF AMERICA

10 9 8 7 6 5 4 3 2 1

*To Gail Fortune, a woman of
style and grace and
impeccable taste;
I owe you so much.*

"I will not budge an inch."

—Shakespeare,
The Taming of the Shrew

One

Mr. Bell, the keeper of Cullscombe's gaol, jerked his head up from his desk, blinking like a sun-starved mole. He scratched at his chins—all three of them—as he tried to determine what had so rudely interrupted his dreams of young Sally, the Pelican's buxom serving wench.

He cleared his ears with a tug at his earlobes and cocked his head to the side. A coach could be heard rattling down the sleepy country lane, its iron-rimmed wheels squeaking like a family of mice. Wishing that he were still in Sally's plump arms, Mr. Bell yawned broadly and tilted back on the legs of his chair to squint through the grease-streaked windowpanes. A carriage approached amid a cloud of gray Devonshire dust. He squinted harder into the glass. He could just make out the crest emblazoned on the door—

The chair slammed back onto all four legs. Mr. Bell, suddenly wide awake, threw himself across the paper-strewn desk and snatched hold of a half-empty bottle of gin. He tossed the bottle to the back of the desk drawer, then leaped to his feet, brushing feverishly at the bread crumbs on his vest. Outside, the coachman called to the horses. A harness jingled cheerily.

Cupping his hand over his mouth, the gaoler tested the

spirits on his breath. *Blast.* . . . He sent a hasty glance over the cluttered desk, searching for something— A rusty tin of lavender pomade caught his eye. In a flash, he opened the tin and scooped out a thick, oily dollop which he spread across his tongue. He had just managed to swallow when the front door swung open.

The hinges creaked ominously as sunshine sliced into the anteroom's deep gloom. A figure appeared on the threshold—a dark silhouette, cloaked from head to toe in a swirling cape of midnight black. Mr. Bell gulped and resisted the urge to cross himself.

Bugger his luck, it was . . . *her*. It was the She-Devil of Mooresby Hall!

"M-Miss Mooresby," he squeaked. He remained behind the desk, taking a vague comfort in its scant protection.

"And good day to you, Mr. Bell."

Though she spoke softly, the sound of his name on her lips caused poor Thomas Bell to shiver with dread. What could she be wanting with the likes of him? Whatever it was, dear Lord, he'd gladly give it to her, for all of Devonshire knew that whatever Melisande Mooresby wanted, she eventually got.

One way or the other.

On the diminutive side—she couldn't have even reached five feet, he reckoned—the lady of Mooresby Hall was not one to let size stand in her way. Sure, she might have looked no bigger than a mite, but anyone who'd ever had dealings with the She-Devil knew the truth of the matter. Melisande Mooresby was a large wolf in a tiny lamb's garb. She was as bold and confident and determined— Well, some in town said too bold and too confident for a mere woman. Some like Mr. Bell.

Faith, there wasn't a man in all of Cullscombe who still didn't shudder when relating the story of poor Tim Frye. Riding into town one wet, wintry day last December, Tim had carelessly plodded through a puddle, splashing mud over Patty Porter's skirts. Now, like a fool, Tim had neither stopped to apologize nor taken note of the small black-cloaked figure standing nearby on the walk. Before anyone could blink, Melisande Mooresby had stomped into the middle of the street, right into the path of his cantering mount. 'Twas a miracle she'd not been trampled, some said, while others had claimed Lucifer had merely been protecting his own. At any rate, the She-Devil had dragged Tim—all twenty stone of him—down from the saddle, and by gum, if she didn't have the old cobbler blubbering like a babe by the time he made his apologies to Miss Porter. Needless to say, a lot of folks were riding through town more slowly these days. And giving Melisande Mooresby a wide berth.

But there was no wide berth for Thomas Bell, no sir. Not today. Across the cold stone floor she came toward him, her skirts rustling like autumn's dried leaves. Framed by a thick fringe of lashes, her dark brown eyes shone nearly black. As black as the witch's mane she'd tucked beneath her veiled silk bonnet.

"Mr. Bell, while it is good to see you," she said in a deceptively subdued voice, "time compels me to be direct. I have need of your assistance."

His fingers clutched at the edge of the desk. "Anything, m'lady. Anything 't all."

She smiled. A warm, gentle smile that made the gaoler's skin crawl.

"It is a matter of some . . . delicacy. A matter that will require complete and utter confidentiality. I hope that I may trust in your discretion?" She questioned him with a subtle lifting of her ebony brow.

He hurried to assure her. "Course, yer ladyship. Absolute discretion. You can trust your life with ole Thomas Bell, you can."

She smiled again, causing the constable to question if Satan himself had blessed the lady with such wicked loveliness.

"I assure you, Mr. Bell, that your cooperation will not go unrewarded. I will see to it personally." She gave a pointed glance to the bulging reticule riding against her hip. "Now, as to my business, sir. I would have a look at your prisoners."

Mr. Bell's nose twitched. His eyes darted from the purse to the gaol door. He'd heard around town that Miss Mooresby fancied herself one of those high-minded prison reformers. One of those ramshackle idealists who believed that, with proper guidance and such, the ne'er-do-wells of society could somehow be made over into law-abiding English citizens. Personally, he thought it hogwash. "Sow's ears into silk purses" was what those crazy Quakers preached.

"Miss Mooresby, them in there"—his chins jiggled as he jerked his head toward the prisoners' cells—"why, they just ain't fit to be seen by a proper lady, miss. They're a sorry lot, they are. Petty criminals and ruffians. Pickpockets and riffraff. You cannot honestly be wantin' to soil your skirts among the likes of them, can you now?"

The lady folded her gloved hands in front of her, her expression cold.

"Not only do I wish to view your 'ruffians' and 'riffraff,' Mr. Bell, but I wish to do so immediately. Time is of the utmost importance in this matter and I have not a second to waste. *Not one more second.*"

Her black eyes flashed in the muted light.

He swallowed and fumbled for the keys. "This way then."

Mr. Bell unlocked the door that led to the heart of the prison and ushered Miss Mooresby inside. The Cullscombe lockup was really nothing more than an old brick stable that had been converted into a gaol after the previous lockup, an alehouse cellar, had burned to the ground last summer.

"Mind your step," the gaoler advised. "The stones are a bit slick."

"Little wonder," she murmured as she lifted her hem above the moss-covered floor. "'Tis as damp and cool as a cave in here."

Mr. Bell fought back a grimace, fearing that a speech on penal improvements was about to be delivered. But the lady merely drew her bonnet's veil over her face and pulled her cloak closed, hiding the trimness of her figure.

Shrewd thinkin', the gaoler thought with approval. Some

of these blokes had been locked up nigh on to seven months now. The sight of a comely lass would have surely stirred up trouble.

"So, my lady, is it a stablehand you're wantin'? Someone to work at the Hall?"

"Yes," she answered slowly. "I am looking for someone for Mooresby Hall."

Mr. Bell shook his head. Why didn't the woman simply send her steward into the village like any other sensible body would do? Lord knew there were lads aplenty in Cullscombe looking for honest work; some who'd give their eyeteeth to land a plummy job in the Mooresby stables. But, like those reforming Quakers, the lady of the manor probably figured she was doing a good deed by saving some rascal from a well-deserved flogging or a six-month sentence at the house of correction.

The constable snorted quietly beneath his breath and ambled over to the first cell. Enclosed and fitted with a heavy wood door, the chamber had once been a horse stall. Now barred windows had been fitted into the doors so that the gaolkeeper could maintain a vigilant eye on his charges. In truth, however, Mr. Bell spent as little time as possible among the prisoners' cells, only venturing from the front room twice a day to deliver their meals. Long having suffered from a delicate constitution, he simply could not stomach the persistent stench of unwashed bodies and unemptied pots.

"Look lively now," the gaoler bellowed. "We got ourselves a visitor."

A few indistinct mutterings met this announcement, echoing hollowly against the barren brick walls.

The gaoler pointed a pudgy finger at the door of the first cell. "This fella here was brought in for coin clippin'. I'd imagine that, with a crime as serious as this, Lord Underwood'll send him off to the Guildhall in Exeter for sentencin'."

Since their parish did not boast an appointed justice of the peace, it was left to the young Viscount Underwood to serve as magistrate for Cullscombe and the surrounding area.

Alas, the irresponsible Lord Underwood tended to be rather lax in his duties. Prisoners languished many long months— often nigh on to a year—before their cases were heard, a circumstance which added woefully to Thomas Bell's workload. Until his death six years ago, Jonathan Mooresby had been Cullscombe's magistrate and, to Mr. Bell's mind, the She-Devil's father had done a far better job of it than his youthful successor.

With a wave of his hand, the gaoler invited Miss Mooresby to take a look through the window.

She approached, her back stiff, and raised herself onto her toes. Her profile was but a shadow beneath the lacy veil as she peered into the chamber. "No," she said, dropping to the soles of her feet. "I fear he is too old."

"Ah." Mr. Bell nodded and shuffled a few feet down the row to the next lockup. "Well then, here's a young one for you. His family's been in Cullscombe six generations now. Father is the butcher, Saunders. Respectable sort, Saunders, even if the lad went bad."

"And what is young Mr. Saunders accused of?" Miss Mooresby asked.

"Poachin'. He was caught red-handed on Lord Underwood's property, so I don't reckon it'll go too easy on the lad."

She tilted forward and looked through the bars, then quickly stepped back.

"Why, the boy cannot yet have seen fifteen," she said indignantly. As if *he,* Thomas Bell, were to blame for either the lad's age or crime. "I am sorry, Mr. Bell, but he won't do at all. He is much too young."

Too old, too young. Too infirm, too coarse. And so it went as they traveled down the row of prisoners. The gaolkeeper masked a sigh when they stopped in front of the seventh lockup. The fetid air—and the lump of pomade sitting at the bottom of his belly—were making him decidedly queasy. He wished the woman would just hurry up and finish with her business, so he could have a lie-down.

"Here we got a pickpocket. Brought him in three months ago," the gaoler offered wearily.

Miss Mooresby stretched high to glance through the window bars.

"Hmm," she murmured. "This might be a possibility. How would you describe this prisoner's disposition, Mr. Bell?"

"Downing? He's manageable 'nough, I suppose. He don't fuss or carry on none."

"Ask him to smile."

"M'lady?"

"Ask him to smile, if you would."

Mr. Bell rolled his eyes. *Behind* her back. "Downing," he called out. "Give us a smile, man."

"Wha's 'at?" came the muffled—and astonished—reply.

"A smile," the gaoler repeated. "Let's see it. Right here at the window."

Miss Mooresby peered into the cell once more, then turned away in clear disappointment. "Mr. Downing is missing his teeth."

"Teeth?" he sputtered. *What in blazes did a stablehand need with a good set of teeth?*

Laying his palm against his roiling middle, Mr. Bell watched in dismay as the lady marched resolutely toward the next lockup. Confound it, did the dratted female plan to keep him here all afternoon?

"Miss Mooresby," he whined.

She pivoted around, and the look she gave him had him wondering how such a small slip of a girl could set his knees to shaking.

He licked at his lips. "I was thinkin' that we might get on faster here," he wheedled, "if you would be so good as to tell me what it is that you're looking for. Exactly."

She lifted her chin.

"*Exactly,* Mr. Bell, I am looking for a husband."

The gaoler's blood ran cold. Colder still as she began to walk toward him, her black skirts swishing back and forth, her fingers idly twisting her silk kerchief into knots.

"As a matter of fact, Mr. Bell . . . Does it happen that you are married?"

His stomach lurched six ways to Sunday, and a painful belch lodged beneath his ribs.

"M-me? I . . . I, no—"

Her eyes narrowed in shrewd deliberation. "Naturally, 'twould only be a marriage in name. I would have it annulled at the first possible opportunity, probably within the month."

Mr. Bell felt sweat bead along his brow. He asked himself if she might be mad.

Then, before Melisande Mooresby could drop the noose around his neck, Cullscombe's gaoler was struck with sudden inspiration.

"Wait! I've got just the man for you, miss, just the fella." Somehow he managed to coax his boneless legs into carrying him across to the other row of cells. "He just came in last evenin', my lady. A comely bloke. Just the right age. And he's got all his teeth, he does."

She glanced curiously to the door against which the gaoler leaned. "The nature of his crime?"

"Nothin' graver than a li'l tussle with the mayor's son. He's fresh off the boat from the colonies, headed back home to Scotland, you see. I suppose he tipped one too many at the Pelican last night, for he ended up breaking Charlie Bryant's nose clean in half. Not that that scoundrel Charlie didn't have it comin' to him, Miss Mooresby. No, sirree. Mayor's son or not, he's an out and outer that one is. Course I had no choice but to bring Taggart in when ole Bryant seen what had been done to his boy."

She ceased twisting her kerchief, her mouth pursed in a contemplative moue. "A Scot, you say?"

He bobbed his head up and down with such fervor that a crick pinched the back of his neck.

"And no one has come for him?"

"Nary a soul," he breathlessly assured. "And since he's bound to be in at least a month or two afore Lord Underwood can hear his case, I think he'd fair jump at the chance to get outta here." *Even if it does mean hitchin' his fate to the Mooresby witch,* he thought.

Her boot tip-tapped the floor for an interminably long

second. "Very well. Open the door so that I may speak with him."

Now, under ordinary circumstances, Mr. Bell would have been most reluctant to allow anyone, much less a lady, admission to a prisoner's cell. He was responsible, after all; it was his head on the block if a prisoner were to escape or if someone were to become injured. However, when presented with the unthinkable alternative of becoming bridegroom to the She-Devil of Mooresby Hall—

The key was in the lock and the door was swinging open before either of them had taken another breath.

As Melisande Mooresby slipped into the cold, dark cell that reeked of urine and sludge, the gaolkeeper clasped his hands together and turned his eyes toward heaven.

Oh, Lord, I'll ask nothin' else of you ever again, I swear it. But please, I beg of you . . . Please let her take him and not me.

Melisande was growing impatient and she didn't care for the feeling. Patience, if she possessed any, had never been her primary virtue. She was not one to stand by and watch and wait. Not Melisande Mooresby. She was an achiever, a doer. If a situation had to be resolved, then she resolved it swiftly and efficiently. Decisively.

Today, however . . . Today Melisande knew that she could not resolve her current dilemma swiftly enough. Scandal loomed. Disaster threatened. She had to act and act immediately. Before the sun set on this day, by God, she vowed that she would find herself a husband.

Drawing her cape around her, she stepped into the narrow, shadowed stall. Her nostrils flared in reaction to the vile aroma, but she resisted the urge to cough. The walls glistened with dampness and the air felt unnaturally cool.

A figure sat on the edge of a rickety cot, his elbows braced on widespread knees. Coatless, the man wore a ripped white shirt, plain gray breeches soiled at the knees, and boots desperately in need of a good polish. He looked dejected. Or tired, perhaps. He sat with his head bent, bent so low that his hair, untouched by gray, almost brushed the stone floor. His hands were linked behind his neck.

Melisande allowed her gaze to briefly linger on those hands. Sun-browned and large, they looked strong and capable, as if they belonged to a smithy or a bricklayer. She wondered what trade the man plied.

Surprisingly, he did not raise his head when she entered, although she knew that he must have heard the key's teeth-grating screech in the lock.

"Mr. Taggart?"

His shoulders rose and fell in what appeared to be a sigh.

"Mr. Taggart," she repeated, this time in a voice that rarely went unheeded. "If you could spare a moment of your time."

Once more the muscles of his back shifted, and a low, groaning chuckle accompanied the movement.

"A moment of my time," she heard him rasp. He slurred his words like a colonial, although a hint of the Scottish burr was yet evident in his speech. Strangely Melisande did not find the peculiar accent unattractive.

Very slowly, he lifted his head.

Of an instant, Melisande felt glad for her veil's protection, for without it Mr. Taggart surely would have taken notice of her reaction. And react she did. The gaoler had not spoken false when he had called the man comely.

Long brown hair, streaked with thick bands of gold, hung to his shoulders and framed a face that was, at once, both soft and hard. Hard lines formed his nose and brow, and hard angles defined where jaw met cheek. But there was softness in his features, as well. Softness in the wide mouth and the almond shape of the eyes. *Well, softness in one eye,* she mentally corrected. The other eye had purpled and swollen shut, probably courtesy of Charlie Bryant's fist.

She guessed the man to be older than her twenty-two years—but not by much. His face, though bronzed by the sun, did not show signs of age, and a youthful brawn was visible in the girth of his arms.

Hmm. Obviously a bit rough around the edges, but he just

might do. Might do very nicely, in fact. After all, she had never thought to actually find a gentleman within these walls; merely the clay with which to mold one. She'd always said it could be done, had maintained that she could redeem the sorriest, lowliest, most unfortunate of men. This figure before her provided the right ingredients, the proper packaging. He could be made into a gentleman; he needed only to be shaped by a deft hand. Her deft hand.

"Mr. Taggart, I have a proposal to put forth to you. If you agree to accept my proposal, I will see to it that the charges against you are dropped and that you are released from this cell this very afternoon."

He said nothing, but continued to stare at her from his one good, bloodshot eye.

"Do you wish to hear more?"

"Go on," he invited, although not with much eagerness.

"I do not require a great deal of you, Mr. Taggart. In fact, very little when weighed against what you stand to gain by my offer. I need simply for you to play a role. The role of a gentleman in my home for a period of three to four weeks."

She paused. He remained silent.

"I will arrange to have you properly tutored in order for your masquerade to be successful. And you will need a wardrobe"—her gaze skimmed over the breadth of his shoulders—"appropriate for a gentleman of your assumed station, which I will, of course, provide. All that is asked of you is your cooperation in pulling off this harmless little charade. Then, after I no longer have need of your services, you will be free to go."

He shifted a fraction of an inch, revealing an aged white scar that ran parallel to his jaw. "Sounds to me," he drawled, "like you need to get yourself an actor."

Melisande smiled. Despite the odd, hybrid accent, his voice was, at least, cultured. She would not have to concern herself over that aspect of the pretense.

"Actually, Mr. Taggart, circumstances require someone unknown to my social circle. An actor runs the risk of being recognized from the stage. I understand that you, however, are but recently returned to England, which suits my purposes very well indeed."

He sent a short glance to his hands splayed between his knees. "Sorry. Not interested."

"Now, now, I shouldn't encourage hastiness in your position, my good sir. The gaolkeeper informs me that you may be looking at a lengthy sojourn here. Months, I do believe he said."

The man's regard was direct, unflinching.

Melisande felt annoyance flit through her, but she dared not lose her temper as her options looked to be few. While she'd enjoyed watching Mr. Bell squirm, she'd never truly considered the portly constable a viable candidate. Whereas this man . . .

"Ah, did I fail to mention remuneration? How silly of me. Naturally, you'll be compensated for your troubles, leaving Mooresby Hall with your pockets well-lined, I assure you. And when you consider the alternative, Mr. Taggart"—she waved her hand to indicate the cramped and dirty cell—"I do believe my proposal to be an attractive one.

"There is one small detail," she added. "We will have to be married."

His good eye narrowed. "Married? As in 'wedding'?"

"Yes. You do not already have a wife, do you?"

"No-o. Not that I recall."

"Excellent. As I said before, I do not think we will need to perpetuate the masquerade longer than a month or so. After that, I assure you that the marriage will be annulled posthaste."

"A month," he repeated, rubbing his palm over his whiskered chin. "And all I have to do is agree to this proposal of yours and you'll convince that overfed turnkey out there to let me go? You can do that?"

Melisande's lips quirked with a hint of smugness. "I assure you, Mr. Taggart, that Mr. Bell will accord me his full cooperation."

Taggart shrugged. As if he were agreeing to nothing of any importance at all. "All right. It's a deal."

"A deal," Melisande echoed in relief, surprised by the ease with which he had acquiesced. How effortless it had been. And how fortunate for her that she had stumbled upon an agreeable and compliant sort of character. 'Twould make her plan so much simpler to carry out.

"I'll ask Mr. Bell to bring you to Mooresby Hall this afternoon then." She started for the door, then checked her step. "Oh, I almost forgot. What is your full given name?"

He tilted his head to the side, his gold-streaked hair fanning across his shoulder. At the back of her mind, Melisande thought it would be a shame if they were forced to cut such a glorious mane.

"Will. William Erasmus Taggart."

She nodded. "Until this afternoon——"

"And yours?"

She wavered, then chided herself for being foolish. He would eventually have to learn her name if he were to play the role of her husband, for goodness' sake.

"Melisande Mooresby."

"Melisande," he repeated, gazing at her from that one almond-shaped eye.

She shivered and drew at the edges of her cloak. "I shall see you this afternoon, Mr. Taggart. Until then, I bid you a good day."

Without further ado, she swept out of the cell, nearly bumping into the gaolkeeper, who'd obviously been eavesdropping just outside the door. He hurriedly backed up.

"So he'll do?" the constable asked.

"He'll do very well indeed," Melisande answered, digging into her reticule and handing Mr. Bell a generous ten-pound note. "See to it that he is washed and delivered to the Hall before sunset." She glanced over her shoulder to the cell door, adding quietly, "To the servant's entrance, if you please. Then, once he is out of your hands, I expect that you will have no recollection of Mr. Taggart whatsoever, will you, Mr. Bell?"

The gaoler clutched the note behind his back. "None whatsoever, my lady, I assure you."

Melisande nodded briskly, shut her reticule with a sharp click, and headed for the anteroom door, leaving the constable to finish with his locking up. God help her, she still had much to see to before this day was done. She had a wedding to arrange.

Two

Will's teeth came together with a *crack* as the cart's back wheel hit a rut in the road that nearly sent him flying. Smothering a curse, he settled back on the wooden planks and massaged his aching jaw, while trying his very damnedest to appreciate the irony in his situation. For it was ironic—in a way.

In the kind of way that made a man feel like killing somebody.

"Jesus," he ground out as another bump jolted the cart, making his bones rattle. Making him question how on earth he'd come to this. Here he was, Will Taggart, ex-privateer and bounty hunter, being hauled like a crate of cabbages down an English country lane . . . to meet his bride.

A sardonic smile curved his mouth and he thought it a damned good thing that his friend Wildcat couldn't see him now.

The heat of late afternoon pressed down upon him as he wiped his sleeve across his damp forehead, squinting into the gray-green horizon. After spending the night in that frozen jail cell, Will had come to believe that he'd never be warm again. Lord, had he been wrong.

Beneath the unusually warm April sun, he felt as if he

were being boiled alive. Sweat trickled down his back and chest, causing his shirt to cling uncomfortably to his skin. Worse yet, the smell of moldy onions had begun to issue from the moth-eaten wool coat the gaolkeeper had handed him after his bath. A bath that Will decided wasn't going to mean much after this hot, dusty ride through the Devonshire hills.

"Ach, as if it matters," he muttered darkly, tasting dirt as he licked at his parched lips. It didn't matter since Will figured he'd be wallowing at the bottom of more than one muddy trench during these next few days, probably making chummy with chickens in coops, splashing through creeks, and maybe even climbing himself a tree or two. A man on the run tended not to fuss about a little filth under the fingernails.

The only question was when. It had occurred to Will to save himself the trouble of facing Melisande Mooresby and to simply make a run for it now. Over the years he'd evaded men a thousand times sharper and a thousand times more competent than the thick-skulled English constable. If he did choose to bolt from the cart, Will knew there was no possibility of Bell ever chasing him down on this side of the ocean or the other.

But no. The smarter course was to wait for the cover of darkness. For if Will's luck held—and he'd always been an inordinately lucky bastard—Melisande Mooresby might not discover his disappearance until late tomorrow morning. And even then, she might be reluctant to confess to Cullscombe's gaoler that her potential groom had bolted before she'd managed to get a ring on her finger.

Aye, Will figured he'd do best to simply sit tight and wait. Even though waiting entailed spending the next few hours fending off the mysterious Miss Mooresby and her plans for a trip to the altar.

Granted, he *had* given his word, agreeing to the woman's outrageous offer. But he would have said anything—would have promised to marry mad old King George himself—if it had meant finding a way out of that hellhole of a prison cell. He had no intention of actually marrying the woman.

Not by a long shot. Rather he had been handed an opportunity and he'd seized it.

In fact, he should have seized that opportunity a whole helluva lot sooner, but, at the time, he'd been suffering from a hangover and so hadn't been thinking clearly when she'd issued her proposal. Even now, he could kick himself to think how perilously close he'd come to letting his chance for escape pass him by.

Of course, the word "marriage" often clouded a man's thinking. Terror had a way of doing that.

Will leaned against the backboard, folded his arms across his chest, and looped one booted foot over the other. Now that he thought about it, he might be able to work matters so that Miss Mooresby was only too glad to be rid of him. A gory tale or two about his days as "Tiger" Taggart, meanest bounty hunter west of the Mississippi, and he'd have her weeping with gratitude to discover him gone on the morrow.

Not that he intended to scare her. He wasn't that much of a blackguard. But deal or no deal, he sure as blazes wasn't going to stick around long enough to marry the woman. He hadn't dodged bullets from Haiti to St. Louis only to be brought down by a skirt, for God's sake.

The corners of his eyes crinkled as he thought again of the skirt in question, the veiled woman who'd come to his rescue that morning. What had Melisande Mooresby been trying to hide behind that heavy veil and bulky cape? And how had she—a woman—circumvented the law in arranging to have the charges against him dropped?

All afternoon he'd been wondering about her, curious as to what manner of female resorted to hunting for husbands in the local gaolhouse. She was young; he'd been able to tell that much from her voice, rich and clear. And she was small, petite. He didn't imagine she'd even reach the top of his shoulder if they were to stand side by side.

Nonetheless, it was obvious that the lass had to have something wrong with her—something seriously wrong— for her to be forced into buying a bridegroom. She was probably disfigured in some way. Scarred by pox or a burn . . .

Will shook his head, irritated by a twinge of pity. Hell, he
didn't want her to think he was running out on her because
of her . . . imperfection. Whatever it might be. But neither
was he ready to trot her—or any woman—down the aisle.
Sure, someday he'd have to settle down and take himself a
bride but, at twenty-eight years of age, Will didn't see any
reason to rush.

Or he hadn't seen any reason until . . .

Until the gaoler turned into a winding driveway and there,
atop a sloping rise, a house came into view. A house the
likes of which gave Will Taggart pause. Of deep red stone,
the mammoth two-story structure was halfway to being a
castle. Steeply-pitched roofs bent over tall windows of
leaded glass, and a massive tower soared up from the east,
overlooking the U-shaped courtyard. Well-kept hedgerows
stood like sentinels along the perimeter of the house, their
emerald uniforms brilliant against the scarlet background of
the house's facade. The grounds were impeccable, not a
single blade of grass out of place.

Bell drove the cart around to the rear of the house as Will
pondered, his eyes narrowed in studied consideration. Could
it be that his hopeful bride-to-be lived *here*? In this palace?

The warden brought the cart to a standstill in a small
cobblestone court bordered by the stables and a wing of the
house. Bell climbed down from his perch and ambled
around to the back of the cart.

"This is it," the gaolkeeper confirmed. "Mooresby Hall."

Will nodded warily and jumped from the cart. His
thoughts were racing as he tried to calculate just how rich a
person would have to be to live in a place like this.

"Come on now," Bell urged sharply. "I don't want her
sayin' I brung you late."

Still tallying the numbers in his head, Will followed the
constable up to the house, where the man pounded at the
servant's entrance as if he were trying to gain admittance
through the Pearly Gates. A stick-thin woman, wearing a
white cap and apron, answered the door.

Before she could speak, Bell blurted out, "Miss
Mooresby asked me to bring this here fella to the Hall afore

sunset. Here he is. I done my part. Make sure the lady knows that I done my part."

Then, with a brief tip of his cap, the constable murmured "God be with you" in Will's general direction and bolted for the cart. Will gave a lazy scratch to his jaw as he watched the man scurry away. The English sure were a damned skittish lot.

"So Miss Mooresby is expecting you?"

Will pivoted around. The gray-haired maidservant was looking him over from his bare head to his scuffed boots.

"Aye. I believe she is," he answered. Cautiously.

"Hmmph." The maid stepped aside. "Why don't you come and wait in the kitchen then? I'll send word upstairs. Are you peckish?"

Will nodded. The previous night's carousing had left him with little appetite this morning, and any hunger he'd been left with had vanished once he'd taken a whiff of Bell's watery gruel.

"Well, Mrs. Penster will fix you right up," the woman said. "Follow me."

She led him through the laundry, where enormous tubs spewed forth the scent of lye, past a larder and pantry that looked full enough to feed a city, and finally into a kitchen nearly half the size of a ballroom.

In spite of himself, Will was impressed. Though the Taggarts' home wasn't the largest in the burgh, neither could it have been described as anything approaching modest. Yet, when compared to the opulence of Mooresby Hall . . .

The maid settled him on a bench in front of a large wooden table, and soon Will was digging into a meal of onion tart, cheese, and home-brewed ale. While he ate, he noticed that he was the subject of many inquiring glances. Mrs. Penster, the portly cook, hadn't stopped gawking at him since the moment he'd arrived, and the freckled scullery maids shot him a peek every few seconds from their steamy, ovenside posts. Will wondered if the servants of Mooresby Hall could possibly have any inkling as to his purpose in being there or if it was only his disheveled and dusty appearance that had so captured their attention.

"By Jove, what now?" a male voice cried out from just outside the door, shattering the strained quiet of the kitchen. "What in blazes has she gone and done this time?"

Will glanced up from his dinner to see a harried-looking gentleman charge into the room, trailed by the rail-thin maid who'd admitted Will earlier.

The man, young and fair-headed, skidded to a halt on the threshold as his eyes met Will's. Will nodded a wary greeting, since the stranger's expression was not precisely what he'd have called welcoming.

The gentleman did not respond to his salute but turned stiffly toward the maid. "Thank you, Taylor. You did well to inform me."

The maid curtsied and retreated to one side of the kitchen to join the other wide-eyed servants. Will lifted his mug and casually drained the rest of his ale, all the time watching the newcomer from the corner of his eye.

The gentleman hesitated a moment before striding toward the table, his fists clenched at his sides. As he approached, he moved into a shaft of honeyed sunlight that allowed Will to see that the man was far younger than he had first thought. Barely out of his teens, in fact, downy-cheeked and clear-eyed, if taller than average.

"Melisande?" the boy asked, as if her name alone were a question in and of itself.

Will took his time in answering. He pushed away his plate and swung one leg around so that he was straddling the bench.

"Aye," he finally said, alert to the fact that the youth could not possibly be carrying a weapon beneath his fashionably close-fitting coat.

The young man's features spasmed, and Will got the impression that this response had somehow pained the boy.

"Come," the stranger invited. "Let us speak privately."

Though Will was starting to get a real bad feeling about all this, he rose from the table—slowly. He sent a quick wink to the cook, then followed the youngster from the room. They walked wordlessly down two long corridors, through a rotunda-shaped hall, into a library. A library fit for a king.

The room was a study in overwrought luxury—in massive leather chairs and heavy velvet window hangings and gilt-trimmed tomes that stretched across three of the library's four walls. Floor-to-ceiling leaded glass windows looked onto the west, where the sun was leisurely sinking into the Devonshire hills. Before the fire, a liver-spotted hound slept, peacefully snoring.

"Please, have a seat," the young gentleman invited, heeding his own advice as he dropped limply into a tall wingback.

After a hasty survey of the room—an instinctive precautionary measure—Will strolled over and sat down in the opposite chair. Though he made a point to outwardly match the other man's loose-limbed pose, inwardly Will was on edge. He didn't like this. He didn't like it at all.

A long moment of silence prevailed as the blond stranger sized Will up. "I . . . ," he announced on a tired sigh. "I am Melisande's brother. George Mooresby."

Will dipped his chin. "Will Taggart."

"A pleasure, I'm sure." George Mooresby's words lacked a certain sincerity as his gaze flicked over Will's borrowed and threadbare coat. "I am curious, Mr. Taggart, as to what business brings you out to my home today."

Will's lips lifted. In the barest of smiles.

"Your sister brings me," he answered in a languid, Americanized drawl. "I believe she is expecting me."

"Ah, yes. I'm sure that she is. But before I send word to her that she has a caller, I would like to know the *reason* she has summoned you here. The maid informed me that you were brought to the Hall by none other than Cullscombe's gaolkeeper."

Will curled his fingers into his palm and glanced at his chipped nails, debating how much he wanted to reveal. As far as he could see, there was no logical reason not to tell young Mooresby of Melisande's proposition. After all, the lady had not sworn him to secrecy, had she?

Besides which, as the man of the house, George Mooresby

was not very likely to approve a proposed alliance between his darling sister and a pub-crawling, gin-brawling Scot. Not unless the man was profoundly wanting for common sense. Will's eyes narrowed consideringly. On reflection, he thought that old George's brotherly objections could be rather useful—they could give Will the very excuse he needed to slip out of this unsavory agreement. Instead of fleeing and being pursued, perhaps there was some way he could walk away from all this unpleasant business. . . .

Will stretched his arms along the top of the chair and shrugged. "If you must know, Melisande has asked me to marry her."

"I see." Steepling his fingers in front of him, George tapped the tips of his fingers together. "And have you accepted her proposal?"

Will's brows shot into his hairline. He had remembered the English as phlegmatic, but this kind of self-control bordered on the ridiculous. Had Mooresby not understood him?

Intent on painting a clearer picture for the boy, Will pointed at his swollen black eye. "This morning your sister came to see me in the Cullscombe gaol, Mooresby. In the gaol," he repeated meaningfully. "She asked me to marry her and I accepted, though, frankly, I have been having second thoughts."

George sat forward with a frown. "Second thoughts?"

And in a flash of understanding, Will realized that George Mooresby was . . . disappointed.

Disappointed?

What in the hell was going on here? Could it be that the girl was so wholly undesirable that even her brother would see her married off to a complete and total stranger? A stranger plucked, at random, from a row of felons?

Warning bells sounded in Will's head. Sounded so loudly they nearly deafened him.

He pushed to his feet, mentally plotting his path to the nearest exit.

"See here, Mooresby, I can appreciate that this is a family matter best handled by you. Please give your sister my regrets that it . . . uh, didn't work out. No, don't get up," he ordered gruffly. "I'll see myself to the door."

Three long strides had Will halfway across the library before George Mooresby called after him.

"Wait!"

For some reason—some unearthly reason—Will checked his step.

Never would he be sure why he paused in that moment, only seconds away from making a clean getaway. Never would he understand why, when he'd had the opportunity, he hadn't simply barreled out that library door, instead of ignoring the very same instincts that had saved his life a dozen times over.

In the next few weeks, however, Will would remember his hesitation, would remember that moment fraught with decision, and he would ask himself: *What the hell was I thinking?*

"You've done what?"

As her sister teetered on the verge of a swoon, Melisande grabbed hold of Eileen's slim arm and waved a vinaigrette—which she'd had at the ready—beneath the girl's nose. It was generally considered prudent, when in Eileen's company, to keep a vial of smelling salts close at hand.

"Eileen, come, come," Melisande chided. "This is no time for histrionics. We've still far too many details to dispense with."

Eileen's pink-rimmed eyelids fluttered. Weakly she bobbed her head.

"Of course, you're right, Melisande. You're always right. If only—" Eileen's breath came short and labored, in anxious little pants. "If only God had made me as resourceful and clever as you."

Melisande rolled her eyes and steered her sister toward the bed. She sat Eileen down on the rose satin counterpane and passed the vinaigrette once more in front of her ashen face.

"God gave you a kind and delicate nature, which is of far greater value in our world than anything as mundane as cleverness," Melisande countered. "Besides, I daresay that Benjamin would not love you half so well if your temperament suddenly began to resemble mine."

Tears filled Eileen's lovely blue eyes, making them sparkle like the gems they'd been oft compared to in poorly penned verse.

"Oh, Benjamin," Eileen moaned. "My dear Benjamin, what will he do? What will he say?"

Immediately Melisande regretted her slip of the tongue. Benjamin Roddington, Eileen's fiancé, had already wrought enough havoc on this day without her summoning forth his name once more.

"Eileen, I must insist that you stop this incessant weeping," Melisande said firmly. "It cannot be good for you or the babe. You have your health to consider now, do not forget."

Eileen sniffed and, in her own brave little fashion, fought back the tears. "Yes, you are right again, sister. But how? How can I allow you to do this perfectly dreadful thing? And on my account?"

"You make far too much of it, my dear," Melisande said, tenderly smoothing a light brown curl from Eileen's cheek. "'Tis nothing more than a business arrangement, an arrangement wherein I stand to benefit as much as you. Once I am wed, Grandfather will have accomplished what he desired"—Melisande's jaw clenched—"and I will, finally, have the use of Grandmother's inheritance."

"But, Melisande, I am sorry, but I do not understand. I had thought that Lord Fielding was to offer for you any day now. Why would you choose to wed a criminal instead of the baron?"

Melisande's jaw clenched even tighter, and she could only be grateful that the perfidious Lord Fielding lived far out of her reach. She could just scream when she thought of all the time she'd wasted on that scoundrel! The months she had spent in Bath scouring the field of bachelors, searching for just the right candidate. A man who would not try to manage her; a man who would not interfere in her life, or order her about as if he were, by happenstance of his being born a male, her God-given lord and master.

Then she had met Fielding. By Jove, he had been positively perfect—accommodating, benign, inoffensive.

She had been so pleased to finally settle on the baron, and had made it clear to the man that she expected a proposal before the summer was out.

But, evidently, the weasel had more backbone than she'd given him credit for. Only that very morning, Catherine Dolbane had come to call at Mooresby Hall and had inadvertently let "slip" the rumor that Lord Fielding had recently asked for the hand of one Elsa Carolly. Furious at the news, Melisande had been poised to ride off to Wiltshire to set the baron straight when she'd stumbled upon Eileen, suffering the throes of morning sickness. The truth had then come out.

Melisande waved her hand, dismissing the baron as if he'd never existed. "Lord Fielding was not going to suit," she told her sister. "And since time was of the essence, I was not about to risk a delay in hunting up another acceptable prospect."

"But a colonial from the gaol!"

"He is not a colonial," Melisande corrected. "He is a Scot. He has only been living in America."

"A Scot?" Eileen did not seem at all reassured. "Dear heavens, is he a *Catholic*?"

Melisande blinked. Dash it, she hadn't considered that possibility. She should have thought to inquire before she sent off for the license.

"A Scot," Eileen murmured fretfully, twisting her fingers together. "He's not one of those barbarous highlanders, is he?"

"No, I don't believe so. His accent would suggest the south, I think."

Eileen's palm fluttered to her forehead and she looked in danger of swooning again. "Oh, my dear sister, however shall you manage? To pretend to be married to such a man. Is he . . . terribly unrefined?"

Melisande wavered. She didn't wish to alarm her sister,

yet neither did she wish to play false. "Well," she prevaricated, "his vocabulary seems adequate and his diction is unobjectionable. As to whether he can read or write, I cannot say, nor can I speak to his intelligence. He *is* a bit rough around the edges—"

"Oh, it is all my fault," Eileen wailed. "If only Benjamin and I hadn't succumbed."

Guilt forced Melisande to shake her head in a denial. "No, Eileen, it is I who am entirely to blame. If I hadn't been so negligent in selecting a bridegroom, you and Benjamin would not have been left waiting to marry these past two years. It was my selfish reluctance to wed that has placed you in this difficulty. My reluctance and," she added balefully, "Grandfather's obstinacy."

Eileen's palm fanned across her flat stomach. "If only Grandpapa had relented. Does he not realize that no one adheres to that antiquated notion anymore? Really, as if in this day and age it's at all sensible to expect the older sister to always marry before the younger."

Melisande glared at the tips of her shoes. "I think the old wretch insisted upon it merely to torment me. He knew that the lure of Grandmother's inheritance wasn't enough, so he forced me to stand in the way of your happiness."

"Oh, no." Eileen laid her hand on Melisande's arm. "It wasn't your doing. I . . ." She flushed and glanced aside. "I ought to have been more patient."

Melisande patted her sister's hand as a frown settled between her brows. Though sympathetic to her sister's plight, she simply did not understand how Eileen could have been so carried away on a tide of passion that she had risked both public humiliation and disgrace to the family name. Eileen was not the sort given to impulsiveness or immoderate emotions. She was a mild-mannered and gentle soul—a dove to Melisande's hawk.

How then had it happened? To be honest, Melisande questioned whether passion such as Eileen described even existed. At twenty-two she had lived nearly five years longer than her younger sister, and not once had she come close to experiencing a like emotion.

Admittedly she'd been fond of a gentleman or two. Thought a handful of them pleasant enough and not too terribly overbearing. She had even gone so far as to kiss that rat Fielding once or twice. But the yearning, the powerful aching need that Eileen had spoken of, was entirely beyond either Melisande's comprehension or her experience.

Perhaps, she reasoned, she didn't have it in her. Truthfully, she had long since resigned herself to the fact that she wasn't the typical English female. She was too hotheaded to be typically English. And too—

Well, suffice it to say that if Eileen embodied the most desirable of feminine qualities—docility, sensitivity, and delicacy—Melisande was to be found lacking in them all.

"But what of Grandpapa?" Eileen asked. "What will you tell him?"

Melisande flipped her long, unbound hair over her shoulder. "As little as possible. By the time he gets wind of the goings-on here and makes the trip from London, the worst of it will already be done. I've sent a message to our cousin, the bishop, and asked him to procure a license, which should arrive within the next two or three days. And after leaving the gaol this morning, I made straight for the Cullscombe vicarage and left a message, instructing the minister to begin posting the banns for your and Benjamin's wedding."

"Banns? Oh dear, must we wait as long as that?"

Melisande gave Eileen a reproving look. "Eileen, dear, we are laboring to protect your reputation. A rushed, slap-a-dash wedding would be tantamount to a confession, don't you think? After all, after you are married, it's not likely to be commented upon should the baby arrive a bit earlier than the standard nine months."

"But what of your reputation? Aren't you concerned for yourself?"

"Oh, pooh." Melisande waved her fingers in a show of indifference. "I daresay there is little that the 'She-Devil of Mooresby Hall' could do to raise eyebrows in Devonshire anymore. A hasty marriage, an even hastier annulment— none of it should come as shocking to our neighbors."

Eileen still appeared to waver as she gnawed fretfully at her lower lip. "I don't know, Melisande. It does not seem right to allow you to make this sacrifice for me."

Sacrifice? As if from nowhere, a vision of broad shoulders and tawny-streaked hair flashed before Melisande's eyes.

"I am *not* making a sacrifice," she argued. "I am being practical. No matter what my views on the institution of marriage, Grandfather insists on seeing me wed. Very well, I shall wed. And then I shall annul. By choosing this route, at least I will have my long-awaited inheritance."

"Do you . . . Do you still plan to use the money to found a house of reform?" Eileen's features twisted with ill-concealed distaste.

"I do," Melisande returned staunchly. "And I am certain that Papa would have approved of my venture."

Eileen let loose a sigh of defeat. "You have made up your mind, haven't you? About all of it. About the Scot and the wedding and your plans for the reformatory?"

"I have." Melisande stood, smoothing the wrinkles from her crimson skirts. "And you know better than anyone, Eileen, that once I have set my mind to an endeavor, I refuse to be deterred. I will see it through straight to the end."

A weak smile wobbled on her sister's lips. "Straight to the bitter end," she repeated.

Three

"Wait, Mr. Taggart, if you please."

George Mooresby leaped from his chair as if he planned to give chase.

Balanced on the balls of his feet, Will eyed the library door. Freedom lay just on the other side. Deliverance. Although the warning bells continued to toll in his head, urging him to flee, he remained where he stood.

A prickling of premonition crept along his skin, raising the fine hairs at the back of his nape. Instinct made him reach for the Indian hunting knife he ordinarily carried, but his searching fingers found his belt empty.

Not that he actually anticipated an attack. Not in a library, and certainly not from this dandified Englishman but fresh out of leading strings. Nonetheless, Will sensed approaching danger. A threat, impending peril—

"George? George, where are you?"

The library door flew open smack in Will's face. If he'd been standing even an inch closer, his nose would have been shattered to bits instead of his toes merely smashed.

The woman entering did not see him. Her bright red skirts swished with determination as she marched into the room, straight toward young Mooresby, who looked as if he'd been turned to stone.

"George, we must talk."

That voice . . . Its husky timbre was familiar, as was the direct manner in which she delivered her words.

She stood with her back to Will, her hands planted uncompromisingly atop her hips. Nice hips, he noticed. Well rounded, yet not too round. A slim waist, a gently curving back. Will's eyes slitted as he measured her. She was small enough to be Melisande Mooresby—

"This concerns Eileen," she said, "so I suggest that you sit down. It is not going to be at all easy for you to hear."

George uttered some wholly unintelligible sound as he cast a desperate glance at Will.

"Sit down, George," she said again, pointing him to the chair he'd recently vacated. "This day has already taxed my patience to its very limits, and I haven't the—"

She must have noticed the direction of young Mooresby's gaze, for she stopped mid-sentence and spun around, her midnight-black hair swirling about her shoulders like a satiny sheet. At the back of his mind, Will thought it unusual for her hair to be unbound, for it to spill like an inky waterfall down to her waist. Where he had just come from, only the Indian women walked about with their hair loose, their heads uncovered.

As she turned to fully face him, Will felt his gut contract. Could this be Melisande Mooresby?

No pox, no burns, no scars . . .

Aye, she was beautiful. So damned beautiful his mouth watered. Her skin was the texture of fresh cream, her eyes the color of thick Creole coffee. Her full lips, parted in surprise, offered a strikingly sensual contrast to her sharp nose and the no-nonsense squareness of her jaw. A jaw that hardened when recognition set in.

"Mr. Taggart."

Of a sudden, Will did not find himself as eager to take his leave as he'd been but a moment earlier. He stepped from behind the door, bending forward in a brief salute. His toes still throbbed from their encounter with the door.

"Miss Mooresby."

"I had not been informed of your arrival"—she shot her

brother a look of patent displeasure—"or I would have
greeted you myself. I gather that you have already made the
acquaintance of my brother, George?"

At last young Mooresby managed to break out of his
stupor, his chest puffing out as if he had only that moment
recalled his position as lord of the household. "Melisande, I
was going to send for you after I had spoken with Mr.
Taggart. I really was. I mean when a complete stranger calls
for you—" He shuffled his feet like an awkward child, his
voice cracking. "I do have my responsibilities, you know.
Responsibilities to you and Eileen—"

"Yes, George, yes," she broke in impatiently. "Now that
you've spoken with Mr. Taggart, are your responsibilities
fulfilled?" She folded her arms across her chest, across the
enticing curves that had been hidden from Will that morning. "I have pressing business I need to discuss with this
man."

"Yes, I know," George interjected. "I know of your
'business.'"

Melisande glanced at Will, her lips pursed. 'Twas obvious
that she would have preferred to be the one to inform her
brother of their bargain.

Will gave a negligent shrug, seeing no reason to apologize.

"I think it imperative that you and I discuss this matter,"
George said to his sister. "Though you might have consulted
me *before* the fact, don't you think? After all I have reached
my majority and I am entitled—"

"Oh, George, do be quiet!"

Like a testy colt, Melisande tossed her head, her hair a
silken black mane that made Will think of desert night skies
and inky bayou waters. This woman was no shrinking
violet, he thought to himself. This woman had fire in her
spirit. *Mantowagan,* as the Lenape would say.

"Very well, George. By all means, let us discuss my
pending nuptials. But I would first like a few moments alone
with Mr. Taggart."

Young Mooresby appeared afraid to refuse. "I will allow
you five minutes," he said, pushing his "lord of the manor"

role a fraction too far. For as George walked past his sister,
Will thought he heard Melisande Mooresby actually hiss
beneath her breath. *Hiss.* Like the she-cat she was starting to
remind him of.

Will's gaze followed the sulking George out the door, his
eye catching on a row of glittering decanters sitting atop a
bureau on the other side of the room. Suddenly aware of his
keen thirst, he started toward them, reflecting that a stiff
drink might be of some benefit in the upcoming interview.
His hand hovered above the crystal stopper, when he turned
to find Melisande Mooresby looking him up and down in
frank appraisal.

"May I?" he asked belatedly.

Her lips pursed. "As you wish."

Will poured himself a generous portion, the delicate
aroma indicating that the brandy could only be French, and
of the highest grade. He lifted the glass to his nose. It
smelled like heaven. It also smelled like money.

In fact, everything about Mooresby Hall fairly reeked of
wealth. The scent of coin was inescapable, in the musty
Spanish leather and the lemon-polished cherrywood. In the
flat cool scent of Italian marble and the heady perfume of a
well-tended garden.

In the woman standing before him.

Leaning indolently against the sideboard, Will wrapped
his palms around the snifter and waited. If he'd judged her
correctly, Melisande Mooresby was the type of woman to
get right to the point.

She did.

"Whatever my brother might have said, Mr. Taggart, I
want you to know that we *will* be married. And soon. Have
no fear of that."

Will's brows lifted and he surmised that she was attempting to reassure him. *Guess again, darlin'.*

She linked her hands behind her back and started to pace,
her stride swift and agitated. "George is not yet aware of the
reason for my urgency," she explained. "Once he is, then he
ought to appreciate our need for haste. This isn't a matter to
be trifled with and I cannot abide any delay. If George

continues to pose objections—" She shook her head. "Well, it matters not, for I assure you that we will be married. The very moment the license arrives."

The crystal snifter poised on his lips, Will recognized his cue. This was where he was supposed to jump in and explain to her that she had made an error. That, flattered though he was by her offer, he just didn't make for good husband material and, besides, her brother would never allow it.

Instead Will took another sip of the brandy, his gaze boldly caressing the stubborn sway of her hips.

"Why are you in such a rush to wed?" he asked.

She ceased her pacing, and her chin came up a notch. "My reasons are confidential. Personal."

At first Will imagined the color in her cheeks to be only the glow from the hearth, the firelight reflecting off her rich crimson gown. But, no. She was blushing. A blush of embarrassment—

Well, hell. Just how blind could he be? It was obvious, wasn't it?

"A babe?"

Her silent hesitation was answer enough. *So much for waiting for nightfall,* Will decided. He was going to have to take his chances on the open road right this minute. Slamming his goblet onto the sideboard, he made tracks for the door, his boot heels ringing out like pistol shots, echoing up to the rafters.

"Sorry, lady, bargain or no bargain, I sure as hell—"

"Not mine!"

Her indignant protest drew him up short. "What do you mean 'not yours'?"

"Oh, bother." She shoved her fists onto her hips, drawing Will's attention to those delightful curves again. "I suppose you would learn the truth sooner or later." Her mouth pinched into a tight bow. "It is my younger sister, Eileen. She and her fiancé have . . . rushed matters. And my grandfather, curse his stubborn hide, refuses to let her marry until I wed."

"Not even under these circumstances?"

Melisande's back stiffened. "We have not *told* him of the circumstances, for heaven's sake. I do not know what the Scottish or American attitude might be," she said, arrogance tilting her nose skyward, "but here in England, Mr. Taggart, a family's good name is priceless. Invaluable. My grandfather is a viscount and a peer of the realm. He would never forgive Eileen for her transgression. If she were to bring scandal into this family— Why, Grandfather would disinherit her and ship her off to a foreign nunnery with nary a second thought. The man is thoroughly uncompromising."

Will scratched behind his ear. "But you can marry on a whim, then arrange for a speedy annulment, without offending Grandpa's sense of pride?"

Melisande gave him a look. A look that brought into question his intelligence. Or lack thereof.

"No one expects anything of *me*," she said. "With Eileen, it is different."

"Why?"

She frowned as if taken aback, then turned away from him to stalk to the window, where early dusk painted the sky in vivid shades of ruby and violet. In the fading light, her hair glinted a deep blue-black.

"Why?" she repeated. "Because that is how it is meant to be. Eileen is lovely. She's always been lovely. She is a perfect lady in all respects. Since the day of her birth, we have all believed that she would do well. And she has. Her fiancé, Benjamin, is heir to an important earldom."

Will still didn't understand. Why did no one expect Melisande to "do well"? Did the lass harbor some defect invisible to the eye?

Slowly he walked over to join her at the window, careful to maintain a safe distance between them. She was staring out onto the dusk-washed hills, her profile clear and sharp. He had no chance to ask about her family's expectations— why no one had any for her—before she pivoted on her heel, looking him square in the eye.

"Terms."

"What?"

"We have yet to discuss terms," she said. "The terms of

our agreement. What do you think would be fair compensation for a month of your time, Mr. Taggart?"

Will grinned and cupped a hand around the back of his neck. "How much have you got?"

Disdain sharpened her pupils to pinpoints. "Enough. Shall we say a hundred pounds?"

"Let's say . . ." He glanced to the diamond studs sparkling in her ears. "A thousand."

"Nonsense. Two hundred pounds and not a penny more."

"Five hundred."

"I said two hundred, Mr. Taggart, and that is where I stand. Take it or leave it."

Shrugging, Will conceded. After all, he was merely playing along. "I'll take it. Though you sure do drive a hard bargain, lady."

Her answering sniff was dainty, yet triumphant. "I should hope so. After nearly four years of managing the estate, I'd like to think I've learned something of the art of negotiation."

Will went instantly still. "You manage the estate?"

"I most certainly do. I see to all the Mooresby financial affairs. The tenants, crops, investments, everything. My father recognized early my faculty for estate administration and encouraged me to become involved. I must say I've been rather successful to date, realizing profits in all our recent fiscal ventures."

Will's pulse quickened and he glanced around the room, once again cataloguing the Mooresby fortunes. "You don't say . . ."

The germ of an idea was forming in his thoughts. A proposition so absurd he knew he had to be thoroughly insane to even consider it.

Are you crazy, Taggart? Have you lost your blasted mind?

Hell, he wasn't ready to take a bride. He needed a wife like he needed a cutlass through his heart. And he'd have preferred the cutlass.

Ever since he was old enough to bed his first woman, Will Taggart had been dodging apron strings as if they were

bullets. Promises of undying love and eternal devotion had
never been in his trunk of wooing techniques. He had never
deceived a woman to get her to lie down with him. He'd
always been honest: "Live for the moment and take the
loving but, in the morning, sweetheart, I am gone."

In fact, he and Wildcat even had a longstanding bet as to
who would be the first to fall victim to the altar. And Will
simply hated to lose.

Yet . . .

It wasn't as if he would be taking just any woman for a
bride. No, he was talking about an unqualified beauty here,
a lady of wealth and impeccable breeding. A woman
intelligent enough and courageous enough to manage this
vast estate. A woman who virtually dripped gold from her
fingertips.

*My God, Melisande Mooresby could be the answer to my
prayers.*

The longer he weighed the idea, the more convinced he
became that the fates had presented him with a twenty-four-
karat golden opportunity. An opportunity that only the worst
kind of fool would let pass.

And Will Taggart was no fool.

"Very well then, we've agreed," Melisande said, breaking
into his thoughts. "Three weeks. A month at the longest.
Then once Eileen is wed, I'll handle the particulars of the
annulment and you will be free to return to Scotland or the
States or"—she fluttered her hand, indicating that it made
no difference to her—"wherever you choose, Mr. Taggart."

"Will," he corrected silkily, sneaking another peek at
those appealing curves of hers. "If we are to be husband and
wife, don't you think you should call me by my given
name?"

Her brows inched together. "Yes, I suppose that's reasonable. 'Twould be more convincing." Still gently frowning,
she drummed her fingers against her lower lip, muttering,
"What else, what else . . . Do *you* have any other questions or concerns?"

Will watched as she awaited his answer, her thumb

tapping at the pink, delicate fullness of her lower lip. Desire hit him. A powerful surge, sweet and unexpected.

"No, I think I'm getting a fair idea of what I need to do," he answered, shifting nearer as she continued her pensive muttering.

"You'll stay here at Mooresby Hall, which ought to be sufficiently proper since George is at home. And we can have the tailor out tomorrow. The tutoring I can most likely take care of myself, and—"

She ceased her monologue, glancing up with a start.

Will stood over her, his gaze fixed to her lips as they parted on a light, breathless gasp.

Hell, if I'm going to go through with this, if I'm going to take this woman to wife—

He had to be sure of one thing.

Grabbing hold of her shoulders, Will bent and captured Melisande's mouth with his. Captured and possessed it completely, his lips molding her softness and warmth, his tongue playing along her velvety fullness. At first she was frozen beneath him, her breath short and quick, her body rigid.

But Will drew her closer, rubbing her breasts against his chest, deepening the range of his kiss. As his tongue probed what he knew had to be virgin territory, he felt her mouth move tentatively under his. That small movement sent desire spiking through him. He pulled her tight, feeling her heart thud in time to his own raging pulse.

He groaned and lowered his palm to her breast—

She twisted and lurched back, her hand lifted as if to strike. Her hair was disheveled, her mouth swollen.

They were both breathing fast, both staring at her hand poised above them. The air crackled. Slowly she lowered her arm and raised her chin, striving to reclaim her dignity.

"That, Mr. Taggart," she said shakily, "is not part of our agreement. You will not repeat it."

Will was on the verge of telling her with what regularity he planned to repeat it when the library door opened to admit George Mooresby.

Melisande's brother froze, his gaze darting back and forth

between them. Will guessed that it did not take a clairvoyant to determine what had occurred to put the flames in Melisande's cheeks or the fire in her eyes.

Pressing the back of her hand against her mouth, she made an angry, muffled sound, and bolted from the room like a comet's flare.

George, looking dazed and somewhat awed, turned to Will. "Am I to assume the marriage is still on?"

Will's pulse hammered, his groin ached. Already his lips craved the taste of her again.

He glanced to the empty doorway and answered with more conviction than he'd ever felt in his life. "The marriage is on."

Four
꘎꘎꘎

Flustered and out of sorts, Melisande marched upstairs to her room, making straight for the cheval glass hanging in a corner of her green-and-gold chamber. After first kicking aside a pile of books she'd left on the floor, she approached the gilt-framed mirror with a peculiar sense of dread.

"Bother," she grumbled as she peered into the glass. "Bother and botheration."

To her utter dismay, her reflection revealed an undeniable and telltale pinkishness about the cheeks. She was blushing. When she *never* blushed. Melisande did not blush as she seldom had reason to. She wasn't the missish sort who turned red at the drop of a colorful phrase, or grew embarrassed at a hint of innuendo. And rarely, if ever, did she succumb to feelings of either guilt or shame. Guilt or shame for what? To her mind, her actions were generally well thought out, rational, and quite justified. At least . . . to her mind.

Deliberately she smoothed the wrinkles from her brow.

That's better, she thought, her gaze slipping inexorably lower, from a pair of dark, clouded eyes to a firm, straight nose to gently parted lips. Melisande's frown reappeared as she studied her mouth's familiar shape and form. Although it looked much the same as it had only an hour earlier, it felt different now. Her mouth felt somehow plumper and fuller. More sensitive.

Curious, she ran a tentative forefinger across her lower lip, amazed to find the smooth surface cool—not warm. Not afire as it had been a few minutes earlier. . . .

Afire, yes, she mused morosely. "Afire" quite described her cheeks as she pictured once more how she'd let that presumptuous Scot maul her as if she were some cheap alehouse doxy. God help her, on any other day, she would have floored the man, left him searching for his teeth on the Axminster carpet. And on reflection, she wasn't exactly sure why she hadn't fought the scoundrel; why she hadn't let her fists fly the moment he grabbed hold of her shoulders. At the very least, a deftly placed knee would have served her well—and served him warning. But instead she'd only stood there like a rag doll while he played her mouth as if it were a musical instrument. Cajoling, caressing, teasing it to reveal its full potential—

Her scowl deepened.

What had the impertinent rogue been hoping to prove anyway? That he knew how to kiss a woman? Kiss her so that her knees went weak and her stomach turned inside out?

Melisande drew back from the glass, her nose twitching in sudden irritation.

"Gracious," she exclaimed aloud. "What am I carrying on about?"

She drew herself up and straightened the collar of her gown, huffing beneath her breath. If her knees were weak and her color high, it had naught to do with stolen kisses, she told herself, but rather with her concern for Eileen. It had, after all, been a most difficult day. A day provoking enough to ruffle even her level temperament: a suitor gone astray, a sister in the family way, and a groom plucked from a gaol cell. Was it any wonder she was flushed?

"Ridiculous," she said, spinning away from the mirror and nearly stumbling over a thick, leather-bound book.

And it *was* ridiculous to think that her nervous state was

in any way connected to William Taggart. To think so would be to give the man entirely too much consequence when, in fact, he was a virtual stranger to her; a coarse, plain-speaking Scot who had a weakness for drink and a penchant for trouble.

But she would turn him around. Yes, indeed. She would teach him all that he needed to know to improve himself, to better his station in life.

Truly, if anything, she ought to sympathize with the poor man. It was quite obvious that he had not the first notion how to behave around a gently bred lady. To take such outrageous liberties— Well, she might be able to excuse his paucity of manners this once, especially since she'd made it clear to him that no further breaches of conduct would be allowed. But if Eileen were to hear of it . . .

Melisande tugged at her earlobe, her gaze wandering to the black cloak she'd worn into Cullscombe that morning. Its woolen folds still reeked of the gaol's stench, the odor summoning forth the vision of her intended as she'd first seen him—his shirt ripped and hanging open, his knuckles stained with blood.

A trace of uncertainty flickered through her.

What did she really know of William Taggart? Aside from the limited information she'd gleaned from Mr. Bell? Though the man did speak with a reasonable degree of intelligence, there was a definite coarseness to Taggart's manner; a rough, uncivilized edge about him that suggested he'd blackened that eye of his more than once in the past.

Perhaps, Melisande thought, it would be best if her "fiancé" was kept out of the way for the first day or so. At least until she could school him in the finer points of etiquette and deportment. After all, Eileen's sensibilities were astonishingly delicate, and the man *had* been living in the colonies.

Determinedly Melisande strode across to her writing table and quickly penned:

> *Understanding that you must be weary from the day's travails, I see no reason why you must inconvenience*

*yourself by joining us for the evening meal. I have
therefore instructed that a tray be brought to your
room in the hopes that you may retire early. I trust
that in the morning I will find you well rested and
ready to set to work. We will begin at seven o'clock
sharp.*

—M

Melisande crisply folded the note in half, then rang for
her maid. When Molly answered the summons, Melisande
ordered the maid to deliver the message, along with a cold
collation, to Mr. Taggart's chambers. She also asked that hot
water be sent to his room in case he chose to bathe
again—she had noticed an odd oniony smell to his person.

Satisfied that she'd taken all prudent measures to ensure
the success of her matrimonial plan, Melisande returned to
her writing desk with a baleful smile. She had just enough
time before dinner to compose one last letter to a certain
Lord Fielding. She had yet to congratulate the baron on his
recent betrothal and she did so want to make clear to the
gentleman her sentiments regarding the happy news.

Seven o'clock the next morning found Will racing across
the dewy Devonshire fields, the wind whistling in his ears,
the thunder of pounding hooves pulsing through him,
echoing into his very bones.

He had just swerved aside to avoid a small boulder when
another rider surged past. The horseman reined in and
turned his mount with a skill Will had not often witnessed
from a white man. He, too, pulled up, nodding his approval.

"That's some impressive riding, Mooresby."

George Mooresby grinned and tipped his high-crowned
hat. "You've a fine seat yourself, Taggart. Not many can
hold Ulysses once they've given him his head."

Will narrowed his eyes into the morning sun, reflecting
on how easy, how tempting, it would have been to give
Ulysses free rein. To let the powerful chestnut carry him
across the valley and into the dark northern hills toward
Scotland.

A few hours earlier he had contemplated doing that very thing. He'd woken at dawn with a violent start, sitting straight up in the unfamiliar bed. His hand had shot beneath the pillow, groping for his missing knife, before he'd abruptly recalled his whereabouts. Mooresby Hall. The home of his bride-to-be. With a self-derisive snort, he'd flopped back onto the mattress to stare grimly up at the frescoed ceiling while a painted Cupid mocked him from above, its cherubic eyes dancing with glee.

Will had not long lain abed. Still questioning what in the hell he'd gotten himself into, he'd dressed, slipped out of his room, and immediately bumped into George Mooresby prowling the early morning corridors. After accepting George's invitation to join him for a ride, Will had borrowed a set of clothes, then followed the younger man to the extensive Mooresby stables, stocked with the finest horse-flesh money could buy. As they rode into the sunrise, George had pointed out how the vast Mooresby property stretched from one horizon to the next . . . And suddenly—suddenly Will had remembered what it was he had found so appealing about the prospect of marriage.

Pivoting in the saddle, Will studied his young riding companion as George leaned forward and whispered words of praise into his horse's ear. Though the two of them had spoken little during their vigorous ride, it had been obvious to Will from the first that Mooresby had something on his mind. The lad was virtually a-tremble, brimming with jitters like a pot about to boil over. He wanted something, all right. He just didn't know how to ask for it.

Side by side, they turned and began walking their sweat-lathered horses back in the direction of the manor.

"So you're"—George lightly cleared his throat, a cough that might have masked a nervous cracking of his voice— "from Scotland, eh?"

"Aye."

"I wager I wouldn't have guessed it from your speech if Melisande had not already mentioned the fact."

"I've done some traveling, picked up bits and pieces of accents as I went along." A sardonic gleam entered Will's gaze. "So what other interesting tidings did your sister share with you, Mooresby?"

"Well, ahem, she said that the two of you are to be wed by special license."

A tenseness squared George's shoulders, leading Will to suspect that the true objective of this morning jaunt was about to be revealed.

"That's the plan," Will laconically agreed.

"Ah, yes, very good. So glad to hear that the two of you have worked it out. Do you happen to know when the license is scheduled to arrive?"

Apparently it couldn't arrive soon enough to suit Mr. Mooresby's purposes.

"Any day, I'd imagine."

"Hmm, the license, the ceremony . . . and then I daresay you'll be wanting to take Melisande home to meet the family, eh?"

Will slanted the lad a curious, calculating glance. He knew that Melisande must have told her brother that theirs was to be a marriage of convenience only. Why then the pretense of ignorance?

"What are you getting at, Mooresby?"

"Me? Well, I, uh—" George's cravat jiggled as if he'd swallowed hard. "Dash it all, I can't take it anymore!" he burst out, his simmering emotions getting the better of him at last. He jerked his hat from his head and slapped it heatedly against his thigh, earning a nickering protest from his horse.

"She's driving me mad, I tell you, mad! I'm like an infant in short pants around her, stuttering and hemming and hawing, always the little brother she feels she must take care of and manage and order about.

"I vow you've got to help me, Taggart. The brotherhood of men and all that. You've simply got to marry her . . . if only for her own good, dammit!

"Now, uh, don't think that I'm not thinking of her, too, you know," George added somewhat belatedly. "I swear she'll never be happy going on as she has been, and she's too bloody stubborn to recognize it or to hear the truth of it from me. I ask you, what is to become of the girl? Can't she see that if she goes on like this, she's going to end up a miserable old ape-leader surrounded by spineless fools who've not got the pluck to stand up to her and say no?"

Caught off guard by the intensity of Mooresby's outburst, Will merely squinted into the horizon. "So, in your opinion, your sister needs to hear no?"

"Lud, does she ever! She needs a man she can respect, I tell you. A man who will fight to be accepted as her equal, not some lily-livered toad she'll use as a doormat."

"And what makes you think," Will asked mildly, "that I'm not just as lily-livered as the next toad?"

George had the grace to look embarrassed as he waved his crop at Will's mount. "I guess you could say that Ulysses was my notion of a test. I have always believed you can tell a lot about a man by how he sits a horse. Ulysses here won't let just anyone climb atop him, no sir. I figured that any man who could handle that spirited bit o' blood ought to be able to handle the She-Devil of Mooresby Hall."

Will's brows rose. "The She-Devil?"

George's youthful expression said "oops."

"Er, nothing really," he stuttered. "Meaningless nickname the locals invented. Nothin' to it, you know."

Will questioned whether Melisande would think there was "nothing to it," then idly wondered if George Mooresby was the sort who bled a lot.

"I don't know." Will gave a thoughtful scratch to the underside of his chin. "Sounds like a lot of work for the man willing to take her on."

George jerked aright, nearly leaving his saddle. "Now, see here, don't get me wrong," he protested. "She's a first-rate gal, and a rare catch at that. Why, 'pon my word, there isn't a female with half her character in all of Devonshire, I'll swear it. One thing you can say about our Melisande is that she's loyal to a fault. She can be depended upon in a pinch, she can, true blue."

Will did not answer, and George evidently took that to mean he hadn't pleaded his case well enough.

"And though she might not be a diamond like Eileen," he

continued to argue, "she ain't too hard on the eyes either. She's got a sizeable dowry coming to her. *Sizeable*," he repeated, swinging his crop for emphasis.

With a casual flick of his fingers, Will sent an insect away from Ulysses' ear. "So aside from a bit of a stubborn streak, there's nothing . . . wrong with your sister?"

"Wrong?" George retracted his chin like a confused turtle. "Well, she is rather sensitive about her ankles— Is that what you mean? Very well, they might not be as trim as she'd like, but, demme, if I haven't seen thicker ones in my day."

In *his* day.

Will subdued the twitching of his lips, thinking it unlikely the pup had even seen his twenty-first birthday yet, much less a woman's ankles. Nevertheless, he did feel sorry for the lad. It was clear that Mooresby was trying his damnedest to assume his role as man of the house, but wresting the reins from the headstrong Melisande couldn't be an easy endeavor.

"So what do you want from me?"

Will had been expecting a catch, a hook of some kind. An opportunity like Melisande Mooresby didn't fall into a man's lap without a price. Naturally he'd been hoping that the price of his bachelorhood would be sufficiently steep . . .

"Only to carry through with her scheme," George said. "Up to the point, that is, where she obtains the annulment. Now, I realize, Taggart, that you probably hadn't been looking for a lifelong leg shackle—what man is? But we've all got to come up to scratch sometime and Melisande would be a prize for the right fella. A downy fella looking to improve his circumstances, let's say."

"Are you suggesting that I should somehow foil the annulment?"

"Y-yes."

"Do you have a suggestion as to how?"

The lad turned a color so red, he looked almost purple.

"Ah-hah." Will was now quite certain that young Mooresby knew naught of women's ankles.

Frowning, he turned to glance once more at those beckoning northern hills. From the sound of it, George Mooresby wanted nothing more than what Will had already planned for himself: to make a true marriage of the false one. If George were willing to lend assistance, shouldn't he accept it? With the two of them working toward the same goal, it would be that much easier to convince Melisande that her future lay in his hands. Her future and her riches and her softly curving hips—

George made a harrumphing sound. "Of course, I'd be presenting you with a wedding gift."

Will's ears perked up, yet he kept his tone indifferent. "What did you have in mind?"

"I thought that Ulysses might be to your liking?"

Pushing out his lips, Will made a show of considering the offer. He didn't want to appear overeager—not when he so clearly held the upper hand.

"Hmm, I don't know. 'Twould be a shame," he mused, "to pair this fine animal with a lesser beast. . . ."

George winced.

"Perhaps the other chestnut?" Will suggested. "What was his name? Attila?"

"Oh, lud—" George cut short his anguished groan. "Yes, yes, Attila *and* Ulysses," he conceded, rolling his shoulders back and forth as if he were working a knot from his neck. "After all, I mustn't forget that it is my sister's happiness which is at stake here. She might not like it at first, but she'll come around eventually, mark my words. Once she appreciates how well suited the two of you are, she'll settle in to her wifely role and be right glad of it."

Settle in? Well suited?

Will shot a sidelong look at the younger man, his gaze openly speculative. "Indulge me, Mooresby, but you do seem determined to foist your sister off on me and I would very much like to understand your rationale. What in blazes convinces you that Melisande will even have me? That she'll let me close enough to render an annulment impossible?"

For the first time that morning, George assumed a

confident air, as he returned his hat to his head, placing it at a jaunty angle. "Last night when I returned to the library and found you two together . . . you'd kissed her, hadn't you?"

Will admitted as much with a shrug.

"I thought so," George said. "You see, Taggart, the last fella who tried to steal a peck from Melisande couldn't walk for a month." He smugly held up a trio of gloved fingers. "Poor bloke paid for his insolence with no less than three broken toes, crushed under the heel of my sister's dainty foot."

Will gave a small, indulgent smile. "So Melisande chose not to grind my toes to dust. I wouldn't say that means much of anything, Mooresby."

George shook his head and answered in all seriousness, "From Melisande, old boy, I'd call that virtually a declaration."

Five

Stifling a yawn behind her hand, Melisande—who had slept but fitfully—entered the morning room at precisely fifteen minutes before the hour of seven. To her dismay, she found the breakfast table empty. No George. No Will Taggart. Only a handful of pale saffron sunbeams slanting in from the mullioned window.

"Has my brother not come down yet?" she asked the footman stationed beside the buffet. Like her, George normally rose with the sun.

"Mr. Mooresby has already been and gone, miss. He and the visiting gentleman broke their fast earlier and left for the stables a good half hour ago."

Melisande nearly dropped the cup of freshly poured chocolate just handed her. "George and Mr. Taggart have gone riding? Together?"

"Yes, ma'am," the servant repeated. "About thirty minutes ago."

"Confound it," she muttered. Had she not informed Taggart that they were to begin his instruction first thing this morning? At seven o'clock sharp?

Sitting down at the brass-inlaid table, Melisande scowled at her coddled eggs as if somehow they were to blame for this unsettling turn of events. For Taggart's failure to heed her directive boded ill, she thought. Very ill indeed. The man was supposed to be eagerly awaiting his tutelage, not gallivanting about the estate with her brother, for goodness' sake. Her brother, who should have known better than to distract Taggart from his—

Oh, dear. Melisande bit at her lip as another disquieting thought came over her: George wouldn't dare meddle in her plans, would he? Last night, while she'd been informing him of her general stratagem to get Eileen to the altar, he had been unusually silent. Did George disapprove? Of her plans? Or of the Scot?

Of course, no one in the family had ever condoned Melisande's ambition to establish a remedial academy, so perhaps George simply didn't care for the idea of her bringing Taggart up from the gutter. So to speak. If that were the case, then why had the pair gone riding together?

And why had Will Taggart failed to appear when she'd told him to?

As her eggs grew cold and her toast limp, Melisande sat and watched the mantel clock chime first seven o'clock and then a quarter past. It ticked on to twenty past, twenty-one, twenty-two . . . Her fingers were drumming the table in an irritated, staccato rhythm when finally, at twenty-five past the hour, the breakfast room door opened.

In walked George, his step buoyant, his smile at ease with the world. Until he saw her. As soon as their gazes clashed, the bounce left his stride and his expression fell, assuming an almost sheepish cast. She wondered what the devil the foolish boy had been up to.

"Good morning, George."

"Melisande," he said in greeting, sweeping a nervous hand through his dark blond hair. He headed straight for the coffee urn. "I say, you're looking well this morning."

"Thank you, but I'm not looking at all well," she contradicted, in a voice meant to be deceptively pleasant. "My color is off and I've bags under my eyes the size of feedsacks."

"Aye, but what fetching feedsacks they are," a voice

chimed in, its distinctive drawling burr making Melisande's pulse leap to attention.

She jerked her gaze to the doorway, and then had to bite her tongue to keep her jaw from dropping open. Her husband-to-be stood on the threshold looking positively . . . civilized.

The moth-eaten jacket of yesterday had been replaced by a tailored riding coat, one that looked familiar and must have been borrowed from George's wardrobe. Melisande could not help but note how the garment's fine cut emphasized a pair of shoulders that had no need of false padding. His ripped black breeches and pirate-like blouse had also given way to borrowed attire. He wore a fresh linen shirt and a pair of too-snug trousers that molded his thighs with shocking—and eye-widening—precision. If not for his shoulder-length hair swinging freely about his shoulders, he might have resembled any London buck on his way for a jaunt through Hyde Park.

Melisande felt an unexpected spurt of annoyance that he should appear so well turned out. Only yesterday, the man had been wallowing in his own filth in the bowels of the Cullscombe gaol!

Yet why, she asked herself, *should* she be annoyed? Her goal was to transform him into a gentleman, and he did resemble one at the moment—if she discounted the dangerous gleam in his eye and the wicked allure of his heathenishly long hair.

Dragging her gaze away from the threshold, Melisande forced herself to finish her ice-cold chocolate before she rose from the chair with a feigned calm. Feigned, because she was perturbed. Terribly perturbed.

She didn't want to believe that her peevishness was due to the fact that her lips had tingled the whole night long, keeping her awake. Nor did she want to think that the sight of those sculpted thighs bothered her in the least, even though her stomach was flooding with a strange and potent warmth.

She turned toward the door, deciding that if she were to be annoyed by anything, it would be the way Will Taggart was looking at her. *The rogue.* His cocky, lopsided grin plainly told her that he was recollecting the liberties he'd taken last evening. The liberties she should never have let him take.

"I've been waiting for you," she accused, glaring pointedly toward the mantel clock, which now showed half past seven. "As I informed you, we have work to do today, Mr. Taggart. A tremendous amount of work. If we hope to introduce you to society as my betrothed, we must immediately set about making you as presentable as possible."

His grin broadened and he sent a wry glance from his chest to his toes. "Aye. We sure wouldn't want anyone to see me in this state."

Melisande's brows spiked together and she shot a hasty peek at George, who was taking a fascinated interest in the cuff of his coat sleeve.

"Your appearance is much improved," she coolly conceded. "However it takes more than the donning of a fancy coat to make a gentleman."

"The donning of fancy words, as well?"

Melisande blinked. Did he mock her? Did he *dare* to mock her? But, no, of course not. It was only his lack of upbringing that made him unaware of his impertinence. William Taggart was not to be condemned, but to be pitied. He came from a different walk of life, had been raised with a different set of values and mores. If she were to test her reformative skills, she must remember that her mission was to mold this man into a gentleman; not to disparage him for any failings or shortcomings he might possess.

"There are rules regarding what constitutes polite conversation," she explained, responding to his question as if it had been sincerely posed. "Naturally we will review them as part of your tutelage."

"Naturally."

Again her eyes narrowed, as she thought she heard a hint of derision in his voice. But she held her tongue.

Turning to her brother with a brisk swish of her skirts, she said, "George, I will be working with Mr. Taggart in the music room, I think. Would you please ask Eileen to take her viola lesson in the parlor today? I'd prefer that we were not disturbed."

"I'll tell her," George said. "But you know Eileen is simply champing at the bit to meet Will."

So "Will" was it?

"Eileen is not a thoroughbred, George, and you'd do well to save your equine analogies for your horsey set. As far as Eileen being curious, I'm sure you can manage to keep her distracted until supper this evening. I don't think it fair to place Mr. Tagg— er, Will," she corrected, "in a position where he would feel awkward or unprepared. Let us not forget that our circumstances are foreign to him and unfamiliar. A few hours instruction is the very least we should allow before making his introduction to Eileen."

Her brother cast an uneasy glance to the figure filling the doorway. "Uh, perhaps you and I should have a word, Melisande—"

"George." An impatient sigh fluttered her fichu. "Can it not wait until later? We have already wasted half the morning when every precious moment ought to be put to good use." She waved a hand toward the central hall. "Heavens, for all we know, Grandfather could arrive on our doorstep at any moment, taken by a whim to pay us a visit. How, pray tell, might we then explain to him that the man I plan to marry is little better than a boorish rustic?" Without glancing his way, she wiggled her fingers in Will's direction, adding breezily, "No offense intended."

George rubbed the tip of his nose. "Yes, well—"

"Yes, well. You may instruct Mrs. Penster to bring us our midday meal in the music room."

Gathering her skirts, she marched to the door, sailing past her betrothed without so much as a glance. She categorically refused to allow her gaze to stray anywhere near the vicinity of his mouth, anywhere near that arrogant, self-satisfied grin.

Nonetheless, she was keenly aware of him as her hem brushed over his boots. Aware of the faint scent of horse and grass and leather that all combined to form a pleasant and utterly male aroma.

"This way . . . Will," she called as she continued into the hallway.

At her back, she heard him answer in a low, chuckling voice, "Aye, aye, captain."

As Will followed those swaying hips down the long and twisting corridor, he detected a distinct heaviness expanding in his groin. A heaviness that made Will appreciate what a truly sweet deal he was setting up for himself. Sleek-footed thoroughbreds and rambling castles aside, the prospect of getting Mel into his bed was nearly as appealing as the thought of the money she brought with her.

George had said she was "no diamond," and Will understood the comment now. Melisande of the inky black mane and stubborn square chin was not some colorless, decorative bauble. Rather her beauty was strong and fierce like flint, like the rock that kept a man alive in the cold, barren nights of winter.

Aye, Melisande Moorseby promised fire. He could see it in those dark chocolate eyes that spat sparks, glimpses of the greater heat burning within. She might not be a beauty in the traditional china-doll sense, but she had strength. She had spirit. More spirit than any female he'd met in his twelve years traveling through three different continents. George had the right of it, all right—she'd be a handful, for certain. But there was nothing Will loved more than a challenge. The thrill of the chase. The call to adventure.

He watched her now as her long, jet tresses undulated back and forth with each purposeful step of her tiny booted feet. No lace caps for this woman. No spinsterish braids. That she would wear her hair loose told him that Melisande Mooresby was not a woman afraid to flout convention. Despite her prissy, purse-lipped talk of proper etiquette and polite conversation, Will did not believe for a second that Melisande would hesitate to fly full-speed into the face of convention if it suited her.

Just as she had not hesitated to pluck a husband from the gaolhouse in order to save her sister's reputation.

At the farthest corner of the house, Melisande pushed

open a door and preceded him into a vaulted chamber that looked out onto a flower-filled garden, its natural bounty overwhelmed by the room's gilt and glitter. A pianoforte took center stage beneath a mammoth crystal candelabra that reminded Will of one he'd seen years earlier in a fancy New Orleans bordello.

Melisande explained over her shoulder, "We should be able to work here relatively undisturbed. At least, until it begins to grow dark."

Will's step hitched. *Until it grows dark?* Damn, the woman was talking as if she planned to take him apart piece by piece, then put him back together again!

Aye, 'twas obvious that the lovely Melisande was laboring under the impression that William Erasmus Taggart didn't have a cultured bone in his body. That he had to be some variety of backward Scottish peasant who'd been living in a cave, or perhaps a slavering, ignorant brute who'd been running wild across the American frontiers. (Actually, that last assumption wasn't too very far from the truth.)

Granted, she did have reason to think him less than a prince, seeing as how she'd not found him under the most auspicious of circumstances. The black eye, the hangover, the gaol cell stinking of urine . . .

"Come, come," she prodded as he lingered warily at the door. "We haven't time to dillydally."

All the same, he sure as hell wasn't about to suffer this attitude of hers. Her haughty airs were mildly amusing when directed at George, but when that same regal condescension was turned on him—

Will's lips curled slyly at the corners. If Her Highness was looking for an uncouth bumpkin—or a "boorish rustic" as she'd called him—he could oblige her. Why not? He did so hate to disappoint a lady.

Plucking a blade-like leaf from the floral arrangement resting atop the piano, Will tucked the greenery into the side of his mouth and slowly sauntered over to the chair directly facing Melisande. He dropped into the chair—something expensive and old, he could tell—draping one leg over the

chair's arm and letting the other leg stretch out in front of
him. Considering the intimate view he was affording her, he
was relieved that the tautness in his trousers had eased
somewhat. For as it was Miss Mooresby was getting herself
an eyeful.

Or two eyes full, Will thought proudly.

"Now," she began, whirling toward him. "We'll need to
review both our histor—"

Her gaze fell to the vee between his legs. He saw her
blink once, then twice, before she swiftly turned away to
study the garden view.

"It seems," she said, her spine so rigid that Will thought
he could have used it for a fence post, "that our first order
of business will be instruction in the correct way to occupy
a chair."

Will's look was pure innocence as she turned back to him,
her eyes focused purposefully high.

"A gentleman does not sprawl," she told him. "Your
limbs must be . . . contained."

"Contained?" Will transferred the bitter-tasting leaf to the
other corner of his mouth. "I'm not sure I take your
meaning."

"I mean that your limbs should be kept together," she
said. "And a gentleman never sits while a lady is still
standing."

Will motioned her toward the other chair, deliberately
passing his hand over the bulge in his crotch to give it a lazy
scratch. "By all means."

Her brows shot toward the ceiling, her mouth condensing
to the size of a pea. "You ought not—"

Evidently she could not find the words. She sputtered.
She gaped. She wiggled her nose. At last, heaving an
indignant sigh, she acquiesced by stiffly perching herself on
the edge of the seat.

Will crossed his legs at the ankles and folded his hands
behind his head, assuming a pose of indifferent leisure.
George's linen shirt, a shade too small, stretched tightly
across his chest, pulling under his arms and puckering his
nipples.

"Is this better?"

"I—er, yes." With a swift lick of her lips, she flicked a strand of hair over her shoulder. "I think that we should begin by establishing some guidelines. Guidelines that I will expect you to meet while under my employ." As she spoke, her voice grew more confident, her tone as brisk as a northeastern wind. "Let us first address the issue of punctuality. In the future, when an appointment is set, you will make every effort to meet me at the designated hour. Time is precious, especially in this enterprise, and I have little patience with tardiness.

"Secondly, I cannot allow any excess of drink during these next few weeks." She raised an imperious palm face-out as if to fend off his impending argument. "Now, my father did explain to me how, for certain people, the thirst for spirits can be like a disease."

"A disease?" Will echoed, undecided if he wanted to shake the wench or kiss her senseless. Now she believed him to be a drunkard as well as a brainless lout?

"There's no need to deny it, for Mr. Bell revealed to me that 'twas your affinity for spirits that landed you in his gaolhouse. I would hope that your short stay there taught you a lesson. Or"—her brow furrowed—"I hadn't thought of it, but have you been incarcerated previously?"

Will gave the twiggy leaf in his mouth a contemplative twirl. "Well . . . there was that time I shot—"

"You shot someone?"

Will scratched at his jaw, in an effort to disguise a grin. "Actually, in this case, I was referring to the time I shot up a saloon in Chicago."

She blanched, but recovered quickly. "Well, all that's water under the bridge, isn't it? Today you start your life anew. Without spirits."

"Damn," he drawled, "it's not going to be easy for me to give up the bottle when you figure that my father is a whiskey-maker. Why, I've been drinking since before I could walk."

"Goodness." Disgust and pity vied for supremacy in Melisande's horrified expression. "Be that as it may," she said briskly, "I must insist that you curb your cravings while we perpetrate this little masquerade. There is simply too much at stake. Furthermore, Mr. Taggart, 'damn' is not a term to be used in good company. In fact, that brings me to point three: the use of foul language. . . ."

As Melisande continued sermonizing, Will studied the ripe curves of her mouth, acutely aware that the only cravings he need worry about were currently creating havoc in his trousers.

He stood up in the middle of her speech.

"Mr. Taggart—"

"Will," he said as he strolled past her, heading for the piano. Behind him he heard the gentle squeak of wood on marble as she rose from her chair, following after him.

"Will, you do not appreciate the seriousness of this undertaking!"

He sat down at the piano, his fingers hovering darkly over the clean white keys. The instrument smelled of oil and lemon, while the flowers in the arrangement gave off a sweet, waxy aroma, oddly pleasing.

Will pulled the leaf from his mouth and flicked it away. "Sure I do, Mel."

Oh, *that* got to her.

Under the brilliant turquoise of her gown, her chest swelled with a deep, quavering breath. "My name is Melisande. Melisande Mary Mooresby."

"Quite a mouthful, isn't it?" He screwed up his face as if chewing on all those sounds. "A heckuva lot for a fella to have to remember, don't you think?"

She swallowed, the column of her throat working.

"Now, . . . *Mel*." Will bobbed his head thoughtfully. "I think I can remember that. It is only three letters—isn't it?"

A shadow of disbelief drifted across her features. "You can read, can't you?"

He gave her his most beguiling smile.

Clearly frustrated now, Melisande asked, "Would you be good enough to read the name of this piece for me?"

With her chin, she indicated the sheet music open upon

the stand, an arrangement by the Englishman Thomas Attwood.

"Well," Will drawled in an exaggerated Yankified twang, "it looks like a big ole word, but I reckon I can try."

"You reckon!" Melisande thrust her balled fists onto her hips. "What, pray tell, has befallen you, Mr. Taggart? In the last ten minutes, your accent has deteriorated to that of an illiterate colonial hayseed! And your vocabulary—have you wholly lost your ability to speak in multisyllabic words?"

Chuckling softly, Will did not answer her but launched into the opening bars of the arrangement, his fingers moving adroitly across the cool, ivory keys. Though he'd not played in countless years, he gave a decent showing of himself through the first page of music, before letting his fingers fall lax and silent.

The last notes faded, the quiet broken only by the aggravated tapping of one small foot. Will tilted his head to the side and glanced up at her through the curtain of his hair.

"So 'twas a game, was it?"

"Not so much a game as giving you what you wanted."

If possible, her back grew even more rigid. "What I wanted?"

"Hmm-mm. You seemed convinced that I was nothing more than an uneducated churl and I hated to think you might be disappointed. Your eagerness to civilize me was rather touching . . . in a snobbish sort of way."

"I am not a snob."

"Uh-huh. And I suppose the only reason you sent me off to bed last night like a misbehaving bairn was that you were concerned I might be 'overtired'?"

Her nose crinkled. As if a fly had flitted across her vision.

"You weren't fatigued?" she countered belligerently.

He lifted a shoulder, reluctant to admit that he had been tired. Tired to the bone.

"Very well." She stared at him the same way she'd done that morning in the gaol. Cool, assessing. "So you read music as well as words. I trust then that you've had some education?"

"Some."

Her too-broad chin lifted a notch. "Am I to believe that you have been gently reared?"

Will mentally debated the term "gentle," as he rubbed at the side of his stubbled jaw.

"Are you or are you not a gentleman?" she persisted.

"Well, I don't know about me," he said with deliberate provocation. "But my father is."

"Your father, the whiskey-maker?"

Will winked. "Scots country squire. University educated. Owns a distillery."

"I see." She folded her arms across her chest, eyeing him up and down. "Your father must be very proud," she said dryly, as her foot began an agitated tapping.

Will grinned, thinking it no accident she'd been dubbed the "She-Devil."

"Very well, you claim to be a gentleman." To Will's ears, she sounded disappointed by the fact. "Then let us have an accounting of yourself, William Taggart."

An accounting of himself? What in blazes did the woman mean?

"If we are to pretend to be husband and wife," Melisande explained, "then I must have some knowledge of your background in order to construct a credible story explaining how we came to meet. And how we came to be affianced."

"Ah." Will cleared his throat, curiously relieved. She didn't want a justification of his existence—merely a few factual details. "What do you want to know?"

"Everything."

The ruthless determination she infused into the word made Will feel like squirming. Hell, even *he* didn't want to know everything about himself.

"Where are you from?" she asked.

"South of Edinburgh."

"Family?"

"My father still lives in Dunslaw, where I was raised."

"Sisters or brothers?"

"No."

"Mother?"

"She's gone."

"Oh. I'm sorry."

Will gave the barest of shrugs, avoiding her gaze. "It was a long time ago."

"So you have been living in the States?"

"For the most part."

"Where exactly?"

With his forefinger, Will jabbed at a key, waiting until the bright, piercing note fully withered between them before answering, "New Orleans, St. Louis. Worked as a bounty hunter in the western territories for a while and spent some time privateering in the Caribbean after that."

"Really." Melisande's eyelids fluttered with surprise. "You've certainly enjoyed a . . . checkered career."

Will ducked his head, thinking she didn't know the half of it. Nor did she probably want to.

"And when—"

"Enough about me." He flattened his palm on the keys, signalling his uneasiness with the harsh, nerve-jangling chord. "What say we have an accounting of your life now, Mel."

Her scowl was as dark as her thick witch's mane.

"I would much prefer to proceed in an orderly manner," she said. "Jumping willy-nilly from subject to subject is neither logical nor productive. Let us first finish reviewing your history before I acquaint you with my own. Now then, as I was saying—"

"No." Will stood up and lazily stretched his arms over-head. "I don't think so."

"I beg your pardon?"

By the startled look on her face, Will gathered that George Mooresby had the right of it: Melisande was not accustomed to being gainsaid.

"No," he repeated, lowering his arms to his sides. "I want to learn something about you." Slowly he began to pace counterclockwise around the piano, circling behind her, catching a whiff of her spicy female smell.

Her head moved from side to side as she followed his movements, trying to see him when he passed behind her, close enough to stir her hair with his breath.

"How old are you?" he asked.

She didn't want to answer, but she did. "A score and two."

"Twenty-two and unwed." He clicked his tongue at the back of his teeth, still circling the piano like a hungry hawk. "And you've never been asked to marry?"

"Untrue!" she protested. "I have been asked any number of times."

"You have?" He came around the end of the instrument, approaching her from the left. "I don't believe you."

Her outraged intake of air swelled her chest, lifting her lace fichu as she spun to face him. "You brand me a liar, you audacious rogue?"

"Who, then?" he taunted. He stopped before her, his fingers itching to dive into that river of black silk.

"I-I don't have to say."

"Hmm-hmm."

"I have been asked to marry," she insisted hotly. "Dozens of times."

He shifted closer, surprised by his need to know. "Who, Melisande? Who?"

Her eyes were like bubbling vats of darkest pitch, which once fallen into, a man could never escape.

"Very well," she snapped, "if you must know. George, Eileen, and Grandfather have all begged me to marry, so there!"

Will might have laughed, or he might not have, but before he could decide either way—

"Aaaaaghh!"

A shriek ripped through the halls. A hair-raising, blood-curdling shriek that sent them both racing for the door.

Six

꧁꧂

Melisande charged down the corridor, vaguely aware of Will's footsteps silently trailing after her. She thought of asking him to wait in the music room, but another cry from the front hall—this one not quite as blood-curdling— convinced her to make haste.

Emerging from the shadowy hallway into the sun-streaked foyer, she quickly determined what all the fuss was about: Eileen had fainted. Again. Draped in the aged butler's arms, her sister was a boneless lump of peach organza froth, her head lolling drunkenly over the servant's shoulder, her plump arms limp and white. Bates, no young-ster, looked as if he were having a deuce of a time support-ing Eileen's weight as he swayed back and forth like a sapling in the wind.

Melisande's first thought was *Oh dear, let it be merely a mouse or some other comparable horror*. For although Eileen swooned on average once a week, Melisande was concerned that this particular swoon might be due to her sister's delicate condition. She'd heard that a woman's health often suffered during the early months of pregnancy, and Eileen had ever been susceptible to all manner of ailments and illnesses.

"Betsy, don't just stand there," Melisande chided as she hurried across the foyer. Instead of offering assistance, the young housemaid was standing at the butler's side, gaping like a slack-jawed ninny.

"Run fetch my vinaigrette," Melisande ordered, "and do be quick about it."

The silly girl didn't budge.

"Betsy, did you hear—"

Melisande's breath caught. She skidded to a halt, her slippers' heels seeking purchase on the slick marble floor.

There, on the front step of Mooresby Hall stood a . . . being. A creature that had to have come straight from the pages of a Daniel Defoe novel.

He wore a fringed animal-skin vest with no shirt beneath, his smooth hairless chest as brown as roasted chestnuts. From wrist to elbow, his bare arms were covered with red tattoos in dizzying geometric patterns. Straight black hair hung past his shoulders, with maroon and gold feathers swinging from a single braid over his ear. His face . . . My goodness, his face was enough to make even Melisande swoon with fright. Harsh and craggy, its focal point was a pair of eyes so pale blue that they didn't look to fit with the rest of his features: the high cheekbones and wide, strong nose.

"I'm looking for tiger," the being said gruffly, his accent as alien as his appearance.

Tiger?

Melisande craned her neck to peer out to the driveway, but no vehicle of any sort awaited. Only an old, bow-backed plow horse, which stood grazing at the lawn's edges.

She regarded the stranger doubtfully. "You're looking for your groom?"

The man's dark features twisted into a frown, the ferocity of his scowl causing Betsy to emit a strangled, squeaking noise.

"I said tiger." His bronzed fingers brushed across the tips of his sable braid. "Striped hair."

"Oh, miss," Bates murmured in a nervous aside. "I do fear he means the *beast*. Must be all about in the head."

Melisande indicated for Bates to step back, and he did so, hovering behind her like a liveried wraith.

"I am sorry," Melisande said in the slow, patient voice she reserved for the very young or the very old. "But we have no tigers here in England. Have you lost your way?"

About thirty miles to the south of Cullscombe there was a small private asylum that was known to cater to the mentally infirm of wealthy families. 'Twas possible that the man had escaped from the facility, although where he could have come by his outrageous costume Melisande could not guess.

The stranger grunted, his pale eyes slitting to thin azure bands. "The only thing I've lost is tiger. I was told I could find him here."

Melisande shook her head. "I regret, sir, that you have been misinformed, for there are no tigers at Mooresby Hall."

Against the butler's side, Eileen stirred and groaned softly.

"Now I am going to have to ask you to be on your way," Melisande told the stranger, shooing him off as she would a stray dog. She did feel a tiny bit guilty for sending him away, but, dash it, she had her sister's welfare to consider. Eileen might take another shock if she were to reawaken and find the brutish-looking fellow still here.

Melisande started to reach for the door—

The man was across the threshold before she could even grab hold of the door handle.

"I'm not leaving without tiger." His voice had dropped to a menacing timbre, as he loomed before in all his unclad savagery.

Melisande, her hand still outstretched, glanced furtively to the knife at his waist, then to the brass umbrella stand a few feet away. While loath to harm a lunatic, she had to wonder if the man's mental infirmity made him dangerous.

As if in answer, the stranger suddenly looked past her and growled, "You bastard!" before storming into the front hall like a bull on the rampage.

Melisande leaped toward the umbrella stand, Betsy's startled shriek blasting in her ear.

"I say now," Bates could be heard blustering ineffectually in the background.

Gripping the heavy brass stand as if it were a fencing foil, Melisande whirled around, prepared to do battle.

"*En garde!*" she cried.

She lunged forward, knee bent, weapon poised— The air left her lungs in an immense *whoosh* of surprise.

Could it be? Was the half-clothed lunatic in fact embracing her betrothed?

"Damn you, Tiger," the stranger said, clapping Will atop both shoulders in a typically male greeting that was certain to leave bruises. "Damn your sorry hide. I'm sure as hell going to make you pay for this."

Will grinned a slow smile. "I wondered what was keeping you, W.C."

Confused, and more than a touch irritated, Melisande lowered the umbrella stand, its weight beginning to grow heavy in her arm.

Across the foyer, Will's gaze found hers.

"Tiger?" she questioned archly.

The sound of her voice caused the stranger to turn around, pinning her with his pale, unnerving regard.

Will rolled his shoulder in an indifferent shrug. "It's a nickname."

"Ah." Her lips pursed. "I see."

And she did see where he would have come by such a label, the way those tawny-gold stripes streaked his thick chestnut hair, and the supple, catlike grace that seemed to characterize his every movement.

"Allow me to introduce Niankwe MacInnes," Will said, slapping his flat palm on the stranger's broad back. "But you can call him W.C. or Wildcat."

"Wildcat? Tiger? My, such clever monikers you two have."

Her sarcasm was acknowledged by a faint narrowing of Will's eyes.

"And W.C., may I present Melisande Mooresby, the lady

who"—his lips curved in an evil grin—"is to be my bride."

Wildcat's smile faded. "Sure, Tiger, and I'm the god-damned Czar of Russia."

Then the man spat—actually spat!—on the foyer's black-and-white checkered floor.

"Sirrah!" Melisande exclaimed, staring aghast at the brownish tobacco lump staining her foyer. "Who in heaven's name do you think you are, barging into my home and—"

She was silenced abruptly as long fingers pressed into her waist, causing her to nearly jump from her skin. Intent on the mess on her floor, she hadn't noticed Will come to stand beside her. With an indignant gasp, she tried to pull free but his grip was too firm.

"God's truth," Will told his friend, cheerfully ignoring her struggles. "Mel and I are going to be married."

"Right." Wildcat then drew his knife from his waist and brandished it menacingly before them. "And I'll have your scalp for lyin' to me, you no-good skunk."

A tremulous, high-pitched wail drew all eyes toward the door where Eileen, having regained consciousness, stood trembling against the butler's side.

"T-Take his scalp," she stuttered breathlessly, her face whiter than chalk.

"Now, Eileen—"

But before Melisande could reach her sister, Eileen's eyes rolled back in her head and she slipped to the floor in another dead faint.

"For the love of Moses," Melisande fumed. "Now see what you've done!"

Thrusting her elbow forcefully into Will's ribs, Melisande wrenched from his grasp to go kneel beside her sister. A pair of footmen rushed into the entrance hall, at long last responding to all the shrieks and cries.

"It's about time," Melisande snapped. "Come, carry her upstairs," she ordered the footmen. "And you, Betsy, go along and see that my sister is made comfortable and put to bed with a soothing tisane."

"As for you—" She glared at Will and his barbarous companion. "The music room. Now."

Not waiting for them to follow, she strutted down the corridor, her fists clenched so hard her knuckles ached. She couldn't remember the last time she'd been in such a state. By gosh, she felt as if she'd been duped. Not only did she not get to "reform" Will Taggart, but now it seemed the insufferable man came with baggage! A red man straight from the wilds of America!

Melisande never made mistakes. Never. But at the back of her mind, she couldn't help asking herself if 'twas possible she had erred in her gaolhouse selection yesterday. For the more she learned of Will Taggart, the more she began to wonder if the toothless pickpocket might not have made for a wiser choice.

Niankwe testily fingered the handle of his knife as he strode alongside his friend in the wake of the witch-woman's path. "I swear to you, Tiger, I'm getting too damned old for these games of yours. Too old and too tired."

"Ah, you were born old, W.C. Of course, thirty-four would find you ancient."

"Hell, you are serious then? You plan to marry this woman?"

"Serious as can be."

Wildcat scowled down the hall in the direction of Melisande's twitching skirts, thinking that his friend must have gotten hold of some bad liquor.

"Crazy," he muttered. "You are *gakpittshehellat*. Why would you decide to tie yourself down after all these years? And"—his lip curled into a sneer—"to a needle-tongued female such as that one?"

"Why do you think?" Will asked, pausing before a painting on the corridor wall, a Dutch master's work that even W.C. recognized.

"Money?" He made a disdainful huffing noise. "You've won and lost fortunes a dozen times over, Tiger. You know how to line your pockets when they're empty. You sure as hell don't need a wife to make you rich."

"Maybe I need more than just money."

W.C. shot his friend a penetrating, sidelong look. "Your father?"

The subsequent silence confirmed Wildcat's worst suspicions. *No. Not even Tiger would think—*

"Hell!" W.C. glanced ahead to where Melisande was disappearing into a doorway. "That she-wolf will skin you alive once she figures it out."

"Don't worry, I can handle Mel. She's a woman, isn't she?"

Wildcat was not so certain. From what he'd seen, she could be an evil spirit, a *machtapekwonitto*. His people told stories of such spirits taking human form, wreaking havoc on unsuspecting men.

"You think your father will accept her?"

Will shrugged, though the gesture lacked its usual ease. "What does the old man have to lose? As it stands now, the house, the farm, the distillery. He says that they're all in danger of falling to the creditors. And if he does lose it all . . . Well, I've got to wonder if the shame of it might not kill him."

"Men do not die of shame, my friend. And believe me, there are fates far worse than death." Wildcat's gaze darted to the open doorway a few yards ahead. "That woman there could well be one of them."

Will laughed again, his deep rumble echoing down the long corridor. "I'll just have to take that chance, won't I?"

Will chucked Wildcat playfully on the shoulder, and W.C. barely restrained himself from blackening his friend's other eye.

Damn you, Tiger. Taggart never did consider the consequences of his actions; never took the time to look before he leaped. It wasn't because he lacked for basic intelligence; why, Will was sharper than a porcupine quill and the smoothest talker Wildcat had ever met. No, the problem with Tiger was that he believed in taking risks. Huge, insane risks that no normal man would attempt.

Tiger could risk everything . . . because he cared about nothing.

"Crazy," Wildcat repeated grimly. "And I'm just as crazy for promising to help you."

"Hey, don't say I didn't warn you." Will held up both hands to signal his guiltlessness. "Giving your word is a dangerous business, Cat. A dangerous business."

"Particularly where you are concerned," W.C. shot back. "I swear, Taggart, you're a goddamned magnet for trouble. I let you out of my sight for a few hours and what do you do? You land your sorry butt in jail, then find yourself a shrew for a wife." His braid swung back and forth as he shook his head in a combination of regret and wonder. "How do you do it?"

Will turned and strode to the open doorway, ushering him ahead with a wry, deferential bow. "Just lucky, I guess."

"Lucky" was not precisely the word that sprang to Wildcat's mind as the two men stepped into the music room. Chin thrust forward, foot tapping, black eyes blazing— Melisande Mooresby looked to Niankwe MacInnes like a woman who could summon lightning from the skies with a mere snap of her fingers. She stood in front of the piano, the sun behind her casting an indigo-blue halo around her dark hair. She looked to Wildcat like trouble. Pure, unadulterated female trouble.

With another bemused shake of his head, Wildcat strolled around her, dropping into a chair at the far end of the room. Though he suspected that Tiger was planning to make the biggest mistake of his life, he sure didn't see any reason not to at least enjoy the show. It promised to be fairly entertaining.

Foot still tapping, Melisande launched her attack. "This is outrageous," she said, addressing Will where he lounged in the doorway, his shoulder leaning comfortably against the jamb. "Simply outrageous. I demand an explanation. You said nothing to me about bringing along a companion."

"W.C. is an old friend who's traveling home with me to Dunslaw."

"But he—" Without turning around, she made a brusque, uncertain motion toward Wildcat's chair. "His attire. Those feathers and tattoos. He's a . . ."

"A savage? Aye, I admit Niankwe's manners leave something to be desired. He even manages to make me look good, don't you think?"

Wildcat issued a low growl of warning which Tiger chose to ignore.

"I presume then that's the reason you associate with Mr. MacInnes?" Melisande asked acidly. "To make yourself look good?"

Wildcat did not like the way they were discussing him as if he were an insignificant fly on the wall. A Lenape brave commanded a certain amount of respect.

"Nah." Will hooked his thumb over his waistband. "To tell you the truth, Mel, I've been trying my damnedest to lose old W.C., but he's harder to shake than a case of the pox."

"And I'm sure you would know all about *that* particular disease."

W.C. winced. Surely this woman possessed the devil's own tongue.

But Will, unfazed, merely scratched lazily at his neck. "Well, I don't know much about pox, though I could tell you a fair amount about snakebite. You see, W.C.'s mother"— Tiger finally acknowledged him with a casual jerk of his chin—"saved my life after I stumbled into a nest of cottonmouth. She's a Delaware medicine woman, but his father's a Scots trapper."

Wildcat saw how Melisande Mooresby's nose wriggled with distaste before she turned to him, her witch-lips pursed sour and tight. He did not hide his own scorn, bestowing on her a thin, sinister smile. A smile that would have sent any normal white woman fleeing for her life.

"You can't stay at the Hall," she told him bluntly.

"As long as Tiger stays"— Wildcat thumped his closed fist against his chest—"I stay."

"Unless you'd rather call off our deal?" Will proposed, grinning the same bland grin he used when bluffing at poker.

The witch-woman's jaw clenched, her foot tapping thrice

into the silence before she answered. "There is a room above the stables. He may sleep there."

Wildcat felt the chill of her gaze as it skittered across him, lingering on his tattoos.

"When you find yourself some proper clothing, Mr. MacInnes, you may join us at the table for meals. Until then, your appearance is too unsettling and would likely distress my sister."

With a dismissive sniff, she turned again to Will. "And so that there are no more surprises, *Tiger* . . . Should I be expecting any more guests to come calling? Or perhaps you're still awaiting the arrival of Mr. 'Cheetah' or 'Panther'?"

While Will laughed out loud, W.C. shook his head, asking himself which of the two he felt more pity for: his foolish Scots friend or the viper-tongued Englishwoman who didn't yet know it, but had just met her match.

Seven

༩༠༦༧

A poker player of some renown on the other side of the Atlantic, Will considered himself a bit of an expert at "reading" people. He knew how to watch for telltale clues, the small signs that usually meant the difference between winning or losing. A flicker of an eyelid, an imperceptible shaking of the fingers—these were what he looked for when facing an opponent either across a card table or across a dueling field.

When it came to understanding Melisande Mooresby, Will had learned he didn't have to search any farther than her feet. Depending on her mood, those feet tapped, shuffled, shifted, and stomped. They kicked angrily at her skirts and they stubbornly dug in their heels. They were—*if he allowed himself the hyperbole and he did*—the window to Melisande Mooresby's soul.

It was those very clues that he'd relied on earlier in the music room when he'd asked Mel if she wanted to back out on their deal. He knew before he posed the question that she'd śay no. The tense shuffling of her feet had told him that she was afraid. Afraid for her sister's reputation. As infuriated as she was by Niankwe's sudden appearance, she wasn't about to risk having the deal blow up in her face. No, she'd stood firm. And Will admired her for it.

"Hell, Tiger, will you watch where you're swinging that thing? You're supposed to be aiming for the tree, not my head."

Roused from his musings, Will realized that he'd come dangerously close to lifting the scalp of his Lenape friend.

"Well, stand back, for God's sake," Will grumbled, angling his elbows out to the sides. "Give a man some room."

As W.C. retreated a pace, Will, with a flick of his wrist, sent the dagger he held sailing across the yard to pierce the target dead-center. Two inches closer to the center, in fact, than Niankwe's knife had landed.

"Two out of three?" Wildcat offered.

"You fetch the knives," Will agreed.

Wildcat strolled over to the tree they were using for target practice and pulled the weapons free. "By the way, brother, you have yet to thank me for keeping this safe for you," Wildcat said, walking back to Will and handing him his hunting knife. "If I'd let you go out with this the other night, you might be facing the hangman right now."

Will balanced the weight of his knife in his palm. "Not very likely," he retorted. "The lad was just looking for trouble and, after a few buckets of ale, I was willing to oblige."

"Uh-huh." Wildcat lifted his chin, indicating Will's black eye. "And what were you looking for? Besides a shiner?"

Will glanced at his boots and shrugged. "I guess I just needed to blow off some steam."

"Hmm-mm." W.C. let his blade fly and it hit nearly the same spot as before. He grimaced, obviously dissatisfied with the throw. "One of these days, my friend, you're going to have to confront the source of your anger."

"Oh, hell, Cat, don't start," Will said, jostling his friend aside to take his turn at their imaginary throw line. He pulled back his arm and, end over end, the knife skimmed through the air, again beating out Wildcat's mark.

"Lucky bastard."

Will smiled. "Luck has nothing to do with it," he taunted

as he went to retrieve his knife. "You're just getting rusty, old man."

The very next second Will was laid out flat on his stomach, his nostrils filled with dirt.

"Damn you, Cat," he growled, bucking hard to fling the Indian from his back.

While W.C. tried to pin Will's arm behind him, Will slipped free and succeeded in rolling over onto his back.

"Old, huh?" Wildcat asked, baring his teeth.

Will groaned when Wildcat's knee found purchase in his belly.

"Old *and* slow," Will answered breathlessly, working to get his feet into position to kick Wildcat off his chest.

Together they rolled left, then right, growling and cursing. Over the years, they'd played this game many times, the score just about even between them. In the beginning, Wildcat had held an edge, but of late Will had begun to gain ground.

Will twisted and spun, dragging Wildcat beneath him, pushing his forearm against his neck.

"I've got you now," he muttered, as sweat stung his eyes. "Like he—"

Twa-a-ang.

Sunlight glanced off steel. Both men jerked. Less than a foot from Wildcat's head, a knife quivered in the earth, its blade buried deep in the plush green lawn.

"What the—" Wildcat muttered.

In unison the two men looked up to find Melisande Mooresby standing beside the tree they'd been using for target practice. Where before two blades had pierced the target, now there was but one.

"Are you finished trying to kill each other," she asked icily, "or must I do it for you?"

Slowly Will rose to his feet, pulling the blade from the ground. "Damn, woman, where did you learn to throw a knife like that?"

"Never mind," she hissed, marching toward them. "What I want to know is what you two think you are doing? I leave you for one hour and I return to find you rolling about in the mud like swine! This is not the American backwoods. This is my family's ancestral home and I'd thank you very much to behave like civilized men while you're guests here. Or is that possible?"

Will wiped the knife clean on the side of his trousers. "It's . . . possible."

"Oh, how relieved I am to hear that. Now if I might only see evidence to the fact. You, Mr. Taggart, are supposed to be a man of breeding." Her eyes raked him from head to toe. "But to judge from the mud and grass stains visible on your person, I'd call you a man of *weeding* instead."

W.C. snorted with laughter.

"As for you, Mr. MacInnes—"

Wildcat sobered instantly.

"I suggest you find something with which to cover yourself even if it's only an old horse blanket." She pointed a commanding finger toward the stables. "And I suggest you go locate one now."

Wildcat's eyes widened then narrowed to slits. "*Malliku,*" he murmured.

Witch.

"Just go," Will told him in the Delaware tongue. "I'll take care of this."

Wildcat retrieved his knife from the tree, walking a wide circle around Melisande. She watched him every step of the way, her turquoise skirts rippling as her foot tapped a testy rhythm beneath them.

Once W.C. had disappeared in the direction of the stables, Melisande whirled on Will. "You and I have an agreement."

"Aye," Will warily conceded.

"Well, Mr. Taggart, I do not believe that wrestling in the back garden falls within the terms of our agreement. It's wholly unacceptable, this sort of behavior. Puerile and offensive. I thought I made it clear to you, sir, that you are expected to conduct yourself like a gentleman while at Mooresby Hall. Was I not clear? Did you not understand me?"

Will had to bite his tongue to keep from laughing out loud. Never had he known such a woman. Never. In his experience, he'd found that members of the opposite sex generally responded to him in one of two ways: The mousy ones were terrified of him while the bold ones usually tried to get him into bed. None had ever dared scold him, for heaven's sake. Scold Tiger Taggart. If Will hadn't been so very amused, he might have felt a measure of indignation.

But it was difficult to be angry when this bantam Valkyrie stood there before him. This woman of uncommon strength and spirit. Aye, Melisande Mooresby might have had a touch of the shrew about her, but for what he had planned, he needed a woman with courage. He needed *this* woman.

Will took a step toward her and saw the tiniest flicker of alarm spark her gaze.

"Aye, I understood you," he said, closing in another step.

"G-Good." The tip of her tongue wetted her upper lip. "Then why don't you go inside and clean yourself up before meeting me in the music room? We have yet to devise a plausible story explaining how we came to meet and we must have our facts"—her eyes widened as he advanced another foot toward her—"straight."

Will smiled. "Hmm-mm, straight," he murmured.

He saw her pulse flutter in the hollow beneath her ear. The sweet smell of loamy earth surrounded them. Swiftly he moved to close the final inches between them but Mel moved at the same moment, backing up until she bumped into the tree behind her.

"Oh." Her eyes grew even rounder as she realized she had no more room in which to run. Her glassy-eyed gaze fell to his mouth, fear and anticipation doing battle in her expression. Her breath came fast and shallow. Will's smile broadened. *Aye, you want it as much as I do, don't you, lass?*

He leaned forward—

Suddenly Bates, the butler, appeared in the periphery of Will's vision.

"Miss Mooresby?" the servant questioned hesitantly.

Damn.

Will straightened as Mel darted under his outstretched arm.

"Ahem, I am sorry to disturb you, miss, but a messenger has arrived from Viscount Rutherford."

"From Grandfather?" Melisande flattened her palms across her skirts. "Where is he?"

"I've put him in the parlor, miss."

"Very good."

Then, without so much as a backward glance or a polite "by your leave," Mel started for the house, Bates tripping anxiously after her. Will let loose a foul curse and kicked at the tree trunk. It looked as if his bath would have to be a cold one. Ice-cold.

"By Jove, it's a coil, I tell you. A bloody nasty coil."

Pacing back and forth in front of Eileen's four-poster, George appeared to be on the verge of a nervous collapse. A sheen of sweat glistened slickly on his brow, and his wavy, blond hair was virtually standing on end due to the constant raking of fingers and the incessant rubbing of forehead.

"For heaven's sake, George, sit down and collect yourself. You're not doing any of us a bit of good carrying on so."

Seated beside the bed-bound Eileen, Melisande censured her brother with a nod and a frown, indicating to George that his theatrics were upsetting their younger sibling. George sent a sheepish glance to Eileen before obediently falling into a velvet tufted boudoir chair. Against the fabric's deep pink, George looked shockingly pallid. Almost green.

"But George is only speaking the truth, Melisande," Eileen pointed out, as she sniffled behind a perfumed handkerchief. "Surely this business is all bound to end in a terrific muddle. What if Grandpapa arrives before the marriage license? What if you cannot wed and then I cannot wed and—Oh!" Eileen burst into a fresh torrent of tears as Melisande blindly patted her sister's arm, wondering what more could occur to upset her nicely laid plans.

God help her, she'd not drawn an easy breath since yesterday morning when she'd learned of Eileen's condition. From there it had been but one calamity after the other, beginning with Lord Fielding's defection, and leading right up to the message she'd received but minutes earlier from her grandfather's envoy. The message stated that the Viscount Rutherford was, at that very moment, en route to Devonshire. Evidently he'd been in Bath taking the waters when it had occurred to him to pay his charges to the south a short visit. The missive said he was to be expected Wednesday.

Today.

"Now, let us not assume the worst," Melisande advised, knowing that she, at least, had to remain clearheaded amid the chaos. "Grandfather might be delayed by any number of incidents: a lame horse, a flare-up of gout, some urgent estate business. We cannot be at all certain that he'll arrive this evening."

"And if he does?" George asked, gnawing like a rabbit at the side of his thumb.

"Well, if he does . . . Then we'll have to hope that the license arrives before him."

"Blast!" George vaulted from the chair to begin his pacing anew. "Where *is* that dashed license?"

"I instructed Cousin Harry to deliver it with all possible speed," Melisande said, noticing that her ankles were not fully covered and, out of habit, drawing her skirts around their offensive thickness.

With ten fingers thrust through his tangled coiffure—five fingers evidently weren't sufficient to convey the depth of his anxiety—George suddenly exclaimed, "Lud, I know! Should we not send a man into Exeter? To fetch the paper directly from old Harry-the-Bishop?"

Melisande gave a small, strained smile. "I've already done so, George. I dispatched a groomsman within minutes of reading Grandfather's note."

Her brother's answering grimace seemed both annoyed and relieved. "I should have known you'd be thinking ahead of me."

"Melisande is always thinking, isn't she, George?" Eileen chimed in with weepy admiration. "She has ever so much common sense."

"Yes, well . . . You'd think a bloody bishop could arrange something as simple as a license and not take forever about it," George whined, tugging at the hem of his striped valencia waistcoat as he turned and marched toward the bedroom window. Outside the sun had commenced its downward slope into the hills.

"Are you feeling better?" Melisande asked, as Eileen's tears looked finally to subside.

"Oh, yes." Dark lashes swept up to reveal dewy, periwinkle eyes that Melisande had secretly envied since the two girls had been in the nursery together. Eyes she'd envied since the day she'd been told that her own were the uninspiring color of Devonshire mud.

"So much better, sister, and I do beg your pardon for behaving like such a ninny."

"Ninny? Don't be silly," Melisande said. "You took a fright as anyone would have done in similar circumstances."

"It was rather a shock," Eileen agreed, her fingers fluttering to her chest, where they splayed out like a flower's petals. "He looks so very . . . dangerous."

"Now, now, you needn't worry about him. He's gone off to the stables, where I trust he'll remain. Out of our sight."

"The stables?" Eileen's brows knitted delicately.

"Yes. You didn't think I'd let him stay in the Hall, dressed as he was, with all those horrifying tattoos on display."

"Oh, him! Gracious, yes, he was rather terrifying, although I was, in actuality, speaking of your Scot."

An odd twinge caught at Melisande's middle. "My Scot?" Was Eileen saying she found William Taggart frightening?

"Dear me, yes. I'll grant you that the Indian's appearance was most disturbing, but when I laid eyes on that man you think to marry—" Eileen shivered against her satin-trimmed pillows.

"What? What of him?"

"Why, can't you see it?" Eileen whispered, her gaze darting furtively to where George stood staring out the window.

"I, uh . . ." Feeling ever so stupid, Melisande chewed at her lips and wondered what her sister could possibly see in

Will Taggart that she could not. Admittedly, of the two, Eileen was the more knowledgeable sister when it came to understanding men. She was, after all, expecting.

"Goodness, Melisande," Eileen whispered timidly from the side of her mouth. "He's one of *those*."

"Those?" Melisande nearly toppled onto the mattress as she leaned closer, trying to catch her sister's murmured words. "What do you mean 'those'?"

Eileen, who'd begun to blush, peeked over to George once more before she answered, "One of those men. You know, the dangerous kind. The kind who can make even the most proper young lady forget she's a lady. Oh, heavens, Melisande, surely you know what I'm talking about. The sort of man a woman finds simply irresistible."

"Irresis—" Melisande reared back, scoffing. "He's only a man, Eileen. And not a very polished one at that."

"But polished has nothing to do with it," Eileen assured her. "Certain men—not many—are simply born with it. This . . . this quality that makes it impossible for a woman to say no."

Her forehead puckering, Melisande asked herself how it was that she'd never heard of this particular male trait before. Irresistible? Dangerous? Could Will Taggart truly be one of *those*?

But perhaps there was something to it. . . . For hadn't she, only an hour earlier, come perilously close to letting Will kiss her after giving him strict instructions never to do so again? Gracious, what had she been thinking? She had stood there as if in a trance, the prickly tree bark pressing into her spine, and waited. Waited for his lips to take hers.

Oh, dear. Melisande rested her fist against her mouth, questioning what this might mean. She certainly could not return to Mr. Bell's "house of husbands" in search of another spousal candidate. She hadn't the time for that. And if it was merely a question of being able to say no, why, Melisande had never had any trouble employing that word to its fullest and best usage. No, she couldn't allow herself to be rattled by Eileen's imaginative observations. Will Taggart was, after all, only a man. . . .

On the other side of the room, George let out a loud, exasperated sigh as he flung the heavy window hangings back into place. "I swear I'll go mad just sitting here, waiting to see who first comes tooling up the drive. Who will it be, do you think?" he questioned gloomily. "Grandfather or Harry's messenger?"

Melisande's head jerked up with a snap. "Sit and wait?" she echoed. "What nonsense you speak, George. We cannot wait for anything. We have dozens of details to attend to and we've already spent too much time talking when we ought to have been taking action."

Melisande began ticking off items on her fingers. "First, George, I want you to ride over to the Wilders' and ask to borrow a coach."

"Borrow a—"

"I recommend you leave posthaste in case the family has plans to go out for the evening. Also, before you leave, have one of our coachmen change out of the Mooresby livery and into a plain dark coat. I'll attend to the packing while you're gone."

"Packing?" Eileen questioned.

Melisande nodded. "No matter how events unfold, I simply must be married when next I see Grandfather. Therefore, if the license does not soon arrive, I have to be prepared to sleep elsewhere this night."

"And what about Will?" George asked.

"He, too, will have to sleep elsewhere. If Grandfather arrives this evening, Will and I can reappear on the morrow already happily wed."

"And how will you explain why neither Eileen nor I attended the nuptials?"

"Gracious, George, I don't know," Melisande grumbled, feeling as if her head were spinning in ten different directions. "An elopement? I don't know. Let us hope it doesn't come to that, shall we? Let us instead pray that the license reaches Mooresby Hall by the time you return with the carriage. Now, be off with you, George. I must go ready my groom."

Eight

∿᠙᠊ᐸᏔᏳ

Will *threw back* another shot of whiskey, smacking his lips in contentment as he felt its liquid heat travel down his throat and into his stomach. *Mmm-mm, those Mooresbys sure know their liquor.* Top-rate stuff right across the board, from French champagnes to Portuguese ports to the finest Scotch malt.

"Ach, life is good," Will said aloud, gazing thoughtfully into his empty glass, where the crystal's chiseled lines reflected his satisfied smile in a dozen fractured images. Angling the glass to the left, he studied his reflection, pleased to note that the discoloration in his eye had finally begun to fade.

"Ah-h-h," he sighed, tilting back his head so that his neck was cradled in the curve of the tub. A man's life couldn't get much better than this, he decided. Good whiskey, a hot bath, a toasty fire. Servants eager to attend to your every whim at the pull of a bell or the wave of a hand. Aye, he'd be right sorry when it came time to leave all this luxury behind and head north with his bride.

After setting his glass down beside the decanter, Will closed his eyes and sank beneath the hot foamy suds. It was so very peaceful in his watery cocoon with his gut warmed

by whiskey and his ears full of nothing but soap bubbles and
the gentle slosh of the bathwater and . . . a distant pounding.

He sat up and shook his head, flinging water in all
directions onto the gleaming hardwood floor. He glanced to
the bedroom door. Had someone been knocking—

Like a plains tornado, Melisande Mooresby burst into the
room, waving a piece of paper above her head. "It's
arrived," she announced brusquely, "and we'll need to
leave—" She skidded to a halt about three feet shy of the
copper tub.

Her eyes grew huge.

Will, anticipating either a shriek or, at the very least, an
embarrassed apology, was surprised when Melisande didn't
instantly turn tail and run. Instead her curious round-eyed
gaze wandered over him with—what he judged to be—an
interesting lack of maidenly modesty. It was as if she were
seeing him with a heightened awareness, a woman's awareness.

Melisande Mooresby, he realized, was seeing him as a
man.

As she continued to stare at him with those bewitching
chocolate eyes, Will felt himself stir . . . to greater lengths.

"Yes?" he asked, his amusement plain. "May I be of some
assistance?"

"I—" Stumbling back a handful of steps, Melisande
finally dragged her eyes away from her prurient inspection.
"Y-you didn't answer my knock," she explained in her
defense, "and the footman was convinced you were in here
as he said he'd delivered a bottle of whiskey to you only a
half-hour ago."

"Ah, and you feared I'd fallen into a drunken stupor and
drowned in my bath?" He gave her an intimate, half-lidded
glance. "Why, Mel, I'm touched that you should care."

Her brows snapped together and she appeared to recollect
herself, spinning a crisp ninety degrees to stare at the far
bedroom wall. Will noticed that, for the first time since he'd
met her, Melisande had put up her waist-length hair. The
simple crown of braids should have diminished her wild,

witchlike appeal, but he found quite the opposite to be true. The prim, severe style only served to emphasize the sensuous column of her neck and nape, the unearthly translucence of her skin.

"For heaven's sake, the footman didn't mention that you were bathing," she muttered hotly, still staring at the wall. "You surely cannot believe that I would have come in if I'd known you were indecent."

Indecent? One brow cocked, Will assessed himself. Aye, he was naked. But put together rather *decently,* in his not-so-humble opinion.

"If you weren't looking to be titillated"—he grinned as he saw her spine stiffen—"am I to assume the reason you barged in during my toilette has something to do with that paper you're clutching between your fingers?"

She glared at him from the corner of her eye. "It is our marriage license and while I haven't time to explain the whole of it now, recent developments require that we leave for the chapel immediately."

Damn. His engagement was to be even more short-lived than he'd anticipated. "Immediately?" he asked without much enthusiasm.

"Now," she insisted.

He started to pull himself from the tub.

"No! Wait!" Her hand shot out, urging him to retreat even as she stole another peak at his attributes.

Will sank back into the water and Melisande spun fully around this time, presenting him her back. "I will wait for you in the hall," she told him, her voice warm with a blush. "I, um, presume you've borrowed some clothing from George?"

Will ran a hand through his wet hair, admiring the lushness of the hips before him. "Aye, he loaned me a few things."

"Good." She grabbed hold of the doorknob, then paused, adding, "Hurry . . . please."

In less than five minutes Will had dried himself off and shrugged into George's borrowed finery. The cravat he left loose around his neck since he hadn't worn one of the damned things in years and he figured, if it was that important, Melisande could damn well tie it for him.

While he dressed, Will pondered that "please" she'd reluctantly parted with, deciding that "recent developments" must be pretty desperate. She'd been worried. Which worried him. After finally resigning himself to the idea of marriage, Will sure as heck didn't want any obstacles getting in the way. Especially not now that he had a pair of thoroughbreds riding on this deal.

He stepped into the hall to find Melisande holding the license close to her face, as she pored over its contents in the dim corridor light. Her lashes, scrunched together as she squinted, were like a fringe of black sable against the pale smoothness of her cheek.

"George is waiting for us in the carriage," she said without preamble and without looking up. "Are you ready?"

Was he? Will kicked at the heel of his boot, weighing the question in all seriousness. His hungry gaze followed the curve of Melisande's jaw to her neck, a long, kissable column of ivory, and then lower to the shadowy vee disappearing into her bodice. Tonight, he realized, would be his wedding night.

"Aye," he agreed in a strangely raspy voice. "I'm ready."

They passed by a footman lighting wall sconces, the smoky tang of oil weaving through the corridor, dogging their footsteps. For some reason, the aroma reminded Will of his mother making candles during the long evenings of Scotland's winters.

"So, Mel," he said, as they headed for the staircase. "Are you going to tell me why we're racing to the altar sooner than planned?"

Melisande, striding along so briskly that she was practically trotting at his side, appeared reluctant to answer.

"We've had a message from my grandfather. He is to arrive at Mooresby Hall," she said, "possibly as early as this evening."

"I see. And you want to greet him as the newly espoused Mrs. Taggart, is that it?"

"Yes, of course." She slanted him a look of impatient

annoyance. "Do you not understand what is at stake here? If our marriage is not a fait accompli, the viscount might put a stop to the reading of Eileen's banns. As it is, Grandfather is certain to kick up a fuss about my own hasty alliance. He can be so frightfully disagreeable, that man. I can but pray that he doesn't try to have our marriage invalidated before Eileen and Benjamin are wed."

"Why would he try to have it invalidated? Didn't you say he wants you to marry?"

"Yes, although . . ."

"Although not necessarily to the son of a lowly Scots squire?"

"I didn't say that," she countered, lifting her chin. "I'm only concerned because Grandfather is bound to suspect that something havey-cavey is going on and he isn't the kind of man who likes to be made a fool of."

Will didn't figure that most men did.

In the entrance hall the butler stood waiting, his arms piled high with an assortment of coats and hats. He rushed forward and assisted Melisande with a gray wool cloak.

"You've given the staff their instructions, Bates?"

"Yes, miss. All is in place, precisely as you've instructed." The butler handed Will a coat and beaver, frowning when he took notice of Will's unbound cravat.

"Remember, under no circumstances is Eileen to be left alone with the viscount," Melisande warned, tugging on her gloves. "It matters not to me how you manage it, but she cannot be left to Grandfather's questioning."

"Yes, miss. I'll do my best."

She leveled a steely eye on the butler. "I know you won't disappoint me, Bates."

The poor old fellow turned another shade of paste. "No, Miss Mooresby. Never."

The air felt cool, the day marching toward dusk, as a footman led them to a plain, unmarked coach waiting in front of the manor. Will's keen eye noted that the horses couldn't have been from the Mooresby stables as they weren't of the same quality he'd observed yesterday.

Melisande preceded him into the carriage. As he followed

after her, Will saw that she started to sit opposite her brother, then changed her mind, moving to take the place beside young George. She left the open banquette for him and for him alone.

Aye, if it makes you feel safer, Will thought with a cynical smile. *But you won't be able to elude me for long, Mel. Not for long.*

He sat down and nodded across the coach to George, who looked as if he was about to cast up his accounts all over his shiny black boots. The lad looked petrified, stiff with nerves. Was young Mooresby getting cold feet?

Melisande set to drawing the faded velvet curtains over the windows, casting the threesome into a murky gloom as the carriage swayed into motion.

"Glad you could join us," George offered, a nonsensical greeting if Will'd ever heard one.

"Glad to oblige," Will answered, stretching out his legs and folding his arms behind his head.

"Before you settle in for a nap," Melisande interrupted, "I think we should review our story for the viscount." She reached for the strap to steady herself in the rollicking coach.

"You mean the story of our whirlwind courtship?"

Will's lazy grin was met with a cool nod.

"Precisely." Melisande lightly rapped the rolled license against her brother's arm. "You pay attention now, George, since Grandfather will, in all likelihood, question you as well."

George grunted, and crooked his finger around the curtain to peek out, muttering something about "bloody slow horses" even though the carriage was now barreling down the lane at bone-rattling speed.

"Let us begin," Melisande suggested, "with our first meeting."

Will watched her without appearing to, his lashes low, concealing the direction of his gaze. In the silvery shadows, Melisande's eyes gleamed like the eyes of a cat, glowing like the darkest of midnight flames. Aye, a fire blazed inside her, all right, drawing him forward like a hapless moth. He didn't want to be, but dammit he *was* curious. Curious to learn just how hot Melisande Mooresby burned.

"It was in Exeter," she began, "a month ago. I'd accompanied George into town for a livestock auction. You and he were both interested in a pair of grays and had decided to settle the matter in a gentlemanly fashion over dinner that evening."

"What did I eat?" George wanted to know.

Melisande visibly stifled a sigh. "It makes no difference, George. Whatever you please. Now"—she turned her gaze on Will again—"I joined you and George for dinner that same evening and we formed an immediate attachment."

"Love at first sight?"

Her nose wriggled. "More or less."

"Who got the pair of grays?" George asked.

"For heaven's sake, George, will you forget the grays? Neither of you were high bidder, so we returned home the following day."

"And you and I did not meet up again," Will finished for her, "until I showed up at Mooresby Hall to ask for your hand."

"Yes," Melisande agreed. "You are on your way home to Scotland after traveling abroad for a few years. I think that, wherever possible, we should try to adhere to the truth; it will be easier for us all to remember."

"And since I was in a hurry to return home to my ailing father," Will added, "we were married as soon as arrangements could be made."

"Yes, that's good," Melisande approved with a nod. "Very good."

"Speaking of arrangements . . ." George waggled his brows at Will in a comically furtive communication. "I am curious, Melisande, as to how you plan to proceed with the annulment?"

Not a muscle twitched, as Will waited for her answer. Of course Melisande-the-Shrewd would have already decided on a strategy. And it was damned clever of old George to draw it out early, as a matter of fact.

Melisande straightened and held tighter to the strap as the

carriage lurched hard to the right. "The law prescribes but
three options, George, two of which would prove unsatis-
factory for my purposes. When the time arrives, I need only
to produce a suitor who will claim a preexisting contract.
You see, once I confess that I'd already given my word to
marry another, but then had been carried away by a brief
infatuation with Mr. Taggart . . . voilà, we have grounds
for an annulment."

"It's that easy?" George asked. Melisande didn't spy the
panic that flitted across her brother's features, but Will did.

"Well, I should imagine that Cousin Harry, in his position, will be able to take care of the details easily enough,"
Melisande explained with breezy confidence. "And since
there won't be any . . . complications"—she cleared her
throat—"an annulment ought to be a very simple and
straightforward matter."

Oh, there'll be complications, Will silently vowed. *You
can bet your sweet life on it, lass.*

Aloud, he said, "Quite a plan you've put together. But tell
me, have you already lined up someone to play your jilted
suitor? Or will you be needing to make another trip down to
the gaolhouse?"

Her lips pursed sourly. "No need to worry—"

She went still.

Thunder rumbled from afar.

Melisande lifted the corner of the curtain, then dropped it
as if burned.

"Duck!" she cried.

Will stared at her as if she'd suddenly taken leave of her
senses. Then before he knew what was about, Melisande
planted both her palms atop his head and shoved with all her
might. The next thing Will saw was his knee rushing up to
slam full-force into his face.

Nine

༒

"*You ought to* have ducked."

As she fidgeted with her hem, Melisande tried not to feel guilty, although it was very hard not to do so when Will's eye grew more purple and more swollen with every passing second.

"I did tell you to duck," she repeated. "Why didn't you?"

"I thought you were commenting on the local fowl," he murmured dryly, leaning back against the squabs, while his fingers experimentally probed the multi-hued flesh expanding over his cheekbone.

Melisande pressed her lips together. "I do apologize."

"And God knows she doesn't do *that* often," George piped in, as if such an observation might somehow prove helpful. George, ever obedient, had fallen to the coach floor the moment Melisande cried "Duck." He'd learned how to follow direction.

"I cannot imagine why I exercised such force," she tried to explain. "It must have been the effect of seeing Grandfather's coach bearing down upon us. I'd half-expected that we might meet up on the road, yet it still came as a surprise, and I never have much cared for surprises."

Will eyed her warily. With the one healthy eye he still possessed. "I'll keep that in mind."

Leaning forward, George strained for a better look in the
ever diminishing light. "Must hurt like the devil, eh, Will?
Sure looks like it would, all puffy and raw like that. And just
when the old bruise had started to fade, darn the luck."

Melisande frowned at her brother's back, thinking that a
career in politics was surely not to be George's destiny.

She had to admit Will was behaving astonishingly well
about the whole thing. She'd fair to cracked his skull open
and yet he'd not blustered or howled or even so much as
groaned. He'd acted very manly about it. Very *gentlemanly,*
in fact, an inner voice pointed out, as she shifted on the seat,
rolling shoulders gone stiff with tension. Dash it, but she
hated such useless sentiments as remorse. They did make
her feel just intolerably wretched.

"So I take it that the viscount didn't recognize us?" Will
asked, after he'd satisfied himself his eyeball was still in its
socket.

Melisande chewed at her lower lip. "Fortunately they
drove right past."

"Hmm. No Mooresby crest, eh? That was shrewd thinking to borrow a coach, Mel. Smart lass."

"Why, thank you," she acknowledged with a prim, self-
satisfied nod.

"So how much time do you think we have before your
grandfather figures out what we're up to?"

"Enough time, I should hope. Luckily we passed each
other just outside of Cullscombe. Barring any difficulties,
we ought to be wed before Grandfather's coach reaches the
gates of Mooresby Hall."

Even as Melisande spoke, the carriage began to slow.
"See? We must be nearing town already."

She peered out the window to a shady outline of jagged
rooftops silhouetted against the gently graying sky. "Yes, St.
Andrew's chapel is straight ahead."

At this end of the village, and at this time of day, the
streets were quiet since the rowdier establishments were
located farther west, closer to the river. As Melisande
stepped out of the coach, she looked to the west, and could
not help but pause a moment in appreciation of the sunset's
beauty. Generally the pre-dinner hour was reserved for her

daily meetings with the housekeeper and steward, so she rarely had an opportunity to enjoy the colors of dusk. They were all her favorite hues, the rich, daring colors of persimmon and indigo and crimson.

"Isn't it pretty?" she wondered aloud, as George and Will climbed down behind her.

"I'll say," George said. "In fact, that violet color there"— a gloved finger pointed to the horizon—"precisely matches the color of Will's eye, wouldn't you say?"

Melisande's lips pursed. "Thank you, George. And since your vision is so very acute, why don't you run around to the rectory and see if you can't locate Mr. Chandler?"

"Me?" George motioned to the footman. "Why don't you send—"

"Go, George."

Her brother stomped off, frowning petulantly, his boots clattering on the brick walk loudly enough to wake the dead. He had only just left sight when a booming and deep voice could be heard calling out a greeting.

"Hello there, Mr. Mooresby."

Mere seconds later, George reappeared around the corner of the chapel, accompanied by the burly, bearded Mr. Chandler. The reverend, a native of Cullscombe, was a decent enough man, if possessed of a rare fondness for snuff. His sermons were oft interrupted for a pinch or a sneeze and 'twas rumored he favored the same costly blend as the Prince Regent himself.

Walking alongside George, Mr. Chandler pulled up short when his gaze fell on Melisande standing at the chapel gate. She smiled sweetly. He clutched at the crucifix hanging from his neck.

"I see that you're well acquainted with the good reverend," Will murmured in her ear. The warmth of his body reached out to her in the coolness of dusk.

"Silly, superstitious man never lets go of a grudge," she whispered, fighting back a scowl. "The year I was fourteen, he threatened to have me exorcised because I questioned why Eve had to take all the blame for man's fall from grace."

Will's muffled laughter followed Melisande as she pasted

a bright smile to her lips and marched forward, license in hand.

"Mr. Chandler, I am sorry to disturb you at this hour, but we've come on important business that requires your attention."

"Business?" The priest's voice had risen an octave or two.

"Yes, rather urgent business. If we might step inside . . . ," she suggested.

En masse they filed into the church, where Mr. Chandler lit a pair of footed candelabra positioned at the narthex. Their light seemed lost in the cavernous space, where every sound was magnified tenfold. Linseed oil and fresh paint scented the air, as well as the lingering scent of snuff.

Melisande had turned around to search for Will, when he materialized on her other side, giving her a start. Even in boots, his step was so light, 'twas almost soundless.

As she looked up at him, Melisande felt her gaze drawn to the streaks of gold shimmering and dancing in his hair. Like her, the candlelight could not seem to resist those tawny veins, as it flickered and played over their gilded lengths.

He said something in a low voice. Distracted, she did not heed him.

"Wh-what?"

"I said I'll take it from here," he quietly repeated, plucking the license from her grasp before she could offer a protest.

His grip still firm on her elbow, Will led her forward. "Mr. Chandler, as Miss Mooresby already stated, our business is urgent and serious. The lady and I have come to ask that you unite us in matrimony."

The minister gasped, then tried to cover it by feigning a belch. "My good man, marriage is not an institution to be taken lightly and, in your case, I would urge *thorough* consideration before . . ."

His words died as he appeared to take notice of Will's freshly bruised eye. "Oh, dear," Mr. Chandler mumbled pityingly beneath his breath. "The depths to which some will sink . . ."

Melisande stiffened with indignation. Was the reverend insinuating that she—

"I did not blacken his eye!"

"Oh, yes, you did, Melisande," George contradicted. "Don't you remember? Just now in the coach, you popped him a facer."

Melisande wished she'd had the foresight to bring along a muzzle.

"Nonsense," she insisted in her firmest, most convincing manner. "In no way did I coerce Mr. Tagg—"

Fingers pressed into her elbow, exerting pressure just short of pain.

"Here." Will slapped the license into the reverend's open palm. "We have the necessary papers and we wish to be married. So let's get started, shall we?"

A flinty undercurrent in his tone left no room for argument. The priest cast one last doubtful look toward George, who, for once, had sufficient good sense to keep his mouth shut.

"Yes, very well, then." Reluctantly the minister unrolled the license and tilted it toward the light to read. "Oh. But there seems to be some mistake."

Melisande's stomach plummeted to her toes. *A mistake?*

"This is not a special license," Mr. Chandler said, his beefy features softening as if with relief. "I cannot perform the ceremony now."

"Why not?" Will asked before Melisande could.

"You see, my good man, this license requires that you wed between the morning hours of eight and noon. Only a special license, authorized through the Archbishop of Canterbury's office, grants the right to marry at any hour in any house of the Lord."

Cousin Harry!

Melisande silently debated whether cursing a bishop to hell was an unpardonable offense in the eyes of God. She was about to put down her foot and issue her demands when she sensed a subtle change take place in the man standing beside her. Will became suddenly . . . alert. As if his muscles had all grown taut and were quivering expectantly, awaiting his call to action.

Curious, she glanced toward him, watching as he slowly drew back his jacket and pulled from his pocket a worn and battered timepiece. For the love of Moses, didn't he well realize that it was nearing seven o'clock? Or did he truly need to verify the lateness of the hour?

Then Will shifted—in a movement so very subtle—and something shiny glinted at his waist. Something metallic.

Oh, dear heavens.

Melisande felt momentarily light-headed. Breathless, speechless. She shot a panicked glance to the reverend. By his extreme pallor, she deduced that he, too, had spied the knife sheathed at Will's side.

"Isn't it fortunate then that my watch shows it to be a quarter to noon?" Will asked in a soft, saber-edged drawl. Smiling like the very devil himself, he slipped the watch back into his pocket without offering to show it to Mr. Chandler.

No one spoke.

Melisande was in a daze. One part of her was delighted that Will may have convinced Mr. Chandler to carry on with the nuptials; another part of her was horrified by his threatening display of competence and authority. Who was this man? And what, pray tell, was she getting herself into by marrying him?

From that point on, everything began to move at a dizzying pace. The reverend snatched up his prayer book and rattled through the ceremony so swiftly that Melisande hadn't the time to think. The footman was rushed in to serve as a second witness and then they were all whisked aside to sign the register. Within ten minutes—perhaps as few as five—the deed was done. Melisande Mary Mooresby, heiress and hopeful prison reformer, was now Melisande Mary Taggart, wife to a Scots whiskey-maker.

As Will's hand cradled the small of her back, directing her outside, Melisande studied the ring weighing heavy on the fourth finger of her left hand. How very odd, she thought, that she would have forgotten to procure a ring, for it wasn't like her to be neglectful of details. And 'twas even more remarkable that Will should have remembered and had a ring at the ready.

It was a simple gold band, wide and unadorned, far too large for her finger. Yet despite its size, somehow the band managed not to slip off over her knuckle; it merely spun and rubbed and slid, as if to consistently remind her of its presence.

She was still contemplating the ring when she realized that they had returned to the coach. She glanced up as the door slammed shut and the horses shot off. Then George began to laugh. What began as nervous giggles soon progressed to hysterical guffaws, until her brother was clutching at his sides, his face almost puce.

"George, good heavens, what's come over you?" Melisande asked with no small measure of concern. Granted, they'd all been under tremendous pressure these last twenty-four hours, but now was not the time to lose control of one's senses.

Virtually apoplectic, her brother did not—could not—answer her.

"George, I beseech you—"

Without warning, Will reached over and grasped George's chin in one hand, hauling him halfway across the coach to meet him eye to eye.

"It's all right, lad," Will said gently, his burr more pronounced than the norm. "It's all right now."

Like a sorcerer waving an enchanted wand, Will continued to grip George's face until her brother blinked a few times then calmed. Will released him and George sat back on the banquette, his expression contrite.

"I say, I'm sorry," he mumbled. "Didn't mean to act the loose screw. I thought we were done for back there and then to have it all come around . . ." Emitting a shaky breath, he shook his head as if overwhelmed by the evening's events.

Melisande herself was overwhelmed, but couldn't afford the luxury of hysteria. Not when Grandfather awaited them at Mooresby Hall.

"Yes, well. Although the nuptials did not proceed precisely to plan"—Melisande snuck an uneasy glance across to Will—"the important thing to remember is that we have achieved our objective: Will and I are married."

At the other side of the coach, her husband maintained a brooding silence. Melisande tried to decipher his expression, but the coach's interior had fallen into darkness. They had left Cullscombe in such haste that the interior lantern had been left unlit, and evening's shadows were now sitting thickly upon them.

For no logical reason, Melisande felt herself annoyed by Will's silence. And by her suspicion that he was staring at her under the veil of darkness. She *felt* as if his gaze were upon her; her skin was inexplicably itchy, her cheeks unnaturally warm.

"We're fortunate that nothing went amiss," she said as an implied reproach. "I do not know whether threatening Mr. Chandler was the wisest course of action."

"Threaten?" Will's voice seemed to emanate from the very shadows. "Don't tell me that you threatened the good vicar, Mel."

Her lips drew into a pucker. "Not I," she clarified. "And I can't say I approve of you carrying *that*"—she gestured to his coat—"about."

Will hooked an ankle over a knee, forgetting her lesson about keeping his limbs in proper and modest alignment.

"I don't know why not. It was a gift from my grandfather to my father," Will said. "And on my tenth birthday, Da passed it on to me as a keepsake."

Melisande caught her breath. "Surely you must be joking. At ten? Ten years old?"

"Don't you believe that I could tell time at that age?" he asked in an amused drawl.

Tell time—?

Her fingers curled, the wedding ring chafing against her palm. "I was referring to the *knife*."

"Ah, the knife."

As if the wretch had truly misunderstood her.

"Aye, the dagger is mine. W.C. had been keeping it for me while I kept company with your friend Mr. Bell."

"Do you really think it wise to display it so prominently?"

Silence reigned for a heartbeat.

"I've learned," Will said in a quiet voice, "that I'm less

likely to have to use a weapon, Mel, if it's obvious that I'm carrying one."

Her fingers fell limp in her lap. *Goodness.* It hadn't occurred to her that he might actually have used the frightful thing. On a person!

Her pulse beat a little faster and again she asked herself what she knew of this man. Could Will have possibly drawn blood with that knife? Human blood? Dear Lord, might he even have wielded it with deadly results, perhaps taking another life?

She shuddered slightly, unable to lift her eyes from her wedding ring. *Now, now,* she told herself, *remember that he's been living in the colonies, traveling through untamed lands. To go about unarmed in the American wilds would surely be the height of foolishness. Of course he is in the habit of carrying a weapon. Which doesn't necessarily signify that he is dangerous.*

And yet Eileen had called him exactly that. Although Melisande rather suspected that the arsenal her sister referred to was not stocked with knives or pistols, but with devilish grins and impossibly wide shoulders. And with gold-threaded locks and a strong dimpled chin . . .

"By Jove, it would seem the old man has been busy!" George trumpeted into the quiet.

"What?" Melisande listed toward the window.

"Have a look," George invited, lifting aside the curtain. "He's lit every bloody lamp in the hall."

Framed in the distance, Mooresby Hall was indeed lit up like a torch, dozens of squares of saffron light dotting the blue-black night.

"What can he be up to?" she wondered aloud.

"Perhaps he's on a manhunt," Will suggested from the shadows.

"A manhunt? For whom?"

Will shrugged. "You? George? . . . Wildcat?"

Oh. Melisande pressed the back of her hand against her lips, the unfamiliar ring cold against the tip of her nose.

"The devil," George burst out. "Do you think Grandfather's called out the hounds?"

An unsavory vision came to Melisande then, a vision of Wildcat MacInnes run to ground by the dogs and treed in the dining room chandelier.

"I told him to stay in the stables," she said to no one in particular.

"Lenape braves aren't known for following orders, Mel."

She glared into Will's corner. "I daresay you do not seem overly concerned for your friend. Grandfather might be advancing in years, but he's still an exceptional shot."

"Uh-huh." Will sounded patently unimpressed.

The coach barreled the final yards down the drive, then shuddered to a halt in front of the manor's doors. Melisande did not wait for the footman, but leaped from the carriage, her skirts billowing shamelessly about her ankles. She was headed up the steps when her upper arm was trapped. Trapped in a brown, gloveless hand.

She snapped her gaze upward, as the light from the front windows illuminated the bronze flecks in Will's green eyes. Beautiful eyes, she thought to herself. *Despite the scarlet and violet mottling.*

"Don't you think it best that we enter Mooresby Hall together?" he asked. "As man and wife?"

Melisande caught her breath, disconcerted by her own carelessness and lack of forethought. Gracious, she was supposed to be playing the part of a new bride flush with happiness and madly enamored of her husband. To rush into the manor alone, as if anticipating a crisis, would only serve to arouse her grandfather's suspicions.

"Yes, of course," she answered. "You're quite right."

He gave her a wicked, lopsided smile, and offered her his hand. "Mrs. Taggart?"

Then, in a flash of comprehension, as goose bumps skittled up her arms, Melisande finally understood what Eileen had recognized from the very beginning. She saw it—the inexplicable something that drew her to this man even against her will. It was magnetic. It was hypnotic. . . . It was terrifying.

Ten

Before they'd taken two steps into the front hall, they were accosted by a frantic Bates.

"Oh, miss," the butler whispered, his thin arms fluttering up and down, reminding Will of a scarecrow tossed about in the wind. "I vow I've done all I could, but when the viscount arrived—"

"Where is he?" Melisande asked.

"His lordship and—ahem—Mr. MacInnes are in the parlor."

In Will's grip Melisande's fingers spasmed as she glanced up at him, her dark eyes enormous with apprehension. Will didn't know whether to laugh at her sweet owlish face or to pull her into his arms and tell her to stop worrying.

Before he could decide, she released his hand and bolted in the direction of the parlor. Will lengthened his stride to keep pace with her, bemused by her obvious concern. Did the woman honestly believe that her grandfather was going to best a Lenape warrior?

"For God's sake, Mel, relax. Wildcat can take care of himself."

She didn't look at him, but kept marching. "He is a guest in my home. *I* am responsible."

Responsible for too much, Will thought with a frown.
From what he'd seen, the woman bore the weight of the
world on her shoulders. And they were tiny shoulders at
that.

Melisande attacked the parlor door, pushing it open with
both hands. Her breath hitched audibly.

A silver-haired gentleman—tall, stout, and impeccably
attired—stood above Wildcat, clutching his friend's hunting
knife as if poised to plunge it straight into W.C.'s chest. Or
so it, at first, appeared.

In the time it took to blink, Will sized up the scene. What
could have been mistaken for cowering in terror was merely
Wildcat's loose-limbed sprawl across the velvet brocade
sofa. And the old man, Will noticed, was gripping the knife
with the blade pointed inward, not outward, as he looked to
be examining the handle's intricate carvings.

"Grandfather!"

Melisande's cry of alarm caused the Viscount Rutherford
to pivot toward them. Instantly Will perceived that this man
was not your standard tea-sipping, snuff-dipping English
lord. This was a man to be reckoned with. Authority shown
in every aspect of the viscount's features, from his eagle-
sharp eyes to his stone-hard mouth to the dark and dis-
pleased scowl veeing between his graying brows. He
reminded Will of a government man, one who influenced
policy and hobnobbed with those in positions of power. He
was a man who knew how to get what he wanted—or, in
other words, he was Melisande's kin.

"Granddaughter," the viscount replied in a voice like ice
shattering on a frozen pond.

Will sensed Melisande's momentary confusion. In a
wordless and instinctive movement, he placed his hand atop
her shoulder, urging her to calm down and reassess the
situation.

The viscount's sable eyes—so similar to Mel's—narrowed as they fixed to Will's possessive hold upon his
granddaughter. Without turning around, the older man
handed the knife back to W.C., his shrewd gaze not once
easing from its scrutiny of Will.

"Who the hell are you?"

The muscles in Melisande's shoulder contracted, but Will's gentle squeeze kept her silent. Since the viscount had already acquainted himself with W.C., Will figured odds were that the old man knew damn well who he was. Will smiled to himself, admiring his tactics.

Wrapping his arm around Melisande's waist, Will practically dragged her into the parlor. George, he noticed, had taken the coward's route and mysteriously disappeared.

"The name's Taggart." Will didn't extend his hand, choosing instead to hold onto Mel. He kind of liked the way she felt tucked into the crook of his arm. "Will Taggart," he clarified. "Melisande's husband. And you must be the Viscount Rutherford."

On the divan, W.C. was very casually cleaning his teeth with the tip of his hunting knife, looking almost bored.

The viscount's gaze flicked from Will to Mel and back again. "You married her?"

It was impossible to tell from his inflection whether he found the news shocking, infuriating, or gratifying.

"Aye, I did."

"When?"

"Half an hour ago."

"Half an hour?" The viscount snorted. "Just how long have you know the gel?"

Melisande tried to wriggle away, but Will held on tight. "Long enough."

Rutherford's scowl deepened. "Rushed matters, didn't you?"

Will shrugged. "I know what I want when I see it."

"Hah! And when you want something, you up and take it?" the viscount blustered. "By Jove, I'd like to know who gave you that right!"

Will nodded to Mel. "She did."

"She did, huh? Did you compromise her? Is that where you came by that shiner?"

"Yes. Not yet. And no."

"Hmph. Cheeky Scot." The viscount then turned his

suspicions, and his considerable bulk, on Melisande. "Is this all true?"

She bobbed her head, the scent of jasmine wafting from her crown of braids. "It's true. I am sorry that we could not wait for you to arrive after receiving your message, Grandfather, but we had already made our plans, you understand."

"Hmm-mm. I think I *do* understand." 'Twas evident that the old man smelled duplicity in their story. "Let me see the ring," he abruptly demanded, stalking toward them.

Melisande flung out her hand. Will noticed with a vague admiration that her fingers were not shaking, although he knew she had to be wound tighter than a spring.

"Not much to look at," the viscount said with a disparaging sniff.

Melisande jerked her fingers from his grasp. "Neither am I," she retorted, "so it suits me well."

For a moment, Will regretted that he'd not had anything finer to give her. Did she believe he'd not thought her worthy of better? Or did she believe her sister's insipid fairness to be more attractive than her own dark, fine-edged beauty?

Standing together at close range, the resemblance between Mel and the viscount was made obvious to Will in the bold jut of two similarly shaped jaws and the like intensity of eyes so dark they appeared bottomless. Though Melisande clearly hadn't inherited her grandfather's size, Will now appreciated where she'd come by the spirit that seemed to be so sadly lacking in her siblings.

A tingling at Will's nape made him aware of the fact that, while he studied the viscount, the viscount was studying him.

"Like what you see, Sir Insolence?" the old man challenged.

"It's Taggart," Will corrected. "And, aye, I do. So far."

The viscount stared at him and Will stared back. Rutherford's features hardened. Will's eased. Their silent standoff might have gone on all night, but for George's timely arrival.

"Champagne?" young Mooresby offered, as he cheerfully

sauntered through the doorway with the tray-laden Bates on his heels.

"Thank heavens," Will heard Melisande sigh in the faintest of whispers. "He'll calm down once he's had a bottle or two."

"Grandfather, how very good to see you again." George's smile was brittle with pretense. "I suppose you have heard the happy news, eh?"

The viscount stroked his silvery sideburns, stroking and stroking until George began to turn pink around the ears. "I've heard," he said at last.

An awkward silence prevailed while the butler swiftly distributed the champagne and they all stood around exchanging dubious glances. Then Bates fled and George raised his glass. Wildcat lifted his glass as well, although he remained where he was, with his feet propped up on the sofa.

"I propose a toast. To my sister, Melisande, who chose wisely and well."

Over the rim of his goblet, Will's gaze met Melisande's. She bit at her quivering lips, before contemplating the bubbles in her champagne.

There was a brief hesitation on George's part, as he waited to see if the viscount would drink. When the old man drained his glass, George downed his own in a single swallow.

Melisande did no more than study her bubbles.

"Don't you care for champagne?" Will asked.

"No." She wrinkled her nose. "In truth, I have no tolerance for spirits of any kind."

And you've married a whiskey-maker? Will suppressed a grin of irony.

"Grandfather," Melisande said, "dinner is soon to be served. Have you yet been shown to your room?"

"Hah! I've been shown every room in Mooresby Hall," the viscount countered belligerently. "I didn't believe that nincompoop butler of yours when he told me you'd eloped, so I insisted on searching every blasted corner of the manor myself. Never have trusted that shifty-eyed Bates," he muttered. "Most likely pinches the silver."

"Bates does not steal," Melisande corrected in a firm, no-nonsense voice.

"Hmmph. We'll see about that." The viscount tugged at his waistcoat, laboring to pull the embroidered vest over his significant girth. "By the by, what current ailment plagues that sickly sister of yours now?"

"Eileen?" As if Melisande had any other sister, ailing or not. "I believe she is so overcome at the prospect of finally being able to wed Benjamin that she's taken to her bed with a case of the vapors."

A silver brow crooked suspiciously. "Do not forget, Melisande Mary, that though you may hie off and wed any Scotsman who comes your way, Eileen has not yet attained the age of consent. And it is *I* who must give consent, gel. Not you."

Melisande's fingers tapped at the goblet's crystal base. "Of course, Grandfather, although I daresay you could hardly pose any objection to Benjamin or his family. They come from one of the oldest, most respected lineages in all of England and—"

"Poppycock," Rutherford snapped. "I've met more horse's asses from old, respected families than I have time to count."

George choked back a nervous laugh.

Melisande silenced him with her witchiest look. "Well then, since we've no interest in counting horse rear ends," she said tartly, "and since you've already been shown your room, shall we go in to supper?"

The viscount grumbled, but Melisande managed rather deftly to herd their party, including the taciturn Wildcat— who'd donned an actual shirt—down the hall and into the dining room.

This room, like all the others Will had seen at Mooresby Hall, positively oozed wealth. Decorated in shades of crimson and cream, it was dominated by a mammoth table, long enough to serve at least forty or fifty, Will estimated.

Only one end of it had been set for the five who sat down to their meal.

They'd barely taken their seats—Melisande's grandfather at the head—when Lord Rutherford resumed his interrogation.

"So, Taggart, your savage friend here tells me that you're a man of some importance in the colonies."

"Does he now?" Will cast a questioning glance across the table to Wildcat, who grinned fiendishly and began paring his nails with a silver table knife.

"Indeed," Rutherford said. "In fact, I would like to hear more about your work for Mr. Adams. How was it now that you are credited for saving the president's life?"

"God help us," Melisande whispered at Will's left.

George feverishly beckoned the footman to serve him more wine.

"Ah, that." Will's smile promised Wildcat painful and prolonged retribution. "I am certain that Mr. MacInnes exaggerates my consequence. For a few short months I worked as a—"

A small, bony elbow jabbed him in the hip. A warning, Will assumed, not to mention his stint as a smuggler or a privateer or a bounty hunter.

"As a surveyor," he continued smoothly, "for the United States government. I didn't report directly to Mr. Adams, even if Mr. MacInnes likes to inflate the importance of my role."

"And what's this business about saving Mr. Adams's life?" the viscount persisted.

"I assure you it was nothing heroic. I had been surveying a remote area of Kentucky through which Mr. Adams and his party happened to be traveling. At any rate, I shot and killed a certain *wildcat* that had been causing them trouble."

W.C. paused in trimming his nails and scowled.

The viscount went back to stroking his sideburns.

"Grandfather, perhaps we ought to take a moment to discuss Eileen's wedding," Mel suggested in a conspicuous attempt to steer the subject away from unsafe waters. "We've only a month to plan."

Rutherford abruptly slapped his heavy palm onto the table, startling George into spilling his claret. "By Jove, I want to know what's lit a fire under everybody in this house," the viscount complained. "Why are you all in such a devilish hurry to rush to the altar?"

Melisande set her fork down on her plate with deliberate precision. "As you are fully aware, Grandfather, Eileen and Benjamin have been waiting years as it is."

The viscount bristled like a bear provoked. "Don't you reprimand me, gel," he told her, waggling an accusing finger. "It's you who's been holding up those two and well you know it. I say if Eileen and her prissy little viscount are ready to wed, then let us have at it already. They have my blessing. No reason I should wait around here when that holier-than-thou cousin of yours—What's his name again? That bishop fellow?"

"Harry," George supplied.

"Yes, that's the one. He can arrange matters in a trice." Rutherford plunged a spoon into his pudding. "We'll have the wedding on Saturday."

"In three days?" Melisande half-rose from her chair. "But we cannot possibly arrange a wedding in that time."

The viscount looked his granddaughter up and down, taking note of her everyday, and unexceptional, attire. "I'd wager you arranged yours in three minutes, Melisande gel."

Mel flushed with embarrassment but did not back down. "I am not Eileen, Grandfather. She'll be heartbroken if she doesn't have a proper celebration. You know she will."

"A week then."

"Two," Melisande countered.

Matching black eyes dueled over a platter of sweetbreads. The moment stretched and stretched.

"Two weeks," the viscount conceded gruffly.

Eleven

༄

"Has my imagination run amok or is Grandfather actually spying on us?"

Melisande threw a look over her shoulder, and the hasty movement sent pains shooting through her neck. Good gracious, she was stiff. She bit back a grimace, watching the late evening shadows gambol across the corridor walls as the lamp swayed uncertainly in her hand.

"Aye, he's trailing us, all right," Will said. "I would guess to confirm for himself that we are planning to spend a blissful night in each other's arms."

"Oh, for heaven's sake," Melisande hissed. "I know he must harbor suspicions, but this is the outside of enough. He cannot *force* us to share a bed."

"No. But he might start asking a lot of questions if we don't. It is, after all, our wedding night, Mel lass."

A frisson of trepidation shivered up her spine. "What are you suggesting?"

Will held up his palms in a show of innocence. "I'm not suggesting anything. God knows *I* have nothing at stake here; it isn't my little sister whose reputation hangs by a thread."

Melisande grit her teeth. He would have to put it in just

those terms. And have the right of it, as well. It would not do to bungle matters now, not when they'd made it this far in their charade. Not when Eileen still had so very much to lose.

As they approached the door to Will's suite, Melisande swallowed around a lumpy dryness in her throat. "Tell me then, what is deemed proper?" she asked, somewhat testily. "Am I to join you in your room or vice versa?"

"Your room."

The alacrity of his response unnerved her.

"This is madness," she muttered. Madness to contemplate spending the night with this dangerous and captivating stranger. This stranger who, as of a few hours ago, was her husband.

If only, she lamented, she could have remained oblivious to his appeal. If Eileen had never pointed out this magnetic quality of his, might she not have seen it? Might she have failed to notice how his every look had the potential to make her knees turn to mush?

His shoulder brushed hers in the smallest of movements.

Melisande shivered, wondering whom she hoped to deceive—herself? Even prior to the conversation with her sister, she'd known something was different about Will Taggart. She'd known it from the moment he'd first kissed her in the library, for he had done what no man had ever done before; he had made her *feel*.

Madness, she told herself again. Nevertheless she said nothing, allowing Will to accompany her down the hallway and around the corner to her chamber. She paused outside the door, grasping for an alternative. "Perhaps if we—"

She'd not even finished her sentence when Will strolled right past her into the room.

"Evenin', sir," Melisande's abigail greeted.

Will saluted the girl with a saucy wink, and the young maid beamed. Evidently even servants were not immune to his charm, Melisande noted sourly.

"You may go, Molly," she said.

The maid curtsied. "Thank you, miss. Er, ma'am. And felicitations to you both."

As soon as the abigail had left, Melisande regretted sending her away. She ought to have asked the girl to bring her a salve or a compress for her neck. A headache had come upon her and, despite her best efforts, she could not ignore it. Her head pounded, the words "dangerous, dangerous, dangerous" incessantly hammering against her skull, echoing through her thoughts like a haunting refrain from an oft-sung melody.

When Melisande tried to shut out the pain, images even more unsettling than her sister's warning flashed through her thoughts. A mesmerizing pair of gold-green eyes. The menacing glint of a blade in candlelight. The anatomy of a Scot as viewed through a tub of soapy water.

With a start, Melisande realized that she had closed her eyes and she opened them wide upon hearing the key turn in the lock.

Will straightened from beside the door, holding the brass key between his thumb and forefinger. "We wouldn't want anyone to come stumbling in, would we?"

A tiny panic assailed her. In two steps, she had crossed the room and plucked the key from his grasp. "No, we would not," she agreed. "However, *I* will hold onto this, thank you."

She deposited the key and the lamp on her dressing table. Above all, she knew that she had to keep her head about her. She could not lose control of the situation.

As calmly as she could manage, she turned her back to him and began removing her ear bobs in the dressing table's mirror.

"Through that door on your left," she told him, "is a small servant's chamber furnished with a cot. Unfortunately the cot is rather small, but I daresay you'll survive it for a single night."

"One night? And where am I to sleep the rest of the time?"

Melisande stilled in the act of pulling a pin from her hair. Goodness, Grandfather didn't expect her to sleep with her husband each and every night, did he? Was it customary for married couples to do so? Since she'd been but a child when her mother passed away, she could not remember her own parents' arrangement. *Fourteen* nights? Fourteen nights sharing her bedroom with Tiger Taggart? She bit into her lip.

"I will have to puzzle on it," she said. "Until then." She pointed Will toward the antechamber.

Shrugging, he yanked his hair free from its leather tie and walked over to the bed. He sat down on the green damask counterpane and began tugging at his boot.

"Wh-what are you doing?"

He glanced up, his overlong hair rippling along the side of his cheek. "Getting ready for bed."

"Not in here," she corrected, again waving him toward the adjoining chamber. "In *there,* if you please." With an exasperated sigh, she turned back to the glass and resumed the tedious task of removing the hairpins from her braided crown.

In the mirror, she watched Will frown and scratch at his chin. He then tossed a boot against the entrance to the servant's alcove. The door swung open as the boot clattered noisily to the floor, and he made a face, oddly boyish, like a toddler eyeing his first plate of peas.

"What now?" she asked.

"Did I happen to mention that I have a strong dislike for tight spaces?" He laid his strong, brown hand against the base of his throat. "They make me feel all short of breath, like I'm suffocating, no room to move."

In the reflection, his expression was one part regretful, two parts expectant. Was the scoundrel toying with her again?

"Very well," she said. "I shall sleep on the cot and you may have the bed."

"Ach, what kind of unchivalrous cur do you think I am? No, don't answer that," he added hurriedly, grinning from ear to ear. "I'll tell you what—you take the bed and why don't I just sleep in this chair?"

Melisande glanced skeptically to the piece of furniture in question, a petite boudoir chair, about half Will's size. Another sharp twinge at her nape caused her to reflect on how deucedly uncomfortable the cot was likely to be. If she were lucky enough to sleep at all on the dratted thing, she'd likely awaken in the morning with her neck and back in spasms.

"All right then. If you prefer, you may sleep in the chair, though I doubt you'll find it restful."

"Compared to some places I've slept, it'll be heaven," he assured her.

Her image in the glass caught the small furrow that worked between her brows. For some reason, she didn't like to imagine the different places in which Will Taggart may have slept. Or with whom.

"Did you really work as a surveyor?" she asked abruptly.

His second boot plopped onto the Axminster carpet. "Aye, for a short time."

A surveyor, a privateer, a distiller . . . Was there nothing this man had not yet experienced, an adventure he'd not yet lived? For one still shy of a score and ten, he'd handled himself remarkably well this evening, she had to confess. Men much greater in years and maturity than Will had not stood so confidently against the powerful and intimidating Viscount Rutherford. Indeed he had acquitted himself admirably. Almost too admirably.

After yesterday Melisande had abandoned her hopes of "making Will over," once she'd been made to realize that he was not the destitute, uneducated soul she'd believed him to be. Although she had been looking forward to playing Pygmalion, and was disappointed she'd not have the opportunity to "redeem" him, Melisande could not have anticipated that her gaolhouse pugilist would reveal himself to be such a complex personality. Complex and distressingly competent.

For anyone to go toe to toe with her grandfather as he had done—

"*Gracious,*" she suddenly gasped.

While she'd been lost in reverie, Will had divested himself of all but his unmentionables and was now standing before the fire warming himself.

By God, he was splendid with the firelight caressing the planes and curves of his back and arms. . . .

Heat shot through her abdomen and Melisande ruthlessly squeezed shut her eyes. "For heaven's sake, put something on," she ordered a bit more imperiously than she'd intended.

She heard a faint rustling behind her. After a full minute's quiet, she cautiously lifted her lashes.

He'd pulled on his boots.

"Oh, you—"

Spreading his arms wide, Will offered her a shameless view of his chest in all its sun-bronzed, sculptured glory. "You cannot expect me to sleep in my clothes, now can you, Mel?"

She sputtered, mortified by her body's almost immediate reaction to his beauty. Her palms had grown damp, itchy with the desire to explore the tufts of brown curls sprinkled across his front.

"I . . . Douse the lamp," she at last managed.

As he turned away, she would have sworn his lips curved upward, accentuating that tantalizing cleft in his chin. She wondered what it would feel like to touch it, to tickle it with the tip of her fingernail.

Irresistible had been Eileen's word of choice. Well, blast it all, Will Taggart might be irresistible to most women, Melisande decided, but she was no ordinary female, no milk-and-water miss. She was made of sterner stuff, by Jove, she was a Mooresby. Why, if need be, she could resist Lucifer himself.

As long as he hadn't a dimple in his chin.

Will extinguished the lamp, so that the only light came from the banked fire as its rosy glow filtered through the darkness.

"You may use that blanket," she told him. "The one folded at the foot of the bed."

He padded over to the four-poster with his feline tread, then settled himself with the blanket in the striped boudoir chair. Melisande sidled behind the painted changing screen, comforting herself with the knowledge that it really was quite dark.

She flinched as she started to slip out of her gown, for the skirts' silken swish struck her as too intimate a sound to share with the man on the other side of the partition. She froze, then tried again. There was no help for it. Every murmur of cotton, every rasp of a tie, seemed exaggerated in the shadow-washed stillness, until Melisande's heart was pounding fast beneath her ribs. She'd never felt so foolish. She was actually short of breath as she removed her petticoat and chemise, flushed as she drew her night rail over her head.

With profound relief, she tied the bow at the neck of her nightgown and crept from behind the screen.

"That was lovely."

Melisande stilled, unable to feign ignorance. So he had been listening to her undress. *The cad.*

She climbed onto the mattress, its squeaks and groans taunting her even further. Angrily she shoved aside the counterpane and linens. Faith, but it was insufferably warm tonight.

At last she lay there, rigid as a board, scarce even daring to draw air into her lungs.

"Mel?"

She sighed, despairing of ever hearing her given name from his lips. "Yes?"

"What will the servants say when they find the sheets clean in the morning?"

She blinked. "What do you mean?"

"I mean, aren't you worried that the viscount will hear that the sheets were not stained and draw his own conclusions?"

"Oh." Heat stole into her cheeks as understanding dawned. "No, um, I don't think so. Grandfather will assume we've anticipated our vows, which he most likely already believes. And, in our particular case, I see no reason to convince either him or the household staff of my unsullied state." She stopped and thought her logic through. "After all, when I petition Cousin Harry for the annulment, it will be infinitely less complicated if I claim the marriage to be unconsummated, therefore, why try to dissemble and pretend that it has been?"

Will rubbed thoughtfully at his jaw. "So let me get this straight. I'm going to spend the night in this dollhouse-sized furniture in order to give the appearance we're sleeping together; even though in a matter of weeks you're going to deny that we ever did?"

"Precisely."

Of course, with Grandfather's arrival and the date of Eileen's wedding being changed, she would have to revise her annulment plans. And there was that bothersome little detail of finding a third party to act as wronged suitor . . . But until the viscount had left Mooresby Hall and until she had her grandmother's inheritance in hand, no action would be initiated with the church or with Cousin Harry. However, it was not too early to start seeking a site for her reformatory. The old mill west of Cullscombe might do nicely. . . .

"Mel."

"Hmm?"

"You are unsullied, aren't you?"

Her eyes snapped open. *The nerve—* "Heavens, what do you think?"

She could almost hear his answering smile.

"G'night, lass."

She grumbled "Good night" and flipped onto her side. A frustrated punch at her pillow, then she tucked her hand beneath her cheek. Something cool and hard pressed into her flesh.

Her wedding ring.

"And what are the women like? Are they pretty?"

Wildcat tilted back in his chair, carefully balancing his mug of ale. "Not as pretty as you, *Woachawes.*"

Eileen blushed, her eyes growing round like a pebble drawing circles on a pond's mirrored surface. "What is that you called me?"

"It means sunflower."

"Oh." Her lashes fluttered down, then up. "Your language is very interesting, Mr. MacInnes."

As are you, little one. With regret, Wildcat had to remind himself that this soft-eyed woman carried another man's babe within her. Lucky bastard.

He indicated her plate with a wave of his mug. "*Mitsi,*" he told her. "You must keep up your strength."

Eileen glanced apologetically at her breakfast. "My appetite is poor of late."

"No," he insisted. "You must eat. Your sister will surely blame me again if you fall into a faint."

She giggled and took a small bite of toast. "So you've not been to Scotland before?"

"No, though my father has maintained contact with his family and they are expecting me to visit."

"And your father is not homesick?"

Wildcat finished off the rest of his ale. "He has lived among the Lenape for three decades. He's not much of a Scot anymore, as Tiger likes to point out."

A whisper of a breeze stirred the back of his neck, carrying a familiar scent. "Speaking of the devil . . ."

A hand clapped Wildcat's shoulder.

"Are you telling this bonny creature that I'm a devil?" Will asked from behind Wildcat's chair.

W.C. wiped the back of his hand across his mouth. "Miss Eileen is an intelligent woman. She can see for herself the horns you hide under that mane of yours."

Grinning, Will took a seat at the table, on the other side of Eileen. "You mustn't believe everything this heathen tells you," Will warned her. "He has a tendency to make up stories."

"Oh, really? But he was just telling me how he chased down on foot the deer whose hide he was wearing yesterday. Is that not so?" The fair-haired Eileen looked crestfallen that the story might not be true.

"Aye, that much is fact," Will admitted. "W.C. has always been light-footed. He can outrun just about anything."

"A useful talent when keeping company with you, my brother."

As the footman offered Will a beverage, Wildcat noticed

that his friend chose the bitter coffee over the smooth homebrewed ale.

He was going to comment on Will's night of sleep—or lack thereof—when the viscount hobbled in, aided by a walking stick.

"Grandfather." Eileen rose to place a kiss upon the earl's crepe-like cheek. "Oh dear, has your gout flared up again?"

"Yes, blast it," the old man groused. "Your cook gave me some potion which will surely poison me. Mayhaps I'll test it on George first. But you, at least, appear in better health this morning, granddaughter."

"Oh, I am," Eileen said, helping him to his seat. "I am much recovered and looking forward to at last marrying my dear Benjamin. I thank you for giving us your blessing."

"Yes, yes, whatever you want, gel, whatever you want. Frankly, I'd have thought a miss with your looks could do better, but . . ." The viscount carefully lowered himself into a chair, his sharp gaze assessing Eileen's plate.

"Are you sure you're all the thing, child? You've not eaten much."

"I'm fine, Grandfather. Truly."

"Good. For we can't have you swooning in the church like some silly Bath miss. It would reflect badly on us all, gel, badly on our stock."

"Oh, no. I'm sure I'll be quite fit by then."

"See that you are," Lord Rutherford instructed, leaning his cane against the table and turning his attention to Tiger. "Well, boy? Where is your bride?"

Will reached for the salt cellar. "She's still abed."

Rutherford nodded, his jowls swaying like a turkey's wattle. "That's a good sign. Did she please you well enough?"

"Oh!" Standing behind the viscount's chair, Eileen turned a bright cherry-red. "I do believe I hear Bates calling," she murmured before quickly exiting the room.

Will took his time seasoning his eggs, more interested in apportioning the salt than in answering Lord Rutherford's question.

"She pleases me."

The viscount barked a laugh. "I wouldn't put much store in her continuing to please, Taggart, for if you haven't marked it yet, the gel is a managing piece—likes to have things her way. Ain't many who can abide a bossy nature in a woman."

Will smiled noncommittally.

The viscount twirled the nob of his cane. "Did Melisande happen to mention her grandmother's endowment? The twenty thousand pounds?"

No one but Wildcat would have noticed the telltale twitch of surprise at the corner of Tiger's bruised eye.

"It's a respectable sum," Will said.

"Respectable indeed," Rutherford sniffed. "Lends the gel a certain charm, I'd say." He struggled to his feet, leaning heavily upon the ornate walking stick. "When you're done with your breakfast, come find me, Taggart. There are a few matters we need to discuss."

As soon as Rutherford hobbled out the door, Wildcat expected to see Will jump up onto the table and whoop with joy. Or at the very least, to let loose with one of his famous crooked grins. Instead, Will took a measured sip of his coffee.

"Don't tell me you already knew about the money," Wildcat said, "because I'll sure as hell not believe you."

"Aye, I knew. Just not how much."

Yet you do not sing praises to the sky? Something was definitely amiss. "Did you bed her?"

Another infinitesimal twitch of the eye. "No."

"Dammit, Tiger, do you not see that this woman has bewitched you? She has cast some kind of spell, some odd English enchantment. I say we get out of here while we can."

"Leave? Why would I leave when everything I desire is being handed to me on a silver platter?"

"The fates do not give freely, my friend."

"Hell, you fret like an old woman, Niankwe. Trust me, there is nothing to worry about." He shoved away from the table. "Now, if you'll excuse me, I'm off to go a few rounds with the viscount."

Wildcat cursed under his breath, wishing for the hundredth time that someone had beaten some sense into that boy while he was still young. His hide was too thick now for a lash to be of any use. Damn the luck.

The problem with Will, as Wildcat saw it—or, at least, *one* of the problems with Will—was that Tiger believed himself to be invincible. Nothing could touch him because he *let* nothing touch him. Hell, he'd seen Taggart grin that same friggin', lopsided grin with a cocked pistol pressed to his temple. Tiger never let anything get to him because nothing had ever been that important to him.

"Good morning, Mr. MacInnes," a familiar voice said at his back.

Nothing had been that important to him . . . until now.

"I passed Will in the hall and he said that you were in here, though, at this late hour, I was surprised that anyone would still be at breakfast," Melisande said, sitting down with a cup of chocolate. "Did you oversleep?"

"No. I have not yet grown so soft that the sun rises before me. It was this fine ale that detained me. And your sister's curiosity."

"Ah, Eileen has been downstairs? So she is feeling better?"

"Yes."

The footman stepped forward to clear the plates.

Melisande waited for the servant to leave before she bobbed her chin. "Thank you for attiring yourself in a less startling manner, Mr. MacInnes. I know you think me a prude, but it was truly my concern for Eileen's sensibilities that caused me to be so short with you yesterday."

Wildcat merely grunted. Whatever else he might think of this woman, her love for her family was a quality he had to grudgingly admire.

"Are you comfortable in the stable quarters?"

"Comfortable?" He lifted one side of his mouth. "I make myself sleep upon the floor for fear such luxury will ruin me for the rush mats of home."

"Really. Do you plan to return to the States soon?"

"I don't know. My uncle has had a vision that tells him

my destiny lies on this side of the ocean. I hope to hell he's seeing it wrong."

"So you do hope to return home?"

Wildcat shrugged. "I am promised."

"Promised? Do you mean engaged?"

He glanced away, his gaze seeking the verdant view on the other side of the window. "More or less. Our families have reached an agreement."

"Do you care for your chosen mate?"

"Do you?" he shot back.

Melisande's smile turned guarded. "You do not particularly like me, do you, Mr. MacInnes?"

"It's not that so much, as I can see that you are headed for big trouble, Melisande Taggart."

She brushed a lock of hair behind her ear and coolly regarded him. "And what makes you say that?"

Wildcat leaned back in the chair and scratched at his stomach. "You don't know Will. You cannot even begin to."

"But he is 'big trouble'?"

Wildcat's eyes narrowed and he gave her a tight smile of warning. "Oh, yeah. You might not know it, but when you married Will, you got yourself a tiger all right. You got yourself a tiger by the tail."

Twelve

❧❦❧

Will sat on a bench at the far end of the Mooresby gardens and contemplated the sheen on his new boots. They'd been delivered earlier that afternoon, along with six pairs of trousers, four waistcoats, four coats, a dozen linen shirts, a veritable mountain of stockings, cravats, handkerchiefs, gloves, drawers, and who knew what other nonsense. Although Melisande had mentioned something about the tailor and the coincidence of Will and George being of a comparable size, Will hadn't anticipated the boxes and boxes that had come pouring into his room one right after the other. He'd shoved aside most of it, except for the Hessians.

Just give him a good pair of boots and some deerskin leggings and he was content. Well, as content as any man could be who'd not slept more than an hour or two a night, five days running.

After that first night of sharing a room with Mel, Will had abdicated the pint-sized chair and had taken instead to bedding down in front of the fire. The carpet was plush and he could stretch out his limbs; and he had a far better view of the sleeping siren who was driving him to complete and utter distraction. Try as he might, he couldn't sleep while she lay there, her silken hair begging to be stroked, her soft curves calling out to him in the darkness.

Will wasn't used to going without a woman and he damned sure wasn't used to a woman who so easily resisted his charms. His marriage needed to be consummated. But his wife was not cooperating.

They had settled into a routine these last few days whereby they'd see each other at breakfast and then Mel would disappear for the remainder of the day as she rushed around preparing for Eileen's wedding. They would all meet up again for supper, but this schedule understandably did not allow for much private time between Will and his bride. Those few minutes preparing for bed had become his only opportunity to woo, and even those minutes Melisande had managed to cut short.

He hoped he was making headway. A touch upon her elbow as he led her into dinner, a whisper at her ear.

The way Will saw it, he now had a dual purpose in bedding his wife. First, he needed to throw obstacles into the annulment path. Not only would a consummated union be more difficult to dissolve but, frankly, he figured that once Mel had a taste of passion Tiger-style, she'd follow him to the ends of the earth for more. He just needed to make sure she got that first taste.

Secondly, and most importantly, he wanted her. He *had* to have her. She'd become a test of his manhood, a challenge he could not walk away from. Hell, yeah, he'd counted coup with Wildcat and gone one-on-one with a brown bear twice his size. He'd hunted men into the deepest woods, knowing they'd as soon slit his throat as look at him. But Melisande . . . Now, she was a challenge. With every provocative sway of her hips and every fiery toss of her head, she upped the ante. And this was one game Will was determined to win.

Scuffing his heels through the dirt, Will reflected on his many conversations with Lord Rutherford. Not surprisingly the old viscount had deduced after only a day or two that the marriage was a sham. But rather than confront Mel, Rutherford had come to him with his suspicions. Will had admitted nothing; he'd denied nothing. And then, precisely as George had done, the viscount had offered to sweeten the pie: If Will was agreeable to taking on the responsibility of his granddaughter, he would see to it that, in one year's time, another twenty thousand pounds was deposited to Will's account.

Will laughed softly and bent forward, dropping his head into his hands. Damn, it was absurd. No one wanted Mel . . . but him.

And to think Melisande had been worried sick that the viscount wouldn't find Will good enough for her. On the contrary, once Rutherford had determined that Will wasn't wanted for murder, he'd been satisfied. Like George, the old man seemed to believe that Will was the only man in all of Britain capable of taming their "She-Devil."

A twig snapped and Will looked up to find Melisande a few yards away, frozen as if she'd been caught in the act of sneaking away.

"Don't let me disturb you," she said, endeavoring to retreat behind the hedge.

"Hold up, Mel." He beckoned her forward. "Come have a seat."

"No. I haven't the time." She glanced to the garden path, the way she'd come. "Eileen's nuptials are consuming every bit of me."

Will groaned. God, would he love a chance to consume every bit of her.

"Come on," he urged. "You can rest for a minute." He flashed his best come-hither smile. "I insist."

Her raven brows dipped together. Her nose twitched with indecision. But ultimately she walked across the courtyard with care, picking her way gingerly as a deer picks its way across an open meadow. He scooted over and she sat down, leaving a discreet distance between them.

"Oh, my." She closed her eyes on a small, tired sigh. "It does feel welcome to rest my feet." She dipped her head back, rolling it left and right along her shoulders, as the tips of her hair slid along the marble bench.

A vampire-like instinct came over Will in that moment—

a desire to sink his teeth into that tantalizing expanse of snowy-white flesh.

"Neck ache?" he asked.

"Mm-mm." Opening her eyes, she cupped a hand to her nape. "It has been stiff."

God, hasn't it, though? Will thought.

He inched closer. Mel shot him a wary, sideways glance.

"Here," he offered. "Allow me."

"No, I don't think—"

He brushed her hand aside, substituting his. She scowled at him, reaching for his wrist.

"I do not want—"

"Give me a chance. I've been trained by some of the most skilled healers in the world."

Her scowl eased to a dubious frown. Gently he kneaded the muscles at her neck, her hair like baby mink against his knuckles. Jasmine, the scent she favored, mingled with the lavender flowering at their backs, its heady perfume unrestrained in the warmth of late afternoon.

"You are tight," he murmured, then regretted his choice of words. They drew to mind other images too tempting to contemplate.

She kept her head down, her fists clenched in her lap.

"Relax, Mel. Isn't this better?"

He saw her small white teeth dig into the fullness of her lip, as her chest rose and fell in a rapid cadence. Suddenly she lurched to her feet.

"I must be going."

For one brief second, as she whirled away, their gazes met. Will felt as if he'd been poleaxed. My God, he'd seen it. He'd seen what she'd been fighting to hide from him: *Desire.*

Leaping up, he grabbed for her, catching hold of her upper arm. She tried to break free, her fists flailing, but he clamped his fingers around her other arm.

"Easy," he said. "Or you'll blacken my eye again, you impossible woman."

She stopped struggling, although he could feel her shaking like an aspen leaf.

"Mel?"

She lifted her face to him and what he saw in her was nothing short of magnificence, making his breath catch with longing. She was fire and fury, confusion and desire. She was need and need denied.

"I am going to kiss you."

Her chin raised. "I have forbidden you to do so."

"Forbidden?" A faint smile escaped him. "I wonder, Mel, if you don't want me to break some of your rules."

After a long, pregnant moment, he took her silence to mean *yes.* Break the rules because she was too proud to relent on her own.

He leaned toward her slowly, appreciating the torment blazing in her obsidian eyes. Ach, how she would have loved to have denied him. But her curiosity burned too bright.

She did not elude him; she did not let her lashes drift closed like a frightened virgin. She met him as he might have expected. With defiance and spirit and energy.

Their lips met and clung together, as if in reunion, so long apart after that first stolen kiss. They tasted and tested. They explored and excited. For Will, it was even more powerful than he'd remembered, more fulfilling than he'd dreamed.

"Open for me," he begged.

For once, she did not put forth an argument, instead accepting his tongue's tender invasion. His hands slid up her arms to twine through her hair. Her nails flexed gently against his chest.

He kissed her as he'd wanted to kiss her every night as he lay sleepless on his pallet beside her bed. He'd had many hours to envision how he'd hold her, how he'd touch her, how he'd make her whimper for him. His lips eased from hers, drifting to the corner of her mouth, then to her cheek and eyelids. His tongue explored the curve of her ear as his hands swept down her back until he was cupping her buttocks. She whimpered then, the sweetest music to his ears.

"Sorceress," he murmured in the hollow beneath her jaw.

Trapped between their bodies, her hands slid over his

chest up to his shoulders where she filled her fists with his hair, pulling him, dragging his lips back to hers. When he obediently possessed her mouth again, he felt her smile.

Yes, command me all you want, sweet witch. For Will was bewitched, entranced, spellbound.

The sun warmed his back, the breeze whispered in his ear. He felt drunk and uncontrolled. He pulled her closer, bending over her, seeking her breasts. She gasped as he kissed her through the muslin gown—gasped and arched, inviting him to take more. Impatiently he tugged down the neck of her dress and chemise, hungry for her softness. And there in the garden, with the April sunshine bathing them, he worshiped her, suckling her as she sang a throaty song of desire.

"Melisande? Are you out here?"

It took both of them a few seconds to heed Eileen's call. Melisande was the first to react, her fingers going limp in his hair. Will turned his head to the side and rested his cheek on her breast, his loins ready to burst. She gave him a light shove on his shoulders. Reluctantly he straightened.

Their eyes met and he read regret in her expression. Regret that they had been interrupted? Or regret that she had succumbed to temptation, lost control?

"Melisande, where are you?" Eileen called from a short distance. "The seamstress has arrived and is waiting to meet with us."

Melisande licked her lips, puffy and pink. "I am coming."

With clumsy fingers, she blindly fixed her bodice, her gaze not once leaving his. No embarrassment, no maidenly tears. Not from Melisande. Disappointment, perhaps. Confusion, certainly. *And how could she not be confused?* Will asked himself.

He, who had known women by the dozens, who had enjoyed sex often and well as a pleasant and necessary diversion, was dumbfounded by the intensity of what they'd just shared. How must Melisande feel? Melisande who was as yet "unsullied"?

She said nothing, but turned and walked away. Will let her go. This time.

•   •   •

Melisande met up with her sister on the garden path halfway back to the house.

"There you are. I was beginning to—" Eileen's sentence broke off. She flattened a palm to her chest. "Oh, my."

After casting a swift glance behind her, she took Melisande's hand in hers and started pulling her toward the other end of the gardens.

"The seamstress—"

"She can wait," Eileen declared, leading her across the lawn, past the maze, to the circular Greek folly tucked behind the rose garden.

"Sit," Eileen bid her, "before you collapse."

Melisande sank onto a cool, shaded bench. Eileen joined her and immediately began wringing her hands.

"I should call it off," Eileen said. "I should call it off before it is too late."

"Call it off?" Melisande shook herself, trying to awaken from the feverish daze clouding her thoughts. "But . . . but you cannot."

"I must. I ought never to have agreed to this plan in the first place. You've already risked too much on my behalf."

"No. *No*," Melisande repeated more firmly. "The wedding is in but a week. Benjamin's family arrives Sunday, you'll wed on Wednesday . . . Under no circumstances will we call it off!"

"But, Melisande, look at you." In dismay, Eileen pressed her fingers against her lips.

Melisande was afraid to look. She knew that if she glanced down, she'd find her nipples still turgid, straining against the front of her gown.

"I tried to warn you," Eileen said.

"Yes, you did and I am grateful for your counsel, I truly am." She patted her sister's tangled fingers. "Unfortunately, I hadn't understood how . . . effective a man's kisses could be."

Eileen woefully appraised her stomach. "Very effective indeed."

"If I had known— I mean never would I have imagined

that kissing could make one feel so . . . so . . . *nice*,"
Melisande finished for lack of a better word.

"Oh, but, sister, it gets better," Eileen whispered with a
sober little frown. "Or worse, I suppose. Depending upon
your point of view."

"Better?" She could scarce credit such a claim.

Eileen blushed a vivid rose, unable to look her square in
the eye. "I daresay you wouldn't believe me if I tried to
describe it."

"Try," Melisande insisted.

"Oh, I don't think—"

"Try."

"Oh." Eileen's lashes fluttered apprehensively. "Well, it is
similar to the kisses' feeling, but perhaps a hundred, if not
a thousand, times more potent. Did you"—she averted her
gaze—"become warmish?"

Melisande nodded, thinking that her toes must be singed.
"Yes, quite warm."

"Hmm-mm." A delicate clearing of the throat followed.
"This is so awkward, so difficult to discuss—"

"Not so difficult," Melisande said. "I am a married
woman, Eileen. At least for the time being. I must know of
these matters."

"Yes. I suppose if Mother had lived, she would have been
the one to speak to us of this."

"But, sadly, she is not with us, so it is up to you. So,
please. Go on."

Eileen sighed, obviously overcome by the sensitive
subject. "Well, as I was saying about being warm . . . You
do become warm. Very warm. Hot. So hot that you feel as
if your insides are melting. And then a pressure builds. An
odd sort of pressure that comes from a deep, secret place. It
builds and builds until suddenly you dissolve and *boom*—"

With a dramatic flourish, Eileen threw her hands into the
air as if to simulate an explosion.

Melisande had to struggle for breath. "My, that does
sound intriguing."

"Oh, but it's not always so pleasant."

"No?"

Eileen leaned forward, her blue eyes wide. "I have heard that if you attempt this intimacy with the wrong gentleman, the whole episode can go frightfully awry. Disastrous, I've heard."

"Really." Melisande wrinkled her nose. She was sorry to hear that, since she'd harbored a secret hope that her experience with Will had not been that unusual. Commonplace even.

"So only certain men can produce this . . . *boom*?"

Eileen raised her shoulder in a petite shrug. "From what I understand."

Melisande tapped her chin thoughtfully, her brain clicking away. "How disagreeable 'twould be to go through life and never experience what you've described."

"Oh, dear, you mustn't worry about that," Eileen told her reassuringly. "Someday, after all this false marriage business is over, the right gentleman will come along and make you the happiest of women. I'm sure of it."

"Do you think so?" Melisande asked, a queasy uncertainty drawing at her stomach.

"Positive," Eileen said. "He'll have to be the very best of men, of course. Educated and kind and agreeable. Why, I wouldn't be surprised if he were a marquis or a duke. Or a prince!" Eileen clapped her hands, delighted with her fantasy. "Oh, yes, Melisande, yes. You, my darling sister, deserve no less than a prince."

Melisande smiled and tried to play along with her sister's daydream. But the only prince she could envision was not crowned with metal, but with a mane of streaky gold.

Thirteen

༄

"Psst."

The hiss had come from across the rear courtyard, the same courtyard to which Will had been delivered by Mr. Bell that fateful, fateful day nearly two weeks ago.

Peering over his shoulder, Will spied George Mooresby at the other side of the court, barely peeking out from behind the smokehouse's oak door, as if he were playing the children's game of hide-and-seek. With a jerk of his chin, George motioned for Will to join him.

"By Jove, I was beginning to worry that you'd snuck away in the night," George whispered, closing the smoke-house door after sending one more cautious glance around the quiet yard. "You've certainly made yourself scarce of late."

Will dodged a ham hanging from the rafters, as his vision adjusted to the warm, steamy darkness of the small curing shed. "I've been busy," he answered.

Since the arrival of the groom's family two days earlier, Will had been keeping a low profile at Mooresby Hall. He'd never been particularly fond of pomp and circumstance, and the upcoming union of two prominent English families seemed to call for plenty of both. When the genealogy charts had appeared, Will had disappeared, spending the last few days with Wildcat as they mapped out the Devonshire terrain to the north and east. In the event they were required to make a speedy departure.

Will leaned against the smokehouse wall, careful to avoid the meat hooks. "Sorry, George, old boy, but I've got better things to do than listen to Rutherford and the Earl Ketching debate bloodlines all night long."

"Blasted dull stuff, isn't it? I wish Eileen would hurry up and marry Benjamin and be done with it. Although after this morning . . ." George grimaced, apparently hesitant to continue.

Will made an impatient rolling motion with his hand, urging him to get on with it.

"Well," George said, "this morning, I finally had a private moment with Eileen and was able to ask a few questions about Melisande's intentions. What I learned does not bode well for our plans, I fear. Not well at all. It seems that Melisande aims to send you away as soon as the wedding party leaves Mooresby Hall Thursday afternoon."

"Send me away?"

George bobbed his head. "The very same day. Apparently she's decided that she can pursue the annulment just as easily without your presence. And in fact—if you can believe it—the silly girl has already sent a discreetly worded letter to an old school chum of mine asking him to step forward and act as the injured party in the annulment proceedings."

"A Mr. James Fowley perhaps?"

George cocked his chin into his chest. "My word, how did you know?"

From his coat pocket, Will withdrew a sealed letter, waggling it before George's eyes.

"Y-you pinched it?"

"Oh, I wouldn't say 'pinched.' Wildcat merely caused it to be missing."

"Thank God," George huffed, "since Fowley is the sort with more hair than wit and he might actually have fallen in with Melisande's cork-brained scheme. Nonetheless, how are we to keep her from sending you off come Thursday? She'll do it, you know. One way or the other."

"She can't if I've already gone."

"What? You can't back out now! W-We've made a gentlemen's bargain."

"Easy, Mooresby, easy. I've no intention of backing out; I'm just thinking aloud."

"Oh." George tugged at his cravat. "Blast, but the air is close in here."

Will considered pointing out to the lad that the dairy would have made for a more comfortable trysting site, but chose to hold his tongue. Young George still had a lot to learn.

"So what are you thinking, Will?" Mooresby asked, dabbing at his damp forehead with a kerchief. "What are we going to do about Melisande?"

"You mean what am *I* going to do to rid you of your sister?" Will asked with a cynical lift of his brows.

"Oh, er, right." At least, the boy had enough grace to look abashed.

Will squeezed the bridge of his nose, feeling irritated though uncertain of the reason. "All right, George, what I need from you is a traveling coach, kept ready and waiting from this moment on. I can't be exactly sure how this will develop in the next day or two, but I might have to leave in somewhat of a hurry."

"Yes, yes, I can see to a coach. Anything else?"

"No, the rest I can take care of," Will said, idly studying the pattern of the floor planks. "Did Eileen tell you anything more about what Mel has up her sleeve?"

"Let's see . . . She did mention that Melisande is starting to consider sites for her remedial academy."

Will glanced up. "Her what?"

"Oh, it's a pet project of hers, completely absurd if you ask my opinion. She's had a bee in her bonnet about it for as long as I can remember, though how a woman of sense could pursue such folly—"

"Are you talking about some kind of house of correction?" Will asked, recalling Melisande's desire to "rehabilitate" him at the outset of their charade.

"Yes, something like that. But she's no radical reformist, no Hannah More or the like. To tell you the truth, I don't believe Melisande is really all that interested in penal reform or in improving conditions at Newgate. I think for her the true attraction to this venture is the chance to impose her will on others. To 'fix' people, as it were.

"Of course, I'm sure she doesn't see it that way," George said not unkindly. "In fact, I know that she means to do good. You see, Melisande has spent her entire life managing other people's lives and, I confess, she's done a damned fine job of it for the most part. She does have a talent for making you view the world her way. And yet she doesn't understand that one cannot change people just by wishing them changed."

"So she hoped to use her inheritance to finance this crusade of hers?"

"Hmm-mm. She'd never use the estate monies. Melisande is far too ethical for that."

"Has she mentioned anything to you about the inheritance?"

"She told Eileen that she'd spoken to Grandfather at least two or three times about the bequest and he'd not been very accommodating."

"Really?" In Will's pocket, a bank draft in the amount of twenty thousand pounds felt like it was burning straight through to his flesh.

George frowned and tugged at his earlobe. "But apparently she's worn him down and he's agreed to transfer the monies either today or tomorrow. Melisande isn't renowned for her patience, you know."

"Well, patience isn't one of my more pronounced virtues either," Will said as he pushed away from the wall.

"You're not going to change your mind, are you?" George asked before starting to gnaw at a thumbnail. "You know, I really do believe Scotland will be the best thing for her."

Will considered a moment before answering in all honesty, "So do I, George."
So do I.

The morning of Eileen's wedding dawned free of clouds, the horizon as crystalline and clear as the square-cut diamond sparkling in the bride's engagement ring. Not normally one prone to superstition, Melisande nonetheless took the fine weather to be a favorable omen. She needed a good omen. A dozen of them.

Once or twice during these last days, she'd actually questioned whether or not her sister would make it to the altar. She'd not anticipated that Benjamin's father and her grandfather would respond to each other like oil to flame. Just last night, the two older gentlemen had dipped too deeply into the port, launching into another heated debate over whose blood was bluest. Benjamin had been forced to literally drag his father away before the question was put to the test by the spilling of that same blood.

Verily, it had been all that Melisande could manage to keep this betrothal intact. Eileen, overly emotional due to her condition, had been a weepy mess, alternately sobbing and swooning until even the patient Benjamin had grown exasperated with her tears. And between the two sparring patriarchs and the extremely sensitive Eileen and then George, who'd been as tense and tight as a bowstring—

Throughout it all, Melisande had felt like a juggler at the fair, trying in vain to keep her balls from crashing to the ground. The only saving grace had been that, due to all the upheaval, scant attention had been paid to her new husband. No one had much cared that she'd gone off and married a rough-edged, wild-eyed Scot. No one much cared that she'd wed at all.

With a final tug to straighten the hem of Eileen's pale pink skirts, Melisande rose from her knees with a weary sigh.

"Can you tell?" Eileen asked, her brows furrowed with concern. Turning to stand in profile in front of the cheval glass, she spread her hands across her flat stomach.

"All I can tell is that you'll be the loveliest bride Devonshire's ever seen," Melisande answered reassuringly. "So do stop fretting and enjoy your day."

"Yes, of course, you're right, sister dear. This has been so stressful, has it not?"

Melisande had to literally bite her tongue. If anyone had borne the brunt of the recent stress, it surely hadn't been Eileen, who'd lain abed till noon or later each day. But what would it accomplish to say so to her already emotionally vulnerable sister?

"Come now, we mustn't tarry." Melisande handed Eileen a leather-bound Bible and a pair of kid gloves. "I do believe that Benjamin and his family have already left for the church."

As she pushed her sister out the door, Melisande's eye caught on the silver vinaigrette case resting beside the bed. She snatched it up. As a precaution.

Melisande guided Eileen down the staircase, her gaze skimming over the trio of gentlemen patiently awaiting them in the front hall. The threesome made for an unlikely ensemble. Although her grandfather, George, and Will were all dressed in similar finery, it was Will who stood out among them. Despite the cravat and conservatively cut superfine coat, he still somehow succeeded in looking not quite civilized. She supposed it was rather like dressing a wolf in sheep's clothing; no matter how soft and appealing the exterior, one could not disguise the razor-sharp fangs lurking beneath the surface.

With relief, she passed her sister off to George and her grandfather, subtly shaking her wrist to relieve the numbness brought on by Eileen's death grip upon her.

Will casually took hold of her other hand, tucking it into the crook of his arm. Distracted, Melisande did not pull free, instead taking a secret solace in the strength of the figure beside her. When, she asked herself, had she last had someone to depend on, a strong shoulder to lean on and offer *her* support?

"Where is Mr. MacInnes?" she asked Will, as they headed for the flower-festooned carriages waiting outside.

"W.C. doesn't believe in, what he calls, our pagan rituals."

Pagan? Now there was a laugh—if Melisande had been disposed toward laughter just then. Although he'd not formally been invited to join the wedding party, she'd worried that Wildcat, with his barbaric tattoos and deerskin leggings and brightly colored feathers, might decide to put in an appearance in any case. Obviously the man was accustomed to doing as he pleased, having flouted this past fortnight every convention and unspoken rule regarding the proper role of a guest. He'd made free with the contents of the wine cellar, taken the dogs hunting without soliciting George's permission, and then, yesterday, issued a wholly improper proposal to Benjamin's youngest sister.

No thank you, but Niankwe MacInnes was a complication Melisande did not need today.

While Melisande was occupied helping Eileen with her bonnet, it was decided among the menfolk that she and Will would share a carriage with the bride, while George and the viscount would follow in the second vehicle. No doubt arranged so, Melisande suspected, because neither her brother nor her grandfather wished to be left alone with the watering pot Eileen. Thankfully, however, her sister held up fairly well during the short ride to town, sacrificing but three handkerchiefs to her nervous tears and requiring the smelling salts but once.

The church bells were ringing as they drove up in front of St. Andrew's, black carriages lined up like giant beetles along Cullscombe's main thoroughfare. Due to time constraints, Melisande had decided to keep the affair moderately sized; thusly, they were expecting only eighty at the wedding breakfast, and but sixteen more overnight guests at the Hall, in addition to the six members of Benjamin's family.

They'd just descended from the coach, when Eileen began to totter.

"Oh, dear, I . . . I—"

Will caught her by the shoulders, as Melisande dug into her reticule yet again for the vinaigrette.

"For God's sake," Will said gruffly, giving Eileen a mild shake. "This has gone far enough. All you have to do is get through this next hour, lass. Buck up now. Show some backbone."

"Will!" Melisande started to interrupt, convinced that such a curt scolding would send Eileen wailing back to the carriage. But her sister only nodded and licked nervously at the corners of her cupid's-bow lips.

"There's a girl," Will said. "Now go on. Make your family proud."

Eileen nodded again and obediently took her grandfather's arm, sniffling one last time. Shocked, Melisande didn't know whether she ought to thank her husband or slap him silly.

"I daresay you needn't have been quite so brusque with her," she muttered in an aside. "She's not used to being shaken like a rag doll, you know."

He looked down at her, his eyes narrowing to slits of pale green. "One must sometimes be cruel to be kind."

"Ah! Are you now quoting Shakespeare to me?" she asked in mocking surprise.

"Shakespeare? Well, I don't know who said it first, but they damned sure got it right. Remember that, will you?"

Remember what? As Will hauled her along into the church, a frowning Melisande tried to determine what he had intended by that cryptic statement. What was it she was supposed to remember? Shakespeare or the symbiotic nature of kindness and cruelty?

She was still pondering the question when Mr. Chandler's booming words opened the service. "Dearly beloved . . ."

My God, this was it.

Suddenly overcome with emotion, Melisande sank back against the pews, the tumult of the last weeks passing through her, washing over her, in a mind-numbing tide. As she gazed at her sister standing hand-in-hand with the future Earl Ketching, Melisande knew a brief burning behind her lids, but attributed the sensation to one too many sleepless nights. Closing her eyes, she let herself go limp. Limp with exhaustion and relief.

By heavens, I've done it. I've done it. It hadn't been easy — at times, it had been downright torturous — but she'd weathered the crisis, navigating her family through what might have been a horrific calamity. Eileen would be married, reputation unscathed, future secure, happiness assured. Soon Melisande would see her sister give Benjamin an heir, and someday rise to the rank of countess. Indeed, if Eileen's life were a painter's canvas, it would stretch out before them as the most pleasing of landscapes.

Indeed *Eileen's* life was set.

Almost against her will, Melisande sidled a glance to the man at her side. For days now, she'd been laboring to forget the sweet-smoky scent of his hair as it filled her hands; the caress of that whiskered jaw as it played across her most sensitive flesh. But the more she tried to drive the memories from her, the more insistently they returned, haunting her at every hour of the day, tormenting her with the promise of what could be.

The promise of what could be.

It was that which had first planted the idea in her thoughts. An idea so insidious, so alarming, that she'd refused to dwell on it at all. As busy as she'd been, she'd been able to shove the notion aside, to push it to a corner of her mind and order it to be silent. But the idea sat silent no longer.

Did she not deserve a small taste of the same happiness that Eileen was to know for years to come? A brief sampling of the secret pleasures her sister had hinted at, pleasures that Melisande might not ever have a chance to experience again? Eileen had said that not all men were capable of producing those pleasures in a woman. From what Melisande had seen, and already experienced, she had every reason to believe that Will Taggart could deliver on that score. *Yes, indeed,* she thought, surreptitiously fanning herself with her reticule. She did not think he'd disappoint.

Therefore what were the dangers of succumbing to her desires? Of just this once, seeing to her own wants instead of the wants of her brother or her sister or her grandfather? Admittedly, there was the sticky issue of the annulment. The

loss of her virginity might make the process more complicated, but it certainly didn't preclude the possibility. Dear
Cousin Harry had always proved accommodating—even if
he did botch the license—and he was a bishop, for heaven's
sake. He would be able to handle the annulment one way or
the other, consummation or not.

So what else might stand in her way? Will himself?
Although she hadn't yet spoken to him about leaving, she'd
already made plans to send him away on the morrow.
Really, once Eileen was married, there was no reason to
keep him at Mooresby Hall. He was a bit of a distraction,
that man. Of course, she would have to make clear to him
that he was still expected to leave . . . after the deed was
done. In fact, it would be even more critical that he do so,
for she did not think she would be able to face him the
morning after. An unexpected shiver raced through her, as
she tried to envision what "a morning after" entailed.

No, a clean break would inarguably be for the best.

She'd thought it through for a few days, and had foreseen
no logical reason not to indulge her curiosity. Not to, at least
once, do as *she* wanted, rather than what she was expected
to do.

And what if she chose the route of caution instead of
experimentation? Who knew if, or when, she'd ever again
meet a man whose touch set her afire, a man who could stir
her as no other had ever been able to do?

Twenty-two years and she'd not met a single man she felt
worthy of even a kiss. Then Will "Tiger" Taggart comes
along. . . . Memory shot through her like a jolt of physical
pain, as she pictured his golden head bending over her, his
cheek nuzzling her breast. God save her, but, yes, she
wanted more than kisses from him.

She wanted the *"boom"*.

Fourteen

∾ᴈᴇ᙮

"Damn, Tiger, what have you done to your witch-wife? She is possessed tonight, wiyagasksu."

Concealed in the shadows of the terrace, Will watched Melisande whirl across the dance floor, her midnight hair trailing after her like an ebony cloud. Laughing and smiling, she swooped from one guest to the next, a carefree butterfly flitting from flower to flower.

"I dunno, W.C. It's nothing *I* have done. I believe the culprit is that fancy French champagne."

"Ah. So the lady has no head for spirits. But, from the looks of it, she will in the morning."

"Hmm-mm. Especially since Mel doesn't normally drink."

"And yet . . . she drinks tonight."

Will sensed Wildcat's questioning regard, but did not meet it since he had no answers to give. He didn't know why Mel was guzzling champagne like a thirsty sailor, or why she was behaving as if this were her last night ashore.

"She's probably glad to see Eileen finally married," Will suggested. "The prospect of her sister being exposed to scandal had worried her more than she let on."

"Worried?" Wildcat made a scoffing noise. "It is I who have been worried, my brother. This She-Devil, as they call her, has bewitched you. You try to hide it, but I see how your hungry eyes always follow her, how you hang on her every word. This woman has become an obsession with you."

Will said nothing, because he feared that Wildcat spoke the truth. Not about Mel casting a spell upon him; but about him caring too much. In the past, Will had desired women—lots of women—yet never had he wanted one as urgently as he wanted Melisande. In fact, during the last day or two he'd kept himself aloof, placing more distance between them in order to cool his ardor. It disturbed him. It wasn't safe to want anything as much as he wanted this woman.

"Are you going to come in and join the party," Will asked, "or are you planning to play Peeping Tom all night?"

"I like it out here. It interests me to watch the *wapsitschik* celebrate."

Will flicked the end of W.C.'s braid. "Don't forget that you're half-white yourself, MacInnes."

"You must remind me."

Will smiled, although his annoyed gaze was trained on his wife as she laughed up at some knock-kneed cousin of the groom's. When her fingers gamboled suggestively just inches from the man's chest, Will had to stare down at his boots and command them to be still before they carried him through the terrace doors to perform a native war dance atop Mr. Knock-knees's face.

"I think I'll go in," he said mildly.

"You'll be ready to leave tomorrow?"

Will nodded, his eyes following Mel as she flitted on to another guest. "As we've planned."

Wildcat grunted and then stepped back into the shadows, melting into the darkness to continue his study of the odd *wapsitschik*. Will, well accustomed to his friend's peculiarities, merely shrugged and hooked his coat over his shoulder before heading back to the party.

Although the doors to the terrace had been thrown open, the air inside the room was thick with the smell of smoke and people, the music drowned out by the high-pitched buzz of conversation well oiled by drink. He temporarily lost sight of Mel, then located her again on the other side of the room, leaning against a marble pillar. With her head tilted back and her hair streaming down to her waist to twine like ebony vines around the column, she made an arresting, even breathtaking, image. The contrast of chaste white marble, coal-black hair, and crimson red gown was so vivid, the colors so elemental that Will imagined he could almost *feel* them. Feel their rawness, their earthiness, pulling at something inside him.

He laughed at himself, wondering if that raw feeling in his gut might not be due to that last shot of whiskey he'd enjoyed.

Mel was talking with a pair of capped spinsters when he approached, her lids hanging low over her eyes as if she were in danger of falling asleep. Either that, he decided, or she was flirting with the two old maids.

She saw him and her dark coffee eyes opened wide, her mouth curling into an astonishingly warm welcome. "There you are," she greeted, swaying toward him. "I've been looking for you."

"What a coincidence," he said, answering her with a guarded smile. "I've been looking for you, too." He looped his arm around Mel's waist, surprised by the ease with which she sank against him, her head pillowing into his shoulder. She felt pliant and vulnerable. Not at all like Mel.

He sent the two older women a look of faint apology. "Ladies, will you excuse us?"

"Of course, of course," they answered in rushed unison, blushing and waving them away, while giggling behind their fans about "young love" and "eager newlyweds."

Their whispered titters followed Will and Mel out into the corridor.

"Where are we going?" Mel asked airily, as if the answer mattered not at all to her.

"I'm putting you to bed."

Husky laughter rippled from her and she leaned her head back to peer up at him, her gaze amused. "You think I'm tipsy, don't you?"

"You're not?"

"Gracious, no. I'll confess to a certain . . . giddi-ness"—she laughed again, deep in her throat—"but I do believe I am entitled, you know. I've had a perfectly wretched few weeks and now it's all come round beautifully and, if anything, I am drunk with the most profound and utter relief."

Without warning, she pirouetted in his arms, plastering herself to his front, her nose tucked tightly into the vee of his waistcoat. With her breath warm and damp against his shirt, she looked rather like a small animal trying to burrow into a hole.

"Did you see how happy Eileen is, William?" she asked the button on his brocade vest. "She's not shed a tear since we left the chapel. It's all been settled so-o-o-o very nicely," she crooned with a contented sigh. Then she peeked up at him, and a tiny frown surfaced between her brows. "Well, not all. . . . I have yet to settle matters between us and I really ought to take care of that right away, shouldn't I?"

Will's hand steadied her at the small of her back, the touch as impersonal as he could make it when his body was already responding to her nearness. "Just how much cham-pagne have you had tonight, Mel?"

"Two glasses." Her eyes rolled clockwise as she recon-sidered. "All right, perhaps three. But certainly not enough to affect me in any way."

"Hmm-mm." Will gently turned her around and nudged her down the hall toward the staircase.

"You really think I'm drunk," she stated in a tone con-veying astonishment, amusement, and mild affront.

He kept nudging. "Let's just say I think it's a possibility."

"Pooh. Could one who has overimbibed do this?" she demanded. Lifting her skirts, she hopscotched up the stairs with commendable alacrity, turning every few steps to beam down at him, obviously quite proud of her goatlike nimble-ness. Will, keeping a few risers between them in case she tumbled, followed after.

"See?" At the head of the staircase, she faced him,

balancing on one foot and holding her arms out like a silk-swathed weathervane.

"So you're not falling down drunk," he wryly conceded. "I still think you should get to bed."

Slowly she lowered her arms to her sides. Candlelight from the wall sconces gleamed at her back, illuminating the crimson dress so that it cast a pinkish glow around her. Will couldn't decide if the effect made her appear like an angel sent from above or a temptress from a warmer locale.

As he drew even with her and took hold of her elbow, he saw that she was scowling. At him.

"What's the matter?"

"I, sir, am offended."

"Oh?" Subtly he drew her away from the top of the staircase.

"Yes, I am!" she insisted, even though he'd not actually been arguing with her.

"Once in a very great while I let down my hair, so to speak, and allow myself to indulge in a spot of pleasure and look"—she flung out her hand with enough force to dislocate an elbow—"what comes of it! I am accused of immoderation. I, the most moderate, the most restrained, of persons. Oh, yes," she emphasized, bobbing her head. "I am insulted by your insinuation, Mr. Taggart."

He sketched a mocking half-bow. "My apologies, madam."

Then he took her by the shoulders and spun her in the direction of her bedroom. They made it almost to her door before she listed into him hard, her eyelids fluttering like a loose mainsail.

"Are you aware, William, that I do not normally partake of strong spirits?"

"You don't say?"

He tried to reach for the door handle but, when Mel started to slip from his grasp, he was forced to grab hold of her before she dove to the floor. With effort, he balanced her on his hip and lunged again for the latch.

"No. I *do* say." Her voice dropped confidingly. "I only sampled the champagne tonight hoping 'twould give me courage."

Surprise caused his fingers to linger on the door handle. *Mel desiring a drink to bolster her courage?* Talk about carrying coals to Newcastle . . .

Inside her bedchamber, a lamp had been lit and left atop the dressing table. Mel pulled away from him and veered toward it, breathlessly exclaiming "Ah, yes" as if she'd only that moment discovered the miracle of light. But instead of reaching for the lantern, her fist closed triumphantly around a cloth bag also resting atop the table.

"We have business to conclude, my good man," she announced in an overloud voice.

With the toe of his shoe, Will prodded the door closed. He saw no need for the servants to behold their tightly buttoned mistress gone three sheets to the wind.

"Business?" He chose to remain close to the door, not knowing where Mel's current mood might lead. He'd once already experienced her wickedly accurate aim and he wasn't what you'd call a slow learner.

She sashayed toward him, clutching the bag, her eyes gleaming with an indefinable purpose. "Tomorrow, William Taggart, you will take your leave of Mooresby Hall."

"I will?"

She nodded vigorously, bringing her dark tresses to life. "You will. For I have arranged to put a carriage at your disposal and you, dear husband, will be in same carriage and on your way home to Scotland by dawn's first light tomorrow."

With an easy toss, Will pitched his coat over the back of the little striped boudoir chair that had tortured him the night of his wedding. "You have it all planned, I see."

"Naturally I have it all planned." Drawing to a halt in front of him, Mel stretched herself to her full—if limited—height and bestowed on him a look of haughty confidence. "Someone must take care of life's myriad details and that someone is me, Monsieur Tiger. I am the responsible one. I am the one who must see to every minute crisis, every trivial disaster." Her voice fell. "Everything."

Lowering her gaze, she soberly pondered the satin

drawstring bag until he began to wonder if she'd forgotten her use for it.

"Oh, blast it, here." Her movement rough and abrupt, she grabbed hold of his hand and plopped the sack into the middle of his palm. The bag's weight was so unexpected he nearly dropped it.

"The money is all there," she said with a feigned breeziness, a breeziness that somehow struck Will as sad. "Although you are welcome to count it, if you like."

He held the heavy bag out before him, as if not certain what to do with it. Mel, evidently growing impatient, thrust her hands onto her hips and started tapping her toe in that rhythm that said she was irritated.

"Go on," she urged. "Count it. You have earned it, I daresay. Two hundred pounds per our agreement."

"Ah. The agreement," he said, pretending he'd forgotten. He gave the bag an experimental toss. "So you want me to take your money and leave?"

"Yes, that's what I said."

"Hmm-mm." He continued to contemplate the coin bag, keeping his expression neutral. "And what about the annulment?"

Melisande made a sharp flapping motion with her hands. "Good gracious, I'll see to the annulment, never fear. I have well-placed friends and relations, you know."

"So that's it then? We're done, good-bye?"

"Well, y-yes." She turned aside, but not before he spied a fleeting panic shift across her features. "That concludes our business," she said haltingly, twisting her fingers together behind her back. "Although . . ."

He leaned against the door and folded his arms, curious—and not a little concerned. Mel was simply not acting like Mel. She'd gone from giddy and flippant one moment to hesitant and shy the next. And now, by God, she was twirling a lock of hair around her forefinger like some unsophisticated schoolgirl, her teeth worrying at the fullness of her lower lip. All she lacked was a smattering of freckles and a goddamn pinafore.

Surely no one in Cullscombe would have recognized the

She-Devil of Mooresby Hall in that moment, Will decided. Hell, even *he* scarcely recognized her.

"All right, Mel, it's bed for you," he said, shoving away from the door. "Now."

He strode over to the four-poster and pulled down the quilted counterpane. "Come on," he said. "Just slip off your shoes and climb in."

"No."

A slanting sideways glance found her chin up, her jaw set, her color high. The unfamiliar diffidence of manner she'd briefly exhibited was already gone. *Good.* He liked her better fiery.

"See here, Mel, you're obviously not cut out to be much of a drinker. The champagne's affected you . . . badly. My advice is sleep it off before you say or do something you'll regret in the morning."

"I won't have any regrets."

Will froze, hackles rising at the nape of his neck. Her soft statement, rife with innuendo, shot straight into him, awakening that part of his anatomy which was already overly stimulated.

He took one look at her, at the heat in her eyes, and very slowly started to back away from the bed.

She advanced three quick steps.

He sidled two paces toward the door.

She did the same to cut him off.

They stood there face-to-face, their bizarre little dance at an awkward impasse. Rapid breaths lifted Melisande's chest up and down in a distracting cadence.

"I want you to kiss me."

Oh, hell. Will shifted his weight onto his right leg, trying to ease the increasing tension in his groin. "Mel, I don't think that's such a good idea."

Her chin notched one degree higher. "You don't want to?"

"Now, I didn't say that—"

"Then kiss me."

She had a way of looking at him, her eyes all soft and melting, her back straight and proud . . . Like she was looking at him now.

He moved so swiftly, he saw her blink when suddenly they stood but inches apart. His hands cupped the tops of her shoulders and, as always, the extreme delicacy of her bones came as a shock, startling him. He couldn't get over the expectation that a strong-spirited woman like Mel ought to be sturdier; not of a frame so porcelain fine he feared breaking her in half. He flexed his fingers carefully in the firm flesh of her upper arms while smiling the smallest of smiles. Aye, Mel might be all softness and fragility on the outside, but inside, by God, she was a warrior. A queen. A fire goddess.

His lips swooped down and claimed hers. Her breath hitched slightly and he took it as his, stealing her mouth's air and moisture for himself, savoring her taste. She was yeasty champagne and honeyed pears. A heady combination. Too heady.

He tried to retreat before control was lost to him, but Mel would not permit it. Locking her fingers behind his neck, she clung to him with a keen ferocity that hinted of desperation. With a curse and an effort, he jerked free, the blood already pounding in his head like pain. She reached for him, and he caught her wrists.

"Mel," he rasped. "Do you remember the other day in the garden? If you aren't careful, we're going to take up where we left off and I don't think that's what you're wanting."

She licked at her lips, as if to recapture the essence of their kiss. "That's precisely what I'm wanting, Will. I want all of that. And more." Amazingly her steadfast gaze did not falter, although a blush swept across her sharp cheekbones. "I want to experience everything a woman can experience with a man."

A few years back, Will had been out hunting when he'd been broadsided by a bull moose; the effect of Mel's declaration hit him with roughly the same impact. He felt unsteady, like the air had been knocked from his lungs.

"Do you know what you're saying?"

Under a thick veil of lashes, her pupils glittered as dark as sin. "I do."

"But—"

"But," she interrupted, "I need you to make me a promise first."

Will's thoughts whirled dizzyingly, made even more confused and garbled by the insistent pleading from south of his beltline. That piece of him would have promised anything, would have sworn to give Mel the moon, the stars, the heavens, all tied up in a gold-trimmed ribbon. But the part of Will that had kept him alive these last ten years was not so easily swayed. His gut. His instincts were telling him to slow down: *Easy, Taggart. Hear her conditions first. Think before you throw her down to the carpet and plough her till you both cry with the pleasure of it.*

"What kind of promise?" he asked warily.

Again her tongue slid across her lower lip, playing havoc with what was left of his reasoning abilities. "Whatever we share tonight—whatever happens between us—you must swear to me that you'll leave for Scotland tomorrow as I've arranged."

"Before sunrise?"

She nodded, tucking a strand of hair behind her ear, her fingers drifting teasingly from her ear to the pulse beating in the hollow of her throat to the mouthwatering curve above her breast.

Will debated a fraction of a second, his deepest, most secret fears awakened. Never before had he wanted a woman with this bone-aching degree of intensity. It frightened him, Wildcat's warnings echoing through his mind, and his own unerring instincts urging caution. Would it be more than just sex with Mel? Was that what scared him?

So what if it was? he asked himself. She was his wife, after all. He was going to make love to her sooner or later. And the way his body was feeling, it may as well be sooner.

But the risks . . .

To hell with them.

He cleared his throat. "You have my word that I will be gone from Mooresby Hall before dawn tomorrow."

Triumph shone in Mel's smile. Triumph and an almost imperceptible smidgeon of apprehension. Will held himself still, waiting to see if there was any chance of her changing her mind. Waiting to see if that hint of apprehension might develop into something stronger.

But when Mel reached for the collar of his shirt, he knew without a doubt there'd be no turning back.

Fifteen

꒰ ꒱

Melisande focused on nothing but the tips of her fingers as they made contact with Will's skin, warm and tanned and rough. She focused on her fingers and silently implored them not to tremble. Not to expose the depths of her nervousness.

She knew that Will believed her to be inebriated; it suited her to let him believe the lie. While the champagne had loosened her limbs, giving the world a nice fuzzy glow, Melisande was not so far gone in her cups that she wasn't aware of what she was doing. She was, in fact, undressing her husband.

She tugged determinedly at the neck of Will's shirt, hopeful that she didn't look the fool. Above all, Melisande hated the appearance of ineptitude and, unless she acted boldly, with an assuredness she was far from feeling, her lack of sexual experience was bound to reveal itself in all its spinsterish glory. Granted, Will already knew her to be a virgin; she'd told him so. However that didn't necessarily mean she'd not undressed a man before—did it?

Still fumbling with his collar, she suddenly felt his fingers wrap around hers, checking their frantic tugging. Dread lifted her gaze to his. Oh dear, had Will decided not to cooperate after all? Had she botched it?

His eyes were soft and green as grass as he murmured, "Let's do this right."

"Yes, of course," she agreed in a hoarse whisper. As if she knew what "right" might be.

With their eyes locked, he slowly brought her right hand to his mouth, his lips just grazing the peaks of her knuckles. She liked the feel of that. A shallow sigh escaped her. Then he licked the seam between her fingers, his tongue working into the sensitive crevice where finger met palm.

"I-I—" She thought she ought to say something. A compliment perhaps?

His gaze probed hers, waiting.

"I . . ." She floundered. "Should we move to the bed?"

Quiet laughter brought out fine wrinkles at the corners of Will's eyes. "All in due time, sweetheart. There's no need to rush."

Sweetheart. Melisande couldn't recall ever being the recipient of such an endearment. Her father had occasionally called her "pumpkin," but "sweetheart" was ever so much nicer than being termed a round orange gourd.

Will's touch feathered across her shoulder blades and she found herself closing her eyes, surrendering to the quiet pleasure of his caress. Gently he explored her neck and jaw and arms until she became aware of a chill puckering her skin. A shiver opened her eyes and she saw that he had unhooked her gown, drawing it, and her chemise, from her shoulders. Against her bosom folds of crimson silk gathered just above her nipples, the skin startlingly white upon her breasts. She felt strangely pleased by his skill, thinking it augured well for the rest of the night.

She stood motionless as Will pulled her hair forward, draping it across her front. He spent many long seconds arranging her hair, stroking it lightly like a harpist strokes the strings of his instrument. Then he kissed her. And Melisande abandoned any sense of lingering shyness and kissed him back. His teeth scored along her lower lip and her teeth did the same to his. When his tongue dipped into her warmth, her tongue ventured into his, testing, tasting, enjoying.

"Good God, Mel," he groaned against her lips. "Do you know what you do to me?"

She didn't know and, even if she had, she wouldn't have had the breath to answer him. While he continued to kiss her, he nudged her gown lower, his hands cupping her breasts through the curtain of her hair. The silky tresses slid across her skin as he kneaded her gently, his tongue probing deeper and deeper.

Heat coiled inside her belly, spreading into her thighs and abdomen, weakening her knees. She clutched at him, fearful that she might fall. God help her, she did fall—

No. Her sudden sense of weightlessness was due to Will scooping her up into his arms. Smiling, she hid her face into the side of his neck as he carried her to the bed. All the intoxicating feelings she'd remembered from the garden were returning as wondrously as before. How glorious it was.

He laid her on the bed, then blanketed her body with his. He was heavier than she'd expected. Harder. His thigh pushed insistently against the core of her where she felt moist and hot, as his mouth roamed from her lips to her eyelids to her ear.

"Are you sure?" he asked again, his voice cracking faintly.

She nodded, holding more tightly to his shoulders, determined to hold him if he should change his mind and try to leave her. He did pull away and she clutched at him, but he only brushed aside her hair to bare her breasts. In the dim light her nipples looked so engorged and rosy, she scarce recognized herself. She scarce recognized the way her breasts seemed to swell, to reach for him, imploring his touch.

A pang shot through her when he pinched their swollen peaks between thumb and forefinger. Her back arched up from the mattress. Lightly he twirled and twisted them, the sensation somewhere between anguish and ecstasy. A whimper emerged from the back of her throat, a restlessness invading her limbs.

"What do you want, Mel?" he asked, his breath moist against her naked skin. "Tell me."

She squeezed shut her eyes as his fingers played her nipples, plucking and teasing. "Everything," she whispered. "I want it all."

"Do you want this?" His tongue lapped across her nipple and she had to swallow a scream of delight. Wet and soothing, it felt to her nipple fiery and raw.

She gave a single tense nod, her fists clenched in the bedsheets. He licked the delicate peak again. But only once.

"More," she said through gritted teeth.

A chuckle shook his shoulders, then he took her entire nipple into his mouth and suckled her. His lips and teeth pulled at her until she was squirming beneath him, every muscle clenched and tense. The heat at her center grew hotter and hotter, pulsing with . . . need. The need to be touched.

Hoarse, unintelligible words came from her.

"What's that?" he asked. "What do you want now, my love?"

"I-I don't know," she gasped.

"Come now, Mel. Yes, you do. You always know what you want."

"I don't!" But her protest rang hollow even to her ears.

His chin nuzzled the underside of her breast, his whiskers scraping her flesh. "Since when are you afraid to ask for anything?" he taunted. "You know what you want me to do, Mel. Tell me."

The need inside her was spiraling out of control, demanding to be appeased. Try as she might, she could not seem to keep her legs still. They slid against him, seeking his hardness.

"I want you to touch me."

She sensed his answering smile. "Where, Mel?"

Dear heavens, it was unbearable. Unbearable.

Her hand fluttered past the junction between her thighs. "Here."

"Where?" He rolled slightly onto his side, robbing her of his body's heat.

Oh, God. She bit at the inside of her cheek, unable to look at him. Her heart raced. Blindly she grabbed for his hand and brought it to rest on her skirts at the very center of her.

"Ah." He cupped her with a butterfly's touch. "Is that what you want?"

Yes. But it wasn't nearly enough. Her hips lifted, stretching toward his fingers, the promise they held.

"More," she told him, her voice breaking.

He did not disappoint or disobey. His hand slipped sweetly under her skirts, his calloused palm shimmying along the inside of her thigh. Her legs accommodated his exploration, falling open of their own accord.

"Yes," he murmured with approval. At the exact moment his fingers found her, he bent over and kissed her full on the mouth.

She cried out and bucked against his hand.

"Yes, yes. Talk to me, Mel."

"I want—" She could barely speak for the rapidity of her breathing. "I want you to continue touching me, Will."

He started to roll onto his side, but she grasped his hair with both fists, pulling him back to her. "And I want you to continue kissing me."

"Yes, ma'am." His tongue thrust past her lips and his fingers pushed into her. Again. And again. His tongue and fingers invaded and retreated, invaded and retreated until she writhed beneath him like a madwoman. She never could have guessed that this was what awaited her. This poignant, piercing pleasure.

His breath sang harshly near her ear. "You said you wanted to experience everything, sweetheart. Did you mean it?"

"I always mean what I say," she gasped boldly, throwing all caution to the wind.

He laughed a soft, heated laugh, and before she knew what had happened, he'd pulled free from her and was kneeling between her legs, her silken skirts shoved wantonly up to her waist. A wild light shone in his eyes, something feral and fierce and a little frightening. He grabbed hold of her buttocks and drew her up toward him, looping her knees over his shoulders. She gasped aloud when she realized what he planned.

"I—" A shrill cry of delight consumed anything she'd hoped or thought to say.

His tongue stroked over her and she was helpless. Utterly helpless. He tasted her again and she did not believe she could endure such pleasure. At least, not endure it and live to tell the tale. She writhed against him, but he gripped her thighs, holding her tight.

"Will," she managed to gasp, her hands clenching and unclenching in repeated frenzy. "I don't think I can bear any more . . ."

Gently he kissed the inside of her thigh. "Yes, you can, Mel. You can take anything. Anything and everything I've got to give."

Then he possessed her with his mouth and she cried out. The pressure inside her was mounting too fast. Too fast. She couldn't rein it in; she couldn't control it. The pressure built and built and she lost herself to the sensation. Lost herself altogether in this foreign world, this foreign place where all she could do was feel. She begged, she moaned, she cried out in wonder. Until finally the feeling consumed her, catapulting her high, high into the heavens.

Slowly she came back to earth and found Will slipping from his trousers, his shirt already discarded. She gazed sleepily upon his nakedness and knew both fear and hunger in her heart.

"More?" she whispered.

His tiger-striped hair swept against his cheek as he bent over her, leaning on his palms. Between his legs, his sex was full and large.

"Do you want more, love?" he asked her.

She honestly did not know if she was capable of more, but she gazed into his eyes, hypnotic green-gold eyes, and answered, "Yes."

He smiled then. The most beautiful smile she'd ever known. And then he filled her with one powerful lunge of his tautly held body.

"Will, no!"

Tension pulsed through her, her muscles clenched. She squirmed beneath him, trying to ease the tension, but her movements only compounded it, changed it. In seconds, what had been uncomfortably tight became deliciously snug. What had scorched inside no longer burned with pain, but with pleasure.

The cords in Will's neck stood out as he twisted his head to the side. "God, Mel, you're killing me."

She nodded, thinking that surely people must die of this. That only the strongest could survive such excess of feeling.

Will took a deep breath, the planes of his hewed chest shifting like some perfectly crafted statue come to life. Melisande had to touch him. The need to was undeniable. He convulsed and groaned as her fingers fluttered across his brown nipples.

"You are so warm," she whispered. "So warm and hard."

"Mel. Please. No." His words sounded choppy and short.

Her hands fell. He moved. At first, slowly, cautiously. But slow and cautious was not enough for her. She needed something. Her hips lifted as she invited him to drive on.

"Faster, Will. More."

A deep, rumbling moan met her request before suddenly he plunged into her with all his strength.

"Yes," she whimpered. "Yes."

Again he plunged into her. And again. He pumped into her softness, pumping faster and faster as she bucked against him, meeting his thrusts in an instinctive and natural rhythm.

She grabbed his buttocks, his flanks sleek with sweat, and pushed him into her as if she could take all of him, all of his body, inside her.

"It's there," she told him, her voice raw. "It's there again." And it was there and it took her and it shattered her to bits as she cried out his name.

"Will!"

"Mel, my sweet Mel," he groaned. Then he threw back his head and let out a low, fierce growl, his body shuddering. They both went limp, collapsing into the bed, their breathing labored and harsh.

Melisande felt weak and wet and wonderful. She wrapped her arms around Will, threading her fingers through his hair.

"That was splendid," she said softly. "It was everything I'd imagined."

He mumbled something into the pillow.

"What?"

Will turned his head to the side, his lips grazing the curve of her ear. "Aye, it was splendid, Mel," he whispered. "But it's still not everything."

And in the hours that followed, he proceeded to show her the rest.

Sixteen
꘎

Melisande's own groan awoke her. The mattress was dipping and tipping this way and that, as if Will were turning somersaults upon the bed. Sleepily she recognized that he'd have to be turning somersaults beneath the bed for it to bounce as it was doing.

With a shaky hand, she shoved her hair from her face and cracked open an eye. Daylight had never been so painful. She squinted narrowly, determining that her immediate view was of . . . a pair of knees?

She licked at her lips, her thoughts groggy and unclear. Dust and a gritty dryness filled her mouth.

The coach lurched again.

The coach—

She sprang upright, then almost keeled over onto her other side as dizziness overcame her. Spots of hot light danced before her eyes, and she braced her hand against the carriage wall.

"Will?"

"Aye?"

She blinked and, bit by bit, he came into focus. He appeared tired, she thought, taking note of the weary set to his mouth, then shuddered to imagine what *she* must look like. She pushed ineffectually at clumps of tangled black hair sticking to the side of her face.

"What . . . what am I doing in a carriage?"

"The same as me."

She frowned, valiantly trying to bring her thoughts into order. "But you're supposed to be on your—" In an instant, she came fully awake.

"No!"

He smiled, the smallest hint of apology evident in his expression.

"No!" she cried again and jumped to her feet, struggling for balance as she pounded on the coach's roof with her fist. "Stop! Stop immediately, I say!"

"It won't do any good, Mel. The driver's been told not to stop until the next scheduled change of horses."

She stared at him as if he had spoken from his navel. "You cannot do this."

And yet he had. How?

Last she recalled, they had been lying on the Axminster rug in front of the fire and she'd been planting kisses up the length of his— She glanced down at herself. For the love of Moses, he'd not even had the decency to dress her!

In horror, she sank back onto the seat, furiously tucking her nightrobe around her legs and ankles. Soreness in the most intimate places mocked her as she squirmed, seeking a comfortable position on the banquette. The enormity of Will's deception was beginning to take hold in her mind and her fury was building apace.

"How could you?" she demanded. "Is your word of no value at all?"

He rubbed at his jaw where the beginnings of a beard had set out whiskery seeds. "I did not lie to you, Mel. I promised I'd be gone from Mooresby Hall before dawn and I was."

"But not with me, you foolish Scot! Not with *me*!" She jerked aside the curtain, nearly ripping it from its mooring. The day outside was gray and foggy, making it difficult to ascertain the hour.

"Where are we?"

"A four-and-a-half hour drive from Mooresby Hall."

"Oh, dear Lord." Her heart started to plummet, but she refused to let it sink too low. *Four hours?* Why, 'twas nothing. If they turned around now, she'd be home before dusk, in time for her daily meeting with the steward and housekeeper.

Steeling herself, she set her most commanding gaze upon him, the one she kept in reserve for only the most dire of occasions. This same look had reduced the family solicitor to tears last summer when he'd balked at distributing funds for a new irrigation system.

"William, I demand that you turn the horses around immediately."

"I can't do that, Mel."

Her fingers curled into talons. "You can and you will."

He shook his head with regret. Feigned regret it could only be.

Her fingernails bit into her palms as she struggled not to sink their barbed points into the side of his throat. She could not believe it. She could not believe he had the audacity to defy her outright!

"I would have hoped," she said stiffly, "that during these past weeks you would have come to realize that I am not your typical English lady, Mr. Taggart."

"Aye, Mel, there's nothing ordinary about you, that's for certain."

She resisted the urge to kick him in the shins. "Then you should understand that I'm not likely to sit by and allow myself to be abducted by some roguish ne'er-do-well!"

"Abducted?" Apparently he took no issue with her labeling him a ne'er-do-well. "Come now, Mel. A husband cannot abduct a wife."

"But you are not my husband!"

"No?" He tipped his head to one shoulder, as if puzzled. "You wear my ring, your name is next to mine on the Cullscombe church registry, and as I recall . . . you've warmed my bed."

She flushed scarlet, remembering too vividly how very warm that bed had been. "That is all beside the point," she argued, while tugging at the offensive jewelry on her hand. "We had an agreement."

"And I abided it. Up to a point."

The ring came free and she tossed it at him, hitting him squarely in the chest. He caught it with one hand as it bounced off his coat.

"You cannot change the rules as it suits you to do so, you ridiculous man!"

Will folded his arms serenely across his chest. "Why not? You did."

"I did not! I agreed to furnish you with a wardrobe and to pay you two hundred pounds. I met both those obligations in full."

"And what about last night, Mel? That wasn't exactly part of the bargain, now was it?"

"Wha—" Blood rushed into her face and she fumbled for the neck of her robe, mortified beyond all possible reckoning. Goodness, had it been such an imposition upon him? Had taking her virginity proven such an onerous task that he now felt that she *owed* him something? Granted she had not been very experienced . . .

Embarrassed to her very core, she lashed out angrily. "You'll not get away with this. Grandfather will hunt you down and personally escort you back to Mr. Bell's gaolhouse, see if he doesn't. Or, better yet, he might decide that the Cullscombe gaol is too good for you and have you sent down to Newgate instead," she said, forgetting all her moralistic views on the lamentable condition of the English prison system.

"I don't think the viscount will be chasing after us, Mel."

"Of course, he will." Her chin jutted up. "I am a Mooresby. Grandfather will never suffer the indignity of seeing his granddaughter dragged off to some remote Scottish burgh by a self-confessed rogue."

"You're not a Mooresby, Mel. You're a Taggart. And as far as your grandfather is concerned, you haven't been dragged anywhere—you are merely traveling with your husband to your new home."

Oh, dear God. He was right. No one would think she'd

been kidnapped, except perhaps for Eileen, and, at this hour, Eileen would have already departed on her honeymoon trip. By heavens, no one would know she'd been spirited away. No one would realize.

"Why, then?" she asked, thinking aloud. Why steal her away? Too confused to think straight, and numb with shock, she sank back against the squabs, blinking furiously. *Why?* Will had not professed or exhibited any real affection for her; at least, none that she had noticed. And to judge from the comment he'd just so coldly issued, neither was his passion for her so keen that he'd felt motivated to abduct her to keep her in his bed. What then could have induced him to take her—

Oh, no . . .

"The inheritance," she whispered.

Across the coach, Will's light smile chilled in a clear and shocking admission of guilt. Melisande blanched. Fury bubbled up inside her.

The injustice of it all. The horror. It was unthinkable. Insupportable.

"How could you? That money belongs to me!"

"Aye, it does," Will agreed, his words slowly and judiciously chosen. "But your grandfather has deemed it fitting that I should hold the monies for you. To ensure that they're wisely spent."

"Who are you to say whether they're wisely spent?" she demanded.

"Your husband."

Melisande felt it closing in around her: the trap of her own making. "But my plans for the reformatory—"

"Sorry."

She gaped at him. He dismissed her life's mission with a word? Who, in the blazes, did he think he was?

Your husband, an inner voice repeated.

"You are reprehensible!" she cried. "How dare you speak to me thusly when you have not the first idea of my purpose, my goals."

He shrugged, signifying he cared not.

She wanted to strike him.

"Very well then, if 'tis the money you want, you may have it." She flung her hands forward as if they were full of coin. "The twenty thousand pounds is yours with my blessing. Now tell that blasted coachman of yours to leave me off at the next inn."

Will did not answer her.

"I mean every word," Melisande insisted. "You don't want me, you want my inheritance. So, for the love of God, take it and leave me be."

"But that's where you're wrong, Mel. I do want you."

She reared back in genuine surprise. "Whatever for?"

His shrug was light. "A wife is not without her uses."

"You cannot possibly think—"

"You weren't objecting too loudly last night," he pointed out.

Suddenly Melisande realized where the term "spitting mad" originated, for she was virtually frothing at the mouth.

Will's bold gaze raked her through the nightrobe with disturbing familiarity. "Like it or not, Mel, you're a woman of strong passions. You're only hurting yourself to try and deny them."

"You are deranged! As if I'd ever let you touch me again."

No more favors, thank you . . .

"Careful, Mel." Will leaned forward pinning her with those mesmerizing green eyes of his. "Careful what you say. Someday, I promise you, you'll be on your knees, begging for my touch."

For the first time in her life, Melisande felt herself start to go faint, her head spinning, her palms clammy and cold. Because, at the back of her mind, she very much feared that Will knew whereof he spoke. That someday, sooner rather than later, she would do as he said in her uncontrollable desire to experience once more the delights she'd known last night in his arms.

She started to breathe too fast, an amorphous panic assailing her. "But Mooresby Hall . . . Who will see to the estate, the investments?"

"George is more than ready to take charge."

"George? My brother?"

"You've got to let him have his shot at being a man," Will told her. "He's outgrown your mollycoddling, Mel. He's twenty-one years old; old enough to stand on his own and make his own decisions."

"But Eileen . . ."

"Benjamin will see to her, never fear. She has a husband now. She doesn't need you."

Not needed?

Melisande closed her eyes, unable to accept this bizarre and harrowing turn her life had suddenly taken. She would not abide it. She wouldn't. She was not a puppet to be dragged around at this man's will.

Gathering her strength and her anger, she looked him directly in the eye. "You'll never hold me. You'll have to keep me under lock and key."

"No, I won't, Mel."

She stiffened, alarmed by the quiet certainty in his voice. The gold ring he held in his fingertips caught the sunlight in tiny flashing prisms of white.

"What?" She pretended to search the coach's cabin. "Will your savage friend keep me prisoner? Where *is* the fierce Mr. MacInnes?"

"He's gone ahead to visit his family. He'll meet up with us again in Dunslaw."

"No!" She shook her head violently. "Not *us*. I won't be in Dunslaw. I'll be home at Mooresby Hall."

"I don't think so, Mel. How would it look for you to return home with your belly swollen and no husband in sight?"

Melisande clutched at her middle. "You fiend, you didn't!"

Will's lips drew together in a thoughtful moue. "I might have."

Aghast, she wondered if such a thing were possible. After only one night? And three . . . sessions? Blast it, why hadn't she thought to demand all of the shameless details from Eileen?

A babe.

Her shoulders fell, her head pounded from the inside out. With a sort of desperate resignation, she was forced to acknowledge the bitter truth of Will's statement. This was why he would not need to keep her under lock and key. Because he knew she could not possibly return home increasing. Her grandfather would be livid at the ensuing scandal and, knowing the Viscount Rutherford, he'd give her a good scold and ship her straight back to Scotland—in chains if necessary.

And if there really was a babe involved . . . Did she have the heart to deny her child the right to know its father? Could she do that? She herself had been without a mother during most of her youth and thus well understood the pain of a parent's absence. Would she wish that same pain upon her own offspring?

So until she knew whether or not she was increasing—

"And if I'm not?" she asked belligerently.

"Then you're not."

"And I'll return home."

Will stretched out his legs. "Where is home, Mel? Eileen has gone and George is on his own now. I suppose you could go back to Mooresby Hall, but is that really what you want? To keep house for your little brother the remainder of your life?"

"Yes! Er, no." She rubbed her temple with the heel of her hand. Of course, she didn't see herself as George's caretaker forever, a sad little spinster in fussy white caps. But what was Will saying? That he wanted her to remain with him in Scotland? As his wife, in truth?

"Look, Mel, why don't we wait and see what happens? I don't think either of us wants to do anything rash until we know if there'll be a tiny Taggart joining our ranks." He glanced in the general direction of her stomach. "When do you expect we would know?"

Frowning, she counted. "Three weeks?"

Will nodded, and the easy manner in which he accepted it all only provoked her ire again. *He* had done this, by heavens. He was the one who'd destroyed all her nicely laid plans.

She summoned a pitiless glower, thinking to the weeks ahead. "You'll not find me easy to live with, I vow."

Will wagged his head and smiled—tenderly? "Lord, lass, I never expected that I would."

Seventeen

༄

The homecoming.

Will glanced out the carriage window and felt a bittersweet ache swell inside him, a feeling he'd not prepared for
or anticipated. Never had he imagined that it would affect
him so—the sight of his father's house, the home in which
he had been born and raised.

All the years he'd been away, Will had spent precious
little time in reminiscing. He'd fled Berwickshire at the age
of sixteen, determined to make his fortune and his way in
the world. He'd left believing that he'd never lay eyes on
Scotland again.

He'd been wrong.

Very little had changed during these last twelve years;
from the looks of it, time may have well stood still. The
river was the same river from which he'd pulled trout as a
young lad, its waters swift and ice-cold, fed by a string of
bubbling waterfalls higher upstream. The sky was the same
sky, as blue as the Caribbean Sea and ten times as wide. The
hills were as Will remembered, gently rolling sandstone
mounds sporting their colorful mantle of heather and clover.

Nestled among those emerald Lammermuir hills sat the
Taggart family house virtually unchanged, its red brick

faintly softened by wind, rain, and age. While nowhere near as grandiose as Mooresby Hall—the house could just as easily have been described as a good-sized cottage—there was a pride in its sturdy squareness, a purity in its un-cluttered lines. It was a home, Will realized, that a man could be proud to call his own.

On the seat opposite, Melisande was trying her damned-est to appear disinterested in their surroundings. She'd clad herself in a regal stoicism these last three days, speaking only when necessary, ignoring Will with unflagging resolve. Even though they'd shared a room at nights, Melisande had acted as if he were invisible, climbing into bed each evening without a murmur though he lay but inches away.

For his part, Will had been grateful for her silence as she'd not complained about the grueling pace they'd kept since leaving Devonshire. From dawn to dusk, they'd rode, changing horses at every opportunity. And although they'd not spoken specifically about their future plans, a tacit agreement had been established between them during these last few days: They both understood that Melisande would remain at Dunslaw until they knew whether or not she was carrying his child.

When Will had first come up with that "pregnancy" argument, he'd known immediately that it would do the trick. In fact, at the time, he'd considered it a veritable stroke of genius. Mel may well loathe him for what he'd done—in her sleep last night she'd mumbled something about wanting to slip a blade between his ribs—but her feelings were unimportant when compared to the risk of bastardy for her child. Above all, Melisande took her responsibilities to heart. Performing one's duty with honor was the creed by which she lived, and Will knew that Mel had to feel an unspoken duty to any possible child of hers. A duty far stronger than her desire to return home. Aye, she probably would have loved to escape him, to flee on the first mail coach home; but she was too selfless. No matter how desperately she longed to return to England, Mel, being Mel, would always place the needs of her child before her own.

The question was . . . would he?

He hadn't really thought about the consequences of their night together until he'd brought it up to her. A babe. *Hell.* What would he do if she was in truth carrying his child? He sent a vigilant glance to Mel's trim, uncorseted waist and felt his mouth go dry.

Up until three weeks ago, he'd been accountable to no one, his knife and the clothes on his back his only worldly possessions. Now, God help him, he was responsible for a distillery, his father, his father's home, a pair of thorough-breds courtesy of George Mooresby, and approximately twenty thousand pounds of English gold.

Oh, yes. And a wife.

Adding a baby to the pot was enough to make Will's skin start to crawl. His feet already itched to hit the trail. Any trail. Any road that would set him back on the path to freedom.

"Is that it?"

Will's gaze snapped to her emotionless profile as she studied the horizon.

"Aye, that's your new home."

Her nose twitched minutely. "Are you sure that your father expects you? The place looks to be deserted."

Will quirked a brow in surprise. He'd not had this many words from her since she'd woken that first morning. Was her icy facade starting to thaw?

"According to my father's letter, the business has been in decline this last year." He looked westward where a towering chimney stood smokeless against the robin's egg sky. "To tell you the truth, I don't know whether or not the distillery is even operating."

The carriage bobbed along, passing fields stuffed full of heather and clover and greedy bees. As they grew nearer, a lone figure came into view: a man standing at the front of the house, his wispy white hair whipped by the prevailing southwesterly wind.

"Da must have a visitor," Will murmured.

"Does your father live alone?"

Evidently Melisande's curiosity was getting the better of her.

"We have always had a housekeeper—Mrs. Baker was her name—and a man to help with the stables." Will squinted toward the house. "But whoever it is doesn't look to be a servant. He's—"

Will's words died suddenly as the man started walking down the drive to come greet them. *That stride.* It was distinctive, unforgettable. A wide-legged saunter that Will remembered well from days of riding his father's shoulders and swaying along to its rollicking cadence.

And yet there was no way in hell that man could be his father. He was too old, his back too bowed and frail. When Will had left home, Peter Taggart hadn't a single gray hair in his head. He had stood straight and tall as the firs in the valley below.

"He has aged," Melisande said quietly, either reading Will's mind or his expression.

"Aye," Will answered. He could not say more.

The carriage pulled to a stop, the trunks rattling and shifting atop the roof. For the briefest of moments, Will considered ordering the coachman to drive on. Could he do this? Was he capable of being all that his father needed him to be? Will knew that he was no saint, by God. He was no Melisande Mooresby.

"Will?"

He blinked, jerking his attention to the coach's open doorway, where Melisande had paused in her descent and was eyeing him with curious impatience. "Are you planning to sit there all evening or will you be joining me?"

Will curtly waved her on.

She waited for him just outside the coach, her gaze fixed to the man approaching. The man who was his father.

Will took comfort in the fact that, though older and grayer, Peter Taggart was yet recognizable to him. The eyes were the same olive-green and his chin, like Will's, still bore the cleft that had marked countless generations of Taggart men. His cheeks were thin, his color poor. And he appeared to have lost some weight. Dressed like a country gentleman, his tweedy coat hung loosely from his bent shoulders, and his boots were scuffed and muddied.

Neither man spoke for a good thirty seconds. Then Peter Taggart held out his hand with a tentative smile.

"Faith, but 'tis good to have ye home, lad," he said huskily in his pronounced Border burr.

Will nodded and accepted the frail-boned handshake. "Good to see you again . . . sir."

Their gazes held. Peter broke away first, as if embarrassed, and turned to smile at Melisande. "And what have ye brought us, Will?"

Will placed a protective, and restraining, arm around Mel's shoulders. "I've brought you a daughter. Allow me to present my wife, Melisande. Mel, this is Peter Taggart, my father."

Melisande dipped into a gracious curtsy. "I am so very pleased to make your acquaintance."

Will relaxed with a quiet sigh. He'd been worried Mel might make a scene, perhaps throw herself at his father's feet and beg to be taken home to England. But the "She-Devil of Mooresby Hall," bless her stubborn hide, had too much dignity for that, too much pride to resort to melodrama. If the two of them were going to do battle, it looked to Will as if their war would be privately waged.

"Ach, a wee English lass." Smiling, Peter clasped Mel's hand in both of his. "I'd have reckoned young Willy'd bring home a bride from the Americas." He tilted his head questioningly in Will's direction. "Have ye been that long on our shores?"

"Only a handful of weeks, in fact. But Mel, you see, is a headstrong lass, and the minute she laid eyes on me, she wanted me to husband. Well, you know me, Da. Always the obliging sort."

His father smirked and bent down to look into Mel's face. "He's stolen ye away, has he?" he asked, not knowing how close to the truth he hit with his jest.

Mel slid Will a vengeful glance. "I'm not a woman easily stolen, Mr. Taggart."

Peter chuckled, but his laughter quickly dissolved into a coughing fit that had him struggling for breath.

"Here, please." Melisande pressed her linen handkerchief into his hand and took him by the elbow, steering him toward the house. "Let us go inside. Evening has brought a chill that cannot be good for any of us."

As they headed for the house, Will trailed behind, listening to Mel first question his father about the state of his health, then launch into a speech on the importance of regular exercise for sound lungs. Peter Taggart listened and nodded. Mel lectured and frowned with concern.

Hooking his thumbs into his trousers, Will gave himself a mental pat on the back.

Aye, you did well, Tiger. You did very well indeed.

Melisande wrinkled her nose as they entered the cottage, the musty air indicating that the house was long overdue for a thorough cleaning. Above her head, cobwebs clung to the ceiling of the small front hallway like so many bands of mourning bunting, their lacy nets grayed and heavy with dust.

They passed from the hall to the parlor, where sooty lamps sent a dull glow over a French-style carpet riddled with moth holes and stained beyond hope. An antiquated piano occupied one corner, its every surface covered with books and odd periodicals.

Melisande chewed at the inside of her cheek, questioning how many years had passed since the Taggart home had last known the benefit of a woman's touch. In fact, she was pondering that very question when she looked up and saw the portrait above the fireplace.

"My, what a striking woman," she exclaimed.

Striking and quite obviously Will's mother. Though Mel had remarked on the resemblance between father and son, the similarities between Will and his mother bordered on the uncanny. The shape of his face, the tawny mane of hair, the eyes alive with that indescribable joie de vivre.

"Aye, that's my Maggie," Peter said in a reverential

whisper at her side. "Scotland has ne'er seen a bonnier lass or a gentler soul than Margaret Louise Taggart."

"I am sorry. You must miss her greatly."

To Melisande's dismay, Peter's eyes started to turn lustrous with tears.

"Ach, not a day passes that I—"

"What's this?" Will asked from the doorway. "I travel halfway round the world and I can't even get a dram for my troubles?"

The tone of Will's voice gave Melisande pause as she turned away from the portrait. Emotion, raw yet restrained, had threaded his words, revealing some deeper sentiment she'd not heard from Will before. Could that have been fear roughening his speech? Fear from Tiger Taggart?

Peter wiped hastily at his eyes with the handkerchief, then stuffed it into his pocket. "If it's whiskey you be wantin', lad, we've still plenty of that to offer ye." He hobbled over to a leaded-glass cabinet, where he poured out three portions of a caramel-colored beverage, his movements shaky. One glass he carried to Melisande, spilling some of the beverage onto the already stained carpet.

"Here ye are, Mrs. Taggart."

She had no choice but to accept, although the fumes wafting from the crystal were potent enough to make her head reel. After her experience with champagne, she'd sworn off spirits for the remainder of her days.

"Eh, now, what's this?" Peter asked, lightly touching her left hand. "No ring?"

Melisande glanced helplessly across to Will, wondering what she ought to say.

"Don't worry, Da, I've got it right here." Will delved into his pocket and instantly produced the gold band. "It's a shade too large, so I've been carrying it for Mel until I can have it properly sized."

"Well, ye'll be wantin' to take care of that soon, won't ye, son?" Peter asked, handing Will the second glass of whiskey.

"Aye, Da. Very soon."

Once Peter Taggart had his own drink in hand, the older man raised his tumbler to Melisande.

"If I may borrow from our own Rabbie Burns; 'But to see her was to love her.' And now that I've seen ye, lass, my heart is yers to keep. Tread lightly on the poor old thing, I beg ye."

He smiled, and a salty lump unexpectedly rose in Melisande's throat. There was a sadness about Peter Taggart that reminded her poignantly of her own father, of the sadness that had never left him following her mother's death.

Melisande inclined her head and the two men drained their glasses.

"Ah," Will sighed. "That's some damn fine whiskey, Da."

"Eh, now, watch your language, lad," Peter chided. "Yer lady wife can't be used to yer rough tongue."

Melisande pressed her lips together, refusing to look at Will, for she knew what she'd find there. That mocking, lopsided grin. That cocky gleam in his eye. Dash it all, they both knew how familiar she'd become with his tongue. And he with hers. The last thing she wanted was to be reminded of that fateful night and how she'd proven such an *imposition* on her husband.

"You know, Da, I didn't see smoke from the chimney-stack when we drove in," Will commented. "Are the kilns not firing?"

From the corner of his eye, Peter slipped her a nervous, apologetic glance. "Ach, now, let's not bore yer missus with business, Will. Let me ring for Mrs. Baker to show ye both to yer room, and ye can freshen yerselves. You and I can talk later."

Will set down his glass and braced his feet wide. "I'm as fresh as I'm going to be, Da, and not getting any fresher. Tell me, just how bad is it?"

Another embarrassed glance came Melisande's way, and she placed her untouched whiskey upon the mantel. "Actually I wouldn't mind washing the dust from my—"

"No, Mel. I want you to stay."

Melisande stopped in her tracks, surprised by Will's curtness. "I beg your pardon?"

He motioned her to the camelback sofa. "Go ahead and take a seat. You're a Taggart now. You need to hear this."

Across the room, Peter was frowning unhappily into his empty tumbler.

"Honestly, Will, we've only just arrived. Surely we can discuss this once we've rested and had something to eat. *Later.*"

"No, Mel, I think we need to hear it now," Will said softly yet with unmistakable determination.

Uncertain, Melisande darted glances between Will and Peter before cautiously seating herself in the cushioned rocking chair beside the hearth. Although reluctant to contribute to Peter Taggart's obvious uneasiness, neither did she underestimate the strength of Will's resolve. Knowing the scoundrel, he'd probably tackle her on the threshold should she try to leave after he'd bid her not to. *The beast.*

She folded her hands in her lap and tucked her feet beneath her, acutely aware of the tense undercurrents traveling between father and son.

Peter Taggart released a weary sigh. "I dinna know where to begin, lad," he said, still studying his tumbler. "After ye left, I . . . I dinna know." He shrugged and it was a gesture of defeat. Of complete hopelessness.

"I guess I lost it, Willy. I lost the love of making the brew. I hired a stillman out of Straithalla"—he sighed deeply—"but he was a young one, untried and needin' direction. I wasn't up to the task, son. Then the monies got low and, with the highland clearings, there's no labor to be bought in any case. . . ."

"How much do you have laid down?" Will asked.

His father wagged his silvery-white head. "Four? Five dozen barrels?"

"And are you producing now?"

Peter turned to gaze out the window. "We were, up to a month or so ago."

Melisande flinched, unable to bear witness to the elder man's shame. It was too painful. Yet Will did not appear moved by his father's confession. Though his tone was not disrespectful or impertinent, neither did his many terse questions express compassion or understanding.

Furthermore, where was the easygoing demeanor, the teasing wit that told the world that Will Taggart took nothing it offered too seriously? Nothing but his own needs and desires, that is. Since they'd stepped from the coach, he'd not been himself. He'd been tight, contained. On guard. A bit like an animal caged.

Not that it should matter to her how he was feeling—

"Did you bring in the barley?" Will asked.

"Aye. But I've naught to do with it."

"But is it properly stored?" Will persisted.

"Aye."

"The books?"

"They've not been kept up."

Will nodded, his chin lifting. "All right then. We'll have a look at them tomorrow. The sooner we can take care of this . . ." He didn't finish his sentence. "Mel, you've an aptitude with ledgers, haven't you?"

"Pardon?" She blinked a few times.

"Ledgers," Will repeated. "You kept the accounts at Mooresby Hall?"

Had she heard the man correctly? After seducing her, abducting her, humiliating her, and possibly *impregnating* her, he dared ask her for assistance in setting his blasted bookkeeping in order?

She was more than ready to tell him what he might do with his ledgers when her regard settled again on Peter Taggart. She couldn't explain it, but he did remind her so very strongly of her own father. And he did need help.

"I could have a look," she answered noncommittally.

"Good," Will said. "Tomorrow we can start by inspecting the distillery and mill."

"Yes, tomorrow." Peter appeared pathetically eager to cut short their discussion. "Now let me go fetch Mrs. Baker and have her show you to your room."

As he slipped from the parlor, Melisande had the oddest feeling. The feeling that she'd just been well and truly manipulated. Somehow, in those few short minutes, Will had drawn her into his father's plight, pulled her in, engaged her sympathy. But . . . why?

She glanced up and found Will watching her, his green-flecked gaze intent.

"He's in trouble, Mel."

But Will had known as much already. She recalled the emotion she'd heard earlier in his voice, and instinctively seized on the understanding that more was at stake here than bailing out the family whiskey business. There was history here. A sad and bitter history . . .

It means naught to me, she told herself staunchly.

Yet, as she looked around at the tattered window hangings and scuffed wood floor, she could not resist the urge to set things aright. She had probably three weeks until she knew whether or not she was enceinte, so why not make herself useful in the interim? Organizing accounts—and oversee-ing a thorough spring scrubbing—would at least keep her occupied and too busy to fret over the unthinkable conse-quences of breeding a Taggart heir.

She frowned, realizing that Will awaited some kind of response from her. Already he assumed that her emotions were engaged. And to some extent they were, she realized, her eye catching on the portrait of Maggie Taggart above the fireplace.

Smoothing her skirts over her ankles, she answered with as much haughtiness as she could muster, "If I do decide to help, you understand that I will be assisting your father. *Not* you."

Will grinned. *Insolent man.*

"Of course, Mel. Da, not me. You wouldn't want to give me the wrong idea, would you now?"

She awarded him a frosty glare. "No, I wouldn't. And so that you don't get any more wrong ideas, why don't you run after your father and explain to him that we'll be needing separate rooms?"

Will made a mocking grab at his chest. "But, Mel, how could I explain such a request? Da is under the impression that we're newlywedded lovebirds."

"I don't care how you explain it. Find a way."

Will scratched at his chin, still not acquiescing to her demand. "I don't know, Mel. You didn't seem to mind so very much when we shared a room while traveling from Devonshire."

"Mind?" She swept her hair over her shoulder with a regal brush of her hand. "I am a Mooresby. My blood is the blood of kings and warriors. We know how to endure great hardship and tribulation without complaint."

"Ah, poor lass. Was it so very hard to keep your hands off me then?"

Her teeth clenched. "The only place my hands long to be is around your throat, Mr. Taggart."

Will grinned broadly. "Savage little wench, aren't you?"

"Test me. Just try to crawl into my bed again, o' husband mine."

As if he would want to. He hadn't so much as attempted to touch her since that first night, when she'd practically begged him to seduce her. Lord, her cheeks still burned with the memory.

"All right, Mel, I'll talk to Da. But mark my words, you'll regret this hasty decision of yours. Once you've tasted passion, it's the devil's own torment to deny yourself more of the same."

"You exaggerate your talents, Mr. Taggart."

"Do I now?" His brows arched. "Well, I must not have been at my best that night. Perhaps you ought to give me another chance, Mel, to show you how talented I really am."

Heavens, the mere thought of improving on that experience made Melisande's toes curl in her boots. But, by God, she'd go to her grave before she told him any such thing.

Turning her back to him to ensure that her expression did not give her away, she answered him in her coolest, most contemptuous voice. "Talented? Yes, you put on a strong performance, I grant you. But I have already learned all that I need to know of you, Will Taggart. And all that I ever hope to know."

Eighteen

The following day, the chains were weighing heavily upon Will—the chains of responsibility.

After touring all the facilities and gauging the extent of the distillery's financial troubles, Will estimated that he'd be trapped at Dunslaw a good two to three months or more. *Three months, dammit.* Could he last that long?

It wasn't that he didn't love Scotland or whiskey-making or his father. All three were in his blood, undeniably a part of his history and who he was. He had, after all, been raised in these glens blanketed with lush velvety heather, breathed his whole young life the pure Caledonian air smelling of yeast and barley and smoky peat. Of course, he loved this beauty that was home. He loved it, but he could not live among it.

Because of his father.

Will had hoped that Da might have improved, but he was the same as when Will had left home over a decade ago. He had never accepted their loss. Never. For thirteen long years, Peter Taggart had continued to mourn, wearing his grief like a tangible thing. Will couldn't bear it. He couldn't stomach seeing his childhood hero reduced to this fragile, apathetic shell of a man. God, he wanted to shake him. Shake him and shake him until he'd shaken the misery right out of the old fool. But the spark inside Peter Taggart was gone. Dead and gone.

Beside him on the cart's seat, Mel sighed softly as she pored over the notes she'd taken that morning, her raven-black brows creased in deep concentration. Despite his dour mood, Will felt himself grin. As might have been expected, Mel hadn't been able to stay indifferent to the Taggart family's difficulties for long; she'd seen a problem and now she had to fix it.

During their inspection of the distillery and warehouse, she'd asked literally dozens of questions of his father, some woefully naive, others surprisingly insightful. She'd been so relentless in her queries that Peter had returned to the house before them, worn out by her tireless inquisition.

It was, Will thought, almost amusing, the woman's sense of competency and commitment. Amusing if not downright enviable. Everything Mel did she did intensely, never questioning her capabilities or skills. Once she tackled a project, she saw it through to the end, her sense of commitment knowing no limits or bounds. Aye, she was the right choice, all right. The perfect and only choice.

"Will?" Mel frowned at her pad of scribblings, evidently forgetting that she was supposed to be treating him with icy disdain.

"Hmm?"

"I don't understand this remark your father made about the private producers not paying duty to England." She looked up at him, her chocolate eyes nearly black beneath the sheltering brim of her chip bonnet. "If they produce only privately, they'd not be shipping to England in any case, would they?"

"When Da called them private producers, he meant those that don't hold a license."

Her lips puckered into a tight bow. "But didn't he say that you must have a license to export?"

"Legally you do."

"So those shipping illegally are smuggling whiskey across the border?"

Will nodded.

"So they don't pay taxes. And yet we do?" Mel asked.

We? Will barely succeeded in holding back a triumphant grin.

"Aye, it's the way it's always been, Mel, and there's no use in fretting about it. The highlanders have been making whiskey since the days of Saint Patrick. You cannot expect them to give up their livelihood, license or no."

"But that isn't fair!"

"Fair? Nothing in this world is fair, Mel. The way I see it you can either spend your days lamenting the fact or you can get on with your life."

The heat in her gaze abated a notch. "Nonetheless it does put us at a distinct disadvantage," she argued.

"Aye, but we don't have to worry about the excisemen shutting us down either."

She chewed that over for a moment, her nose wriggling as she thought. "What are you staring at?"

"I was admiring your nose."

A look of soft surprise danced across her face before she remembered herself. "Rubbish," she finally managed, although the word lacked conviction.

Will smiled and pulled up on the reins, drawing the rickety cart to a standstill near a grouping of squat oaks.

"What are you doing?" Mel asked, her head swiveling left to right as if searching for the house, still a long half mile up the road.

"Oh, I thought I'd give old Bonnie a rest. She's not accustomed to so much exercise."

"Why, I don't—" Mel started to protest, but the horse was putting on a good show to back up Will's story, huffing and puffing and hanging its shaggy head.

Mel silenced and reluctantly settled back onto the seat.

They sat there together for no more than thirty seconds, the quiet wrapping intimately around them, before Mel suddenly clambered from the cart.

"And where are you going?" Will asked, amused to spy a definite rosiness in her cheeks. The day was warm, but not *that* warm.

"I thought I'd walk back to the house," she answered briskly. "The weather is lovely and I've been cooped up in that musty carriage these past three days. The fresh air will invigorate me."

"Do you think you can find your way back?"

"Of course, I can." She started walking east with a crisp, determined stride.

Will let her go about ten paces. "Oh, Mel?"

Her back stiffened as she realized she had to be going in the wrong direction. She stopped and waited, her foot tapping in the ankle-high grass, her hips jiggling delightfully.

"Unless you're prepared to swim the river, you'll not make it home that way," he called.

Arms akimbo, she half-turned to peek back over her shoulder. "Well then, are you going to play cat-and-mouse with me or are you going to point me in the right direction?"

"I'll do better than that," Will said. "I'll join you." And he leaped from the cart.

"But what of the gig?" Mel asked. "You can't simply leave it."

"Don't worry. I'll untie old Bonnie here and let her wander home. Fergus can fetch the cart later."

"B-but—" Melisande clamped shut her mouth and turned her back on him. Will grinned as he finished unfastening the lead reins.

"There you are, Bonnie girl." He gave the horse a friendly pat on the rump and sent her on her way.

Then he walked over and calmly did the same to his wife.

"How dare—" Melisande spun around hissing like a cat, swatting angrily at the air behind her.

Will jumped back a step, trying his damnedest not to laugh. "Easy, Mel. I was only trying to aim you in the right direction."

"You were not! You were looking for an excuse to . . . to touch me!"

Will cocked his head to the side. "Now, why would I be needing an excuse for that? I *am* your husband, aren't I?" His eyes narrowed, the levity of the moment gone. "Or am

I only allowed to touch you when you've issued an invitation?"

She swallowed. The breeze caught at the ends of her hair, lifting them gently to float around her shoulders. Behind her, a red-crowned ptarmigan flew past before disappearing into the nearby brush.

"It must give you immense satisfaction," she said tightly, "to constantly remind me of my weakness that night."

"Well, I don't know about the rest of it," Will drawled. "But, aye, I got my satisfaction. In fact, I thoroughly enjoyed myself."

She blinked. "You did?"

"You bet I did." He bent toward her, hovering as close as the bonnet's brim would allow. "And if I recall correctly, madam, so . . . did . . . you."

In the soft spot along her neck, he could see her pulse beating. Beating a soft and seductive invitation.

"Yes," she said. "I did."

Will squinted, taken aback. "You admit to it?"

Her shoulder nudged upward.

"But didn't you tell me only yesterday that I thought too highly of my 'talents'?"

Diffidently she glanced away. "My pride was talking yesterday."

"Oh? And what's talking today?"

She looked him right in the eye, her gaze clear and direct. "My need to be honest."

Oh, hell. The quiet confession was like a blow to Will's chest, tilting him back on his boot heels.

When he failed to answer, Mel turned and started following Bonnie's trail homeward. Will watched her walk away, feeling as low as a man could feel and still call himself a man.

Why? Why had her admission made him feel like such a blackguard? Because, he realized, she'd given him honesty. And he'd given her nothing.

Not once, but twice now, she'd opened to him, exposing her vulnerabilities. This confession just now, and once before, during their night together when she'd been so very

candid about her awakening passions. When had he ever
been as straightforward with her? From the beginning, the
two of them had been at cross-purposes, each trying to
maneuver the other person into fulfilling his or her needs.
She had needed a temporary husband; he needed a caretaker
for his father and the family business. Well, dammit, he had
already performed his role, he argued with his protesting
conscience. Wasn't it her turn now?

Besides, Mel didn't realize it, but he was, in fact, doing
her a favor. Her family certainly hadn't appreciated her—
her strength or her determination. Even her grandfather,
who no doubt would have applauded such attributes in
George, had dubbed Mel stubborn and willful. Difficult.
Hell, yes, she had spirit. Hell, yes, she was bold. But these
were the very qualities that Will admired most in her.

By God, after twelve years of traveling the world, he'd
seen what it took to be a survivor, to endure against all odds.
Mel had all of that and more. She was like . . .

The ivy twining up that oak tree there. Left to grow
unchecked, it ran the danger of strangling the tree hosting it.
Just as Mel had been smothering her family with her need to
be in charge, to fix all the Mooresbys' troubles and woes.

And like the ivy, Mel needed not only the proper
environment in which to flourish, but also to be cut back
when she started to grow wild and out of control. Until he
had come along, no one had been able to "prune" her; they
had all lacked either the courage or the knowledge. Or both.
So what did her family do? They uprooted her, casting her
away with him to Scotland.

Aye, whether Mel knew it or not, she'd had no future in
Devonshire. No room to grow within her family. But here,
she was being offered a future. A chance to use her talents
to everyone's good.

She pretended not to notice when he caught up to her, and
he pretended to forget what they'd been discussing.

"So what do you think, Mel? Do you think the distillery
can be saved?"

She shrugged and kept walking. "You should know better
than I."

"True, I should. Although you've obviously a sound head for business affairs and I'd like your opinion. If you wouldn't mind sharing it."

She glanced askance at him, as if to confirm that he wasn't teasing her. "Very well, if you really want to know. As I see it, you're facing two primary problems, Will. Insufficient labor and insufficient capital to hire more labor."

"I can't dispute that."

"Well, I have the answer to both."

"Naturally."

Her lips pursed and he regretted his sarcasm.

"Tell me," Will asked. "What do you see as a solution?"

She stopped walking and turned to face him. The sun glanced off a square of pure white cheek left uncovered by her bonnet. "My inheritance, the twenty thousand pounds. I'll loan it to you. With interest, of course."

Will shoved a hand through his hair, nonplussed by her offer. He'd never thought she'd loan him the money, and while he hadn't much cared for the notion of spending her inheritance without her knowledge or approval, he'd planned to do it nonetheless.

"You will, huh?"

"I will. Provided, that is, you allow me to supply the labor."

Uh-oh.

"As you know, I've long hoped to establish a remedial academy for those unfortunate offenders of the law who've mistakenly allowed their lives to go astray. What I suggest is this: Give me a chance to prove myself, to test my theories of curative behavior. Lead me to your local lockup and I will, in two weeks' time, turn over to you a dozen men eager and willing to give you an honest day's work for an honest day's wage."

"Mel, I don't think . . ."

"No, no. Hear me out before you dismiss the idea. After all, we both can benefit from this arrangement, don't you see?"

"But this is whiskey-making we're talking about here,

Mel. It's an art, a craft that's older than time itself. You cannot learn to make whiskey overnight, you know."

"Yes, I understand that. But did you not say that Wildcat is bringing you a skilled stillman?"

"Yes . . ."

"And you've knowledge of the distilling yourself?"

"Yes . . ."

"Well, it seems to me then there are plenty of other positions requiring less skill that need yet to be filled. There are the men who must do all that shoveling of the grain and the stirring of the mash. And then there is the beating down of those foamy bubbles during fermentation."

Will's mouth quirked. She *had* been paying attention.

"Look, Mel, it's a noble idea, it is. But if you think I'm going to let you—"

"*Let* me?" She looked to grow a full two inches in height. "Are you under the misconception that I am asking your permission, Mr. Taggart? On the contrary, I am merely proposing a business arrangement."

Will linked his hands behind his neck, holding back a sigh. "All I'm saying, *Mrs. Taggart,* is that not every criminal you rescue from the gaol is going to be as agreeable and as charming as yours truly. You'd be biting off more than you can chew."

"You don't know how much I can chew, er, that is, my mouth is bigger than . . . Oh!" She gave a frustrated stamp of her boot. "What I mean to say is that I can take care of myself. I daresay I've done an adequate job of it these past twenty-two years."

"I'm not saying that you can't take care of yourself, Mel. What I'm saying is I don't think you can handle a dozen life-weary men. You're accustomed to people giving in to you, of bending them to your will. Somehow I don't think that your petty criminals are going to be so easily bent."

"Well, you needn't worry on my account. As it happens, I have an unusual aptitude for encouraging compliancy," she argued. "And I assure you I will be prudent in my selection of workers."

Prudent? Like you were prudent in choosing me?

"Sorry, but I've got enough worries without adding to them. Thanks for the offer, Mel, but the answer is no."

She thrust her hands onto her hips and took a deep breath through her nose, as if laboring to rein in her temper. "You'll still be using my money, won't you?"

Will hung his head and kicked at a pebble in the moss. "Aye," he answered. "I will."

She made a faint sound of frustration and whirled away, her gown fanning out in a circle of ocean blue cotton. As she started to march up the hill, she shouted back over her shoulder, "You do realize that makes you no better than a thief, don't you?"

Will kicked again at the pebble. "Aye," he said quietly to himself. "I do."

Nineteen

The following afternoon, Melisande sat on the floor of Peter Taggart's study surrounded by mountainous piles of papers and ledgers and receipts. She'd already spent the better part of the previous day trying to organize the financial records and, after another four hours this day, was beginning to believe it a task worthy of Hercules himself.

Coughing, she waved a hand past her nose. The dust was as thick as glue, choking the very air from her lungs. Tomorrow she'd see the rug taken out and beaten soundly, even if it meant doing it herself. Mrs. Baker, while well intentioned, was obviously too far along in years to perform such heavy household labor; she needed a maid to assist her. As Melisande stifled yet another sneeze, she resolved to talk to Will as soon as possible about hiring a girl from Dunslaw to help with the house.

She frowned, asking herself how she was to discuss a new maid with Will when she'd resolved never again to speak to the knave. Oh, but she'd been furious yesterday, steam practically spouting from her ears as she'd stomped home through the fragrant fields of heather and clover. All these years, she'd avoided marriage for fear of tying herself to a man who would not respect her, one who would not treat her as his equal. And what comes to pass? Precisely what she'd been hoping to avoid in the form of one William Erasmus Taggart.

Admittedly he *had* asked for her opinion regarding the distillery, but she suspected that he had to have been patronizing her, throwing her a bone so that he'd feel less guilty about embezzling her inheritance. For when she'd offered a solution to his labor problem, he'd dismissed it out of hand, not trusting in her skills to rehabilitate the workers.

Oooh. To think he was going to make free with her inheritance after she'd waited so long for those monies. It simply wasn't right. It wasn't, no matter how the laws were written.

Angrily she slapped a stack of papers from one pile to the next. Losing her inheritance was upsetting, indeed, but made much worse when Melisande recalled what she'd confessed to Will yesterday. Not only had she lost her money, but she'd lost her pride as well. Lord, she wanted to die of mortification when she thought of it, when she remembered how she'd told him of the pleasure she'd taken in his arms. And why had she told him? Why?

The reasoning behind it was so very silly and so very prideful that Melisande felt ashamed of herself: For ever since Will had spirited her away from Devonshire, she'd believed that she'd failed to please him their night together. He'd said something the following morning in the carriage, insinuating that he'd done her a courtesy, a favor, by taking her virginity, and thus she "owed" him something in return for all his trouble and effort.

Well, by heavens, she didn't owe him any longer. He had her twenty thousand pounds!

So yesterday when Will admitted that he'd enjoyed their night together—had enjoyed it *thoroughly,* he'd said— well, she'd been . . . glad. Absurdly glad like some gawky-limbed schoolgirl receiving her first compliment. She blushed now to think of it. To think of her relief at knowing she'd not proven a disappointment in bed.

The problem, as Melisande saw it, was that she was not accustomed to being a disappointment. She'd never lacked for confidence, never distrusted her abilities, or questioned her expectations. And yet, in this instance, she *had* doubted herself. She had doubted her ability to pleasure a man. To pleasure Will.

As she reached for another sheaf of documents, Melisande asked herself why she had offered Will the loan. Had she been so comforted by his admission that she'd rashly proposed to lend him her twenty thousand pounds? Was she that insecure in herself as a woman?

"No," she murmured aloud, after a moment of searching her soul.

No. She'd proposed the loan because it was an intelligent maneuver. After all, since she never had control of the inheritance—blast her perfidious grandfather—she would have lost nothing if he'd accepted her offer. In point of fact, she would have benefitted by earning interest on the money. *If* he'd accepted. Which he hadn't.

The high-handed cur.

She did, however, take a small comfort in knowing that the money was to be invested in the distillery. She was committed to seeing the business recover, if not for the sake of Will and his father, for the sake of any child she might be carrying. God help her, though she hadn't wanted to dwell on the possibility, she had to acknowledge that any child of hers would someday inherit this family business of whiskey-making. It would be part of his or her legacy. Thus, she owed it to that potential heir to do what she could to aid the ailing Taggart distillery, and to make it profitable for future generations. Which was why she sat in a dusty study, sorting through papers until her back ached and her eyes burned.

She rubbed at those gritty eyes, her gaze drifting to the window and the verdant rolling hills framed within its view. Was it possible? Would a child of hers someday frolic among these emerald valleys? A child of her and Will's making? Up until now, the likelihood of a pregnancy had filled Melisande with no sentiment warmer than dread. She'd seen a babe only as a trap, a stratagem by which Will could win their battle and hold her to Scotland. A baby had been an abstraction; not a person, not someone real and soft and sweet-smelling that she might give life to. That she might nurture and raise and cherish.

For the very first time, the reality of it hit Melisande. It hit her in her womb. *My God, I might be a mother.*

A cooper's receipt drifted from her fingers, as images leaped before her. A picture of a plump-cheeked babe at her breast, its tiny fingers curled tightly around hers; a vision of a tawny-haired toddler clutching to her skirts, grinning a toothless grin. Despite herself, Melisande smiled mistily. Would it be so very terrible?

An unsteady breath filled her lungs as she tried to imagine what life here in Dunslaw might bring for her. Scotland was lovely; already she'd developed an affinity for the quiet life they led here, its simplicity and calm. It seemed to her a healthy place in which to raise children, and she'd not have to worry about being idle, what with the distillery and all its related operations. Yes, she rather thought she could be happy here . . . if she could learn to be happy with that no-good, lying scoundrel of a Scot.

A sudden gust sent papers flying like oversized snow-flakes on a winter's wind. Melisande looked up as Mrs. Baker entered the study, carrying a coal bin.

"Oh, I'm sorry, ma'am," the housekeeper said, pausing inside the doorway. "I didna mean to disturb ye."

"You're not disturbing me, Mrs. Baker. In truth, I was just thinking that a fire would be nice now that the sun has moved to the other side of the house."

"Aye, it won't take me but a minute to get it started," the housekeeper assured her, bustling across to the hearth. "By the way, Mrs. Taggart, I spoke to me sister who's always had a gift for potions and such, and she claims she's got a surefire remedy for Willy's snorin' problem."

Melisande glanced up from her paperwork. "I beg your pardon?"

"The snorin'. Mr. Taggart explained how Willy keeps ye up at nights and how ye newlyweds are obliged to keep separate rooms because of it." The housekeeper shook her head in apparent sympathy. "Me sister says the remedy tastes mighty foul, but it works like magic, she swears. The fish oil is supposed to be the secret ingredient."

"Fish oil?" Melisande tried to contain her smile. "Well, I think it's very considerate of you to think of poor Willy, Mrs. Baker. I'm sure that he would want to at least try your sister's remedy, don't you?"

"Aye, I do. It's not right, ye young lovers having to sleep at opposite ends of the hall. I'll run over to Rose's tomorrow to see if I can pick up some of the potion."

"Why, that's very thoughtful of you, Mrs. Baker. Very thoughtful, indeed."

"'Tis no trouble, ma'am. Mr. Taggart won't mind me takin' the afternoon off for such a purpose. Not, I imagine, that the poor man'd take notice," she added with a sad shake of her head.

"Oh, dear, is Mr. Taggart unwell? I noticed that he didn't come down to breakfast this morning."

As the coal took flame, Mrs. Baker brushed off her hands and set the screen back in place. "Not that it's me place to talk, but the squire suffers from melancholy somethin' fierce, ma'am. I know he's glad of Willy's return, but it cannot be without its pain, ye understand."

"Because of Will's resemblance to his mother?"

"So ye've noticed it as well?" The housekeeper made a sorrowful moue. "Ye'd think after all this time . . ."

Melisande didn't wish to be indelicate, but she was curious. "How long has it been since Mrs. Taggart passed away?"

"Passed away?" Mrs. Baker's gray brows drew together and she pressed a frail hand to the side of her head, setting her cap askew. "Faith, whatever gave you the idea that the missus was dead?"

"I— She's not?"

"Not as far as I know, she's not. Last I heard, she was livin' in a remote little village about an hour north of Edinburgh. Called Musselbergh, I think."

Stunned, Melisande sat speechless as Mrs. Baker retrieved her coal bin and bustled from the study.

Will's mother is alive.

Then, why, for the love of Moses, had he told her she was
dead? Or had he? Might she have jumped to that conclusion? She couldn't recall Will's exact words, but he could
have phrased it that she'd been "gone for many years."
Semantics aside, it seemed to Melisande that Will and his
father behaved as if Maggie Taggart were dead. Will never
spoke of her and appeared irritated when Peter did make the
occasional mention of her. And certainly Peter mourned the
woman as if she were deceased. How peculiar it all was. A
mystery that begged to be solved.

Melisande was pondering how to go about solving that
mystery when a loud shout sounded from the hallway. The
stomping of footsteps followed, accompanied by the low
rumbling timbre of male voices. Melisande's first crazed
thought was that her family had finally come after her. Yet
oddly enough, the idea did not fill her with the relief she
would have expected.

As the voices disappeared into the parlor, she chided
herself for being foolish, recalling that no one in her family
had reason to come for her. To their minds, she was where
she belonged.

Dusting off her skirts, Melisande scrambled to her feet.
There'd been no visitors here since she arrived, so she was
curious to see who'd come by. At the other end of the hall,
the front door stood open, spilling sunshine into the foyer
and revealing a pair of unfamiliar horses tied up to the
hitching post. The voices came more clearly now and she
recognized one as Will's.

She pushed open the parlor door to find her husband,
Wildcat, and a strange man enjoying a round of whiskey
before the fire. The newcomer, blessed with a head of fiery
red hair and a matching beard, was the first to acknowledge
her. He came to his feet, his highland tartan swinging in
bright hues of red and black.

"Good afternoon to ye," he greeted.

His accent was so thick, Melisande had difficulty at first
understanding him.

"Good afternoon," she responded, questioning Will with
a wordless tilt of her chin.

From his chair, Will ran a weary hand through his unbound hair and tossed off the introductions. "Melisande, this is our new stillman, Alastair MacInnes. Alastair is a distant cousin to Niankwe. Alastair, may I present my wife, Melisande Taggart."

"A pleasure, 'tis," Alastair said, sweeping her a bow.

She nodded, gratified to see that Wildcat had not yet poisoned his cousin against her. The Lenape brave had made no secret of his dislike of her and, for her part, she could not say W.C. had done much to endear himself to her either.

"We're pleased to have you here, Mr. MacInnes. I understand that your family is in the distilling business?"

"Aye. The MacInnes clan has been whiskey-makers five generations now," he told her with undisguised pride.

"Oh, that's wonderful. Will and I are very glad to have the benefit of your experience, since we are eager to resume production of the Taggart stills as soon as possible."

"Aye, so Will said. As I told him, if the barley is dried and ready to malt, I see no reason we kinna get started tomorrow if ye like, ma'am. The sooner we get to mash, the sooner we get to cask."

"I like the sound of that," Melisande said with a smile. "I only hope we have enough hands to get the work done," she added slowly, determined to push forth her prisoner rehabilitation plan.

"Ach, are we short laborers, Will?" Alastair asked.

Will shot her a tight-lipped smile. "We're a bit lean, but with Wildcat here, we'll get by. At least for now."

"And I see you've ordered new washbacks," Melisande said, knowing full well that 'twas her inheritance that was to pay for them. "Do you think they'll be arriving soon?" Again she posed the question to Alastair, who had no choice but to turn to Will for an answer.

"They'll be in next week," Will said. "Anything else you'd like to know, Mel?"

She waved her hands in an airy dismissal. "No. I just want to stay abreast of developments. By the way, where will you be staying, Mr. MacInnes? In one of the cottages down by the mill?"

"Aye. Will says they could do with a little fixin', but I've always been a handy sort. And what I kinna take care of, I'll have Wildcat see to. It's the least he can do after haulin' me 'cross Scotland on that raw-boned nag out there."

Melisande glanced to Wildcat, meeting his stony gaze with one of her own. Inexplicably the sight of the Indian brave brought back in full force the sense of betrayal she'd felt the morning following Eileen's wedding. The morning she'd been abducted. Melisande couldn't quite explain it, but while her anger had eased these last few days, had softened a bit, W.C.'s reappearance seemed to rekindle it, bringing all the bitterness back to life.

Perhaps, she mused, 'twas simply that she found it easier to be angry with Wildcat than to be angry with Will. She and the Lenape Indian had never established much of a rapport, yet she and her husband— Well, with Will, she'd shared the greatest intimacies a man and woman could share. He'd called her "love" and "sweetheart." He'd made her feel things she'd never felt before. Did she honestly *want* to be angry with him?

Of its own accord, her gaze shifted from Wildcat to Will, catching him in the brief moment when he closed his eyes, leaned back his head, and sighed. She knew he had to be tired, for he'd been working almost around the clock these past two days. In spite of herself, she felt a yearning to go to him, to brush his hair from his forehead and soothe the lines of fatigue from his brow.

Did she want to be angry with him? What was it she wanted to feel for this man? And more to the point . . . What was it she wanted him to feel for her?

Twenty

༒

"*Good work, Malcolm.* Keep it up now."

Will waved to the short, stocky man who was working his wooden shiel up and down the length of the floor with steady, rhythmic strokes. 'Twas hard, sweaty work, turning the barley, but important work. After steeping in the chalky Lammermuir waters, the moist grain had to be turned every few hours in order to control the buildup of heat. An entire lot of grain could be ruined if the shiel man failed to do his job properly over the course of the next few days.

"When you're done here, Malcolm, Wildcat could use a hand with the kilns."

"Aye, Mr. Taggart," the older man answered, leaning on the handle of his shovel. "I'll most likely be another hour here, but it's coming along."

Aye, Will thought, it was coming along, slow but steady. Perhaps slower than he would have liked, but with manpower at a premium in this part of the country, they all had to toil that much harder to get the work done. Of the distillery's old workers, only Malcolm here had been willing to return; the other men had already found employment elsewhere, and Will had had no luck in locating new laborers.

Rolling his head back and forth on his shoulders, he fought the fatigue cramping the muscles in his neck. Forty-eight hours without sleep was starting to take its inevitable toll. Yet, he realized with satisfaction, the peat was cut, the barley in the kiln, the mill primed and ready to receive the mash. . . . Maybe now was as a good time as any to steal himself a moment's rest before the malt went to the tuns.

With a final word to Malcolm to let the workman know he'd return later that afternoon, Will dragged himself into the saddle and let Attila carry him swiftly home. Approaching the stables, Will smiled to see old Fergus hurry out to take the reins. The aged, one-eyed ostler had practically danced a jig yesterday when Attila and Ulysses had arrived. In fact, the crusty old fella had almost wept with joy, which surely would have pleased George Mooresby, Will thought, to know that his beloved pair of thoroughbreds were to be well cared for.

The house was quiet as Will entered, and he wondered where Mel might have gone. Over the last couple of days, she, too, had been laboring long hours; not in the hefting of barrels or the scrubbing of tuns, but with hours upon hours of tedious accounting and meticulous paperwork. The sort of labor that Will simply despised.

If she hadn't already earned his respect and admiration, she surely would have done so by now. Most women in Melisande's position—the stolen-from-their-homes-by-a-husband-they-didn't-want-while-waiting-to-learn-if-they-were-pregnant position—would not have conducted themselves nearly so well. Most women, women like Eileen, would have passed the last sennight weeping buckets of frustrated tears, sulking and pouting and throwing temper tantrums by the score. But Mel? No sir, not Mel. Although thrust against her will into an unfamiliar environment, she'd pushed up her sleeves and made the best of the situation.

Aye, he had to hand it to her. When Mel said she'd help get the business back on its feet, she'd meant it.

A few times a day, she would come down to the distillery to familiarize herself with the different stages of the whiskey-making process. And while Will encouraged her, wanting her to learn about the distilling, each time she suddenly appeared before him, he had to remind himself that she was not his for the taking. That he couldn't just sweep her up in his arms and carry her off to a glen and pleasure her until she whimpered and wept and called out his name.

But, Lord, how he wanted to. He dreamed of it, in fact. But Melisande had made clear she wanted naught to do with him, going so far as to choose the bedroom at the greatest distance from his.

That very morning Melisande had come to visit while he was working at the kilns. Dressed in a green plaid gown, with her hair loose and her color high from the warmth of the furnaces, she'd looked to Will like some Celtic woodland fairy. She'd been earthy and free, smiling, more relaxed than he'd ever seen her at Mooresby Hall. Maybe it was wishful thinking on his part, or his conscience hoping to placate him, but the Scots life did appear to agree with her.

Scotland did, even if *he* didn't. Damned if it didn't seem to Will that Melisande's list of grievances against him was growing longer with each passing day. . . . From kidnapping to embezzling, the charges against him were such that Will did not know how he could possibly try to defend himself.

For instance, he could explain to Mel that he hadn't so much kidnapped her as been *paid* to cart her off by certain members of her family—but, hell, even he was not that cruel. And it might appease her to know that he hadn't actually schemed to get her with child; rather, lust for her had so overpowered him that he'd thrown all caution, and precaution, to the wind. But what man wanted to confess to being overeager between the sheets? And the inheritance . . . Well, not to put too fine a point on it, but he had decided to repay her with interest, so he was, in reality, borrowing the money, not stealing it. Which was well within a husband's rights.

Aye, it wasn't that his actions were indefensible. Yet Will

did not *want* to defend himself. He didn't like having to
explain himself, explain the reasons he'd done what he'd
done. And, dammit, really why should he? If he had learned
any lesson these last dozen years, it had been that being a
man meant doing what you had to do and then being strong
enough to live with the consequences. So why bother to
explain himself to Mel? To win her forgiveness? To lure her
back into his bed?

Will was thinking of his bed—and how very empty it had
been—when he heard his name called through the parlor's
open doorway.

He looked in and found his father sitting in the rocking
chair by the fire with a knitted shawl draped across his lap.
He gestured for Will to come join him.

Bone tired and aching from head to toe, Will nevertheless
heeded the paternal summons. He'd not seen much of his
father of late for, although Peter Taggart had visited the
distillery once or twice, according to Mrs. Baker he'd not
been in the best of health. A case of the "green dismals,"
she'd said.

"Sit down, Willy. I want to talk with ye, lad."

Will perched himself on the curved back of the sofa and
waited. And waited. His father spent many long seconds
dragging his fingernail across a nick in the arm of the
wooden chair, unable to meet his gaze.

"I, uh, want to thank ye, son, for what ye're doin'. I know
it kinna be easy for ye to come back home to Dunslaw. To
come home after—"

"Don't, Da," Will broke in gruffly, suddenly tense as he
sensed where this was headed. "I'm here now and that's all
that need be said."

His father nodded, embarrassed. "How's the brew?"

Will's tension eased. The whiskey-making was a safe
enough topic. "We should start filling casks sometime next
week."

"Ach, that's happy tidings, fer sure. And yer lady wife? A
lass sometimes has a rough time of it, ye know, accustomin'
herself to her husband's home."

Will picked at a loose thread in the sofa's upholstery. "Melisande is doin' well."

"I'm glad to hear it. I like her, Willy. She's a fine woman."

Will smiled softly. "She is. Too fine for the likes of me, I fear."

"Nonsense." His father waved a frail hand, chuckling. "She is a good one, though. Mrs. Baker tells me that the lass has been burnin' the midnight oil in me study."

"Aye, we've all been working hard."

Peter dropped his gaze, toying with a corner of the raggedy shawl in his lap. "It's sorry I am I kinna be of more help to ye, lad."

"What are you talking about, Da? Of course, you've been of help. I watched you make the whiskey for almost sixteen years, didn't I? Everything I know of the stills I learned at your side."

"All the same, I wish these old legs of mine were more sturdy."

Regret and bitterness stabbed at Will. He knew he ought to keep silent, but he couldn't. "It's not your legs, Da."

His father's lips pressed together and he lifted his craggy face to stare at the portrait above the mantel. "This cough—"

"And it's not your lungs, either," Will countered.

"Ye don't know, son—"

"Aye, Da, I *do* know. I *do*." Pressing his clenched fist against his chest, Will said, "The problem is here, Da. Inside."

"Ach, Willy, ye kinna understand what it's like."

Within Will, a tiny kernel of anger began to expand, an anger he might have been able to control if he hadn't already been strained with fatigue. "For God's sake, don't tell me I cannot understand," he argued, his voice rising. "She was my mother, dammit."

Peter's chin tucked into his neck, the folds of his neckcloth swallowing the loose lines of his jaw. "Was?" he whispered bleakly.

"Yes, Da. *Was*," Will answered through gritted teeth.

"And someday, by God, you're going to have to accept 'was.' You're going to have to accept that she's not coming back."

Will pushed away from the sofa, realizing that he was in no condition to continue this conversation; he was too tired. Too weak. He whirled around and almost collided with Mel standing in the doorway. Her pity-filled gaze told him she'd been eavesdropping. Prying little witch. How long had she been standing there?

She hurriedly stepped aside as he brushed by, furious that he'd been goaded into dredging up all the old feelings, all the old hurt. Even more furious that she'd seen him do so. Damn, he needed to sleep. A long, soothing sleep in which he could bury himself and his memories.

The soft swish of skirts pursued him up the stairs, but Will refused to turn around, hastening down the short hallway to his room. His fingers were wrapped around the bedroom doorknob when a small hand suddenly clasped hold of his forearm.

Will jerked his head to the side, his eyes flaming. "I suggest you let me be," he warned.

She did not heed him. *What a surprise.* In fact, she continued to cling to him as he shoved into his bedchamber, her tenacity irritating the hell out of him. With a sharp movement, Will shook her off then paced across the room to the small leaded window that looked out over the silvery-green valley.

From the corner of his eye, he saw Melisande close the door behind her. For the first time in nearly a week, the two of them were alone.

"I mean it, Mel. Get out. I am not pleasant company right now."

"As if you ever are," she retorted lightly.

He braced his arms on either side of the window, struggling to bring his emotions back under control.

"I've not slept in two days and I'm in a foul, foul mood. Would you, for once, be a biddable, dutiful wife and just go?"

"Biddable?" She pretended to search the corners of his

room, then assumed a Scots accent to ask, "Who can ye be speaking to, Will lad, since surely it kinna be me?"

An unexpected huff of laughter rocked his shoulders. "Aye," he agreed with a defeated shake of his head. "I may as well beg the sun to set in the east this evening, eh?"

"The sun is more likely to do as you ask," she said quietly. Meaningfully.

Will concentrated on the beads of condensation pooling at the window's sill. "You're a stubborn woman, Melisande Taggart."

"So the pot calls the kettle," she blithely pointed out.

She moved to lean against the wall beside him and he noticed that her scent had changed since she'd left Mooresby Hall. Previously jasmine had been her preferred fragrance. But now . . . He couldn't say what she wore, but it smelled clean and green like freshly cut grain.

"What did you—"

"No, Mel," he said curtly. "No questions."

"Would you tell me the truth if I asked you any?"

He peered at her over his shoulder, at the way the filtered light picked out only the richest hues of ebony in her hair. Though she stood so close, merely an arm's length away, it felt to Will as if she were miles out of his reach. "I've not lied to you, Mel."

She lifted a brow. "Not in word or deed?"

All right, perhaps he'd withheld the truth, but he'd not lied—

But what of India? his conscience asked. What of his and Wildcat's plans to make a fortune in the silks trade? Contemplating the months ahead, Will wondered if maybe he was lying to her. If he was deceiving her with his intentions.

"How have you been feeling?" he asked.

She stiffened ever so slightly. "If you're inquiring as to whether I've been nauseous or unusually tired . . . I'm feeling quite myself, thank you. And, no, I do not yet know whether we might soon be journeying onto the path of parenthood."

Will took a relieved breath, a breath so deep that the sore muscles in his chest and ribs protested the exertion.

"It's an enormous responsibility," she commented, her dark eyes shuttered, unreadable. "Parenthood, that is."

An annoyed frown cut through Will's forehead. "How much did you overhear down there?"

"Not enough to understand the reason for your anger."

Biting back an oath, Will turned away from the window. Away from her. "Look, Mel, I'm ready to drop I'm so damned tired. So if you don't mind, I'd like to catch an hour or two's rest before we have to drain the tuns."

He extended his arm toward the door, thinking, *To hell with subtlety.*

She responded by pursing her lips, her head falling to one side, her eyes intent. Frowning, he followed her gaze and saw that she was peering inside his coat where it had gaped open. His hunting knife rested prominently at his hip.

"Up to old tricks, are you?" she asked. "I'm not as easily intimidated as the vicar, you know."

Will smiled menacingly and drew the dagger from its leather case, holding it high. "By God, I can't ever remember threatening a woman with a knife in order to convince her to leave my bedroom."

Melisande wriggled her nose. "I can take a hint."

An eight-inch blade—a "hint"?

On her way to the door, Melisande paused a few steps shy of the threshold. "You do realize, Will, that you wouldn't need to work such grueling hours if you allowed me to recruit a few men from the gaolhouse."

"No."

"I assure you—"

"No," he repeated.

"But if you'll only give me a chance—"

"Lord, woman, do you never give up?"

She straightened her shoulders and met his razor-sharp glare with an easy smile.

"Never."

•　　•　　•

That night, Melisande dined alone yet again, for Will was at the distillery and Peter had retired early, as he did most nights. Wildcat and Alastair, though they'd eaten at the main house the night of their arrival, generally did for themselves in their rustic cottages near the river.

Alone at the dining room table, Melisande sat and stared at her plate, replaying in her mind the curious conversation she'd overheard between Will and his father. Naturally she'd been intrigued by their cryptic discussion of the mysterious Maggie Taggart, but one comment above all the others stood out in Melisande's mind and it had naught to do with Will's missing parent. It had to do with *her*.

She's too good for the likes of me, I fear, Will had said.

Did he truly believe she was "too good" for him or had he only been speaking for his father's benefit? Initially startled by the statement, Melisande had come to see where Will might believe himself to be unworthy. Unworthy of her, that is. For hadn't she initially believed the same, thinking him to be no better than a drunken vagabond? Later, her opinion had not improved to learn of his checkered background and questionable vocational choices. And even on the day they wed, she remembered her secret dismay upon realizing that the man couldn't even tie a cravat, for heaven's sake.

But all that seemed like a very long time ago. Somewhere along the way, she had looked past Will's lineage and rough facade and found a . . . man. Not a prince, as Eileen had wished for her, but a man. A bit dangerous. A bit uncivilized. A bit uncouth. But a strong man, who took pleasure in life. And knew how to give it.

Melisande tapped her fingernails atop the simple pine table, wondering if she'd stumbled upon the reason for Will's sudden aloofness. Not that she desired his attentions—gracious, no. In fact, she'd been the one to insist on separate chambers, which was only right and proper considering that theirs was not a marriage in truth. At least, to her mind, it wasn't a marriage in truth.

And yet . . . when she'd followed Will to his room that afternoon, a small secret part of her—a part she only confessed to now—had been hoping he might kiss her. And when he failed to do so, had she not felt disappointed? Discouraged?

With a low sound of frustration, Melisande slapped her palm against her forehead, leaning her head into her hand. *For the love of Moses, just listen to me! I am contradicting myself left and right!* And if Melisande despised any particular weakness 'twas indecisiveness—in others, yes, but especially in herself. When she made a decision, she was absolute, certain. No second-guessing. No namby-pamby, wishy-washy, middle-of-the-road waffling about for her. So then . . . What did she really want from Will Taggart?

She raked her nails across her scalp as if digging for the answer beneath her hair. All she dug up was a flake of dandruff.

"What?" she muttered. "What do I want from him?"

She simply couldn't say. She did know that today when he'd looked so awfully miserable, she'd wanted to comfort him. To take away the hurt he'd been reluctant to share. Unsettling the feeling, but it had been there nonetheless. A need, a burning need, to rid the world of whatever problem or difficulty brought the pain to Will's gaze—

Melisande sat up with a jolt.

"Mrs. Baker!"

The housekeeper bustled in from the nearby kitchen, wiping her hands on her apron.

"Mrs. Baker, if I desired to send a letter to someone in Musselbergh, let's say, would you be able to see it delivered?"

"Musselbergh, ma'am?" Mrs. Baker echoed nervously, her chapped hands stilling in mid-wipe. Her gaze flickered with irresolution behind her foggy spectacles. "Aye. I could arrange it."

"Good. I would like to keep this quiet, if you've no objections. I'd rather not stir up excitement until I know how my letter is received."

"Aye. I think I understand."

"I knew you would." Melisande rose from her chair,

eager to seek out pen and paper. "I'll dash off the letter and give it to you first thing in the morning."

She started to leave the table, but the housekeeper stalled her. "But, Mrs. Taggart, ye've hardly touched yer dinner."

Melisande's nose wrinkled, as she glanced at the brimming platter. "Oh, I am sorry. It was delicious, truly, but my appetite is off."

"Ah-hhh," the housekeeper said knowingly, grinning from ear to ear.

"Oh, no." Melisande wagged her head in a heated denial. "I'm sure I'm not—"

But she wasn't sure.

Blast it, she wasn't sure of anything.

Twenty-one

"*There we are,*" Alastair said triumphantly, as he drove the cork into the side of the last oak barrel. "Our first run."

Wildcat laid his palm on the cask, as if in benediction, while Will clapped his arm around Melisande's shoulders.

"Shouldn't you, at least, try some?" she asked, turning her face up to him with a jubilant smile. A smile that made something inside Will's chest go *clunk*.

"We could," Will said, "but this here is a far cry from champagne, Mel lass. The whiskey is still raw, has to age."

"Aye, the angels must first take their share," Alastair said.

"Angels?"

Will bent over her and whispered, "What's lost to evaporation is known as the angels' share."

"Oh."

Of course, he knew it was only the moment, the euphoria of pride and accomplishment following endless hours of toil, but still it pleased him that Melisande did not pull away from his embrace. It pleased him too much.

"So how should we celebrate?" Alastair asked.

"Sleep," Wildcat suggested, stretching his arms overhead and opening his mouth wide.

Will glanced over his shoulder. "I was just about to tell Malcolm to set another batch of barley to steep—"

"What?" Alastair blustered. "Are ye daft, man? We've laid down the first batch and near killed ourselves doin' it. But now we've got to rest. Ye've got to rest, Will. Ye've worked like two men—"

"Three," Wildcat amended.

"Aye, three," Alastair agreed, nodding his shaggy red head, "and ye cannot keep goin' at this pace, man. It's punishin'. I, for one, need a day to nurse me tired limbs back to life."

Wildcat grumbled his accord.

"All right, you needn't mutiny on me," Will said. "We'll take the rest of the afternoon—"

"And tomorrow," Alastair insisted.

"And tomorrow," Will conceded, "and start again on Thursday. Does that make you happy?"

"It does. In fact, what say we go into town, W.C., and do some proper celebratin'?" Alastair proposed, waggling his thick, caterpillar brows suggestively.

Wildcat nodded. "First drink is on you, cousin." As the two men turned to leave, Will felt Melisande slip from under his arm.

"And where are you going? With them?"

She gave him a quizzical smile. "Home."

Home. God, how Will wanted to kiss her. "Home" no longer meant Mooresby Hall in Devonshire, did it? Home was his home. Their home. Or so he wanted to believe.

"Do you mind if I join you in the cart?" he asked. "I'm of a mind to let W.C. take Attila into town. The animal needs a good run."

Melisande lifted an easy shoulder. "If you like."

"Niankwe," Will called before Wildcat got out of earshot. "Attila is yours for the ride into town. Be careful with him, I warn you, for if he comes back lame, I can't be responsible for what Fergus might do to you."

Wildcat signaled his understanding with a crude gesture. Will laughed and turned back to Mel. She stood looking across the distillery, her expression thoughtful, serene.

"It's very satisfying, isn't it?" she asked in a quiet voice, her gaze passing over the gleaming copper stills. "To take these tiny beads of grain and magically convert them to a liquid as smooth and golden as sunshine. . . ." She turned to him, laughing at her own fancy. "It's like that children's fairy tale about the ugly little dwarf who spun gold from straw."

"Aye, I remember it. Though I'm not sure I appreciate being likened to a wizened elf."

"A pity since you will soon resemble one if you don't get your fill of food and rest. Have you not seen yourself in a mirror lately, Will Taggart? Your color is pasty, you've circles under your eyes, you've lost weight—"

"Enough," Will said, imploring her to cease with an upraised palm. "Lord, Mel, you'll give me a swelled head with such fulsome compliments."

"Well, it's the truth," she insisted.

"Then, by all means, let us hie home so that you may stuff me like a roast goose if you like."

"Wouldn't that be a roast *tiger*?" she returned with a playful grin.

Approaching the gig, Mel insisted on handling the reins, claiming she didn't trust Will not to fall asleep. *As if they need worry that old Bonnie would suddenly bolt,* Will thought wryly to himself as the cart ambled away at a leisurely walk.

"Will, that fairy tale about the straw into gold . . ."

"Hmm?" he mumbled. He'd sat down less than a minute earlier but already had begun to nod off, thanks to the fragrant spring sunshine warming his head, and the gentle rocking of the poorly sprung cart.

"Do you remember what the dwarf wanted as payment for spinning the gold?"

He rubbed the top of his knee. "Let's see, there was something about a king—" His eyes snapped open. Warily he glanced over to Mel, who was gnawing at her lower lip, her profile marred by a frown.

"A babe?" he asked, going so tense that his arches started to cramp. "Are you—"

"I cannot be certain," she said. "But . . . perhaps."

"Damn!" Will exploded as the cramp in his arch blossomed into a full-fledged, muscle-ripping charley horse. He pounded his foot on the floorboard, clenching his teeth.

"Well, for heaven's sake, you ought not be throwing fits, Will Taggart, when—"

"A cramp." Will jabbed his finger in the direction of his boot. "It's a cramp, Mel." He shook his leg a half dozen times before the spasm began to ease. "Oh, God. There, that's better. Whew. . . . Now, where were we?"

Mel scowled and, with one hand on the reins, tugged at her bonnet's rim as a warrior adjusts his helmet before going into battle. "We were about to discuss what course to take, if my suspicions prove correct."

Prudence slowed Will's words to a crawl. "What do you want to do?"

"Well, I have been giving the matter due consideration and I have come to the conclusion that two people cannot construct a life together solely around the existence of a child."

Damn. He should have known it would not be enough. "So what are you saying?"

Her lungs looked to fill to twice their normal capacity. "I'm saying that more compelling reasons than a baby are required to make a marriage successful."

"You don't think a baby is compelling?" he demanded, a shade more aggressively than he'd intended.

She bristled like a cornered cat. "Of course, I think a baby is compelling. But I do not believe if a man and woman are unhappy in their circumstances that a baby can somehow work a miracle and make them happy."

You're not happy, Mel? Will experienced another cramp, this one in the vicinity of his chest. God, he'd been so sure that she was adapting, that she'd come to care about the business and his father and . . . Scotland.

His jaw jutted forward. "There is no way in hell that I'm going to let you take my son back to England."

Mel's infuriated gesture brought the reins slapping against Bonnie's flanks, coercing the horse into a light trot.

"Blast it, William, when are you going to understand that there is no way *I* am going to let you order me around as if

I'm some timid little scullery maid? If I decide to take my son—or *daughter*—back to England, not you or Wildcat or an entire army of knife-wielding heathens can stop me!"

Will's eyes narrowed. "Don't bet on it."

"I'd like to see you try and stop me!"

"Mel, I warn you. You have yet to see me become really angry," he told her in a voice lethally quiet. "And I promise you . . . you don't want to."

"Oh, yes, I know," she flippantly rejoined. "Tiger Taggart. He smiles and laughs and jests while all the while his eyes are telling you that he could just as easily slit your throat as not. How many men *have* you killed, Mr. Tiger?"

"Gee, Mel, I don't know. I stopped counting when I hit a dozen."

Her features went slack.

Will cursed under his breath. Dammit, he'd done it again. Exhausted beyond all reason, he'd let his emotions run away with his better judgment.

"I shouldn't have told you that."

"No," she said breathlessly. "You shouldn't have."

Will curled his fingers into fists, wondering what on earth had provoked him to make such a confession., "For God's sake, Mel, they were all filth. Men who deserved to die, men more vile than you could ever imagine. And I swear to you, in every instance, it was either me or them. One of us had to die."

"How comforting," she murmured, refusing to meet his eye.

He grabbed her by the shoulder, turning her toward him. "Don't tell me you don't know what I'm talking about. You may not have gone out there and seen how frightening the world can be, but you know what it takes, Mel. To survive, you have to be ruthless."

Understanding flickered at the back of her eyes. "And stubborn," she added in a whisper.

Will released his breath. She did understand. Not deep down, as someone who's faced death understands, but enough. Would Mel then understand why he couldn't let her leave Dunslaw? Why he had to keep her here?

An abrupt increase in Bonnie's languid pace almost jerked the reins from Mel's lax fingers. She secured the ribbons in her grasp as they both glanced ahead to where the house had come into view, apparently spurring the old mare to hurry the final yards home.

"Is that a carriage?" Mel asked, sitting a bit straighter on the seat.

Will peered down the road to the approaching cloud of dust. "Aye," he said, nonplussed. "It looks as if we're to have a guest."

"It's rather late in the day for a visitor," Mel commented. "Are you expecting anyone?"

A frisson of foreboding chilled Will's spine. "No."

The outdated traveling coach pulled up in front of the Taggart home only a few seconds ahead of Will and Mel. Peter Taggart, his brow wrinkled with curious interest, had come out onto the porch to greet their unforeseen visitor.

As the coach's unliveried driver climbed from his perch, Will jumped down from the gig and walked around to assist Mel. Simultaneously the driver handed his charge down from the coach.

Shielded from view by the driver, a flash of black and white was all that Will could at first see of their guest. Then the visitor stepped away from the coach, and her costume of white wimple and black shone jarringly stark against the cottage's mellowed red brick.

"A nun?" Mel whispered in surprise. "A Catholic nun?"

Will's feet rooted to the ground. He sensed Mel's regard, but continued to stare straight ahead, his eyes stony with shock.

"Will?" Melisande jiggled his elbow. "Will, what's wrong?"

And then from the porch, Peter Taggart let out a low, keening sound. A sound that was a name.

"Maggie."

Maggie.

Melisande felt the blood drain from her face in a sickening rush. No one moved. No one breathed. Shaking visibly, Peter Taggart had grabbed hold of a post and now clung to it with both frail hands. Maggie Taggart, cloaked in her robes of black and white, stood a few feet from the porch, her severe silhouette as still as death.

It was a moment frozen in time. Endless, eternal. Agonizing.

Melisande was the first to return to her senses. Lurching forward a half dozen steps, she extended her hands in greeting. "Mrs. Taggart?"

The veiled figure turned to her, an older, softer version of the woman in the parlor's portrait. Her resemblance to Will was so keen, so strangely touching, that Melisande knew an inexplicable desire to weep. Maggie Taggart took Melisande's hands in hers, her words gentle and hinting of confusion, "Please call me Maggie. And you would be Will's wife?"

A guilty pang caught at Melisande's middle. In her note to Maggie Taggart, she had written that she was married to Will. But never had she once referred to herself as "his wife."

"Yes, I am Melisande. I am so very delighted that you've come." In embarrassment, she glanced at her plain cotton gown, soiled from the distillery that morning. "I only wish I had been prepared to properly welcome you."

"Oh, dear. You didn't receive my letter?"

"No, I did not. Of course, I had hoped to hear from you soon. . . ." Melisande's sentence trailed off as she detected a familiar warmth at her back. Margaret suddenly looked past her, a tentative smile playing around the edges of her mouth.

"Will," she said quietly.

Compelled to witness his reaction, Melisande spun around, her heart in her throat. Tense and guarded, Will stood there like a man bound for the gallows. In place of a smile, he gave a short nod, his unbound hair sweeping seductively across one shoulder.

"I don't know what to call you," he said.

Hurt pinched at Maggie's smile. "I am still your mother. You may call me that. If you like."

"It's been thirteen years," he said without inflection. "Why did you come?"

Maggie's gaze flitted from Will to Melisande. "I was invited. However, if there has been a misunderstanding—" She turned toward the coach.

"No." Melisande reached for her, darting a glance to Peter Taggart on the porch. He'd not stirred. He merely stood there transfixed, still trembling as if with fever.

"No, please," Melisande urged. "Won't you come in and visit awhile?"

"I'm afraid I cannot stay long," Maggie offered hesitantly.

Melisande wished Will would join with her in urging his mother to stay, but it didn't seem likely based on his stoic reception.

"A cup of tea, then, before you have to travel home?" Melisande suggested, then winced thinking that she ought not to have used the term "home."

"A cup of tea would be very welcome."

"Good. And a biscuit? Mrs. Baker makes the finest currant biscuits," Melisande said, shamed to hear how her voice rang bright and brittle with nerves.

Taking Maggie by the arm, she led her up to the house, the older woman pausing as they drew face-to-face with Will's father. A brisk breeze ruffled the thin white hairs covering his head, the effect rather like a halo.

"How are you, Peter?" Maggie asked.

He nodded a few times, evidently unable to speak.

"Will you join us for tea?" Maggie invited.

"Yes, Mr. Taggart, you must," Melisande said. Hooking her free arm through his, she determinedly escorted the pair into the house, while praying that Will would follow.

Mrs. Baker was waiting just inside the door, her eyes round and watery. She and Maggie Taggart exchanged a few quiet words before the housekeeper scuttled off to fetch the tea tray.

"My, how lovely the house looks," Maggie said as they passed into the parlor.

Melisande swiped at a stray cobweb. "Yes, we've brought

in a maid to help Mrs. Baker, and she's proved very eager to learn."

Will's muted footsteps sounded behind her, causing Melisande to release a shaky sigh of relief. She hadn't known what she'd do if he flat-out refused to join them.

Maggie sat down on the sofa, and Peter joined her, moving like a man in a trance. Will positioned himself by the window, his posture stiff, his arms crossed defensively on his chest. Together they formed a picture of a family—a very odd picture. A very sad one.

With sudden insight, Melisande realized that she was *de trop* in this setting. After all, she had not been party to the Taggart family's painful history, had she? And while she would have liked to have understood what had gone wrong in this home, she recognized that whatever needed to be said between these three people was best said in privacy. She had already done her part; she had brought them together.

Across the room, her gaze met that of Maggie Taggart. The older woman must have somehow read her intent for she lifted her hand and smiled. Smiled a good-bye.

Without looking at Will, Melisande slipped from the room before anyone could take notice. She chose not to leave by the front door—since Will was standing at the window—but walked toward the back of the house, exiting through the study's french doors. As she stepped outside, Mrs. Baker's small herb and vegetable garden assaulted her with the scent of chives, parsley, and mint. The smells were sharp and lush. Melisande wrapped her arms around her waist as she meandered through the crookedly staked rows of green, the soles of her walking boots growing heavy with mud.

So Maggie Taggart is a bride of Christ. Good gracious, she never would have guessed. When Will had spoken of his mother as if she were dead, Melisande had assumed that some scandal had been visited upon his mother. That Maggie had committed some grievous sin which had put her beyond the pale, driving her from her family's bosom.

Granted that Catholicism had been outlawed in Scotland, Maggie's choice of faith still did not seem sufficient reason

to banish her from their home. Obviously there was more to
the tale. More to Peter Taggart's misery and more to Will's
anger than Melisande had supposed.

Her boot callously nudged a toadstool from its earthen
cradle, as she let her imagination wander. From what she
knew of Will's past, he would have been only fifteen or
sixteen years old when his mother had gone. And if he'd
been traveling the world these last twelve years, it took only
the most simplistic math to determine that he'd fled Scotland shortly after his mother had left home. Would it not
then follow that the two events were connected?

And just as Will had questioned his mother about her
absence, Melisande found herself questioning Will's return
to Dunslaw. Away a dozen long years and he comes home
in order to save his father's business from collapse. Why did
something about that scenario suddenly strike her as worrisome?

Melisande's stomach grumbled and she squeezed her
arms more tightly around her middle, her thoughts wandering from one motherhood to the next. Could it be? she
asked. Did a child grow inside her? Assuredly if she did not
begin her flow within the next few days, she'd have
sufficient reason for concern. Concern or . . . celebration.

Tilting her face skyward, Melisande looked for an answer
among the cream-colored clouds. Would a child be cause for
celebration? For her part, Melisande accepted that she
wanted to be a mother. She always had. But did she
want—as Maggie Taggart had so clearly pointed out—to
be a wife? Will's wife? And, what, please God, were Will's
feelings on the matter? He did seem determined to keep her
here in Dunslaw, although his reasons were still unclear to
her.

Earlier, in the gig, she'd tried to pose that very question
to him, but they'd ended up quarreling. If only they could sit
down and be reasonable—

"What the hell did you think you were doing?"

Melisande gasped and whirled around, nearly losing her
footing in the moist ground.

"Will! Goodness, you gave me a fright!"

"I'm going to give you more than a fright, Melisande Mary, unless you tell me what in blazes you thought you were doing by writing to my mother."

Fury stained his cheekbones, his lips stretched thin and tight.

"Where is she?" Melisande asked, peering around him to the house.

"She has just taken her leave."

"Already? But she was here less than a half hour!"

"There was nothing more to say."

"Thirteen years apart and you had nothing to discuss?"

A muscle jerked at the side of his jaw. "Nothing has changed, Mel. It's the same as it ever was."

"But didn't you talk about it? About your father's unhappiness and your—"

Will flexed his fingers open and closed. "Did you think that talking about it was going to make it all right, Mel? That if Da could only talk to Maggie he'd cease grieving her loss? Is that what you thought?"

"Well . . ."

"Dammit, woman, you can't make everything well by wishing it so!"

"But—"

"No, Mel. There's nothing any of us can do to change it. She never wanted to marry Da. She never even wanted children. All she wanted was to dedicate her life to God."

Melisande swallowed hard. "But I don't understand."

"Of course, you don't. And if you had, you wouldn't have done anything so monumentally stupid as to summon her here!"

Monumentally stupid? Her entire life, Melisande had never been accused of doing anything monumentally stupid.

"Then why . . . did she marry?" she asked helplessly.

"Because her family forced her to. And the moment she believed I was old enough to get by without her, she left. Snuck off in the middle of the night to join a clandestine group of expatriate French nuns, for God's sake."

"Oh, Will—"

"Do you realize what you've done with your meddling,

Mel? In your arrogant attempt to 'fix' Da's problem, you've managed to reopen the wounds. And then rub salt in them!"

"I am so sorry. How was I to know—"

"Just stop it, Mel." He slammed his fist into his open palm. "Stop believing that you can fix people. Mother can't be changed. Da can't be changed. And *I* can't be changed."

Melisande's heart skipped a beat. "What do you mean you cannot be changed?"

"I mean you want me to stick around here and help you with the distillery and raise babies and—"

"Stick around?"

And then the pieces of the puzzle fell into place with horrifying clarity. By God, how had she not seen it before? How had she failed to realize?

"*You're leaving,*" she accused in a stunned whisper. "You are planning to go away and leave me here, aren't you?"

He snapped his head to the side, avoiding her gaze.

"Where, Will? Where are you going?"

"W.C. and I have talked about India, but that was—"

"Oh, my God." She laughed a terrible laugh.

"Now, Mel—"

"I cannot believe I was such a fool."

"Mel, it's not—"

"Don't!" She threw her hands into the air. "And don't tarry on my account. Go, Will. Go!" She shoved him in the chest with all of her might. "Go on, run. Run off and leave me here to take on your responsibilities, you miserable excuse for a man. Go on! Run! Keep running, Will Taggart, because that's all you'll ever do.

"Indeed, I see it all so clearly now," she said, her eyes wide and wild. "You can't stop running because you're afraid. Afraid that if you don't leave first, you'll wake up in the morning and discover that someone you care about has snuck away in the middle of the night to become a nun!"

His eyes shot viridescent sparks. "You don't know what the hell you're talking about."

"Oh, yes, I do," she said, her lungs burning with the need to cry. "I do. I only wish I'd figured it out long ago."

"Mel, it's not like that—"

"I see precisely what it's like, Will. And don't worry. I've learned my lesson, learned it well. I promise you I won't try to change you. Because you aren't worth the trouble."

Lifting her skirts, she turned and ran. She ran and ran, until the pain in her lungs was greater than the pain in her heart.

Twenty-two

Sweat poured down Will's back and shoulders, soaking his shirt and stinging the scratches he'd earned thrashing through the thorny underbrush. His throat was raw from shouting, his lips chapped and cracked.

Five hours. Five hours since Melisande had torn away from him, her eyes glassy and dark with unshed tears. Like a fool, he'd not gone after her. Angry and ashamed, he'd returned to the house, thinking they could sort matters out once they'd both had time to cool down. An hour had passed. Then another and another, and still Melisande had not returned home. He'd started to worry then. He'd gone to search for her, first at the distillery and the workmen's cottages, and then at the riverside mill. There'd been no sign of her, no footprints, no stray ebony hairs floating on the wind.

As the lilac haze of dusk had begun to wash into the glens, Will's worry had ripened to panic. He'd sent Fergus into town to fetch Wildcat and Alastair and together the three men had now been scouring the area for nearly an hour.

Will cupped his hands around his mouth, shouting for the hundredth time, "Mel!"

A faint echo bounced back to him from the heather-covered hills, and a frightened hare bounded out from behind a log. But no answer came. Only the faint whistle of the wind and the melodic chirping of grasshoppers. A chill was settling over the valley as the sun made its final good-byes. Will cursed to recall the light cotton gown Melisande had been wearing that afternoon. She'd be cold wherever she was. Cold and hungry. Hurt? Bloodied?

God, what if she had fallen into the river? What if the current was, at this moment, sweeping her away toward the sea?

Will gnashed his teeth until his jaw ached, wishing himself in the fires of hell. Damn him for a fool! Damn him! For days now, he'd known that he probably would not be leaving for India with Wildcat next month. Or, if he'd not known, he'd at least been coming to that realization, working toward acceptance of the fact that his wandering days were coming to an end. So why in the blazes had he even mentioned India to Mel? Had it been a final test for himself, the last mental hurdle he had to jump before reconciling himself to his decision?

Mel had accused him of being afraid. Aye, maybe he was. He'd long been aware of a buried anger within him; an anger that, contrary to what Wildcat believed, was not directed toward his mother. No, Will could honestly say he felt no bitterness for Maggie; years ago, he'd accepted that she had to follow her own path. But perhaps, Will reflected, that long-smoldering anger was directed inwardly toward himself. Perhaps he was angry with himself for feeling fear. Dammit, could Mel be right? Was that what had driven him all this time? Fear of losing what he loved?

One thing was for certain—he knew fear now. He was, in fact, terrified to his very core. Terrified that he had driven away the only woman he'd ever been able to care about. The only woman he'd ever been able to trust.

Mel, where are you?

In the distance, a bird trilled a shrill, wavering tune. Not a bird native to Berwickshire, though, but a signal from Wildcat indicating he had found something. Will lifted his head, trying to pinpoint the call. It came again from the direction of the river. Furiously Will lashed out at the branches in front of him, fighting his way out of the tangled brush. Through the semidarkness, he ran, his pulse hammering at treble pace.

Dear Lord, let him have found her. For either W.C. had located Mel or he'd found evidence suggesting that she'd slipped into the river's frigid waters. A broken tree limb, a flattened cut in the earth at the river's edge . . .

His heart froze in his chest. Up ahead, a few feet from the banks of the river, Wildcat was kneeling in the grass beside Mel's body, cradling her head in his lap. She lay limp and unmoving, her hair streaming about her like a black silken veil. An anguished sound ripped from Will's throat, and Wildcat turned toward him, his features immobile.

"I think," Wildcat said with unthinkable calm, "that she is starting to come around."

Will stumbled forward, falling to his knees at Mel's side.

"Oh, thank God," he murmured.

She looked as if she were merely sleeping, her breath gentle and even, her cheeks delicately flushed. Will searched for blood, but saw none, his worried gaze lifting to Wildcat.

"Is she injured? Anything broken?"

W.C. shook his head, his thick braid swinging like a pendulum. "Her knees are scraped and she has a lump on her forehead here"—he feathered his fingers across a reddened bump to the left of Melisande's brow—"but otherwise, she seems well."

"So she must have fallen and hit her head?"

"It looks that way," Wildcat said, pointing with his chin to a mound of rocks and the gnarled tree roots protruding from mushrooming tufts of clover. "I found her lying there."

Melisande groaned and turned her face into Wildcat's thigh.

"Mel?" Will took her hand, lightly stroking the palm. Damn, she was cold. Swiftly he stripped off his coat and draped it over her.

"Mel, can you hear me?"

She yawned. Hugely. And both Will and Wildcat chuck-led with relief.

"Hell of a place for a nap," W.C. said.

Melisande's eyelids fluttered and opened, closed, then opened again. "Will?" she said uncertainly.

"Aye, lass, I'm right here. It would seem you've taken a nasty tumble. How does your head feel?"

Her brows knit together. "It hurts."

"You've bumped it."

"Yes . . . I remember. I wasn't watching my steps and I tripped. But, goodness, that must have been hours ago. Is there no moon tonight?"

"No moon?" Will exchanged a tense look with Wildcat.

"It is so very dark," she said.

Will's stomach seized with dread. "Mel, the sun has just set."

"But it's as black as pitch—" Suddenly her fingers squeezed his bloodless, her eyes growing round. "Will, it's so dark . . . I cannot see."

He lowered his face to within a foot of hers, a thousand jumbled prayers rioting through his thoughts. "Mel, I'm right here," he said hoarsely. "You can't see me?"

She reached out and fumbled for the side of his cheek, her indrawn breath sharp in the quiet, dusk-filled glen. Against his jaw, prickly with beard, her fingers trembled for a long, long moment.

"God help me," she whispered. "God help me."

"If you're going to share secrets in corners, you'll need to be quieter than that," Melisande snapped, irritated by the indistinct buzz at the other side of the room. "I may be blind, but I can still hear, you know."

Two pairs of footsteps approached the bed, one almost silent, the other heavy and slow.

"Sorry, Mel," Will said. "The doctor was just telling me of two other cases similar to yours that he's seen."

"And?" Melisande asked, her fingers clenching around the frayed edges of the quilt. "Did those people recover their sight?"

The doctor cleared his throat in a series of sharp, hacking noises. Melisande wondered how old Mr. Factor was, and if he was as thin as his reedy voice implied.

"You must realize, Mrs. Taggart, that no two cases are ever exactly alike—"

"But did they?" she insisted. "Did they see again?"

The doctor's sigh was accompanied by the wafting smell of peppermint. Peppermint lozenges.

"Well, the first case involved a young lad of about twelve," the doctor said in a flat, lecturing tone. "After being kicked in the temple by a horse, his sight returned quite unexpectedly within five days of the accident. The lad simply woke up one morning and, voilà, his vision had returned. In the other instance, an Edinburgh woman of fairly advanced years fell down a flight of stairs. I am still following her case; however, I regret to report that, after a year's convalescence, she has yet to recover her sight."

"My, that's encouraging," Melisande said tartly. "One out of two."

"Now, Mel," Will cautioned, lifting her hand from the quilt to thread his fingers through hers.

She swallowed, grateful for the contact. Touch had suddenly taken on enormous importance to her. Will's touch, especially.

"So what *is* your prognosis, Mr. Factor? Will I see again?"

"Alas, I can make no predictions, Mrs. Taggart; however, if I had to venture an opinion, I'd say yes. I think it likely your vision will someday return."

"Someday?" She had never realized what a useless word it was.

"What about the bleeding?" Will asked.

Again the doctor let loose with a self-conscious sequence of *harrumphs* before answering, "I see no reason for concern, Mr. Taggart. From what I can ascertain, your wife is merely experiencing her monthly course."

Heat worked its way into Melisande's neck and throat.

"She'd thought she might be with child," Will said quietly.

Melisande dug her nails into Will's hand, determined not to cry.

"Well, if she was," Mr. Factor said, "it would have been very early. And a fall has been known to dislodge a pregnancy, particularly in the initial weeks."

She sensed the doctor's shrug. "Of course, we have no way of knowing," he added.

Melisande labored to calm herself with a deep inhalation, thinking ahead to the weeks to come, to the new life that awaited her. A life without sight.

"How long must I remain abed?"

"Mel—" Will started to protest, but she cut him off.

"You know I can't just lie here and do nothing, Will. I cannot simply wait for the day that my eyes decide to work again. You know I can't."

"Aye," he said. "I know."

"How long then?" Mel asked.

"I'd say a few days of bed rest are certainly in order," the doctor replied. "Then, if your head no longer pains you, I daresay you could begin accustoming yourself to . . ."

"To my blindness," Melisande finished for him.

"Yes."

"But what about treatment?" Will asked. "Surely there is something that can be done?"

"Mr. Taggart, there *is* no treatment. All that can be done for your wife is to pray."

"But that's not enough!"

Melisande felt the tension in Will flare red-hot.

"Don't, Will," she said tersely. One of them had to be able to accept this with courage and grace, and, by heavens, she surely was not yet up to the task.

"My sympathies to you both," Mr. Factor said. "But please remember it is probable that your vision will be restored, Mrs. Taggart. The only question is when."

She heard the doctor retrieve his bag from the bedside table, as Will offered his grudging thanks.

"We do appreciate you driving out at this hour."

"Of course. And do not hesitate to call me out again if there is any change in her condition."

Melisande leaned back against the pillows, her throat working around a lump of emotion. The door closed with a fatalistic *click.*

"I hate this," she said brokenly.

The mattress dipped as Will seated himself beside her. His scent, she realized, was already so achingly familiar to her. A heady combination of malt and leather that had lingered in her nostrils and on her tongue for nearly a month now—since that first night, the only night, they'd spent together as lovers.

"I hate it, too, Mel."

"If I weren't so blasted clumsy!"

"Mel, for God's sake, you can't blame yourself for this. It was an accident, and if anyone is at fault, dammit, it's me. I should not have told you about India."

She gave a sarcastic huff. "I daresay I would have figured it out eventually."

"No, you wouldn't have. Because if you had let me finish, I would have explained that I had already decided not to go."

"Oh, Will, please . . ." The threat of tears swelled in her throat.

"I swear to you, Mel, I'd already made my decision."

"*Before* I became blind?" she asked bitterly.

"Yes."

She pulled her hand free of his, hiding her eyes behind her splayed palm. She ought to have expected this from him, yet still her pride balked at the gesture. She wouldn't have Will like this. She couldn't.

Lowering her hand, she set her jaw to keep it from quivering. "I won't accept your pity."

"Well, that's good to hear, because I wasn't planning to offer any."

"I mean it, Will, I won't take pity from anyone. I . . . I don't want my family to know. At least, not yet."

He was silent a moment. "All right."

"And I refuse to be treated like an invalid. I—" Her voice cracked even as she lifted her chin. "I couldn't bear it."

"No, Mel." He brushed a lock of hair from her brow. "Neither could I."

So gentle, that touch. She had to bite at the inside of her cheek to keep the tears at bay. She wouldn't cry, dammit. She wouldn't.

And yet . . . Lord, she was scared. This neverending darkness was like an abyss, a hopeless, bottomless abyss from which she didn't have the strength to crawl. How was she going to endure it? Day after day? Night after night? And not knowing the difference between the two?

"You need to sleep," Will said, his words rough and uneven with fatigue. "We both do. Is there anything you want, Mel? Anything I can get for you?"

Besides my sight? the cynic inside her asked mockingly. "No."

Defeated, she scooted down beneath the bedding, tasting a salty sting at the back of her mouth. Will tucked the quilt around her shoulders and stood. She waited for the sounds of his leaving. All was silent.

Then something went *plop* on the wood floor, followed immediately by another *plop*. The mattress sagged and Will climbed into bed beside her, wrapping her up in his arms. She held herself perfectly still, rigid with shock. But only for a moment. As the salty sting pushed up into her nose and eyes, she turned toward him, burying her face in his linen-covered chest.

He smoothed his hand over her hair, whispering sweet words that made no sense.

She let him hold her, all the fury of the afternoon wiped clean in the face of true tragedy, true pain. She could not say whether she believed him or not, and she could not say whether it mattered. All she cared about was keeping the tears at bay. Holding them, holding them . . . Will holding her . . . until she finally succumbed to sleep.

Twenty-three

By fighting like hell, and threatening to tie her down if she didn't behave, Will managed to keep Melisande abed the following day. On the morning of the second day, however, he awoke with the roosters, peeked into her chamber and found her out of bed. Not only out of bed, but standing in the middle of the room . . . half-naked.

Tangled hopelessly in the folds of a red-and-white striped gown, Melisande looked to have caught herself in the sleeves. Backwards. With her arms stretched overhead, and wearing but a gossamer-light chemise and petticoat, she presented a thoroughly charming picture. A picture so fetching that Will felt his powers of restraint tested to their ultimate limits.

Mel abruptly ceased her struggles, turning toward the door. "Who's there?" she demanded suspiciously.

"It's me, Mel. And I'm just trying to decide if the gentlemanly thing would be to retreat quietly or to offer my assistance."

"Well, goodness, you can't leave me like this!" She wriggled her arms to underscore her difficulty, and her wriggling brought on a delightful jiggling of her bosom.

Oh, God. Will wet his lips, recalling the weight and texture and taste of her—

"Will, for heaven's sake, help me!" Her bare foot stamped on the wide plank floor.

Releasing an unsteady breath, he approached, fending off an arm that thrashed past his head. "Easy now, Mel. Easy. If you don't stop flailing around, you'll give me another black eye and I've known enough by your hand, thank you."

She muttered something unintelligible. Something not entirely ladylike.

"And what are you doing up and out of bed?" he asked. "As I recall, the doctor recommended a *few* days' rest."

"Pooh," she dismissed from inside the folds of the gown. "He said I could get up once the headache had gone."

"It has?" Will grabbed a fistful of gauzy material and unceremoniously yanked the dress up and off. Her hair tumbled free to slide in mussy black clumps down her back.

Standing there, silhouetted in the velvety light of morning, with only her plain cotton undergarments on, she was . . . exquisite. Not classically beautiful, but something so much more than beauty. She was a woman—a *real* woman. A little disheveled, slightly vulnerable and a whole lot desirable.

He stood there, holding the frock in his hands.

"You're lovely, Mel."

"Don't be ridiculous," she said with a frown, reaching blindly for the dress. "My jaw is too broad, my ankles heavy, and my nose sharp enough to use as an ice pick."

"Aye," he agreed, but his gaze still roved hungrily over her.

As she groped for the gown he held, her fingers accidentally swept across his chest, brushing over his nipple. She snatched back her hand. A blush suffused her cheeks.

"My gown?" she asked tightly.

"Here, let me help you." He took her hand and placed it atop his shoulder. "Hold on so you don't lose your balance," he said. "Let's try stepping into it."

He bent over and clasped hold of her ankle, gently lifting her foot from the floor. "Perfect," he murmured, his touch lingering a shade longer than necessary as he maneuvered the gown around her toes and heel.

"The other one," he said.

She shifted her weight, the creamy skin of her lower thigh skating against his cheek. Unable to resist, Will pressed his lips against the back of her knee in a caress so light, so fleeting. Her fingers tightened on his shoulder. Had she felt that stolen kiss?

"There," he said, his voice ragged. "Let's stand up now."

Damn, but this is wrong, he thought. *I ought to be undressing her, not helping her into her clothes.* Aye, he wanted to peel away that tempting layer of virgin-white cotton and lay open the sweet, ripe curves. . . .

He drew the gown past her hips, her waist, then paused before helping her into the bodice. How had it come to this? How could it be that he, a married man, did not believe he had the right to touch his wife? Just touch her—here— where the tiniest of freckles dotted the swell of her breast.

Yet, Will didn't feel as if he had that right. If he'd ever had it, he'd lost it two days earlier when she'd told him, her eyes shimmering with unshed tears, that he was a "miserable excuse for a man." Of course, she had reason to believe the worst of him, to despise him. He despised himself.

She had accepted his comfort the night of her accident, but, as far as Will knew, any warm body would have sufficed as well. Shocked and hurting, she'd needed someone. Anyone. And he had been that anyone.

Will cursed himself, aching with the desire to take this woman—his woman—into his arms. But what would she do? What would she say if he reached out and caressed the pink pearl-like nubs thrusting against the front of her chemise?

"Thank you."

Will snapped his gaze up. "What?"

"Thank you for your help, Will."

Her quiet words struck him like a slap in the face. *Helping her? Like hell.* He was outright ogling her, taking advantage of her blindness so that he could drink his greedy fill of her. Disgust filled him as he averted his gaze. He'd shamed himself. Shamed himself as a man.

With jerky, angry movements, he straightened the gown's bodice, directing Mel's arms into the sleeves.

"There. We've almost got it now," he muttered, keeping his touch impersonal as he fastened the thread buttons. He stepped back. Hurriedly.

A small frown was etched between Melisande's eyes. "I believe I can manage my stockings and shoes."

"Good. I mean—" Dammit, if he was angry with himself, he shouldn't take it out on her. Gentling his tone, he asked, "What about your hair? Shall I brush it for you?"

Her hand moved instinctively to her head before her fingers stilled and fell limp to her side. "No," she said, almost defiantly. "I am going to have to learn, aren't I?"

Her expression was such a pained mix of despair and courage that Will could scarce stand to look at her.

She stood there proudly and waited. Waited, he realized, for him to take his leave.

"I'll wait for you in the hall then," he offered. "We can go down to breakfast together."

"You don't have to—"

"For God's sake, Mel, I'm not letting you navigate those stairs on your own!"

She lifted her brows at the ferocity of his tone. After a moment's pregnant pause, she told him, "I'll need a minute or two."

As he headed for the door, Will looked back over his shoulder and watched Mel begin to sidle cautiously toward the dressing table, her arms outstretched, her features stiff with trepidation. Quickly he let himself out of the room.

In the narrow confines of the hall, Will leaned against the wall's wood paneling and closed his grit-filled eyes. From below, he could hear the soft *slap-slap* of a butter churn, accompanied by the distant tinkle of tinny cowbells. But the soothing sounds of morning were not enough to quiet Will's unrest, to quiet the turmoil raging inside him.

Emotions were eating him alive, guilt and shame and need waging a war inside him that demanded but one resolution. A resolution he'd been resisting these last two days, one he'd been fighting every step of the way. He'd grappled with it, he'd tried to ignore it. He'd invented a dozen reasons to avoid it, yet always he'd come back to the same terrible truth; a realization that made him want to howl himself hoarse, to pound his fists against the wall until they were bleeding and raw.

He had to let Mel go.

Will's entire body convulsed at the thought, yet he knew he had no other choice. It was the only decent thing to do, the only way to make amends. He never should have brought Mel to Scotland in the first place. He'd done so selfishly, for all the wrong reasons. For *his* reasons. Although he had convinced himself that Scotland would offer Mel a better future, that argument had been so much balm for his conscience. Only look at her future. Look what had become of his fire goddess, his warrior. His she-devil. And he was to blame.

You can't run from it this time, can you, Taggart? No, dammit, he couldn't. He had to accept responsibility for Mel's blindness and he had to do it honorably, just as she had always accepted her responsibilities. At the very least, he could say he'd learned that much from her.

God help him, but there was nothing left to hold Mel here. His last hope had rested with a baby and now even that hope was dead. Melisande was not carrying his child— would never carry his child—and the loss was like a pain in Will's heart. He had driven her away from him, caused her to lose her sight and possibly their baby.

If he couldn't forgive himself, how could he ever hope that she would? When he considered all that he'd taken from her—Melisande, the strongest woman he had ever known, reduced to fumbling across the room like an unsteady toddler.

But . . . he did know of a way to empower her again. A way for her to reclaim herself.

Behind him, the bedroom door creaked open. Melisande appeared on the threshold, her hair neatly combed, her face dewy and damp from its morning wash. She looked undaunted by fate's unfortunate turn.

"Is that currant scones I smell?" she asked with deliberate cheer.

"Aye. Didn't you tell Mrs. Baker they were your favorite?"

A faint smile brightened her eyes. Eyes that stared straight ahead into nothingness.

Will closed his fingers around Mel's elbow, but she tugged free.

"The other side," she explained. "I want to use my right hand to feel along as I go."

Will nodded and took hold of her left arm, guiding her toward the top of the stairs.

"Mel, I've been thinking . . ."

"And they say we've no miracles in the modern age."

Surprised, Will huffed a short laugh. "Saucy as ever, I see."

"At least one of us does," she commented wryly.

Will studied her profile, wondering where it came from—this awesome resilience of spirit in the face of tragedy.

"I was *thinking*," he repeated with exaggerated patience, "of the way we've had to work these last weeks, laying down our first set of casks. I'll confess it's been a lot more work than I'd anticipated, requiring more man hours than I'd ever come close to imagining. And though I know W.C. will stay as long as I ask him to, he'd never planned to remain in Dunslaw—"

"Neither had you," she pointed out, as her foot overshot the first stair riser and Will clutched at her, drawing her closer to his side.

"Careful now," he warned.

"Yes, I've got it."

He waited until she'd successfully negotiated the next step before saying, "At any rate, Mel, I believe we should give this prisoner reform idea of yours a try. In fact, I was thinking I'd go into Dunslaw today and find out what I could from the constable."

"I beg your pardon?" Her empty gaze was directed at a

point over his shoulder. "Are you thinking to rehabilitate men from the gaol?"

"Not me. You. You've always wanted to try your hand at it, haven't you?"

She gave her head a crisp shake. "I've abandoned that idea, thank you. As you so correctly stated, I can neither fix people nor can I change them. And to ever believe that I could was nothing short of hubris. The most egregious conceit imaginable."

"Now, wait a minute, Mel, there's a difference between changing people and helping them. I know I didn't appreciate that difference—even up to a few days ago—but I have had time to reconsider. I wager you *can* help some of those men, Mel."

She paused at the bottom of the stairs, her fingers exploring the wooden sphere atop the newel post. "All the same, Will, no. I cannot possibly be effective like this."

"Sure, you can. Or, at least, you can try. I know that, under the circumstances, I've got a helluva nerve asking you for anything, but I'm going to need some extra laborers. And soon. If you could turn around even two or three of those men, it might mean the difference between the distillery's failure or survival."

"Will, what you're proposing is ludicrous. I can't even dress myself, for heaven's sake. How can I effect any remedial methods? Without being able to see?"

"We'll help."

"And who, pray tell, is 'we'? Only you and Alastair know anything of the actual distilling process, therefore neither of you can be spared."

"Then Wildcat can help you."

"Wildcat?"

"Why not? I realize that you two haven't always seen eye to eye, but since he's finally decided that you're not a *medsit mtschitschank*—"

"A *what*?"

Will grinned. "An evil spirit," he explained, leading her into the dining room, where a platter of fresh scones awaited them in the middle of the pine table.

"Hah! Am I supposed to be flattered?"

Laughing quietly, Will pulled out a chair for her. "I don't know about flattered, but you won't have to worry about him making any animal sacrifices on your behalf."

Her lips pursed. "My relief knows no bounds."

Will took the chair beside her and reached for a scone. "Jam?" he asked.

"Yes. Please. No cream."

He ladled a generous spoonful of blackberry jam onto the edge of her plate. "In all seriousness, Mel, if you could give it a try for a couple of weeks . . ."

"And then?"

Will's grip on the spoon tightened. Could he do this? Could he say what must be said without feeling as if the words were being ripped from his soul?

"Well"—his jaw tensed—"then I'll repay you the twenty thousand pounds, and you'll be free to return home. I know that you are eager to get back to England, but, to tell you the truth, Mel, I would rather you didn't leave— If you could wait a few weeks, until . . ." *Blast it, Taggart, just spit it out!* "What I am trying to say is that I'd feel a helluva lot better knowing that I wasn't returning you to your family . . . blind."

She went stock still.

"I'm grateful for all your help, Mel. More grateful than I can say. And I know I shouldn't try to hold you here any longer—"

"Since there is no baby," she murmured, her features composed to the point of appearing frozen. In her lap, her fingers knitted neatly together. "You are asking me to stay in Scotland a little longer in the hopes that my sight will return? So that you won't have to feel guilty about sending me home as damaged goods?"

"Dammit, Mel," he hissed. Did she have to twist his words around?

"I do apologize," she said with mock courtesy. "Am I mistaken? Or is that not precisely what you are asking of me?"

Before Will could scramble for a response, Mrs. Baker

chose that extremely awkward moment to enter from the kitchen, tea tray in hand.

"Mrs. Taggart, how are ye this morning, ma'am?" the housekeeper asked, her spectacles fogged with steam.

"Well, Mrs. Baker. Blind, but well."

"Oh, ma'am, ye've been in my prayers. We've all been mighty worried about ye."

"Thank you," Melisande said. "But the doctor believes my condition to be only temporary, so let us not don our sackcloth and ashes just yet."

"No, ma'am." The housekeeper set the tray on the table, then wiped at a smudge on the wood with the corner of her apron. "Mr. Taggart, I've been meaning to ask ye. How's me sister's tonic workin' on that snorin' problem of yers? I would think with the missus' health sufferin', ye'd want to be nearer at hand."

Irritated, Will glanced up from crumbling his scone to pieces. "Tonic?"

"Aye, the fish oil tonic?"

Lord, was she referring to that foul, thick-as-molasses potion that had smelled like a sailor's armpit? The one he'd used to fertilize the beans in the back garden?

"I guess it's working just fine."

"It *is*?"

Melisande's high-pitched query drew Will's attention. What had raised her hackles? Then he realized. If he'd cured his snoring problem—

"Aye," Will said, sitting taller in his chair.

Suddenly, and quite selfishly, he was overcome by a perverse desire to assert what claim he still had over his wife. After all, if he was to be allowed only a couple of weeks more with her, he may as well make the most of them. Melisande might not like it, but, dammit, he wasn't the saint she was. If he had to do the right thing, he'd do it according to his rules. He'd let her go if he must, but not without first stealing a few moments for himself.

No, she'd not like it, but he'd always been a selfish bastard.

"But so soon?" Melisande protested. "Is the tonic supposed to work as swiftly as that, Mrs. Baker?"

"I can't rightly—"

"I've been taking twice the normal amount," Will lied without compunction.

"Ach, 'tis glad I am that I picked up another bottle from Rose," Mrs. Baker said, nodding sagely. "If ye've no objection then, I'll go ahead and move your things into the missus' room this afternoon, Mr. Taggart. That room you've been usin' is in need of a good floor-to-ceiling cleanin' anyway."

"Oh, but I don't know," Mel broke in. "I'm afraid I won't sleep as soundly with . . ."

"With your husband in your bed?" Mrs. Baker asked, chuckling. "No, lass, you won't. But you'll be a happier woman for it."

Will watched Melisande visibly struggle to come up with an objection, an argument to keep him from her bedroom. First her nose twitched. Then her eyelids. Then her lips twitched and trembled.

"Mrs. Baker," she said slowly. "As a matter of fact, Mr. Taggart has not yet had his tonic today. Would you be a dear and fetch your bottle? I'd feel better knowing for a certainty that he was taking the medicine."

"Surely, ma'am. I've got it right here in the kitchen."

The helpful housekeeper toddled out the door, and Will tipped his fingers to his brow.

"Touché," he saluted her.

Her head rocked side to side, her profile sober as Sunday. "I don't understand you, Will Taggart."

His lips turned up in a bitter smile. "I know, Mel. I don't understand myself either."

Twenty-four
꡷꡷

The stench of Mrs. Baker's snoring tonic lingered in Melisande's nose far into the afternoon, the mere memory of its scent enough to make the bile start to rise in her throat. For the life of her, she did not know how Will had managed to swallow two heaping spoonfuls of the vile stuff. Nor could she answer the more troubling question of why.

Once Will had pulled the tonic's cork, she had not even been able to remain seated beside him, the stench was so foul. Hastily she'd fumbled her way to the other side of the room, listening as Will, aided by Mrs. Baker's coaxing, downed two helpings of the nauseating potion. *Two.* Had her very life been at stake, Melisande doubted she'd have been able to swallow that tonic. Yet Will had done so. Willingly. Why?

In order to sleep in her room?

Seated at the parlor's front window, the sun warming her back, Melisande pressed the heel of her hand against her temple and tried to make sense of it. But it made no sense. Why would Will be so keen on sleeping with her, when he'd not so much as touched her these last weeks? No kisses, no caresses. Only a measure of innuendo here and there. He had, on occasion, mocked her about the strength of her

"passions"—and her supposed inability to control them—
but he'd not made any overtures. Goodness, two nights past,
he'd slept beside her, his touch as innocuous as that of a
brother. Not a lover. Not a man so desperate to share a
woman's bed that he'd drink something that smelled like
rotting fish guts.

It was all so terribly confusing. *He* was confusing. One
minute, he informed her that he was sending her away; the
next minute, he was contriving to sleep with her. What was
she to think? What was she to expect? Every time she
attempted to make sense of it, a glaring contradiction reared
its head.

For instance, what could be the reasons Will would want
to sleep with her again? To get her with child? Now, that
hardly seemed likely, since he hadn't been pleased the
first time around by the prospect of becoming a father.

All right then, did he hope to coerce her out of her
inheritance? But why bother? The monies were already his
to control.

Could it be that he was merely looking for sexual sport?
If that were the case, then she failed to understand why he'd
not approached her prior to this. She couldn't believe that
her blindness had suddenly made her more attractive to him.

Her blindness. God, how she hated it. She hated being
weak. She hated being dependent on others. But most of all,
she hated not being in control. And to maintain the
appearance of control, Melisande knew that she had to
maintain her calm; she could not allow her loathing for this
hateful, hateful condition to become apparent, to become
obvious to others. Though there was no way to hide her
blindness, she had to conceal her impotence. She couldn't
reveal the secret torment which she now lived with from
minute to minute, hour to hour. Day to day.

No, she decided, her blindness could surely not have
made her more attractive to Will. It might have inspired his
pity, but not his passion. How then? How might she explain
his sudden and inexplicable desire to share her bedroom?

Her heartbeat quickened. Perhaps Will had decided to
leave for India with Wildcat, after all. Could that be his

motive? Could sleeping with her be an opening gambit in his ploy to convince her to remain in Scotland? He hoped to convince her to serve as the distillery's caretaker by . . . *seducing* her?

She huffed beneath her breath, deeming that theory as far-fetched as any of the others. Mayhaps there was no real explanation. Mayhaps, as he'd said that morning, Tiger Taggart was just as confused as she was.

A hushed rustling at the doorway swung her around. "Hullo?"

"It's only me," Peter Taggart answered. "Am I disturbin' ye?"

"No, not at all. I'm waiting for Will to return from town."

Shuffling, hesitant footsteps drew nearer. "I wish I knew what to say, lass."

"About my loss of sight?" She summoned a smile, her fingers moving to massage the lump at her brow. "The doctor believes it to be an impermanent condition, so I am simply biding my time as patiently as I'm able."

"Aye, Will said ye were a brave li'l soldier."

"Did he?"

"Aye. He thinks the world of ye, he does. Was racked up somethin' fierce when he'd thought he'd lost ye."

Melisande resisted the warmth spreading insidiously through her limbs. Though Will might give lovely compliments and believe her to be "too good" for him, she had to remember that the man was not to be trusted. If he thought to abandon her here with a child while he flitted from one continent to the next—

"I wanted to thank ye, Melisande, for what ye tried to do the other day."

"Thank me?" She fought to bring her thoughts back into focus. "Peter, I don't believe you should be thanking me. I understand that you were terribly upset after Maggie departed."

"Aye, I was," he said with regret. "And while ye might not understand it, lass, the joy of having seen her again was worth the pain that followed."

"Oh, Peter, no."

"Now, now, 'tis nothin' to fuss about. In fact, I think ye may have done me a favor, lass. Though it hurt mightily to watch Maggie go, afterward I came to somethin' of an understandin'. Though I was hurtin' bad, I had to admit to myself that the joy of seein' Maggie again meant more to me than the sadness I knew when she left. Just as the happy years me and Maggie shared together were more important than the pain I felt when she left us.

"Now," he added, "I'm not sayin' that it stops hurtin'. I don't think it'll ever stop hurtin'. But I think I'm beginnin' to accept that the joy Maggie gave me is of greater value than the pain."

"Oh, I am so glad to hear you say that." She reached out for him and he took her hands in both of his, his palms soft and supple.

"Ach, don't get me wrong, lass. I'll never be as content as I was when I was with her. But maybe life holds only so much happiness for each of us. And maybe we have to cherish the moments we are given."

Melisande pondered a moment, then gave a small, quiet nod. "That sounds like very wise counsel, Peter. Words I will keep close to my heart."

He patted her hand, then an alertness shimmied down his arm. "Hey now, lass, I think I see Willy comin'. He must have taken the gig into town, eh?"

Melisande followed the sound of Peter's voice, the sunshine striking her full in the face. "Yes, he did, as he's hoping to find additional laborers in town. Alastair put the barley to steep yesterday, so by next week we'll be in the midst of it again, the fermentation and distilling. We desperately need to hire a few extra hands. If we continue working the men we have now at such an exacting pace, I don't think we'll be able to keep them."

"Is that right? Hmm, maybe I can make myself more useful. At least on the instruction side of the business."

"That would be wonderful. I'm sure Will would be grateful for any help."

The air around her shifted as she felt Peter Taggart lean forward.

"Ach, I was wrong, Melisande lass. It's Wildcat who's driving and he looks to have three—no, four men with him. I wonder where Willy went off to."

Frowning, Melisande wondered the same. Within minutes, wheels rattled, metal screeched, and horses snorted as the gig pulled up in front of the house.

"I'll go meet W.C." She attempted to rise, but Peter detained her with a light touch on her arm.

"He's coming inside right now, lass. No need to get up."

The Lenape Indian's scent preceded him into the room. A scent, Melisande realized, that differed greatly from Will's. Although both men carried the smell of the outdoors, Wildcat's essence was more . . . primitive. More basic. As Melisande imagined a river rock would smell if it had an aroma.

"Where is Will?" she asked without preamble.

"He and the constable had to work out some details," Wildcat said. "He'll be back later."

"So these are the men?"

"Interesting group," Peter Taggart commented. From the sound of his voice, Melisande could tell that he'd moved closer to the window.

"Tiger seems to believe they'll do," Wildcat said.

"And you?" Melisande asked, attempting to follow his light tread as he entered the room. "What's your opinion?"

"I think they'd be fools to give us any trouble" came the dangerously soft reply.

Melisande nodded, deciding that Will and Wildcat shared more in common than a woodland smell. "And what did Will arrange with them? Do they know what to expect?"

"Will told them they'd have today to rest, but tomorrow the work begins."

"Good. Mrs. Baker has left clean clothing in the laborers' cottages—six sets as I'd expected more men than four. But it matters not. Instruct them to bathe and make themselves presentable, and I'll go down after tea to introduce myself."

"Whatever you want," Wildcat said.

She couldn't hear him, but she suspected he was turning away.

"Oh, Niankwe—"

"Hmm?"

Her chin lifted. Now was not the time for false pride. "Will told me that you were the one to find me after I'd fallen and hit my head. I am in your debt, Mr. MacInnes. And deeply grateful."

Silence reigned until he said, "I'll come get you at five o'clock."

Wildcat watched as Melisande carefully paced back and forth in front of the four prisoners, not the smallest hint of fear discernible in her stiff, regal bearing. As she marched, she punctuated every few steps with a sharp jab at the ground with her closed parasol. Dressed in a dark navy gown with military-style epaulets at the shoulders, she looked as if she ought to be leading troops into battle or strategizing a war campaign.

Wildcat had to admit she put on a damned good act. One convincing enough to make all but him believe her utterly unaffected by her blindness. No one else, he thought, could have seen past the facade to the truth, but he had been studying Melisande for weeks now.

In the beginning, she'd worried him, then she'd become a riddle he had to solve. She was an interesting woman; if only because he slightly feared her, when he feared nothing or no one—man, woman, or beast. Yet, like him, she was skilled at masking her fear. And she was scared. Or, at the very least, distressed. The same way he would be distressed to awake and find his legs chopped off at the knees.

As Melisande continued to pace, Wildcat was privately thinking it a lucky happenstance that she had temporarily lost her vision. The sight of their new crew was something less than pleasing to the eye.

They made for an eclectic assortment, these *wapsitschik*. There was a tall one, a short one, a round pink one, and one that resembled an oversized praying mantis. All four men were guilty of crimes of poverty, not violence. Drifters, vagrants, and pickpockets, the men had been questioned one by one by Tiger until he'd been satisfied of their "appropriateness" for Melisande's project.

When Wildcat had first learned of the She-Devil's rehabilitation venture, he'd deemed it *kpitschewagan*. Foolish. The absurd workings of a witch-woman's mind. Yet as the weeks had passed, and he'd learned more of life on this side of the ocean, he'd begun to reassess his views. It was not easy for a man here. Either you lived according to the laws—laws not written by you—or you paid the price. There was no middle ground, no place to just *be*. In Wildcat's land, a man could pack up his belongings and roam until he'd found a comfortable spot, a piece of the world where he, and he alone, reigned. Not so here in Scotland. Even less so in England.

So W.C. could understand how Melisande might sympathize with the misfortunes of her countrymen. If she wished to help . . . Well, why not? From what he'd seen of the woman, she sure as hell knew how to make things happen.

After dispensing with the introductions, Melisande started to outline the method by which she would set this motley crew on the path of righteousness and goodness.

"Since, at present, I am unable to read, I will need a volunteer to serve as my eyes. Are any of you gentlemen literate?"

One hand raised tentatively.

"The short one," Wildcat told her in an aside.

"Mr. Brodie." Melisande nodded approvingly. "Very good then. We will begin with John Locke and Francis Bacon," she said. "Two of my personal favorites. And, of course, we'll also look to scripture for spiritual support."

The tall man named Findlay rolled his eyes, causing the round pink *schwonnak* to answer with a knowing smirk. In an instant, Wildcat's hand fell to the hilt of his knife, his insistent gaze silently demanding that the men heed him and heed him now. They did, their eyes inexorably drawn to his glower. The pink man faded to a shade of white, while Findlay shrugged an abashed apology. Wildcat did not speak, but sent a message loud and clear: *Those who do not respect the woman will learn to respect my blade.*

"Initially," Melisande explained, "half the day will be spent working in the mill or the distillery and the other half will be spent working with me. My goal is to provide you with the tools necessary to lead productive lives. Law-abiding, productive lives. I will warn you—I may be a woman, but I am neither softhearted nor overly tolerant. Little leniency will be given. There is to be no drinking of spirits, no carousing. If, after two weeks, you've not met my expectations, you're to be returned to the Dunslaw lockup. Are there any questions?"

Four sets of eyes settled on Wildcat, wordlessly asking if questions were allowed. He gave a curt nod and waved toward Melisande.

"Ma'am?"

"Yes?" she said, with a tilt of her head.

"It's me, ma'am. Brodie. I do beg your pardon, but I was wonderin'—are we to be paid?"

"If, after two weeks, you've not been returned to the constable, yes, you will be paid like any other laborer."

"Can, uh, we go into town?" Praying-Mantis Man asked.

"Not during your initial training period, Mr. Grant," Melisande said. "I don't mean to be severe, but I am responsible for your conduct. Until I have determined whether or not you are benefiting from our program, you are obliged to remain here at the distillery."

"How are we to eat?" Grant asked plaintively.

"The cottage you four gentlemen will be sharing has been stocked with food stuffs and supplies. The first, and most important, lesson you must learn is self-reliance. You will cook for yourselves, clean for yourselves, do for yourselves."

"But my wife—God rest her soul—saw to those chores, ma'am. I sure as heck don't know how to cook or clean."

"Hmm-mm." Melisande's lips pursed disapprovingly. "And before your wife, your mother most likely took care of your needs. No longer, Mr. Grant. If you don't cook, you go hungry. If you don't clean, you live in squalor, and *that* I will not abide. Above all, you and your three companions must learn to take responsibility for yourselves. Are there any more questions?"

Shocked, woebegone, and disgruntled countenances answered her.

"Anyone unhappy with the arrangement," Wildcat broke in, "can be back in Dunslaw before nightfall. Any of you prefer a gaol cell to Mrs. Taggart's terms?"

"No, sir."

"Nay."

Melisande waited a second then bobbed her head. "Good. Tomorrow morning at six o'clock sharp, you are to meet Mr. MacInnes at the mill. Any man who is even a minute late will be immediately discharged from the program."

She slapped her parasol into her gloved palm with a firm *thwack*. One of the men flinched.

"You are dismissed," she said briskly.

Wildcat shook his head as he watched the men trudge back to the cottage. He had to be getting soft, he thought. Crazy as it seemed, he actually felt sorry for the poor bastards.

Twenty-five

꩜

Will *was not* in the sunniest of spirits when he returned home later that night. Put simply, he'd had a helluva day.

Unlike Cullscombe's accommodating Mr. Bell, the Dunslaw gaolkeeper had not proved nearly as eager to be rid of his charges. The constable, concerned that his superiors would not approve, had made Will jump through the proverbial hoops before he had released the four prisoners. Then, after the hoops had been jumped and the prisoners delivered, the constable had dared demand more money than had initially been agreed upon—which just went to show that the man was a very poor judge of character. Tiger Taggart was not the fellow you wanted to try and double-cross.

At any rate, after a bit of unpleasantness, all had been resolved, though Will was of the opinion he'd have done better to send Mel into town. She would have made mincemeat of that weaselly little gaolkeeper.

Rolling his shoulders, Will climbed to the top of the stairs, the single candle he held sending weak, wobbly shadows onto the floor. Unseasonably warm for late spring, the day had been almost hot, evening now but a shade cooler. The air sat heavy in the house, humid and soft.

At the head of the staircase, Will paused, suddenly remembering that he had no bedchamber to retire to. Earlier that day, Mrs. Baker had moved his clothes and personal effects to Mel's room, stating that she was going to turn the other chamber "upside-down" in a frenzy of cleaning.

He rubbed the side of his jaw. He wasn't really in the mood to go a few rounds with Mel. But dammit, after the day he'd endured, neither was he going to bed down on the sofa. Besides, the hour approached eleven o'clock. Surely Mel would be asleep by now, and he could slip in beside her without stirring up commotion.

Her room was dark as he noiselessly nudged open the door. The frail candlelight did not reach the bed from the doorway, nor could he hear Melisande breathing in the one-two cadence that had become familiar to him at Mooresby Hall. He edged toward the wardrobe—

"What are you doing?" Mel asked from the darkest corner of the room.

Will stifled a sigh. "I'm going to bed."

She weighed his statement for the space of a few seconds, then calmly asked, "What delayed you in town?"

Will's tension ebbed. Apparently she'd accepted the fact that he'd be sleeping in her room.

"Well, as it turns out, the Scots gaolkeepers aren't quite as agreeable as their Devonshire counterparts," he said, lighting a second candlestand.

"Is there a problem?"

"Not anymore," he grimly assured her. He glanced over to the corner where Mel sat in a stiff ladderback chair. She had changed into her night rail, her armor of white cotton. "Why are you still awake at this hour?"

"I could not sleep. I don't seem to know anymore the difference between night and day."

"There's been no change?"

"No."

Will's brows spiked together and he wished that he had not been so thoughtless as to ask. He sat himself on the edge of the bed and tugged at his boots. "Have you had any headache?"

She started to answer, but was interrupted by the sound of his boots clattering to the floor. Their conversation, already strained, suddenly became uncomfortable, awkward and tense. It was, he realized, because he was disrobing. Undressing before her as if they were, in truth, man and wife. They'd not shared this degree of intimacy since that night in Mooresby Hall.

"No," Mel answered, a quaver in her voice. "No headache."

His pulse accelerating, Will faltered as he unbuttoned his coat. Blast it, he had made a mistake. A big mistake. At breakfast, he'd been furious with himself and not thinking clearly, when he had manipulated his way into Melisande's bedchamber.

Greedy to seize as much time with her as he could, he had impetuously decided that he had to be with her no matter the cost. Well, it looked as if it *was* going to cost him, all right. Cost him plenty. For how was he going to lie down beside Mel every night, knowing that he would probably never again experience the sweet pleasures of making love to her?

Don't make it worse, he told himself. *Stop thinking like that, Taggart.*

"Did, uh, W.C. come by with the men?" he asked, trying to divert his thoughts.

"Yes, I spoke to them briefly. Though it's too early to say, they all appear to be strong candidates for corrective behavior."

They damned well better be. He'd interviewed nearly three dozen men to cull those four, two of whom he'd had to travel all the way to Lauder to find. Aye, Mel didn't know it, but she had the likeliest prisoners to be had in the entire shire of Berwick. Once assured that all four were mild-mannered and nonviolent of character, Will had set about convincing them that *he* was none of those things. He had made clear that if anyone failed to satisfy Mel's expectations, he'd throttle the fellow with his bare hands . . . and then he'd get angry.

They had seemed to get his point.

Admittedly the entire project was questionable, bordering

on the absurd if you asked him, but Will hadn't known what else to do for her. And he had wanted to do something. Gift Mel with a little piece of her old self again, a little piece of her dream.

"So what did you say to them?" Will asked.

"I told them that we would begin with two weeks of preliminary instruction. However"—her forehead wrinkled—"at the time, I hadn't considered that my sight might return in the interim. . . ."

"If it does, don't worry, I won't keep you," Will interrupted, struggling to keep his words free of rancor. He hated that she was so anxious to leave him. "You're free to go whenever you want, Mel. You know that."

"Yes," she said quietly. "I do."

Will gave an irritated yank at his coat sleeve. Something crinkled from inside the coat's pocket, reminding him of what else he had picked up in Dunslaw. "I almost forgot. There was a letter waiting for you in town. A letter from your sister."

"Eileen?"

Melisande's features came alive as she rose eagerly from the chair, her slender fingers outstretched. Then she emitted a curt laugh. Her hand fell to splay self-consciously across her stomach. "For heaven's sake, what am I doing?" she asked, embarrassed. "You will have to read it to me, won't you?"

Will stilled in the act of removing his shirt. "You want me to read it to you now?"

"Yes. Will you do that?"

He would have had to be even a greater blackguard than he already was to deny her request. He left his shirt hanging and broke open the letter's seal. The bite of warm wax was strong in his nose as he leaned closer to the bedside candle.

"'My dearest Melisande,'" he read. "'It was with considerable astonishment that I learned of your decision to leave Mooresby Hall and to travel to Scotland with Mr. Taggart. Benjamin and I had only just returned from our honeymoon trip to Brighton when I received word from George of your departure. You may well imagine my surprise, dear sister. A surprise that soon developed into delight.

"'Although I had expressed to you my concerns regarding Mr. Taggart—'" Scowling, Will set the paper down on the star-patterned quilt. "Mel, maybe you should have Mrs. Baker read this to you tomorrow."

"No. I won't be able to stand waiting."

Will scanned ahead a half-dozen lines, noting that his name appeared more than once. "But I seem to be the primary topic of discussion."

"Does that bother you?"

"I would think it would bother *you*."

She lifted an indifferent shoulder. "I have nothing to hide. Go on," she urged.

He shook the single sheet of paper and read on. "'Although I had expressed to you my concerns regarding Mr. Taggart, I see now how sadly I misunderstood you, Melisande dear. I can be the silliest of girls, as you well know, and I fear that my preoccupation with the wedding cast a shadow over my judgment. Why, now I can see that 'twas obvious you were nurturing a *tendre* for your handsome Scot—'"

Melisande made a low, anguished sound and hurriedly stumbled around the end of the bed. "That Eileen," she muttered breathlessly. "Sweet-tempered, but her insight leaves much to be desired. Perhaps I will ask Mrs. Baker to read the letter to me tomorrow, after all." She thrust out her hand, wiggling her fingers with impatience. "May I have it please?"

Intrigued, Will's brow furrowed. "Why, Mel lass, you appear somewhat flushed."

He continued to read aloud. "'. . . yet, I, vain creature, was too busy to note your interest or to lend proper counsel when you sought it. 'Tis clear to me now that if Mr. Taggart could inspire in you the depth of feeling we discussed—'"

"Will!" Melisande lunged forward, making a mad swipe for the letter. She just missed his nose. "Will, give me the letter."

"Wait a minute, Mel, this is getting interesting," he said

with a grin. "What does Eileen mean by 'depth of feeling'?"

Tap-tap-tap went Mel's bare foot.

"I have no idea," she said tersely.

"But she writes that the two of you discussed it."

Her tapping grew more agitated before suddenly she made another desperate lunge for the letter. Will dodged her by rolling to the middle of the bed.

"Will, I am not playing games," she bit out. "Give me the letter."

"Not until you explain."

"You're behaving childishly."

"Aye."

Then, without warning, she launched herself forward, pouncing on him with all fours like a cat.

"Ugh," he groaned, as her elbow dug into his stomach and the heel of her hand connected with his jaw. She thrashed atop him, her fingers flying this way and that, as the letter drifted from his grasp to fall to the floor.

"Jeez, Mel—ouch, dammit! Stop that now."

With one swift maneuver, he grabbed hold of her hands and flipped her over onto her back, pinning her to the mattress. Mel lay there, breathing heavily, her arms stretched over her head.

"Cad."

He laughed and brushed his hair back from his face. "Come on, Mel. I'll give you the letter as soon as you explain what Eileen is talking about."

She scowled, her lips thinning, then drawing into an annoyed pucker. "You make too much of it," she said at last.

"Let me be the judge of that, will you?"

"Really, it's nothing," she said, turning her head to the side. Her nose aligned perfectly with a star's pointed tip on the faded quilt. "I had sought Eileen's advice the day you kissed me in the garden at Mooresby Hall. Being, um"— she wet her lips with her tongue—"unfamiliar with the male-female relationship, I'd gone to Eileen to ask about . . ."

"To ask about lovemaking?"

"Yes."

"Then what's this about, 'depth of feeling'?"

Melisande's chest heaved in an overstated sigh. "Goodness, I don't know. Eileen has always been an intolerable romantic. Apparently when I told her I was . . . affected by your kisses, she took it to signify that more than my lips were engaged."

"Huh." A touch disappointed, Will wondered what he thought—or hoped—Mel's answer might be. He leaned back, releasing her arms. She still could not get up, however, since he sat straddling her lower body. And he was in no hurry to move.

"So," he asked, "did she answer your questions to your satisfaction?"

"More or less. And have I answered yours equally as well?" she asked in a lemon-sour tone.

"Not entirely."

"Oh, you impossible—" Her jaw clamped shut.

Fanned across the quilt, her hair was streaked with ribbons of blue and indigo, as dark as the night itself. Will took a lock between his fingers and rubbed it, releasing its clean, sharp scent.

"Was it enough for you, Mel?"

Her lashes fluttered in confusion. "Enough?"

"That night we shared together," he said. "Was it enough for you?"

Her eyes widened, her every muscle going rigid. He wrapped the strand of hair around his finger, fascinated by its uncompromising lack of curl.

"You know," he said in a hushed voice, "it's possible to experience all that again."

She waited a heartbeat before asking huskily, "Why would we choose to?"

"Because we can."

"Wouldn't you worry about . . ." Her throat worked. "A baby?"

"There are ways to prevent that."

She said nothing. Will felt his groin grow heavy in the lush cradle of her hips.

"Do you know, Mel," he whispered, as he drew her hair

across his lips, "how many nights I've lain in my bed, agonizing, asking myself if ever again I will know the weight of your breasts in my palms . . . the softness of your belly . . . the taste of you on my tongue."

Her eyes closed. "This morning you said I will soon be returning to England."

Remorse knifed through him, as he soundly, silently cursed his misguided sense of chivalry. If he had any sense, he'd chain her to him until the end of eternity. Lock her away so that she'd be forever his.

"That does not mean we have to squander the time that remains to us," he argued. "Isn't it better to seize the opportunities that we are given, Mel, to take what pleasure we can from each other? Now?"

"Your father said something to me of a similar vein this morning."

"Da asked to make love to you?"

She grinned crookedly. "No. He said that we should cherish the rare moments we are given. *Carpe diem,*" she added in a whisper.

"Seize the *night,*" he answered her, stroking her hair, his touch as light as morning's breeze. "We should, Mel. We should just let it happen. Don't think. Don't question. Just let me love you while I still can."

Dammit, he knew he was pleading, but he didn't care. Nothing else mattered now. Not pride. Not ego. Only this woman.

Slowly she turned her face toward him, her lips parted in questing wonder, her sightless eyes seeking. Lifting both hands, she carefully found his neck and cupped it, as her fingers combed through to the ends of his unbound hair. A small smile of resignation curled her mouth.

"Seize me," she invited.

Joy sizzled through him, racing along his nerve endings like fire. Bending his head, he gratefully kissed the inside of her wrist, his lips dry with sudden relief.

"Melisande, Melisande," he moaned as he buried his face into the curve of her elbow. The crisp cotton nightgown held the scent of her, the natural perfume that was her and her alone.

"I wish I could see you," she said, part-apology, part-regret.

He pulled back to study her and her fingers fell away from his hair. "You don't need to see me. Only feel. Feel what I can do for you." Taking her hand, he drew her fingers to his turgid manhood. "And feel what you do to me, Melisande Taggart. The power you wield."

She squeezed him experimentally through his clothing. He could not hold back his pleasured gasp. She smiled then. A wicked smile. A she-devil's smile.

Again her fingers moved over him, testing his length. And his self-control.

"Mel, sweetheart," Will said shakily, grabbing at her hand. "If you keep that up, we'll be done before we get started."

She fumbled for the hem of his shirt, tugging. "Well, if I only have touch with which to enjoy you . . ."

Within seconds, Will had the shirt off and flung into a corner. He couldn't believe that he had almost forgotten Mel's spirited sense of lovemaking. Even their first night together, he'd been curious whether prim and proper Melisande, the same woman who lectured about sitting with "limbs contained," would come to his bed or that other woman he'd seen glimpses of. The fire goddess, the siren. She had surprised him, but not disappointed. No shrinking violet, she. No frightened virgin. Melisande made love as she lived. With a boldness and confidence that was the stuff of men's fantasies.

Aye, what the lass lacked in finesse, she more than made up for in enthusiasm.

Will rolled onto his side, taking her with him. She laughed, a nervous, happy sound of surrender.

"This is odd," she said breathlessly, her fingers tangling in the curls on his chest.

Will brushed her hair from her face with a tender hand. "Because you cannot see?"

"Yes."

"You can trust me," he told her, understanding how vulnerable she must feel.

"Can I, Will?"

His gut clenched. He wanted her to trust him again. So much he wanted that. "Aye, Mel, you can."

He kissed her gently at first. As gently as he was able. His mouth shifted over hers with infinite care, cherishing, worshiping. Her lips parted. His tongue probed farther, meeting hers in a lingering, provocative dance. He wanted to be sensitive to Melisande's needs, to move her along slowly, to make it perfect. Perfect for her.

They kissed for hours. Or so it seemed. Time had no meaning as they explored each other with hands and mouths and sighs and endearments.

Will's lungs were heaving when he finally began to draw her night rail up from her knees. The soft cotton slid over her thighs, baring her flesh so white and smooth.

"Oh, Will, I had missed this," she whispered as he delicately feathered his fingers across her hip.

"Not as much as I did, I vow," he told her hoarsely.

She helped him discard the last of her clothing so that she lay there bare beneath him. Her fingers traveled from his chest to his hair then to his waist, where they met the band of his trousers.

She hesitated and he knew why. The balance of power between them needed to be set right. In quick, jerky movements he shucked his trousers, then slid the length of his body along the length of hers.

"That's better," she said, smiling.

"Aye," he agreed, his member hot against the cool heaven of her thigh.

He kissed the underside of her breast. She sighed. He kissed the tip of her breast. She gasped. He drew her nipple into his mouth, suckling her deeply until her agitated movements beneath him pushed him to the edge.

"Mel, my Mel," he whispered, feeling the heat rise within him and threaten to spill over.

"Yes, Will, now. Please."

She spread her legs for him, generous and sweet, inviting

him to take her as he had so longed to do. But he knew if he entered her now, he'd not be able to control the liquid fire pulsing within him. Instead, his fingers played over her, drawing circles on the tender pink flesh at her center.

She bucked against his hand, as her hair whipped from side to side on the quilt. Flushed and dewy with perspiration, her flesh shone like cream in the soft candlelight, her thighs tensing and untensing.

"Will, oh, Will, I beg you, now! Now!"

Her frantic cries broke the dam of his control; he could wait no longer. He positioned himself above her and drove home, gritting his teeth to find her as tight as a virgin.

Melisande clutched at him, bucking her hips, moving with him, the chords in her neck taut. Their rhythm was savage and dark, drawing them deeper and deeper into the shadowy vortex of desire.

Suddenly Melisande reached her zenith with a piercing cry, her muscles squeezing around him, forcing a guttural cry from his throat. At the crucial moment, Will withdrew by wrenching his body up then down, pumping his seed into the pure, snowy sheets.

Beneath him, Mel's breath rasped into the silence.

And Will's heart revealed to him a truth.

Twenty-six

" '*It is one* thing to show a man that he is in an error, and another to put him in possession of truth.' "

"Well done, Mr. Brodie," Melisande interrupted, signaling with an upraised finger for the man to stop reading. "I think Mr. Locke's sentiment a fitting conclusion to today's lesson, since all four of you gentlemen have been shown to be in error, to have erred against society. The question remains: How then will we put you in possession of the truth? Tonight I want you to ponder Mr. Locke's words as they pertain to you personally and be prepared to discuss them tomorrow.

"And Mr. Grant," she added, as an afterthought, "see to it that you mend the hole in your jacket's sleeve. A gentleman does not go about with his clothing torn or rumpled."

"But, ma'am, how did ye know—"

"It matters not, Mr. Grant. Repair it."

"Yes, ma'am."

With a satisfied smile, Melisande rose from the rough plank table she used as a desk and said, "You have all done well this first week. I hope that we may continue as we have begun. I will see you tomorrow afternoon at precisely two o'clock."

"'Day, ma'am."

"Thank you, Mrs. Taggart."

"Good day," Melisande said, listening to the men's booted feet shuffle from the makeshift schoolroom—the last of the laborers' cabins left unoccupied.

A draft from the open door played across Melisande's arms, as she felt her way to the other end of the table, where Mr. Brodie had left Locke's *Essay Concerning Human Understanding*. A hint of rain hung in the air, the breeze stiffer and cooler than the norm. She shivered, groping for the knitted shawl she'd left draped over a chair. She found the shawl, then located the book.

She was marking the page where they had left off when she heard a pair of voices engage in heated conversation outside the cabin. Though Melisande could not make out the words, the tone was definitely argumentative; more than a discussion of the weather was taking place.

Guiding herself with her hands around the table, she headed for the door as swiftly as she could. As far as she knew, there had been no quarrels between the men. But that did not mean there never would be any.

She reached the cottage's entrance in time to hear Wildcat say ominously, "No excuses."

"But I—" another voice answered. The voice of Mr. Findlay, the forgerer.

"No," Wildcat broke in, his voice as flat and sharp as the knife he carried. "You save your excuses for the constable, Findlay."

"Mr. MacInnes?" she asked. "Is something amiss?"

The muffled rustling of clothing told her that the two men had turned toward her.

"Oh, Mrs. Taggart, I—"

"Shut your mouth," Wildcat growled. "And don't move."

Melisande gripped the door, her anxiety expanding. Though Wildcat had proven to be the epitome of helpfulness and cooperation this last sennight, she knew that at the beginning of their experiment he'd not put much faith in her powers to rehabilitate their quartet of apprentices. He'd been helpful, but guarded, expressing a vague satisfaction with the men's work, yet saying little else. His doubts aside, Melisande knew that Wildcat would in no way sabotage her efforts or undermine her authority with the men. Therefore she had to assume that something truly disturbing had occurred with Mr. Findlay for Niankwe to speak as he did.

A twig splintered directly in front of her, a second before she detected the faint click of the beads in Wildcat's braid.

"Sorry," he said emotionlessly.

"What has happened?"

"Findlay snuck into town last night. Went so far as to 'borrow' Attila. I just came from the stables, where I found the evidence."

Melisande felt a pang in her stomach. *No.*

"Are you certain?" she asked, shamed to hear the tremor of disappointment in her voice.

"He's as good as confessed. Said he had to have a drink."

"How?" she bit out. "How could he do such a thing after all the hours we've spent talking of self-control, abstinence, the power to create your own destiny?"

Wildcat snorted. "He created his own destiny, all right."

She grimaced, knowing that W.C. spoke no more than the truth. Findlay had done this to himself. No one else. Yet why then did she feel so utterly wretched? Why was it that she felt as if she were the one who had failed?

The Lenape must have read her thoughts. "You could not have expected to save all of them," he told her. "Three out of four . . ."

"Three out of four isn't good enough," she whispered tightly. The wind whipped her hair into her face and she ruthlessly shoved it back over her shoulder. She was not one to settle for less than total victory. Compromise had never been an elective in the world of Melisande Mooresby.

"What do you want me to do?" W.C. asked.

Melisande's fingers clenched in the folds of her skirt. She was hurt. Hurt by Findlay's betrayal of her trust. "Exactly as we said we would do if one of them strayed from the program. Return him to Dunslaw. *Now.*"

The air moved as if Wildcat were nodding. "Come on, Findlay. Let's go."

"No! It won't happen again, I swear it. Mrs. Taggart, if I might—"

It all happened so swiftly. She heard Findlay protest. Then there was a rush of movement. Someone pushed into her. She stumbled. *Crack*—the back of her head slammed into the corner of the doorjamb.

"Clumsy bastard," Wildcat growled. A thump followed, the sound of flesh meeting flesh, or of a fist making contact with a jaw.

Before she could even register what had taken place, Wildcat's fingers were digging into her upper arms. "God-damned son of a bitch, doesn't he know Tiger'll have my scalp if you've even got a friggin' scratch on—"

"I'm fine," she interrupted in a rush, uncertain she wanted her vocabulary expanded by some of Wildcat's more colorful oaths. "Truly, I'm fine."

Though she was not entirely fine. Stars danced before her eyes, but thankfully they were performing a sedate minuet, not a boisterous country dance.

Wildcat tugged at her. "I'm going to get you back to the house."

"No." Melisande held her ground, as the stars began to clear and Wildcat's grip dropped away. "It was only a bump, and I am not going to return to the house since I agreed to meet Will after the tutoring session." She probed the back of her head. No blood warmed her fingers. "Honestly, Wildcat, I am perfectly fine."

A groan sounded from a point near Melisande's feet. "Be quiet," W.C. grumbled. Then in a more solicitous tone, he asked her, "Are you sure you do not need to lie down, *ochkweu machelensu*?"

She smiled and shook her head. Will had translated W.C.'s new nickname for her as "woman with big pride." She figured she would have to be a hypocrite to take offense.

"Very sure. As I said, I am leaving right now to go meet Will."

"Then I will walk with you to the distillery."

"That is *not* necessary," Melisande said firmly. "Please,

W.C., if you want to be of assistance, kindly take care of Mr. Findlay."

"Don't worry, I'll take care of him," Wildcat promised. "I'll give him my undivided attention."

Fearful that the Lenape's "attention" might not benefit her ex-pupil's health, she quietly suggested, "Return him to the gaolhouse in one piece."

W.C. grumbled, which she took as an assent.

Leaning against the door frame for support, Melisande bit at her lips as Wildcat dragged away a whining, whimpering Findlay. Though she felt pity for Mr. Findlay—she did feel some—her sympathy was overshadowed by dismay. She knew that she ought not take the man's lapse of judgment as a personal affront, yet it bothered her. It bothered her very much. She was so hoping to prove to Will that she could succeed in this venture of hers. She wanted to prove to him that, despite his misgivings, he had not erred in awarding her this opportunity.

Granted, Findlay's fall from grace did not disprove her capabilities. It only reinforced the lesson she'd already learned from Maggie Taggart. Helping people first required finding people who wished to be helped. No matter how forceful her personality nor how imposing her will, Melisande could not alter that simple reality. A harsh lesson, but one that apparently she needed to accept.

Nonetheless, she had so wished to make Will proud of her. In fact, it had become increasingly important to her during this last week that she do so. A week in which their relationship had crossed over onto new and dangerous ground. Ground that left her shaky and confused . . . and excited.

During the day she and Will treated each other civilly, like friends who were working together toward the common goal of seeing the distillery flourish. For the most part, she behaved with Will as she behaved with Alastair or Wildcat—she awarded him a polite courtesy, but the courtesy of an acquaintance not of a wife.

However, once they retired to her room for the evening, it was as if she and Will entered a private world where all rules were tossed aside, all worries forgotten. In the safety of her bedchamber, they would come together like lust-craved lovers, like souls long separated and starved for each other. They made love two, three, sometimes four times a night, Will forever careful to keep his seed from her. It was tender their lovemaking. It was fierce and wonderful.

It was also an illusion. As eagerly as Melisande awaited the sun's descent each night, she knew that what she and Will shared could not be real. The soft words and loving whispers were but gauzy layers to the illusion, to the fantasy they had crafted for themselves. At the back of her mind, Melisande understood that someday she would awaken and find the dream world gone. That, within a week's time, she would wake up with the knowledge that this was the day she was to be sent home to Mooresby Hall.

At least Will had been direct about his intentions, and she supposed she ought to be grateful for that. More than once he had expressed hope that her sight would return before she left Scotland. But always he spoke of her leaving. Never had he suggested that she stay with him in Scotland, that she remain as his wife.

And never had she asked if she could.

Ochkweu machelensu indeed.

With her cane in one hand and her books in the other, Melisande slowly tapped her way along the grass-beaten path to the distillery. Only a few hundred yards, the distance was not great nor the trail difficult; she'd traveled it many times since blinded and had grown comfortable in the knowledge that, despite her impairment, she did not have to be led around by the hand everywhere. She was not completely helpless.

As she walked, she noticed how the wind blew more vigorously, tossing her shawl and hair and dragging at her skirts. The faintest drizzle had begun to fall, no more than a suggestion of dampness in the air. Melisande hurried along. She did not wish to be caught out in the rain, especially since she hadn't even a bonnet for protection. On the other side of the Lammermuir hills, thunder boomed like the clash of drums and cymbals. Lightning flashed bright and painfully white.

Melisande jerked to an abrupt halt. *Lightning?* She blinked rapidly, trying to focus, her heart suddenly hammering against her ribs. Had it been her imagination or had she seen lightning flare in the sky? She stared straight ahead, her eyes dry and intent. A blurred image appeared, just a tantalizing hint of green and brown, before fading again into black.

She closed her eyes. A fat, icy raindrop splashed against her cheek. She opened her eyes and felt her legs weaken beneath her.

"My God," she whispered. *"I can see."*

Though muted by the rain and clouds, the colors dazzled her, took her breath away. She had been what—nine days without sight? And yet how greatly she had missed the vibrancy a world of vision imparted. The green of the clover was rich enough to eat, her persimmon skirts gushing forth hues of orange and red.

She laughed softly, breathlessly. The rain began to fall in earnest now, its raindrop kisses cold and fervent. She knew she should seek shelter, but prudent thinking seemed impossible when the earth was bombarding her with its visual wonders. Speckled white dots on the face of a toadstool. The piercing blue petals of columbine . . .

Ahead, only a hundred yards or so, stood the distillery, its brick facade trimmed with curlicue, lace-like patterns of ivy. Smiling, Melisande tucked her cane under her arm and lifted her skirts. While keeping her shawl from flying off and her books from slipping and the cane from falling, she jogged the remaining distance, the rain so wondrously cool on her face.

Like a fool, she had just pushed open the door to the distillery, the yeasty perfume enveloping her in its warmth, when the realization hit. Not with joy this time, but with dread: *I can see again.*

Suddenly Melisande's chest felt as if it caved in on itself, panic seeping into every cell, every pore of her. The illusion shattered in that instant. The dream world was gone. Will

had said he would send her home as soon as her sight
returned, whether or not she had completed her two-week
commitment to the prisoners—

"Mel!"

Melisande spasmed as if struck. Will was marching
toward her, his dark blond brows furrowed in concern, his
posture and bearing so masculine, so potent. He was bearing
down on her too quickly. She could not turn around and run.
She could not hide. Then, without conscience decision,
Melisande allowed her gaze to go perfectly blank.

"Mel, for God's sake, what are you doing walking about
in a thunderstorm?" He pulled the ruined books from her
grasp, then removed her sodden shawl. "Lord, woman,
you're soaked to the bone."

"I—" *Dear heavens, I cannot believe I am doing this.*
Deliberately she shifted her empty gaze a few degrees to the
right of his face. "I was caught in the rain."

"And where the hell is W.C.?"

Melisande wiped at her wet face with the back of her
hand in an effort to conceal her turmoil. Goodness, he was
beautiful. That gold-striped hair, those shoulders she'd
clutched and clawed at in the throes of passion. The mere
sight of him was sending heat racing through her abdomen
and other private places. But she could not stare. She could
not give herself away.

"He is escorting Mr. Findlay back into Dunslaw."

"What?"

"He did not speak with you?"

"No. What happened with Findlay?"

"He violated the conditions of our agreement by stealing
into town last night."

Unguarded, Will allowed the full measure of his fury to
show in his expression, a rarely seen glimpse of the man
who was "Tiger" Taggart. Melisande shivered in uncon-
scious reaction.

Will glanced at her sharply, his eyes narrowing. "Blast it,
Mel, you're shaking with cold. The last thing I need is for
you to take ill right now."

Right now? What did he mean? Was he afraid that she'd be too ill to travel back to Devonshire next week?

"Wait here," he ordered. "I'm going to fetch my coat and take you back to the house."

"No!" She grabbed for him, then quickly snatched back her hand before he could observe the accuracy of her reach.

"Mel, I am not going to waste my breath in pointless discussion. I am taking you home."

At a complete loss, she could only give a weak bob of her chin. *I cannot do this. I cannot.* The temptation to follow Will with her eyes was irresistible; she'd never be able to maintain the pretense. Never. But if she did not . . . Was the effort of feigning blindness worth the additional seven days with Will? The additional seven nights?

Unquestionably, her heart answered.

Will walked across to the hooks mounted on the wall and retrieved his coat. She had to drop her gaze when he turned back toward her.

"I'm almost done for the day anyway," he said, as he draped the coat carefully around her shoulders. "Since Da has been helping out with the training of the crew, we've established a pretty effective routine. We might make a go of this old place yet," he said with a lopsided grin.

Don't smile back at him, Melisande told herself. *Keep your gaze unfocused.*

She let him guide her outside into the rain.

"You're going to have to ride pillion," Will said after whistling for his mount. "It can be damned uncomfortable, especially bareback, but we've only a short ride to the house."

"Why aren't you using a saddle?" Melisande asked, as the horse obediently trotted in from the field.

"I've been so busy, I haven't been able to order another, and crazy Fergus won't let me put anything but the finest on George's darlings."

She tried not to flinch when Will grabbed a fistful of mane and leaped onto the horse's back. Goodness, but it did appear uncomfortable without a saddle.

"Now, Mel, give a little hop when I tell you." Leaning

down, Will seized her by the wrist, his grip firm and sure. "One, two . . . three."

She jumped on "three" and Will hauled her up behind him with relative ease. She did not settle easily, however, for it felt as if she were sitting atop a bouncing fence post.

"Ouch."

"Don't fidget. We haven't far to go."

She wrapped her arms around him, holding fast, thinking that, in spite of the discomfort, she could have ridden all the way to London in this awkward position. Cradled against Will's strong back, the breadth of his shoulders shielding her from the harsh elements, the heat of his body caressing her—what mattered a little soreness?

"Are you cold?" he asked, his breath a delicious, tickling warmth.

"No."

She shut her eyes tight, not trusting herself, concerned that she might accidentally reveal her secret before she was prepared to do so. For now that she had time to gather her wits, Melisande questioned what on earth she had done. Why had she chosen to perpetuate this hoax, to weave this tangled web of deception? Admittedly the unexpectedness of her sight's return had caught her unaware, her happy relief "blinding" her to the ramifications of her recovered vision.

After all, she had known it was inevitable. She had known that at the end of her two-week experiment, Will expected her to leave Dunslaw forever. Yet, for some demented reason, she had refused to believe it. She had not accepted the reality of packing her belongings and making her good-byes and climbing into a coach. . . .

She had committed a grievous error. She had deluded herself.

Having fallen into the fantasy the two of them created each night, Melisande had permitted that fantasy to take hold of her life outside of the bedroom. She'd wanted to believe that the tenderness and intimacy they shared was more than the physical act. That Will might have come to care for her as she'd come to care for him.

She pressed her cheek against his back with such fervency and such ferocity that her teeth cut into the side of her lip. A sad wonder flooded her, a bittersweet joy. When had it happened? When had she fallen in love with this thoroughly complicated, thoroughly irresistible man?

He did care for her, she knew. But caring would never be enough for Melisande. As always, there could be no compromise; she could not settle for less than everything. Will's affection, and obvious lust, for her would still be an inadequate complement to the depth of feeling she felt for him. To the love she felt for him.

Foolish girl, an inner voice chided. *Simply tell him that you don't want to leave. Tell him that you want to stay with him in Scotland.*

But as the metallic taste of blood floated across her tongue, Melisande knew she would not. She couldn't change people. She couldn't change herself.

Ochkweu machelensu.

Woman with big pride.

Twenty-seven

Something was wrong.

Frowning, Will watched as Melisande fumbled her way up the stairs, Mrs. Baker following behind, clucking and fussing like a spectacled mother hen.

"Soaked through ye are," the housekeeper fretted. "Come on now, Mrs. Taggart, let's get ye into a hot bath afore ye catch yer death."

At the foot of the staircase, Will stood dripping onto the braided cotton rug, worry pulling at his gut. Worry for Mel.

He had felt her tension during the ride home, felt it seep into his back and shoulders just as the rain had seeped into his layers of clothing. At first, he'd assumed that she was upset over Findlay's transgression. She had, after all, invested many hours in those four men this last week. Many, many hours. Enough to where Will had joked he'd have to ride into town and commit some crime in order for Mel to give him any notice. She'd scoffed when he'd made the quip, but he hadn't been completely in jest.

As the days passed, he grew needier, more possessive of Melisande's time and attention. He hated himself for being that way—he hated himself for *needing*—yet he could not seem to control the feelings. Always at the back of his mind was the knowledge that their hours together were numbered. That, within a week's time, Melisande would be gone. Gone from his life.

So while at first Will had believed her troubled by the loss of her "student," now he wondered if a more worrisome reason lay at the root of her disquiet. She had been unusually aloof as he led her into the house, shying away from him, holding herself at a distance. Rack his brain though he did, he could not think what had changed between them in the hours that followed their early morning love-making. By God, she'd not been aloof then. . . .

Frustrated, he glanced to his boots liberally spattered with mud, the boots Mel had bought for him while they were at Mooresby Hall.

Dammit, there is no point in standing here mooning, Taggart. He'd just go up and find out what was on the woman's mind.

He headed up the stairs as Mrs. Baker descended.

"Ach, and ye'll be needin' a hot bath, as well," she said, shaking her gray head. "I'll put the pot on and be up as soon as I can, sir."

"No hurry," Will told her. No hurry, since he might need the time to extract from his mulish wife the reason for her sudden reverse. And if she weren't of a mood to talk . . . well, then he'd put her in the mood. He only had a few days left to pretend that she was his and he'd be damned if he was going to squander any of that precious time on playing games.

He entered their bedroom to find her sitting in front of a fire, wrapped in the spare quilt from his old bed, its neat squares of blue grayed and faded with age. She looked very small sitting there, and surprisingly young. Her long, wet hair hung down her back like the darkest seaweed as she hunched forward in the chair, seeking the fire's solace. The copper tub had been dragged closer to the hearth in anticipation of a bath.

"Are you warming up?" he asked, as he started to strip from his own rain-soaked shirt.

She burrowed down into the coverlet, answering in a muffled voice, "I am beginning to."

Thunder rolled across the valley in a series of booming explosions that seemed to shake the house's very rafters.

"Quite a storm," Will commented, glancing to the ceiling while shedding the last of his clothes. His bare flesh puckering in painful, inch-long goose bumps, he moved to stand on the other side of the hearth.

"Hmm-mm," Mel murmured, tunneling deeper into her quilted nest as if she wanted to escape him.

Will leaned forward and rested his hands on the mantel, his naked body stretched out before the firelight. From the corner of his eye, he studied her—or, at least, as much of her as he could study, which amounted to the top of her head, from her nose up.

"Mel, what's going on?"

She appeared to start, her liquid chocolate gaze darting to him before falling away blank and wide. "What do you mean?"

"I mean you seem . . . preoccupied."

Her lashes swept down, concealing her gaze. "I"—she cleared her throat—"ahem, have been thinking about my return to Devonshire."

Shit. Will's fingers clenched on the wood mantel, his knuckles cracking like tiny echoes of thunder. He should have known he wouldn't be able to hold her for the entire two weeks. Vainly he'd thought he could addict her to his lovemaking, that if he pleasured her enough she'd choose to stay. *Nice try, Taggart.* But no such luck. Not now that there was no possibility that Melisande carried his child.

Blast it, why did I have to pretend to be so noble, so virtuous, by keeping my seed from her? He should have been striving to fill her womb with a Taggart heir these past nights, and to hell with chivalry and taking the gentlemanly route.

"Are you planning to finish training the three remaining men? I know that Findlay must have disappointed you, but the others look to be coming along, Mel. You're doing a helluva job with them."

She sighed, a long quavering sigh that seemed to signal she was working up her courage. But for what? To tell him that she was leaving tomorrow?

"Yes," she finally said. "I'll complete the men's last week of training. Before I go."

"Ah. I'm glad to hear it. For their sake, of course." Staring into the fire, Will watched the flames gyrate like red-cloaked gremlins atop the iron grate. "And, for your sake, I guess you should know that I've repaid the loan from your inheritance. With interest."

"Oh. How did you manage that?"

"Since we're manufacturing whiskey again, I was able to work out a deal with an Edinburgh banker. We'll need to sell off some of the older casks, but they're probably ready to go."

She was silent a moment, the fire popping and crackling, the thunder rumbling.

"That was good of you," she said in stilted tones. "To repay the monies."

Will shoved from the mantel and turned around to toast his backside. Mel sank into the quilt nearly to her eyebrows.

Rubbing his hands up and down his naked thighs, Will wondered what in blazes had occurred to alter her mood. This guessing and jumping from subject to subject was like grasping at straws and he didn't know why it had to be so difficult. But it was difficult. It was difficult because he cared.

"Mel, I, uh, don't know if I ever fully apologized for bringing you here under false pretenses. I shouldn't have. It wasn't right."

Hah! I'd do it again in a heartbeat, the devil inside him said.

Melisande sighed again, the sound somewhat melancholy. "No, it wasn't right. But I have made my mistakes as well, Will. I see that now. We're none of us infallible."

"Yet, I was wrong—"

"What are you doing, Will? Are you hoping to clear your conscience before I go?"

Zing. He figured he probably deserved that.

"Hell, I don't know, Mel." He shrugged and ran both hands through his drying hair. "We've shared a lot this last month. And I guess I'd like to believe that you'll remember me . . . fondly."

Fondly, Taggart? Who was he kidding? He didn't want to be remembered "fondly." He wanted to be remembered passionately, emotionally, eternally. He wanted Melisande to carry in her mind the same memories that would haunt him for a lifetime. Her kittenlike cries as he licked her from head to toe. The laughter they'd shared. The red-hot desire.

As if on cue, his manhood began to swell between his legs.

Melisande sputtered a cough.

"You all right?"

She nodded, her face hidden in the quilt's folds, as a knock sounded at the door.

"It's Mrs. Baker," the housekeeper called. "I've brung the missus's hot water."

Will grabbed his dressing gown, a shiny hand-me-down from his father, and swiftly pulled it on. "Come in."

The housekeeper entered, followed by the young buck-toothed maid they'd hired a few weeks earlier. The two women poured their steaming buckets into the tub.

"Just give a shout when ye're ready for more hot water, Mr. Taggart," the housekeeper said, as she and the maid headed for the door. "I've got plenty heatin' on the fire."

The door closed and Will glanced to the vaporous tub and then to Melisande, who had not yet moved from the ladderback chair.

"You better hop in while the water is still hot," he said, walking over to lay his hand on her shoulder. "Come on, and I'll help you climb in so you don't slip."

Melisande swung her face away from him. "If, um, you don't mind, Will, I'd like some privacy . . . for my bath."

He felt as if she'd slapped him right across the chops. Privacy? After all they had experienced, he knew her body better than she probably knew it. *I do mind,* he wanted to shout at her. *I mind a helluva lot.*

But he didn't shout or utter a word. Instead he let himself out of the room as silently as a wraith.

That night marked the first in over a week that Will did not make love to his wife. Melisande complained of a headache. Will wanted to complain of a heartache.

"Mrs. Taggart?"

Stifling a groan, Melisande turned her face into the pillow and breathed in, drawing Will's scent deep into her lungs. Perhaps, she thought, if she breathed very deeply, she could capture the scent of him forever, hold it within her for all the years to come.

The bedroom door squeaked open. "Ma'am, are you awake?"

Melisande rolled onto her side, her night rail twisting around her legs. "Yes, Mrs. Baker, I am. Is the hour terribly late?"

"It's half past nine, ma'am, and I hated to disturb ye, but I was worried ye might have come down with somethin'. Are ye unwell?"

"No." Melisande rubbed at her eyes. "Only lazy this morning."

"Lazy? Why, ye've been workin' hard, ma'am, and ye sure didn't rest much followin' yer accident."

"Well, I have rested plenty this morning, haven't I?" she answered, guiltily acknowledging that she'd lain abed not to rest, but to avoid. To avoid pretending to be blind.

Melisande frankly did not know how much longer she'd be able to pull off the charade. The evening meal had proved intolerably taxing, sustaining the deception so much more difficult than she had imagined. And earlier, prior to her bath, when Will had stood before the fire in all his naked splendor . . .

Good gracious, she'd near asphyxiated on her own drool. Every minute, every hour, she'd been terrified that her fraud would be exposed, that her hungry eyes would give her away. And then what would she say?

"I've been feigning blindness because . . ."

Because . . . why?

She ground her fists into her eye sockets, knowing she hadn't the answer to that question. The old Melisande— Melisande *Mooresby*—had had all the answers. She'd been invincible, assured. Melisande Taggart, however, was turning out to be an annoying, indecisive twit of a female whose emotions were running frightfully out of control.

If she had any sense at all, she ought to pack her bags and march down to the distillery and tell Will the truth right now. The strain of deceit was too onerous; she knew she would not be able to bear it. Already she had been afraid to make love with Will for fear she'd forget herself in the midst of passion and reveal the secret. So why not cut short the pretense and accept the inevitable? Accept that it was time for her to go.

Yet how hateful it was to think that she might be gone from here as early as tomorrow— Oh, how she hated indecision!

"Ma'am, the elder Mr. Taggart was wonderin' if ye wanted to accompany him to the storage house. He's goin' to be samplin' from the barrels and thought ye might be interested in joinin' him."

Oh, dear, wouldn't you know it?

Melisande was loath to refuse Peter's invitation, particularly when he'd but recently begun to express a renewed interest in the business. But neither was she emotionally prepared to confront Will, the reality of her imminent departure like a bleeding gash in her heart.

Yet she knew that she could not have her cake and eat it, too. If she wished to claim these last days with Will, she would have to cease waffling. She would either pretend to be blind, or she wouldn't. Blind meant a few more days with Will. Not blind meant she'd be packing today.

Blast.

She would have to settle with her conscience at a later date.

"Tell Mr. Taggart I'll be down shortly, Mrs. Baker."

"Aye, ma'am. He'll be pleased, for sure."

Melisande dressed, deliberately arranging her fichu wrong-side-up as if she hadn't been able to detect which side of the lace to display. The small ruse rankled, making her feel like a liar and a cheat, but she merely set her chin at a stubborn angle and headed downstairs.

Following the stormy night, the day shone as brightly as a newly minted coin, making it all the more difficult for Melisande to preserve her charade as she rode alongside Peter in the open gig. She could not squint into the radiant sunshine, she could not allow her gaze to linger on the iris freshly bloomed along the road. She had to be vigilant. She had to be cautious.

They pulled up outside the storehouse, the horse's pace slow through the tacky, wet peat.

"Careful now, lass," Peter said as he helped her from the gig. "The footing is tricky here. There we are. Good girl. This way," he said, leading her toward the brick building. "A few more steps. I'm opening the door now. There's a post to your left. Watch your step. That's it."

Grinding her jaw, Melisande slowly inched through the doorway, struggling to keep her eyes unfocused and vague. While she knew that Peter meant well, his overdone solicitude was almost more than she could abide when already so plagued with guilt.

"Truthfully, Peter, if you take my hand, I'll be able to follow you with no effort at all."

His age-spotted hand wrapped around hers. "All right then, lass, this way. We're walkin' to our left here. Over to where the barrels are stored."

Melisande had not spent much time in the warehouse, as they'd only put aside one run of whiskey so far, but the building's wooded coolness was pleasant, a welcome relief from the sun's testing glare.

As she followed Peter down the cask-lined aisle, she spied movement at the periphery of her vision. Carefully she glanced aside. Alastair, Will, and Wildcat were all gathered around the most recent shipment of barrels, poking and testing the new casks, examining the workmanship.

Melisande swallowed a sigh. The fates had to be conspiring against her, she decided, pushing her to reveal her hand—or her sight, that is—before she was ready. She had assumed that the men would be working at the kilns today. Or, at the very least, she had not thought to find them here.

She bit back a grimace as Wildcat separated from Will and Alastair and began walking toward her. Of everyone, it was the Indian she feared the most. The stoic, stiff-jawed Lenape saw everything through those pale, steely eyes. Duping him was not a task she would have relished under any circumstances.

Peter, unaware of Wildcat's approach, continued to draw her along at a snail's pace.

"Willy said that we'll need to put to market some of the older whiskey. He asked me to test a few of the stores to help determine which we ought to sell."

"Will must put enormous trust in your judgment," she said, her voice thin with nerves as she forced her attention away from Wildcat.

"Aye, I feared I'd lost my palate," Peter said, "but he and Alastair brought me in durin' the cuttin' and, if I do say so, I did myself proud."

Melisande was mindful not to make eye contact as she smiled in Peter's general direction, for W.C. was almost upon her now.

"Ochkweu machelensu."

She feigned a start and turned. "Wildcat," she said, her voice quivering as she sensed Peter draw to a halt behind her.

"Morning, Wildcat," the elder Mr. Taggart greeted.

Niankwe half-mumbled half-grunted his own version of "Good morning" while Melisande dropped her chin to her chest, allowing her lashes to shutter her fearful gaze. She felt like a mouse cornered. Cornered by a Cat.

"Will said you were unwell last night."

Melisande nodded, pressing her lips together. Though blunt, the statement revealed concern. And she was grateful.

"'Twas nothing serious and I'm feeling much more the thing. But thank you, W.C."

"Was it because of what happened with Findlay?"

Melisande blinked at the tips of her boots and answered sincerely, "No, to tell you the truth, I've hardly thought of the man. I admit I was terribly disappointed at first, but I've had other more pressing concerns on my mind."

"Hmph." W.C. made an awkward movement with his hands as if he wanted to pat her on the back. "Well, it's good you're feeling better."

"Yes." Melisande smiled faintly, her palms damp and sticky.

Wildcat mumbled something about "checking on the stills," then moved past her and headed for the exit. As the door clanged shut, Melisande let out a breath and surreptitiously wiped her palms on her dress. This ruse was insanity. *She* was insane.

"Let's first have a look at what the cooper has brought," Peter suggested, leading her toward a different pallet of casks than those that Alastair and Will were still scrutinizing.

Melisande obediently followed, her eyes dry from their vacant staring. Her mouth was dry, too.

The new barrels, redolent of oak and stacked six across and three high, had yet to be unloaded, towering halfway to the ceiling. Their brown, sloping sides reminded her strangely enough of George's hunting dogs, the gentle curve of the hounds' bellies as they lay before the hearth.

"Can ye smell the wood, lass? Isn't it grand?" Peter asked, his grin wide. He tugged proudly at the ropes binding the barrels, his green eyes shining as she'd not seen since coming to Scotland.

"It is," she answered, feeling her nerves start to abate as she slowly recovered herself. "It's a very rich aroma, isn't it?"

"Aye, the oak is crucial, softens the brew just as nature intended," he said, clinging to the rope as he gestured to the casks. "Some like to use those Spanish sherry casks, but we've always preferred the purity of . . ."

As Peter explained the qualities a good cooper searched for in selecting his wood, Melisande's gaze discreetly wandered. She tried to keep her eyes from Will, but it was not easy. Especially when he and Alastair started to circle around toward them, Will's unbound hair glinting like molten gold in the morning light.

Deliberately she turned aside, her gaze falling once again on the stacked barrels.

". . . now some don't age their whiskey as they should," Peter was saying, "but we've always been mighty careful not to rush the process."

Melisande gave a vague, seemingly interested smile before that smile grew suddenly stiff. Was it a trick of the light? Or was the knot actually coming free? *Yes, by God!* The knot holding the barrels was slowly coming loose as a result of Peter's persistent tugging. The knot was slipping and the rope was slipping and the barrels were—

"Peter!"

There was no time to think. Melisande lunged forward, throwing her body and his to the ground, pain spiking through her left wrist. In the same instant, chaos exploded at her back, wood and metal clattering in a deafening roar as the barrels tumbled loose and crashed to the floor.

Flattened atop the older man, Melisande could feel his heart fluttering at an alarming rate beneath her hand. She pushed to her knees as soon as the dust and the clamor had settled.

"Gracious," she breathed. "Are you injured, Peter? Are you all right?"

Peter Taggart shook his head, his eyes shocked and curious. And strange.

Suddenly Melisande realized what she had done.

Oh, dear Lord. Pressing the back of her hand against her mouth, she whirled around to find both Will and Alastair staring at her in surprised confusion.

"I . . . I—"

Panic assailed her. She bolted for the door.

Twenty-eight

Will couldn't move for a good three or four seconds, shock holding him perfectly immobile. *What the hell had just happened here?*

Then, as Melisande began to sprint for the door, Will shook himself from his stupor and turned to follow after her, but found his path blocked by the dozens of oak casks scattered across the floor. Awkwardly he labored to scramble over them, hopeful that he wouldn't break a leg in his frantic rush.

"Melisande," he yelled. "Mel, stop!"

But she refused to heed him, instead racing out of the storage house in a blur of green, her raven hair flying like a pirate's banner, her finely-boned features rigid with distress.

Will cursed as his knee banged sharply against the metal rim of a cask, then glanced across the room as Peter Taggart, his wispy white locks positively standing on end, pulled himself to his feet.

"Are you all right, Da?"

Peter nodded shakily. "Aye, I'm fine. But I don't know about that lady wife of yours, Willy. I think she may have hurt herself. There's a few drops of blood here on the floor."

"Damn," Will hissed and fought harder to scramble across the casks, hurdling his way to the door.

"Will?" Alastair called. "Do ye want my help, lad?"

Will shook his head, seeing again the shame and pain that had branded Melisande's expression. "Not now, Alastair. If I can't run her down, I'll come back for you. For you and Wildcat both."

God help him, though, he sincerely prayed it would not come to that. He sure as hell didn't want to repeat that nerve-racking search of a week and a half ago. His heart couldn't take it. He had to catch Mel. Especially since she wouldn't realize how dangerous the river would be today, its banks swollen with last night's rains.

Throwing his shoulder against the storehouse door, he charged from the building in a frenzied burst of limbs. The bright sun pierced his narrowed eyes as he hurriedly glanced from left to right. Melisande had disappeared. From immediate view, at least. Fortunately however, the rain-softened earth left a clear trail of her recent passing.

With his pulse pounding in his temples, Will set out at a loping run, pursuing the crushed clover and booted imprints past the mill and then the distillery. Once or twice, he spent a few seconds to drop to the earth to check for evidence of fresh blood. He found none and consoled himself by thinking that her injury was probably nothing more than a flesh wound. Dear Lord, he hoped so.

The brisk wind whined mournfully in his ears as he pursued her trail south. From the looks of it, Melisande was running like a hunted animal, without direction, darting back and forth between trees and brush. Though aimless, her flight had to be swift, he decided, for her to have already outdistanced him in these few short minutes.

As her tracks veered toward the water, Will felt his heart clench, for the river's agitated roar warned of its voracious, storm-swollen currents. But her trail only skirted along the banks before twisting away and leading back to the glen, back to the valley's fir grove, home to noisy grouse, dark clouds of sparrow, and a family of eagle.

There the trail abruptly ended. Will swore between clenched teeth as he painstakingly backtracked a few dozen steps to discover what he had missed in his haste: Melisande had apparently sheered off into the trees.

Only the crackling carpet of dried fallen needles kept Will from slipping on the boggy ground as he followed the trail ever deeper into the grove. As he wove his way through the tall conifers, past the ferns and mushrooms dotting the woodland floor, he forced himself to calm down. He would lose her trail if he didn't keep his focus, if he didn't rein in his imagination.

She's going to be fine, he told himself. *She's going to be fine. A drop or two of blood means nothing.* Yet, despite these efforts at reassurance, his mind would not release the image of her as he had seen her once before, cradled pale and weak in Wildcat's arms, her vision lost. Will blamed himself for the accident, for the loss of her sight. Or he had blamed himself until—

Why? he asked, as he leaped over a decaying log. Why had Melisande pretended to be blind? She had always been so honest and straightforward in her dealings, he could not imagine what might have led her to feign her condition. Could the reason be somehow tied to the aloofness she'd shown with him? The "headache" of last night?

Dammit, he'd known something was bothering her. He'd known something was wrong. Why in the blazes hadn't he trusted his gut and insisted on getting an answer from her last night? If he had, he might not be racing across Scotland, worried sick, right now.

Relief suddenly sagged at his shoulders, and in his chest, his heart somersaulted clumsily. Peeking out from behind a tree trunk just ahead could be seen the smallest glimpse of green plaid, well camouflaged among the foliage. Will expelled an unsteady sigh, then advanced noiselessly, afraid that Mel would run again if she heard him approaching.

But evidently she could not hear him . . . over the sound of her own sobs. Curled up at the foot of the tree, her head buried in her arms, she was crying. Crying in huge, painful gasps.

Will's breath hitched. *Mel crying?* Dammit, she never cried. *Never.* Why, she had not wept even one tear the night she'd lost her sight. Melisande was too strong, too indomitable for tears. Or so he had believed.

"Mel?" He hunkered down beside her, trying to peer through the thick, tangled curtain of her hair. "Mel, darlin'?"

"Leave me alone," came her fierce, watery whisper.

Will's mouth twisted with regret as he dragged an impatient hand through his hair. "Now, Mel, you know I can't do that."

"Yes, you can," she said in a petulant mumble.

"No, I can't. I have to know what's ailing you."

"Ailing me?" She lifted her head, her lashes spiky with tears, her nose as red as a summer tomato. "Is it not obvious?"

Will scratched at his chin, thinking that it was not the least obvious to him. "Da said that you were bleeding?"

"Oh. That." She swiped at her nose as she twisted her wrist to give it a glance. "It's only a scratch."

"May I see it? Please?"

Reluctantly she extended her arm like a princess bestowing a royal favor.

Will took hold of her chilled fingers with extreme care, relieved to see that it *was* only a scratch. Although a faint discoloration at the base of her thumb suggested that the delicate flesh would soon bruise.

"You may have sprained it."

Gently he stroked the blue-threaded veins along the inside of her wrist.

"Thank you for saving my father, Mel. If you hadn't pulled him to safety, he could have been seriously injured, you know."

She gave a diffident nod, and dragged her hand from his grasp as her eyes pooled again with tears. Will figured he must have said the wrong thing as she began to weep again. His concern heightened.

"Does your wrist hurt?"

"No," she answered, the tremulous answer stretching the word to three syllables.

"Then, please, Mel sweetheart, why are you crying?"

"*Because,* dammit!"

Will reared back, clearing his throat to mask an inappropriately timed grin. "Ahem. Because . . . you are no longer blind?"

She huffed with scorn, even as her lips trembled, then dropped her head disconsolately back into her arms.

Confusion flickered through him. He didn't understand any of this. And he didn't understand her tears. "When did your sight return, Mel?"

Her muscles tensed visibly. "Yesterday afternoon."

Ah-hah. Yesterday when she had been behaving so oddly. When he'd been grieved by her chilly reserve.

"Why?" he asked in his softest voice. "Why did you pretend?"

"Because I have taken complete leave of my senses, that's why!"

"You have?"

Her shoulders shook. "Of course, I have. I don't even recognize myself anymore."

"You look pretty much the same to me."

Glowering, she raised angry, pink-rimmed eyes to him. "Well, I am *not* the same," she asserted. "I am weak and foolish and silly . . ."

"Why do you say that?"

"Because I am! I was daft to ever consider feigning blindness in order to—" She pressed her lips together, averting her gaze.

"In order to what?"

She did not answer. Her profile, silhouetted against the dusky brown tree trunk, was pale as morning's frost.

Will cupped her chin firmly in his palm and turned her to face him, his expression unyielding, implacable. "What, Mel? Tell me what it was you were hoping to gain by this pretense."

Her soot-fringed eyes filled with despair, and she testily pushed his fingers away from her face. She bit into her lip before answering with halting reserve, "A few more days . . . with you."

Balanced on the front of his toes, Will felt himself totter, barely recovering before he tumbled face-first into the moss and leaves.

"What?" he choked.

Melisande shrugged, tilting away from him. "I know I was supposed to leave at the end of this week anyway," she said. "But I didn't want you to send me away any earlier."

"Mel, for God's sake, I never said I was *sending* you away," Will argued with sudden heat. "I said that you could leave."

"What on earth are you talking about?" she countered, as her brows drew together to form a single ebony arc. "I could have left whenever I chose. It was your suggestion that I return home."

"But all along, you have said that you wanted to go home to England."

"And when, pray tell, was the *last* time you heard me say that?"

Will scraped his fingers through his hair, wanting to either laugh in relief or bellow in frustration. "Dammit, woman, if you wanted to stay, why didn't you just say so?"

"Well, dammit, *man,* if you wanted me to stay, why didn't *you* just say so?"

"Hell, Mel, how was I to guess? You never said anything."

"Hah! And I suppose all those hours we spent making love did not suggest to you that I might have developed certain feelings for you?"

Will lifted an uneasy shoulder. "I've always known you were a passionate woman—"

Mel gaped. "Not so passionate that I'd . . . I'd do all *that* with a man I wasn't in love with!"

This time, Will did have to steady himself with a hand to the ground. "You're in love with me, Mel?"

She nodded jerkily.

"And you didn't tell me?"

An apologetic pout curled her mouth. "Wildcat knew whereof he spoke when he claimed I had too much pride for my own good."

Will laughed and moved to sit down next to her, his legs

having grown mysteriously feeble. Draping his arms over his bent knees, he leaned back against the tree trunk and smiled.

"Well, if it makes you feel better, Mel, you're not alone in being too proud, you know. I've been in love with you since before we left England but refused to even admit it to myself."

"You have?" Her breath seemed to come a little faster against the side of his neck.

"Aye, I have. You were right about me being afraid to fall in love. I was afraid. Frightened and angry. Not only did I fear losing someone I cared for—like I had lost my mother—but I think I also feared that you were . . . above me, out of my reach. I couldn't reconcile myself to that. I didn't want to believe any woman too good for me."

"Oh, but I'm not at all good!" she argued, clutching at his coat sleeve. "I'm stubborn and proud and vain and imperious—"

"And the only woman I want, Melisande Taggart."

Her dark coffee eyes grew glassy and damp. "So you don't want me to go home to Devonshire?"

In answer, Will took her hand and pressed it to the middle of his chest. "Home is here, Mel. With me. Don't forget that."

She smiled a sweet, wobbly smile before her gaze began to kindle with laughter. "Oh, why did you have to make this so difficult, Will?"

"Me?"

"Yes, you. When I selected you from Mr. Bell's gaol-house, I had thought you to be so manageable, so compliant. But from the beginning, you've given me naught but trouble, you wretched man."

Chuckling, Will folded his arms around her and tumbled her down to the ground. "Trouble? You ain't seen nothin' yet, lady."

"Will, it's wet!" she cried, squirming beneath him.

"Aye," he answered, awarding her a long, probing kiss. "And it's about to get a whole heckuva lot wetter."

Epilogue
༺༻

"I won't stand for it."

"Mel, honey, you have no say in the matter."

Melisande glanced askance at her husband seated beside her on the silk-covered sofa. The divan's crimson-and-silver fabric struck her as almost garish now that she'd grown accustomed to the simpler furnishings of their Dunslaw home.

"What do you mean I have no say? Are we not speaking of my niece, my namesake?"

"Yes," Will conceded in his most patronizing tone. "But if Eileen and Benjamin decide to go to Italy, they will take baby Melisande with them, with or without your approval."

"Rubbish," Melisande said, shooting an irritated look to the parlor door. "We haven't traveled all this way to London to attend the child's birth so that they can then whisk the babe out of the country and away from us."

"I don't think they'll be whisking her anywhere just yet, Mel. She's not even twenty-four hours old."

"Nevertheless, I have to talk to Benjamin. I can't allow him to put the child at risk in foreign environs."

Mel started to rise, but Will grabbed her by the waist and pulled her back down to the sofa, his eyes narrowing.

"Mel, what the hell is the matter with you?"

She spun around to stare at him. "I beg your pardon?"

"I love your spirit, sweetheart, but spirited is one thing and shrewish is another. You've been as prickly as a porcupine since we left home. Now, what's going on?"

"I've been that bad?"

"A weaker man would have tossed you from the coach at the English border," Will said dryly.

"Oh, Will, I am sorry." Melisande laid her head on her husband's shoulder, her hand on his knee. "I hadn't wanted to say anything until I was sure, but"—she reached up and whispered in his ear—"I think I might be pregnant."

A cocky grin stretched Will's lips wide. "Well, it's about time. I've not been plowing your belly these last five months for my own amusement, you know."

Melisande retaliated by sinking her teeth into his earlobe.

"Witch," he murmured.

"Cad," she whispered back, sliding her fingers up his thigh.

"Hey, watch it, woman," he warned as her hand ventured higher. "This might be your brother-in-law's house, but I'm not above throwing you to the carpet and having my way with you."

"Ooh, I'm so frightened."

"You should be," he told her, simulating a feral growl.

She kissed him fully on the lips, her tongue just teasing the seam of his mouth. Will let out a purr this time.

She laughed and cuddled closer. "Ah, my ferocious Tiger. It seems I've tamed you at last."

If you enjoyed *Tiger by the Tail*
you won't want to miss

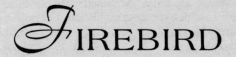

The stunning new novel from Janice Graham
Coming in August from Berkley Books

One

*So far as we know, no modern poet has written of the
Flint Hills, which is surprising since they are perfectly
attuned to his lyre. In their physical characteristics they
reflect want and despair. A line of low-flung hills
stretching from the Osage Nation on the south to the
Kaw River on the north, they present a pinched and
frowning face to those who gaze on them. Their verbiage
is scant. Jagged rocks rise everywhere to their surface.
The Flint Hills never laugh. In the early spring, when the
sparse grass first turns to green upon them, they smile
saltily and sardonically. But as spring turns to summer,
they grow sullen again and hopeless. Death is no
stranger to them.*

—JAY E. HOUSE
Philadelphia Public Ledger (1931)

ETHAN BROWN WAS in love with the Flint Hills. His
father had been a railroad man, not a rancher, but you would
have thought he had been born into a dynasty of men
connected to this land, the way he loved it. He loved it the
way certain peoples love their homeland, with a spiritual
dimension, like the Jews love Jerusalem and the Irish their
Emerald Isle. He had never loved a woman quite like this,
but that was about to change.

He was, at this very moment, ruminating on the idea of
marriage as he sat in the passenger seat of the sheriff's car,

staring gloomily at the bloodied, mangled carcass of a calf lying in the headlights in the middle of the road. Ethan's long, muscular legs were thrust under the dashboard and his hat brushed the roof every time he turned his head, but Clay's car was a lot warmer than Ethan's truck, which took forever to heat up. Ethan poured a cup of coffee from a scratched metal thermos his father had carried on the Santa Fe line on cold October nights like this, and passed it to the sheriff.

"Thanks."

"You bet."

They looked over the dashboard at the calf; there was nowhere else to look.

"I had to shoot her. She was still breathin'," said Clay apologetically.

"You did the right thing."

"I don't like to put down other men's animals, but she was sufferin'."

Ethan tried to shake his head, but his hat caught. "Nobody's gonna blame you. Tom'll be grateful to you."

"I sure appreciate your comin' out here in the middle of the night. I can't leave this mess out here. Just beggin' for another accident."

"The guy wasn't hurt?"

"Naw. He was a little shook up, but he had a big four-wheeler, comin' back from a huntin' trip. Just a little fender damage."

She was a small calf, but it took the two men some mighty effort to heave her stiff carcass into the back of Ethan's truck. Then Clay picked up his markers and flares, and the two men headed home along the county road that wound through the prairie.

As Ethan drove along, his eyes fell on the bright pink hair clip on the dashboard. He had taken it out of Katie Anne's hair the night before, when she had climbed on top of him. He remembered the way her hair had looked when it fell around her face, the way it smelled, the way it curled softly over her naked shoulders. He began thinking about her again and forgot about the dead animal in the bed of the truck behind him.

As he turned off on the road toward the Mackey ranch, Ethan noticed the sky was beginning to lighten. He had hoped he would be able to go back to bed, to draw his long, tired body up next to Katie Anne's, but there wouldn't be time now. He might as well stir up some eggs and make another pot of coffee because as soon as day broke he would have to be out on the range, looking for the downed fence. There was no way of telling where the calf had gotten loose; there were thousands of miles of fence. Thousands of miles.

Ethan Brown had met Katherine Anne Mackey when his father was dying of cancer, which was also the year he turned forty. Katie Anne was twenty-seven—old enough to keep him interested and young enough to keep him entertained. She was the kind of girl Ethan had always avoided when he was younger; she was certainly nothing like Paula, his first wife. Katie Anne got rowdy, told dirty jokes, and wore sexy underwear. She lived in the guest house on her father's ranch, a beautiful limestone structure with wood-burning fireplaces built against the south slope of one of the highest hills in western Chase County. Tom Mackey, her father, was a fifth-generation rancher whose ancestors had been among the first to raise cattle in the Flint Hills. Tom owned about half the Flint Hills, give or take a few hundred thousand acres, and, rumor had it, about half the state of Oklahoma, and he knew everything there was to know about cattle ranching.

Ethan had found himself drawn to Katie Anne's place; it was like a smaller version of the home he had always dreamed of building in the hills, and he would tear over there in his truck from his law office, his heart full and aching, and then Katie Anne would entertain him with her quick wit and her stock of cold beer and her soft, sexy body, and he would leave in the morning thinking how marvelous she was, with his heart still full and aching.

All that year Ethan had felt a terrible cloud over his head, a psychic weight that at times seemed tangible; he even quit wearing the cross and Saint Christopher's medal his mother had given him when he went away to college his freshman year, as though shedding the gold around his neck might lessen his spiritual burden. If Ethan had dared to examine his conscience honestly he might have eventually come to understand the nature of his malaise, but Katie Anne had come along, and the relief she brought enabled him to skim over the top of those painful months.

Once every two weeks he would visit his father in Abilene; always, on the drive back home, he felt that troubling sensation grow like the cancer that was consuming his father. On several occasions he tried to speak about it to Katie Anne; he ventured very tentatively into these intimate waters with her, for she seemed to dislike all talk about things sad and depressing. He yearned to confess his despair, to understand it and define it, and maybe ease a little the terrible anguish in his heart. But when he would broach the subject, when he would finally begin to say the things that meant something to him, Katie Anne would grow terribly distracted. In the middle of his sentence she would stand up and ask him if he wanted another beer. "I'm still listening," she would toss at him sweetly. Or she would decide to clear the table at that moment. Or set the alarm clock. Mostly, it was her eyes. Ethan was very good at reading eyes. He often wished he weren't. He noticed an immediate change in her eyes, the way they glazed over, pulled her out of range of hearing as soon as he brought up the subject of his father.

Occasionally, when Ethan would come over straight from a visit to Abilene, she would politely ask about the old man, and Ethan would respond with a terse comment such as, "Well, he's pretty grumpy," or "He's feeling a little better." But she didn't want to hear any more than that, so after a while he quit trying to talk about it. Ethan didn't like Katie Anne very much when her eyes began to dance away from him, when she fidgeted and thought about other things and pretended to be listening, although her eyes didn't pretend very well. And Ethan wanted very much to like Katie Anne. There was so much about her he did like.

Katie Anne, like her father, was devoted to the animals and the prairie lands that sustained them. Her knowledge of ranching almost equaled his. The Mackeys were an intelligent, educated family, and occasionally, on a quiet evening in her parents' company when the talk turned to more controversial issues such as public access to the Flint Hills or environmentalism, she would surprise Ethan with her perspicacity. These occasional glimpses of a critical edge to her mind, albeit all too infrequent, led him to believe there was another side to her nature that could, with time and the right influence, be brought out and nurtured. Right away Ethan recognized her remarkable gift for remaining touchingly feminine and yet very much at ease around the crude, coarse men who populated her world. She was the first ranch hand he had ever watched castrate a young bull while wearing pale pink nail polish.

So that summer, while his father lay dying, Ethan and Katie Anne talked about ranching, about the cattle, about the land; they talked about country music, about the new truck Ethan was going to buy. They drank a lot of beer and barbecued a lot of steaks with their friends, and Ethan even got used to watching her dance with other guys at the South Forty, where they spent a lot of time on weekends. Ethan hated to dance, but Katie Anne danced with a sexual energy he had never seen in a woman. She loved to be watched. And she was good. There wasn't a step she didn't know or a partner she couldn't keep up with. So Ethan would sit and drink with his buddies while Katie Anne danced, and the guys would talk about what a goddamn lucky son of a bitch he was.

Then his father died, and although Ethan was with him in those final hours, even though he'd held the old man's hand and cradled his mother's head against his strong chest while she grieved, there nevertheless lingered in Ethan's mind a sense of things unresolved, and Katie Anne, guilty by association, somehow figured into it all.

Three years had passed since then, and everyone just assumed they would be married. Several times Katie Anne had casually proposed dates to him, none of which Ethan had taken seriously. As of yet there was no formal engagement, but Ethan was making his plans. Assiduously, carefully, very cautiously, the way he proceeded in law, he was building the life he had always dreamed of. He had never moved from the rather inconvenient third-floor attic office in the old Salmon P. Chase House that he had leased upon his arrival in Cottonwood Falls, fresh on the heels of his divorce, but this was no indication of his success. His had grown to a shamefully lucrative practice. Chase Countians loved Ethan Brown, not only for his impressive academic credentials and his faultless knowledge of the law, but because he was a man of conscience. He was also a man's man, a strong man with callused hands and strong legs that gripped the flanks of a horse with authority.

Now, at last, his dreams were coming true. From the earnings of his law practice he had purchased his land and was building his house. In a few years he would be able to buy a small herd. It was time to get married.

Two

ETHAN PULLED THE string of barbed wire tight and looped it around the stake he had just pounded back into the ground. It was a windy day and the loose end of wire whipped wildly in his hand. It smacked him across the cheek near his eye and he flinched. He caught the loose end with a gloved hand and finished nailing it down, then he removed his glove and wiped away the warm blood that trickled down his face.

As he untied his horse and swung up into the saddle he thought he caught a whiff of fire. He lifted his head into the wind and sniffed the air, his nostrils twitching like sensitive radar seeking out an intruder. But he couldn't find the smell again. It was gone as quickly as it had come. Perhaps he had only imagined it.

He dug his heels into the horse's ribs and took off at a trot, following the fence as it curved over the hills. This was not the burning season, and yet the hills seemed to be aflame, in their burnished October garb. The copper-colored grasses, short after a long summer's grazing, stood out sharply against the fiercely blue sky. They reminded Ethan of the short-cropped head of a red-haired boy on his first day back at school, all trim and clean and embarrassed.

From the other side of the fence, down the hill toward the highway, came a bleating sound. *Not another one,* he thought. It was past two in the afternoon, and he had a desk piled with work waiting for him in town, but he turned his horse around and rode her up to the top of the hill, where he could see down into the valley below.

He had forgotten all about Emma Fergusen's funeral until that moment when he looked down on the Old Cemetery, an outcropping of modest tombstones circumscribed by a rusty chain-link fence. It stood out in the middle of nowhere; the only access was a narrow blacktop county road. But this afternoon the side of the road was lined with trucks and cars, and the old graves were obscured by mourners of the newly dead. The service was over. As he watched, the cemetery emptied, and within a few minutes there were only the black limousine from the mortuary and a little girl holding the hand of a woman in black who stood looking down into the open grave. Ethan had meant to attend the funeral. He was handling Emma Fergusen's estate and her will was sitting on top of a pile of folders in his office. But the dead calf had seized his attention. The loss, about $500, was Tom Mackey's, but it was all the same to Ethan. Tom Mackey was like a father to him.

Ethan shifted his gaze from the mourners and scanned the narrow stretch of bottomland. He saw the heifer standing in a little tree-shaded gully just below the cemetery. To reach her he would have to jump the fence or ride two miles to the next gate. He guided the mare back down the hill and stopped to study the ground to determine the best place to jump. The fence wasn't high, but the ground was treacherous. Hidden underneath the smooth russet-colored bed of grass lay rock outcroppings and potholes: burrows, dens, things that could splinter a horse's leg like a matchstick, all of them obscured by the deceptive harmony of waving grasses. Ethan found a spot that looked safe but he got down off his horse and walked the approach, just to make sure. He spread apart the barbed wire and slipped through to check out the other side. When he got back up on his horse he glanced down at the cemetery again. He had hoped the woman and child would be gone, but they were still standing by the grave. *That would be Emma's daughter,* he thought in passing. *And her granddaughter.* Ethan's heartbeat quickened but he didn't give himself time to fret. He settled his mind and whispered to his horse, then he kicked her flanks hard, and within a few seconds he felt her pull her forelegs underneath and with a mighty surge of strength from her powerful hind legs sail into the air.

The woman looked up just as the horse appeared in the sky and she gasped. It seemed frozen there in space for the longest time, a black, deep-chested horse outlined against the blue sky, and then hooves hit the ground with a thud, and the horse and rider thundered down the slope of the hill.

"*Maman!*" cried the child in awe. "*Tu as vu ça?*"

The woman was still staring, speechless, when she heard her father call from the limousine.

"Annette!"

She turned around.

"You can come back another time," her father called in a pinched voice.

Annette took one last look at her mother's grave and knew she would never come back. She held out her hand to her daughter and they walked together to the limousine.